Also by Timothy H. Drake

Inherited Freedom

SOLITARY VIGILANCE

A World War II Novel about
Service and Survival

TIM DRAKE

authorHOUSE®

AuthorHouse™
1663 Liberty Drive
Bloomington, IN 47403
www.authorhouse.com
Phone: 1-800-839-8640

Published by AuthorHouse 10/08/2014

ISBN: 978-1-4969-4233-3 (sc)
ISBN: 978-1-4969-4234-0 (hc)
ISBN: 978-1-4969-4232-6 (e)

Library of Congress Control Number: 2014917160

To Alice, Anna & Garrett,
Thank you for your unconditional love and support.

"Courage is fear holding on a minute longer."
George S. Patton

CONTENTS

PROLOGUE

The hatch door to the torpedo room opened suddenly with a resounding clang. A brilliant shaft of light blinded me and I blinked rapidly, desperately willing for my eyes to adjust from the darkness that had surrounded me for so long. I recognized the outline of a Japanese Lieutenant, walking hurriedly through the door towards me. His uniform was crisp, clean and easily recognizable. He stopped directly in front of me, knelt down, and silently began to unlock my handcuffs. After the cuffs fell away, he turned his attention to the locks and chains on my ankles. For a month, those cold steel bonds had held me prisoner in this rear compartment of a Japanese submarine. I heaved a shaky sigh of relief now that the bonds were off. The stern face of the Lieutenant told me he was especially upset as he impatiently motioned for me to stand. I had lain in this awkward position for weeks, so it was very difficult for me to even move, let alone stand. Nevertheless, I gathered my legs beneath me and prepared to defend myself from an expected execution. When I rose, the Lieutenant placed his hand on his pistol, but he did not remove it from its leather holster. Instead, he gave me a belligerent shove toward the door, where another Japanese sailor awaited us. I stepped through the narrow hatch with an initial feeling of relief, but I remained on guard as we proceeded down the small corridor.

I was astonished when I saw ten or more Japanese sailors lined up at attention on the left side of the narrow passageway. All of the enemy sailors were looking at me. I could see their hate for me in their eyes and in their body stance. As I walked forward, with the Lieutenant directly behind me, several of the sailors cursed at me in Japanese and spat on my face.

We paused near the sub's conning tower for a short moment as the Lieutenant and the sub's Captain conferred in a seemingly calm but debating tone. The Japanese crew was not aware of my training in Japanese linguistics and that I understood their conversations throughout my entire internment. As a result, I was able to read the sub's depth gauges and clearly understand the discussion between the Lieutenant and the Captain. The two Jap officers concluded their brief conversation, bowed to each other, with neither man looking in my direction. The Captain made it clear he wanted me released but the Lieutenant was clearly against it. My fate was in debate, I did not know what my outcome would be. I could sense the sub rising rapidly. We would soon be breaking the surface of the water and exiting the sub. My mind raced, my heart began to beat even faster.

After a few minutes passed, a Japanese sailor proceeded up the conning tower ladder to open the outer hatch. I watched him intently as he turned the dial and slowly opened it. A sudden rush of cool air met my face, a stark contrast to the humidity I had endured during my time in the sub. Saltwater dripped in, splashing all over me. Bright rays of sunshine lit up the interior of the sub, and I squinted, looking up at a brilliant blue sky. The Captain pushed me from behind and briskly motioned for me to proceed up the ladder after the Japanese Lieutenant. Even though the Captain had ordered me released, I remained on guard to defend myself, in the event they had any last minute ideas of shooting me and throwing me overboard.

During the last month, as a prisoner of the Japanese, I had heard various conversations that revealed to me that the United States had unleashed two atomic weapons over the Japanese cities of Hiroshima and Nagasaki. My capture by the Japanese near Nagasaki linked me to those events.

I exited the sub and took a deep breath of fresh air. My eyes continued to adjust, temporarily blinded by the sunlight. The

Captain exited behind me and motioned me to the rear of the sub. I started toward the rear, still expecting the worst to happen. I knew I could take out both Jap officers if it came to that. This red-blooded American was not going to die without taking them with me.

Chapter 1

CALM BEFORE THE STORM

"Life is a lively process of becoming."
Douglas MacArthur

My name is Allen Voigt and my life's journey began on April 6, 1908, in the small town of Boston, New York. My loving mother, Elizabeth, with the help of a local midwife, delivered me into the world that early spring day with my father Robert, by her side. I was an only child, but my childhood in Western New York was full of fond memories. I liked playing in Cazenovia Creek, hunting in the woods with my grandfather, Henry, and playing in the fields and barns with my neighborhood friends. My family did not have much money, but I did not know any better, life was good. A one-room schoolhouse in Boston, New York provided me with most of my early education.

Early one evening, at the age of nine, my father called me into the living room for a chat. In my mind, I recounted the day's events, trying to remember if I had broken something, forgotten to feed my dog Porgy, or maybe talked back to my mother. I walked into the living room and sat down on our small sofa. I stole a quick glance at my father, who was sitting in his favorite living room chair. He had a very somber expression on his face. It reminded me of how he had looked a few years earlier when he told me my grandmother, Lucille, had passed away. My mother walked in from the kitchen just as my Father began to speak. She lovingly offered me a glass of cold milk and a plate of freshly baked chocolate chip cookies, a combination I never refused. I had just swallowed my first bite of cookie when my father said, "I am leaving to fight a war overseas that will take me away for a long time."

I put down my glass of milk and asked, "Why?"

"America needs me." My father replied.

He paused for a moment and gazed out the window. Then he turned his attention to my mother and took her hands in his. He gave her a smile, than continued, "Our country's freedom is at stake. I must do my part to defend our country. I will be going to fight the Germans in order to protect you and your mother."

My eyes began to tear up, but I still managed to take another bite of cookie. I finished that bite and asked my father where he was going and what he would be doing. He answered, "I am going to France in a big ship as a member of the United States Army."

A few days later, I walked with my mother and father to the train station and saw my father leave to go fight in a war I knew nothing about. I later learned that my father took part in the war in Europe, later known as the Great War. He knew that he would miss almost two years of my childhood. It was a decision that I am sure, weighed heavy on his mind, but he still did what he thought was right.

He served his country, having enlisted in the Army on March 15, 1917, and becoming a member of the 1st Infantry Division. I was eleven years old when my father, honorably discharged from the Army, returned home in May 1919. I asked my father lots of questions about his time overseas. I wanted to know what battles he had fought in, what types of guns he had fired, whether he had killed anyone or been injured. Over the years, my father shared more and more about what he saw and experienced during the Great War. Those stories made me eager for military service and travel. As I grew older, I became more aware of the significance of the Great War. I hoped the day would come when I could perform military service for my country as my father had.

By the time I turned fifteen, with pride, I had told my friends and anyone else who would listen, that my father had fought in the Great War. I learned that my great grandfather, Humphrey Voigt, had served in the Civil War as part of the Union Army's 16th New York Calvary. In time, I discovered that other family members had served in the Revolutionary War and the French and Indian War. Because I grew up in Western New York among so many veterans of the Great War, as well as a few surviving members of the Civil War, I developed a keen interest in history and military service. My education was challenging for me, but I enjoyed learning about history, especially the history of the United States of America and its founding fathers. I gravitated to veterans and their exciting stories of service overseas fighting the Germans. I longed to hear about their adventures aboard ships, in the trenches, and in the air.

In the fall of 1922, my parents moved to East Aurora, a small town southeast of Buffalo, New York. The town was a little bigger than Boston and it had houses on each side of the street, something I had not seen before. I entered East Aurora High School and joined the ROTC program during my sophomore year. Paul Langford, a veteran of the Great War, ran the program. The discipline of the ROTC program came naturally to me and I loved every minute of it. I learned how to communicate with Mr. Langford, a former colonel in the Army, by saying only, "Yes, Sir!" and "No, Sir!" My fellow ROTC members and I marched for many hours around the school's track. My senior year, the program took on leadership initiatives. I learned to communicate effectively as part of a team, but also learned how to function independently in high stress situations. Problem solving and mental toughness took on a new meaning for me during that year as Mr. Langford gave us complex problem solving situations and physical tasks that were timed.

With much relief, I graduated from high school in May 1926, eagerly anticipating the next phase of life. With the full support of my mother and father, I enlisted in the Army, even though America was not at war. I wanted to serve as my father before me had done. Mr. Langford took the time to come by my house a few days before I left for boot camp. He told me he was proud of me and that I would serve our great country well. His last words to me would always burn in my mind, as we stood there together on the front porch of my home. He said, "Throughout America's existence, there have been individuals who refused to let the majority dictate their beliefs or actions. Those individuals stood up, refused to back down, and fought for this country. They displayed character, took responsibility, prayed, and when necessary, went off to war to defend our freedom."

I left for basic training on Wednesday, September 29, 1926. I departed from the very same Buffalo, New York train station that my father had left from nine years earlier. My destination for boot camp was Camp Pine, located in the northeastern part of New York, just to the east of Watertown. My mother lovingly provided a care package; I was glad to see that it included some of her famous chocolate chip cookies.

Just before I boarded the train, my father pulled me to the side. He grasped me by the shoulders and looked me in the eye. "You know how proud I am of you, right?" he asked earnestly.

I nodded my head vigorously, swallowed, and said, "Yes, Sir, I know."

He then cleared his throat and looked at me intently. "Learn all you can, fight hard, and come home to your mom and me, son." He stepped back and held out his hand. I shook it firmly as he had taught me, then I turned and hugged my mother. She tried not to cry as she straightened my shirt collar. I resolutely stepped onto the train and found a seat. I then watched out the passenger car window as my parents waved goodbye. I knew that the earliest I could possibly see them again would be in three months, since the Army's initial boot camp training lasted twelve weeks.

As the train left the station, I found an open seat that was only one passenger car away from the noisy locomotive engine. The train route would be east from Buffalo to Syracuse, New York, stopping in towns like Rochester, Clifton Springs, and Weedsport along the way. As the conductor passed by my seat, I asked, "How long will the ride take to get to Syracuse?"

He cheerfully replied, "Three hours, only because of the required stops along the way."

With that bit of news, I decided to take full advantage of the time and get some needed shut-eye. Before I knew it, the conductor cried, "Last stop before New York City. If New York City is not your final destination, you need to disembark now!" I rose to my feet, picked up my suitcase and ran off the train.

My next objective was to find the train headed to Watertown, New York. It only took me a few minutes to find someone who could point me toward the right train. I literally jumped on the train bound for Watertown with only seconds to spare. Although this leg of the trip was a short one, it turned out to be rewarding. As I walked the aisle of the train, looking for a seat, a man motioned for me to join him. He looked harmless, so I decided to take the open seat next to him. Before I could even speak, he announced, "My name's Tom Beckett. Are you headed to Camp Pine?"

With a surprised look on my face, I replied enthusiastically, "Yes, how did you know?"

Tom replied, "Well, you and I are the youngest folks on this train, you're heading north, and you have a confused look on your face!"

We started up a conversation centered on where we were from, our age, our education and our passion for military service. I was glad to find out that I would not be the only new recruit arriving at Camp Pine that night.

It was 9:30 PM when the train pulled into Watertown. We were to find a green bus with the words "Camp Pine" painted on its side. We got off the train and found a general loading and unloading area for buses and taxies, just outside the small train depot. We sat down on a nearby wooden bench to wait. Thankfully, the wait was not long and before we knew it, an old green school bus with "Camp Pine" painted on its side, pulled up to our bench. Before I could even stand to my feet, the driver opened his window, stuck his head out, and said, "Are you boys heading to Camp Pine?"

We simultaneously answered, "Yes, Sir".

Tom and I boarded the cold bus and saw that we were the only two passengers. The driver said nothing as he drove the bus out of the empty train station.

I was excited and nervous at the same time. I was eager to begin my training, but nervous about the unknown. The United States was at peace and its military ranks were very small, having downsized after the Great War. I expected the level of individual training in the Army to be above par. I was proud to have the chance to serve my country and follow in the footsteps of my father and so many other family members who had served and fought for America's freedom.

The bus ride to Camp Pine only took about fifty minutes. Long before the bus pulled up to the front gate, I could see bright lights off in the distance. As the bus got closer, I could see that the camp was much larger than I had imagined. I was so excited to begin my Army training. The bus driver spoke up and shouted, "Here we are boys, Camp Pine, New York". He pulled up to the main gate and opened his window so he could speak to the soldier on duty at the guard station. The bus driver blurted out, "Two fresh recruits reporting for duty." The soldier at the guard station walked around the bus and motioned for the bus driver to open the door. The door swung open and the soldier stepped aboard. His uniform was straight and bore the rank of Sergeant in the United States Army.

He looked at me first and said, "I am expecting an Allen Voigt and a Tom Beckett. Which one are you?"

I answered, "I am Allen and this is Tom," as I pointed to Tom sitting next to me.

The Army Sergeant responded in a loud, clear voice, "Welcome to Camp Pine. Pick up your bags and follow me."

No words exchanged as Tom and I walked off the bus into the cool night air. The bus driver continued through the gate to places unknown, leaving behind two fresh Army recruits who were about to be introduced to life in the Army. The Army Sergeant asked us to follow him into the guard shack and stand at attention. After what seemed like minutes, but was in reality only a few seconds, the Sergeant said, 'Welcome again to Camp Pine, I am SGT Shoemaker. You are the only two recruits to enter Camp Pine this week." He then turned and picked up a phone sitting on a desk nearby and dialed a series of numbers. Seconds later he stated, "This is SGT Shoemaker calling from the guard station. I have two recruits here who are ready to begin their life in the Army." After listening for a few seconds, SGT Shoemaker stated, "Thank you, Sir, they will be waiting here for their transportation." The Sergeant then put down the phone and asked us to continue standing at attention while we waited for our transportation. "A Jeep will be here to pick you both up in approximately five minutes. The Jeep will take you straight to your quarters due to the late hour."

I spoke up and said, "Thank you SGT Shoemaker".

The Sergeant fired back, "Did I ask you to speak Private Voigt?"

I answered, "No, Sir!" and continued to stand at attention, two things I had learned how to do back in my ROTC program in high school.

A few minutes later, an Army Jeep pulled up to the guard shack. SGT Shoemaker directed us outside and said, "Take a seat in the Jeep."

Tom and I tossed our suitcases into the back of the Jeep, after which Tom took the back seat and I took the front seat. The only words from the driver were, "Welcome to Camp Pine."

We went down a series of dimly lit streets. We passed a large open field, a series of four story buildings that looked like storage facilities, a loud and active officer's club, and finally a series of two story barracks near the back part of the Camp. The driver then stopped the Jeep and said, "Enter barrack #3, find an open bunk and get some rest, you'll need it."

Tom and I gathered our belongings and walked up a short flight of wooden stairs, entering the building. The inside was very dark and smelled like an old barn; I managed to find a light switch. I turned and saw two rows of bunk beds running the entire length of the building.

No one else was in the barracks that first night, so Tom and I had the pick of beds. My head hit the pillow, it was 12:50 AM and I was exhausted. My stomach growled due to hunger but I was glad to have finally made it to Camp Pine.

Shouting, bordering on screaming, startled me awake at 6:00 AM. As I gathered my senses and swung my feet out of the bed, I saw a Drill Sergeant at the far end of the barracks.

"Get out of bed, you miserable maggots! Stand at attention at the end of your bunks and prepare for roll call!"

As a litany of four letter words proceeded from the Drill Sergeant, I walked to the end of my bunk in just a pair of boxer shorts. Tom made it to the end of his bunk with not much more on than I did, but he had the advantage of wearing a t-shirt. We both stood at attention as the Drill Sergeant made his way down the aisle between the two rows of bunks. I was nervous, but not because of the abuse. I had heard yelling like that from my ROTC instructor Paul Langford. I just did not know what to expect next.

The Drill Sergeant finally made his way to me and, putting his face right up to mine, screamed, "Welcome to your first day of basic training Private. What is your name?"

"Allen Voigt, Sir." I replied.

He then proceeded to give Tom the same treatment all over again. He walked around our bunks for what seemed like an eternity and then let loose another primordial scream. "Why are these bunks not made?"

I wanted to say, "Because we have only been asleep for a few hours and were just startled awake." However, I thought better and instead answered, "No excuse, Sir. It will not happen again."

I expected a response from the Drill Sergeant but he said nothing as he continued to pace the aisle. He finally blurted out, "Follow me, you worthless, no good Privates!"

Boxer shorts and all, Tom and I followed the Drill Sergeant out of the barracks and down the same stairs, we had walked up just a few hours earlier. We turned right and walked in our bare feet for what seemed like over a mile until we finally reached another large building.

As we followed the Drill Sergeant into the building, I deduced what was in store for me. I saw barber chairs, racks of shoes, clothing and a mysterious white curtain, that hung from the floor to the ceiling. The Drill Sergeant asked us in a very aggressive way to stand at attention. He then proceeded to inform us what our morning's schedule would be.

"You will first get the haircut of your life. You will then proceed to the white curtain for inoculation shots. From there, you will proceed to the clothing and shoe station for uniforms. Lastly, you will pass by an administrative section where you will obtain your dog tags and general paperwork."

I thought to myself, "What about breakfast?" Tom and I were the only Privates in the entire building, so we did not have to stand in line. Instead, we kindly obliged two barbers and sat down in their chairs. I received the fastest haircut in my life. Five sweeps of the electric razor over my head and that was it. I did not have to look into a mirror to see that I was bald. I saw a pile of brown hair on the floor and confirmed my suspicions by running my hand over my now hairless head.

I exited the barber chair and in a somewhat half-hearted voice said, "Thank you, Sir." The barber nodded his head and motioned me toward the white curtain. At this point, I was still only in boxer shorts and becoming very self-conscious. I walked up to the white curtain and a man in a white lab coat stepped out from behind it to greet me.

"Private, I am Dr. Mahon and I will be administering several shots this morning. These shots are designed to keep you immune

from all the diseases you could encounter if you are assigned overseas."
I never liked shots very much as a kid, but I knew I had no choice
but to take them like a man. Dr. Mahon proceeded to ask me where
I wanted my shots, "Buttocks or arm Private?"

I replied, "Buttocks". I remembered getting shots in the arm as
a child and my arm hurting for days. I hesitantly pulled down the
right side of my boxers and braced for the impact of what would be
multiple shots. The shots stung but I took them, not letting anyone
see my eyes tearing up a bit.

Dr. Mahon stated, "That is all the shots for today but expect more
over the coming weeks." He then proceeded to draw blood, check my
vision, and ask me a series of simple medical questions.

I then walked over to the clothing station, where I would obtain
my first Army uniform. At this station were several stalls, each one
containing different series of clothing. An Army Corporal was at
each stall as Tom and I began to pass by. At the pants stall, the man
behind the counter looked at me and said, "You look like a 30/32."

I had no idea what he meant, as I had never had to buy a pair of
pants before. Mother had always purchased my clothes. My entire
wardrobe at home consisted of three pairs of pants, five shirts, and
two pairs of shoes, a suit and tie. I responded to the man, "I do not
know what you mean."

He shouted back, "Your waist size and leg length, Private!"

With increasing anxiety, I responded, "I have no idea, Sir."

At that, the Corporal threw me four pairs of pants. "Try on a set
of pants, Private, so I can see if they fit," he ordered.

I tried on a pair, and to my surprise, they fit perfectly. The
Corporal at the next station did not even bother to ask me my size,
and simply threw me four shirts. I slipped on one of the shirts and it
fit fine. At this point, I was glad to have some clothes on!

I went to the next station, and the Corporal working behind the
counter asked, "What size shoe do you wear?"

I knew the answer to that question and replied, "Eleven, Sir."
Handed a pair of boots and dress shoes, I was instructed to put on

the boots, but not before being handed five pairs of wool socks. My feet had been cold since I had left the barracks earlier that morning, so wool socks and warm boots were a welcome relief. As I neared the end of the clothing stalls, I was given an oversized bag that contained a tie, t-shirts, underwear, toothbrush, toothpaste and a comb. I was informed that the clothes I entered Camp Pine with, along with my suitcase and all its contents, were going to be shipped home to my parents.

I asked the Corporal handing out the bags, "When will that happen?"

He responded, "Sometime today, if not already." My shoulders slumped in dismay. In my suitcase, I had a picture of my mother and father. I was hoping to secure it before my personal belongings were shipped home.

Tom caught up with me and I told him about our belongings being shipped home. With a panicked expression, he whispered in my ear, "I have a vintage bottle of 1908 Glenlivit scotch whiskey in my suitcase. My father gave me the bottle as I left home." Prohibition was in full swing. If Tom was caught with the whiskey, he might be kicked out of the Army and sent back home.

We approached the last station and I was asked what my name was. "Allen Voigt, Sir", I replied. I was handed dog tags, an ID card and small service record book. When I slipped on those dog tags around my neck, it finally hit me: I was in the United States Army! I walked with my head held high, full of pride in the knowledge that I was now following my father's footsteps, serving my country. I had a few minutes to walk back to my barracks and put away all the clothing and supplies I had received.

We were instructed to report to Camp Pine's chow hall for breakfast. It was a short walk and a welcome sight. I smelled the food before I even walked into the building. The Drill Sergeant had found us by this time and in a calm voice said, "Privates Voigt and Beckett, you have fifteen minutes to eat breakfast. You are my only two Privates that are here at Camp Pine this week, so I am giving you a full fifteen minutes to eat."

I was thrilled about having a meal, not having eaten a full meal since leaving my mother's kitchen, approximately thirty-six hours earlier. As soon as the Drill Sergeant turned to walk away, I bolted for the door. I entered the chow hall at a fast clip, but just after I stepped foot inside, I suddenly stopped to assess where the food was. Just as I stopped, Tom's excitement to eat propelled him right into by back, forcing us to both stumble further into the chow hall. We got some strange looks from several officers eating nearby. I quickly gathered my wits and saluted the officers, before hastily proceeding to the serving line on my left. I picked up a silver serving tray and, at this point, did not care what was being served, as long as it was hot and plentiful. The cooks behind the counter slopped the food on my tray; all I had to do was stick my serving tray out towards them. My mouth and eyes were open wide as I watched the cooks serve up scrambled eggs, bacon, toast, orange juice and coffee. I took as much as my serving tray could handle and headed for the nearest table. The chow hall that Sunday was rather empty so Tom and I had our pick of tables, just as we had our pick of beds the night before. When I took my seat, I placed my serving tray on the table and bowed my head to pray, thanking God for my safe trip to Camp Pine and for the bountiful breakfast before me. Tom and I never said a word the entire time as we quickly consumed our breakfast.

No sooner had I swallowed a few sips of hot coffee, than I heard our Drill Sergeant yelling from the front door of the chow hall. It occurred to me that the Drill Sergeant had not given us his name. "Stand up Privates and follow me!"

Tom and I rose to our feet and headed for the exit. When I reached the exit, the Drill Sergeant was standing on the front sidewalk. He blurted out "What took you miserable, smelly Privates so long to get here?"

"Sir", I replied. "We came as soon as you called us."

"Did you run?" replied the Drill Sergeant.

I hesitated for a minute and replied, "No, Sir, but I promise I will next time."

With a look of disgust, the Drill Sergeant bellowed, "There may not be a next time unless you maggots get your butts in gear and start acting like soldiers!"

I was shocked, realizing I had a lot to learn about life in the Army. The Drill Sergeant did an about face and headed for the nearby parade grounds, which was a large field, centrally located at Camp Pine.

Tom and I assumed it was prudent to follow the Drill Sergeant, so off we went. I thought it odd that we were the only two recruits at Camp Pine. Now we were the only two recruits in an open field, constantly belittled by an Army Drill Sergeant!

"Stand at attention you pacifier-sucking Privates!" At this point, the Drill Sergeant finally shared his name. "Private Voigt and Private Beckett, my name is SGT Nolan. I am a veteran of the Boxer Rebellion in China in 1900 and the Great War between 1917 and 1918. I have been in the Army for thirty years and it is all I know." Before I could even respond to SGT Nolan with the information that my father had also fought in the Great War, SGT Nolan bellowed out, "Hit the deck and give me one hundred pushups."

"Could this really be happening?" I thought to myself. I hit the grassy ground, which was still wet from the morning dew, and started my pushups. In my ROTC class in high school, the most pushups I had ever completed in a row were twenty-five, and I thought that was hard. As I was counting the pushups in my head, I assumed SGT Nolan was doing the same. I hit twenty-five pushups and my arms began to burn. I could see Tom out of the corner of my eye and he was breathing heavily. I passed thirty-five pushups; my stomach was beginning to debate whether or not it was going to give up the large breakfast I had just eaten minutes earlier. My repetitions really started slowing down when I hit forty-five pushups. My goal at that point was to hit fifty and then stop and bare the wrath of SGT Nolan. I managed fifty-one pushups before my arms collapsed in the wet grass. Tom managed a few more repetitions before he collapsed, as well.

SGT Nolan shouted out "I said one hundred pushups." "Private Voigt you only gave me fifty-one, Private Beckett you only gave me fifty-six!"

I could not do another pushup. I had just stood to my feet when SGT Nolan yelled out, "Give me five miles - that represents five times around the parade ground! Double time it girls!"

My first thought was that running had to be better than those muscle-burning pushups. I ran from the middle of the parade ground to the closest piece of track, which was to my left. My newly issued Army boots were not ideal for running, let alone broken-in. That morning, I pushed myself further than I had ever pushed myself before.

By the time I finished three laps around the track, I knew I only had two laps to go. My feet were burning, aching, and most likely bleeding at that point but I was not going to let SGT Nolan heap any additional punishment on me for not completing an order. Tom had managed to outpace me on the track, but even he was beginning to slow at that point. I managed to catch him as we entered our last mile, when he suddenly stopped running. He put his hands on his knees and began to throw up all over the track. I slowed for a bit, looking back over my shoulder at him. As I continued on, straining for that last half mile, I saw Tom running again. He was white as a ghost, slowing his pace as he worked his way around the track. I decreased my pace the last half mile and eventually crossed the five mile mark; the very spot I had begun from over forty minutes earlier. I came to a stop and put my hands on my knees, breathing harder than I ever had before. It was at this point that my breakfast wanted out, and out it came vigorously. My boots did not escape the mess. I collapsed to my knees, overcome with chills and cold sweats. I tumbled my body onto the ground and rolled a few feet away from my breakfast, where I lay looking up at the sun.

At this point, the unforgiving SGT Nolan, who had been standing over by the far side of the parade grounds, blurted out,

"Privates, you are dismissed! Head to your barracks and wash up. Meet me in Building #32 at 1100 hours and do not be late."

"Relief at last," I said to myself. Tom and I staggered back to our barracks. As soon as I had reached my bunk, I collapsed into it. I lay there for a few minutes before gingerly removing my new Army boots and socks, wet with sweat. My feet were blistered and a bloody mess. I eventually hit the showers and washed all the sweat, dirt and blood off my sore body. I had approximately thirty minutes to clean up, sit for a few minutes, and put on a clean uniform. My belongings were already boxed and stacked in the far corner of the barracks. Tom noticed his whiskey bottle had been removed from his suitcase, which was a big disappointment to him. We concluded some officer took it for his own enjoyment, possibly even SGT Nolan.

After resting on my bunk for a few minutes, I dressed and waited for Tom to join me in front of the barracks. As I stood out front, it became obvious from the noise that Camp Pine was now coming alive. Jeeps and trucks were going by and other soldiers were moving about. Tom soon joined me and off we went in search of Building #32, where we were to meet SGT Nolan. We had to ask a few soldiers walking by where it was. We were told the building was on the backside of the chow hall.

We knew where that was, so we reversed our direction and headed back towards the familiar chow hall. We had ten minutes left to make it to Building #32; it would be close but we felt we could make it in plenty of time.

We arrived at the designated location, and there waiting for us was SGT Nolan. "Welcome Privates, have a seat." The building was one big room with lots of wooden chairs, desks, maps and chalkboards. I took my seat not knowing what would happen next. SGT Nolan selected a nearby chair and sat down next to Tom and me. In a much calmer demeanor, he told us that Camp Pine was not anywhere near full capacity because our country was not at war. Including Tom and me, there were only ninety soldiers and officers. He gave us a brief history of the camp and outlined his expectations of us. "Your pushups and five mile run this morning are just a taste of what is ahead of you for the next twelve weeks", he informed us. "My objective is to make you into elite soldiers, soldiers that will be able to defend our country at all costs. You will be subjected to long hikes, weapons training, and strenuous exercise. Are you prepared for the journey that lies ahead of you?"

Tom and I answered simultaneously, "Yes, Sir."

SGT Nolan told us that over the next few weeks approximately one hundred new recruits would enter through the gates of Camp Pine. Our barracks would soon fill up. He spent the next hour explaining how military time worked, and that going forward, the time of day would be in twenty-four increments versus a twelve hour AM and PM delineation. Before dismissing us, SGT Nolan gave us his charge. "America is currently not at war, but that could change at any minute. Germany, Russia and Japan are volatile countries and America could get sucked up into another world war at anytime", he cautioned. "Camp Pine is one of only a very few places where America's young men are being trained for war. Take full advantage of every opportunity that is presented to you here." With that, SGT Nolan dismissed us and sent us back to the chow hall for lunch. We then undertook a five-mile, double-time hike around the camp with SGT Nolan, followed by dinner and another attempt at one hundred pushups. I finally crawled into my bed at 2200 hours. I slept hard and dreamt of my participation in America's next war. I never realized at the time the hardship, horrors and heartache that I would experience in the coming years.

The next morning started off just like the day before had, except that Tom and I had made a promise the night before to wake each other up by 0545 hours so we could dress and be ready for whatever SGT Nolan had in store with us. Unfortunately, SGT Nolan bolted into our barracks at 0500 hours instead of at 0600 hours, like the previous day. Neither Tom nor I were ready; consequently, we were once again forced to stand at attention in what we had slept in, bleary-eyed and sore from the previous day's activity.

This day had a new twist, SGT Nolan gave us three minutes to dress and meet him outside. The sky was dark and the fall morning air was chilly. The blisters on my feet, that I had received the day before, made every step excruciating; walking was nearly impossible and the thought of having to run was tantamount to torture.

SGT Nolan took us on yet another five-mile, double-time hike around the camp. The run was not any easier than the day before, but my feet were cushioned this time with two pairs of wool socks. I survived the hike and managed to limp into the chow hall by 0645 hours. I consumed a lighter breakfast than I had the day before, anticipating pushups or more running. Unfortunately, I was right, managing to complete sixty-eight pushups before pausing to catch my breath, and then completing the remaining thirty-two.

Just as SGT Nolan had told us, more recruits arrived at the end of the week. By the end of that first week, our barracks reached twenty-two recruits. Our morning runs, hikes and pushups were conducted with all of the new recruits; I tried to out-perform as many of them as I could in all our activities.

October 1926 arrived, and the routine continued. I was getting my body into shape and able to endure the unending abuse of SGT Nolan. The barrack that Tom and I occupied was now filled to capacity. Our daily activity was the same, but we Privates were divided into four platoons, with twenty-five members each. SGT Nolan was still our leader, but he directed most of his energy to the four platoon leaders he had selected during the third week in October. I was the designated leader of 1st Platoon and Tom the leader of 2nd Platoon. I was confident my prior ROTC training and inherit leadership qualities weighed heavily in SGT Nolan's selection. It may have been prideful of me but I was ready to accept the challenge.

A lot of variety was added to our daily routine during October, when we were introduced to the firing range. The firing range became part of our daily ritual as we were taught how to handle, load, fire, clean, disassemble and reassemble Browning machine guns, 1903 Springfield rifles and M1911 Colt 45 pistols. The use and proper handling of bayonets and hand grenades was demonstrated. We began taking long hikes outside of the camp, venturing ten and fifteen miles deep into the woods of northern New York. My feet toughened and I was eventually able to endure the long hikes without my feet tearing up. The key I found was to keep my feet cushioned and as dry as possible. The message ingrained in me day after day, as I moved through boot camp, was also to keep my weapons dry at all times.

As the weeks progressed, I made it a point to have the best platoon out of the four. I made sure my platoon members had the right equipment, did not complain and excelled in every exercise we competed in against the other three. Individually, I met my goals of finishing the hikes and runs before anyone else. I gravitated to the rifle range and found all the weapons easy to handle and care for. If I did not hit the targets dead center when I shot, I was disappointed with myself and made sure to make the necessary adjustments.

In early November, Camp Pine saw its first snowfall of the year. I spent my first Thanksgiving away from home that year. Thankfully, the chow hall knew that new recruits were homesick and they treated us right. The cooks prepared turkey, cranberry sauce, gravy, sweet potatoes, buttered asparagus, rolls, pumpkin pie, apple pie, Coca-Cola and coffee. I had been at Camp Pine for approximately eight weeks and I have to admit, that was the best meal I had during my entire time there. The real reward of that cold Thanksgiving Day in 1926 was that I could eat as much as I wanted and not have to run, hike or do any pushups. I went to bed that night with mixed emotions; I was sad to be away from my mother and father but excited to be part of a group of men that were training to defend America. I had four weeks left in my basic training and was determined to finish it at the top of my class.

December was a significant month, both because it was our last month of training and because the training took place in harsh conditions. These conditions tested me mentally and physically. The lessons I learned about teamwork, attention to detail and self-discipline proved invaluable. Even in snow, we new recruits had to complete an obstacle course in which we crawled under barbed wire, climbed ropes, scaled wall installations, and kept our heads down when we were fired upon by live ammunition. The hikes took on a new meaning when we had to maneuver through two feet of fresh snow, while carrying an eight-pound rifle, a full backpack, a shovel, and bedroll.

That month we hiked into Canada, the farthest I had ever walked before and my first visit to another country. It was a sixty-mile hike from Camp Pine to Charleston Lake, Ontario, Canada. The hike included many miles through snow and ice. Our instructors taught us how to cross the northeast corner of Lake Ontario, using a pontoon bridge. The hike took five days and four nights. Along the route, we camped outside in our two-man tents, listening as the wind howled and the snow fell. By the time we reached Charleston Lake, over thirty recruits had dropped out of the forced hike. Those of us who successfully completed the long hike were trucked back to Camp Pine; as we rode in the back of drafty, two and half ton trucks, we could see the recruits who had originally dropped out of the hike, slowly marching north, as we rode south.

We were sent to the rifle range in the latter half of December, even though it was below freezing. We learned how to handle all of our weapons in frigid conditions. The barracks were cold that December, but not as cold as the outside temperature, thanks to a large potbelly stove in the center of the barracks. I had written my parents earlier in the month to let them know I would not be home for Christmas. Many of us new recruits did not have enough money to take a bus or train home for the holiday. Furthermore, our graduation from boot camp was on December 30th. Although we had a five-day leave for Christmas, I was one of a few recruits that chose to use that time for extra practice at the rifle range. I also studied up on military strategy with the help of books that I had found earlier at the camp's small library. I learned the most from material on General Ulysses S. Grant, General William T. Sherman and a Japanese General by the name of Sun Tzu. To my surprise,

SGT Nolan spent some time during those five days sharing stories with me about his time in China and France. He asked me if I had ever considered making a career out of the Army, as he had. I had never really considered making a career of it up to that point, but it triggered an immediate response from me. "Because America is not at war, what can I do to further my career, Sir?"

SGT Nolan took a moment to consider his answer, then in a calm voice said, "We will be going to war again, I feel it. There will be a need for soldiers willing to do whatever it takes to guarantee the safety of our country." His response really stimulated my interest; I spent the remaining days of 1926 thinking about traveling to distant countries and serving my country in ways that were different from the ordinary soldier.

My graduation from boot camp took place, as scheduled, on Thursday, December 30, 1926. Of the one hundred recruits that started with me in early October, only sixty-six of us graduated. Recruits had washed out for various reasons, such as medical issues, disorderly conduct and even some felonies. Our graduation was simple and not attended by any family members. In twelve weeks time, I had gone from a skinny recruit to a fit Army Private well versed in weapons, team-building, proper communication skills and independent decision-making abilities. My ability to receive instruction and provide direction enhanced and my overall endurance was pushed far beyond what I thought was capable. On this day, I received my Private First Class chevron.

The day after boot camp graduation, I was in the chow hall having breakfast with Tom Beckett. We were discussing our future in the Army and possible post assignments. Several of the friends I had made during those twelve weeks were choosing various Army posts; like Carlisle Barracks, Pennsylvania, Fort Bragg, North Carolina, Fort Benning, Georgia, and Fort Bliss, Texas. Of all assignments, Tom's selection was to remain at Camp Pine for the immediate future and train to become a Drill Sergeant. I had no interest in that direction, desiring to secure an assignment that would take me overseas. Locations like Manila, Philippines and Pearl Harbor, Hawaii were appealing. I had seven days to submit three Army destination choices to the Camp Pine Reassignment Office. As Tom and I were finishing our breakfast, recalling some of the highlights of boot camp training, SGT Nolan walked in and sat down next to us.

"Private Voigt, I guess you have heard that your friend Private Beckett here has decided to follow in my footsteps and become a Drill Sergeant?" he asked.

I replied, "Yes, I have Sir. I find it hard to believe but I am happy for him."

SGT Nolan managed to crack a slight smile before he replied and asked me, "What have you decided to do Private Voigt?"

I sat there in silence for a few seconds. "I am not exactly sure, Sir." A few moments went by as I sipped on my coffee.

"Well, I am going to help you make up your mind," said SGT Nolan. He rose to his feet and to my surprise, said, "You and I have been summoned to Building #1 at 0900 hours. I will meet you at the front of the building at 0845 hours. Understood?"

I immediately replied, "Yes, Sir." I had not visited Building #1 during my time at Camp Pine, but I did know where it was, simply from word of mouth. Building #1 was the location of the senior officers and the Commanding General's office.

It was freezing that Friday morning. I met SGT Nolan promptly at 0845 hours outside of Building #1. We walked in together and checked in with the Army receptionist in the lobby. I took a seat and looked at all the pictures of famous U.S. Army Generals on the surrounding walls. One of the larger walls in the lobby had a large American flag hanging on it. The flag had clearly seen some action; its edges were tattered and it showed some modest discoloration. There was a plaque underneath the flag and I had to know what it said. I walked over and read the following:

This United States Flag proudly waved outside of the U.S. Army 1st Infantry Division's headquarters

during the Great War. The headquarters were located in the Cantigny Sector in Picardy, France. This flag flew proudly at that headquarters from April 27-July 8, 1918.

I stood there in awe, for I knew my father had probably spent time in that headquarters during his time in France and had probably walked right under that very flag a few times. A voice behind me disrupted my thoughts. "Do you like military history, Private?"

I turned around and saw a U.S. Army General standing behind me. I saluted him and replied, "Yes, Sir. My father, Robert Voigt, served in the 1st Infantry Division during the Great War." The General then reached out to shake my hand. I gave him a firm handshake.

"I am Brigadier General Pete Massey," he informed me. "It is a pleasure to finally meet you, Private Voigt. I would like you and SGT Nolan to follow me, please." SGT Nolan and I followed the General down a narrow hallway full of pictures on both sides, and up one flight of stairs. An office was located just off the top of the stairs. As I walked into the room, I saw that there were already two men seated behind a long table, facing me. I recognized one of the men as Colonel John Pruitt, Camp Pine's commanding officer. The other man was a Lieutenant. SGT Nolan and I were instructed to take the two seats facing the table. We all sat silently for a moment, and I heard the blades of the ceiling fan above me turning slowly. The room was warm thanks in part to the sunshine that was pouring in through the windows.

Colonel Pruitt turned to me and asked, "Do you know why you are here, Private First Class Voigt?"

I answered in a firm, loud voice, "No, Sir."

Colonel Pruitt then explained, "You are here for one main reason, but let me give you some background information first. In your boot camp graduating class of sixty-six recruits, you ranked number one."

I knew I had worked hard, but did not know where I had finished in the overall ranking.

Colonel Pruitt continued, "Your number one ranking was based on several factors compiled over the last twelve weeks. You scored the highest on weapons training. You also finished at the top of the obstacle course ranking. Your outstanding leadership traits, ability to make quick decisions, and your timely and accurate interpretation of instructions were attributes that SGT Nolan saw in you. He felt compelled to bring your accomplishments and leadership attributes to my attention. I, myself, observed your progress through various events, including the long march to Canada just a few weeks ago. I agreed with SGT Nolan's assessment of your abilities and I shared that with Brigadier General Massey."

All the accolades were embarrassing but appreciated. I simply strived to do by best in everything I did, a habit instilled by my father. I looked over at SGT Nolan, who stared straight ahead at the three imposing figures, betraying no emotion. I had no idea where the meeting was headed and thought that this information could have been shared with me in a less formal setting. Colonel Pruitt had been the only one to speak up to that point. The unknown Lieutenant had a stack of papers in front of him that he periodically shuffled; he looked intently in my direction from time to time however. I wondered why I was the only recruit there from my class. Why were a Brigadier General and a mystery Lieutenant here at Camp Pine? I had no idea where they came from or to what branch of service they belonged.

Brigadier General Massey spoke and said, "Private 1st Class Voigt, you have distinguished yourself here at Camp Pine. SGT Nolan, you have trained a fine soldier. If I recall, SGT Nolan, you and I spilled blood together at the Meuse-Argonne Offensive during September 1918. Private Voigt, your father may have been right there with us."

SGT Nolan respectively replied, "That is correct, Sir. You were a 2nd Lieutenant back then, if I recall correctly." He continued, "Yes,

Private Voigt has shown a unique ability to learn quickly, solve problems creatively, and accomplish tasks far ahead of his peers."

Brigadier General Massey nodded his head as SGT Nolan concluded then turned to me and said, "Private Voigt that is why you are here today. I represent a division of the United States Army that specializes in overseas counter intelligence operations called MID or Military Intelligence Division. We do not call ourselves spies but perform duties that parallel that label. You have been selected, the only one I might add, from Camp Pine's long list of prospective recruits, to become a Military Attaché. This role involves long overseas station assignments, multi-language skills and dangerous assignments. Does this role interest you, Private?"

This is what I had dreamed of most of my life and now the opportunity was sitting right in front of me. My future suddenly became very clear. I processed the information that was being presented to me and answered enthusiastically, "Yes, Sir!"

Brigadier General Massey then nodded his head and turned to the Lieutenant. "Lt. Yates, please provide Private Voigt with a more detailed description of what will happen next."

I waited silently and tried not to appear too eager. Lt. Yates took one piece of paper out of his stack, rose to his feet and walked toward me. He handed me the paper and returned to his seat. Lt. Yates then said, "My name is Lt. Joe Yates and I am an instructor at the United States Army War College, located at the Carlisle Barracks in Southern Pennsylvania. You have been selected to attend the Army War College for the next four years." He gestured toward the paper he had handed me. "The piece of paper in front of you provides you with dates, arrival times, items to bring and a list of our expectations. After completing your studies, you will be assigned a critical overseas post as a Military Attaché. Our goal is to prepare you for whatever you might encounter." Lt. Yates paused for a moment and looked at the other men in the room before he continued. "America will be drawn into war again. We do not know the time and place, but your role, as a Military Attaché will allow us to have boots on the ground in potential hot spots. Your time at the Army War College will be an exception, simply because the college is typically reserved for senior officers. As of today, you are promoted to the rank of Corporal. The Army needs to do a better job of training and equipping its Military Attaches and we are starting with you."

I felt overwhelmed and did not know how much more I could absorb in a single day. I sat in my chair, stunned and excited to be granted such a unique opportunity. Colonel Pruitt then addressed me, "Stand to your feet Corporal Voigt and receive your new chevrons."

I stood and saw that SGT Nolan would be giving me my new Corporal chevrons. As he handed them to me, he firmly shook my hand and leaned into me whispering, "Learn all you can, go far, stand tall, fight to the death and make me proud."

I turned and faced the senior officers at the table and saluted them. Brigadier General Massey, Colonel Pruitt and Lt. Yates exited the room, leaving SGT Nolan and me alone to soak in the moment. After a few moments of silence, SGT Nolan spoke. "You should not be surprised, Corporal Voigt. You have worked hard these past twelve weeks. I saw something in you that first day you ran around the track in your combat boots. You obeyed orders, gave it your very best and refused to quit. These are traits that you carried with you during your entire boot camp experience." He looked out the window for a moment then turned back to me and said, "These are attributes you will have to take with you as you proceed through the Army War College and then overseas." I thanked SGT Nolan for his confidence in me and for helping me secure this opportunity. I walked out of Building #1 that morning, eager to begin my next assignment in the Army."

According to the document given to me by Lt. Yates, I had over a week to report to the Army War College; Monday, January 10, 1927. I decided to take the next four days off and make a quick visit back home to East Aurora. Before leaving Camp Pine, I went by to see Tom Beckett. He was excited to hear about my unique opportunity and wished me much success. We celebrated New Years at the camp with friends we made during boot camp. Tom had become a good friend and I hoped to see him again. I also went to see SGT Nolan and thanked him for making me into a confident and fit soldier. He patted me on the back and told me I would do well. I left Camp Pine on January 2nd. During a brief stop in Syracuse, I called my parents and told them I would be in Buffalo by 8:00 PM that night. My folks had not heard my voice in over twelve weeks and were thrilled to know that I would be coming home, even for a few days.

My train pulled into Buffalo as scheduled, and there waiting on the train platform were my parents. I had not realized just how much I missed them. We embraced and they held me tightly saying nothing for a few moments. My mother spoke first and said, "You look so handsome in your Army uniform. Have you lost weight?"

I answered, "I have actually gained weight, Mom, but it's mostly muscle."

My Dad noticed my Corporal chevrons and asked, "How did you manage to get promoted twice in twelve weeks?"

I grinned and replied, "That is a long story and I cannot wait to tell you and Mom about." It was very cold outside; snow was still on the ground and I was just eager to get close to a roaring fire at home. We all got in the car and my father drove us back to East Aurora. There waiting for me as we opened the front door was my faithful dog, Porgy. He jumped into my arms and licked me repeatedly all over my face. It was good to be home.

The next four days were taken up with good eating, visits with relatives, and lots of story telling about boot camp and SGT Nolan. With excitement in my voice, I spent a lot of time over dinner one night telling my folks about my recent promotion, my assignment to the Army War College, and my eventual appointment to be a Military Attaché overseas. My father humbly expressed that during his two-year stint in the Army, he was never promoted higher than the rank of Corporal. Nevertheless, he was proud of his military service. I spent a full day deer hunting with my Grandfather Henry and his brother Mark, who was a legendary fur trapper in Western

New York. During our time together, my Grandfather expressed how proud he was of me and of my accomplishments. I impressed him even further, bagging a large buck that day. My firing range expertise had paid off!

My visit home went by far too fast. On Friday morning, January 7th, my mother made me the breakfast of all breakfasts: scrambled eggs, bacon, cinnamon rolls and cold milk. My father and I had coffee on the front porch while Porgy sat close to me. My Grandfather asked if he could take me to the train station that morning and my parents graciously allowed him. I packed up my Army duffel bag, hugged each of my parents, and patted Porgy on the head. This time, everyone knew that I might not be returning home for a long time. The last words my Grandfather said to me as he dropped me off at the Buffalo train station were, "Stand strong for the principles you have been taught, shoot straight and pray to God often." I hugged him goodbye and boarded the southbound train for Harrisburg, Pennsylvania.

Chapter 2

FAR FROM HOME

"The struggle of today is not altogether
for today – it is for a vast future also."
Abraham Lincoln

The six-hour train ride from Buffalo to Harrisburg was uneventful.
I had plenty of time to ponder what lay ahead of me as the train
maneuvered southbound along the steel tracks. The big windows
of the passenger train afforded me great views of the rolling hills of
central Pennsylvania. The trees were bare, and snow was everywhere,
covering everything except the train tracks. The other passengers
on the train were cordial to me, asking me questions such as, "How
long have you been in the Army?" and, "Why are you in the Army
when America is not at war?" My answers were polite but succinct as
I explained that I had only been in the Army for twelve weeks and
was now heading to the Army War College in Carlisle, Pennsylvania.

Unable to nap, I stared out the window and reflected on the flurry
of activity over the last three months at Camp Pine. After suddenly
being tapped on the shoulder, I turned and saw an old man in a gray
suit. He asked if he could sit in the open seat next to me. After I
assured him that he could, he sat down. He gathered his thoughts,
and then slowly and firmly stated, "My name is George Walters. It
is a pleasure to meet a fellow soldier of the United States Army."

"Thank you Sir," I replied. "I am Allen Voigt, and I have to ask -
how can you still be in the Army?"

He laughed and explained, "Son, since I am 81 years old, I am no longer in the Army. I am a veteran and very proud to have served my country in the Civil War. Please call me George."

I had never met anyone who had fought in the Civil War before and meeting George was a real honor. George then expressed his appreciation by saying, "Son, you should be proud to serve in the United States Army. My unit served at the Battle of Gettysburg during July 1-3, 1863. I served with the 140th New York Infantry Regiment. We fought some aggressive battles during those three long days. I lost many friends and that is why I am on this train. It has been sixty-three years since I was there and I feel it is finally time to go back."

The Army War College was not far from Gettysburg, so I decided to make a point to visit the battlefield and cemetery during my upcoming time in Carlisle. When George asked me where I was going, he was surprised to hear there was an actual Army college. He asked if he could buy me a cup of coffee in the nearby Pullman car. I agreed and spent the rest of the train ride listening with rapt attention as George described his experiences participating in the Civil War and having to have to kill other men.

I had heard about the Battle of Gettysburg, and even memorized Abraham Lincoln's famous speech but I was now meeting someone that had participated in the famous battle. George was on his way back to Gettysburg to pay his respects to his friends and fellow soldiers that had died there so long ago.

As my train entered the station in Harrisburg, Pennsylvania, I rose and helped George to his feet. I thanked him profusely for spending time with me and sharing so many stories and thoughts about his time in the Army. We worked our way off the train and toward the train station exit, where I said goodbye to George. My instructions from Lt. Yates were to find a cab and instruct the driver to take me to the front gate of the Army War College. Outside the train station, it took awhile but I was finally able to hail a cab. I instructed the driver to take me to the Army War College on

Claremont Road. The cab driver said, "Well, that's a first! I've never taken someone to the Army War College before." Very little else was said along the approximate, thirty minute ride. By the time the cab driver pulled up to the front gate, it was almost six o'clock in the evening. I handed the cab driver a few bucks and entered the guard shack.

A young Private at the guard shack greeted me and said, "You must be Corporal Allen Voigt. Lt. Yates phoned me late this afternoon, instructing us to be on the lookout for you." I confirmed that I was, in fact, Corporal Voigt. The Private then called for some transportation for me and asked me to have a seat on the bench located just outside the guard shack. I thought back to my first night at Camp Pine - this night was in sharp contrast to that one.

Shortly, a black Ford sedan, driven by another Private, pulled up to where I was sitting. He stuck his head out the driver's side window and said, "Corporal Voigt?" I stood and nodded in agreement. I threw my duffle bag in the back seat and sat down in the front passenger seat. The Private glanced over at me and stated, "Welcome to the Army War College, Sir." As we rode through the grounds of the Army War College, I was amazed at the number of buildings, large oak trees and old Civil War cannons scattered throughout the property. The college had been there for twenty-five years.

I was dropped off in front of a white-columned building with the word "Administration" posted in big black lettering on the front of it. Lt. Yates had told me to proceed to office #18, where I was to meet someone who would assist me with my entrance paperwork, lodging instructions, etc. The walkway leading up to the Administration building led me up several brick covered steps. The large ornate building stood out in stark contrast to any of the buildings I had seen at Camp Pine. I walked inside and asked a young woman behind a large wooden desk where office #18 was. She asked if I was Corporal Voigt. When I confirmed that I was, she directed me up two flights of stairs located nearby. I was tired by this point in the day, but excited to be on the campus. After I reached the top of the stairs, I saw a sign that indicated the office was to my right. I walked down a long hallway, practically the length of the entire building. Office #18 was the second to last door on the left. The glass door was frosted, but I could tell someone was inside. I knocked and a voice on the other side said, "Enter". I walked in and found an Army Lieutenant sitting behind a metal desk. The room was not large, with only the desk, a few filing cabinets and a couple of chairs filing up the cramped office. Various black and white photos of Army officers lined the walls. The man's name was Lt. Fuller, according to a brass plaque sitting on the desk. Lt. Fuller asked me to have a seat in front of him, so I placed my duffle bag on the floor, saluted, and sat down.

"Welcome to the Army War College, Corporal Voigt. How was your trip?"

"Fine, Sir", I replied. Suddenly, someone knocked on the door behind me. As Lt. Fuller told them to enter, I turned my head and to my surprise, there in the doorway stood Lt. Yates. I came to my feet and saluted him. After returning my salute, Lt. Yates sat down next to me, and asked, "How was your trip Corporal Voigt?"

"Excellent, Sir." I replied.

"Your admittance into the Army War College is the first of its kind, Corporal Voigt. Typically, college attendees are officers who are here to learn Army tactics and strategy. You are the first to be admitted below the rank of Lieutenant." Lt. Yates paused to let this sink in with me and continued. "As we expressed to you up at Camp Pine, there is an Army initiative to strengthen the role of its Military Attaches. You are entering a four-year program that is experimental and aggressive. Your education will be both academic and physical. Your basic training was only a small fraction of what you will learn here at the Army War College. Are you ready to get started?"

I firmly answered "Yes, Sir".

It was now Lt. Fuller's turn to speak. "Excellent. We have some miscellaneous paperwork to complete, after which we'll get you to your dorm, and then you'll have supper." After Lt. Yates left the room, Lt. Fuller asked me some confirming questions about my age, height, weight, religion, level of high school achieved, and so on. He seemed satisfied with my answers and proceeded to file my paperwork. We left the room together and went down the stairs and outside. We walked across campus at a steady pace, but along the way Lt. Fuller pointed out statues, buildings and landmarks. We eventually arrived at a building labeled "Pershing Dorm". We walked inside and continued up three flights of stairs. By this time, my duffle bag felt like it weighed over one hundred pounds. After we reached the top of the stairs, we walked down a long hallway, finally arriving at a door labeled "Voigt". I was shocked to see my name on the door.

"This is your private room, Corporal Voigt, and it will remain so for the next four years. This room is assigned to you due to the nature of your unique education. The material you learn must be kept secret." said Lt. Fuller. I was used to having my own room at home, but twelve weeks of boot camp had gotten me used to having roommates and fighting for showers, sinks and food. This new living situation would be a pleasant change.

"Drop your bag, Corporal Voigt and let's go grab some supper," said Lt. Fuller.

We left the room and headed out of the dorm. I had not eaten since breakfast, so I was very hungry. It was almost eight o'clock in the evening and the sun had already set. It did not take long to reach the dining commons, which had a format similar to Camp Pine. I grabbed a silver tray and followed Lt. Fuller through the line. He turned to me and said, "I hope you do not mind me eating with you, Corporal Voigt?"

"Not at all, Sir", I replied. "I welcome the company."

The food was similar to that at Camp Pine, but there were more choices. Lt. Fuller and I found some seats near the center of the dining commons. It was a large room, containing several circular tables. There was no one else at our table. I intended to carry on a good conversation with the Lieutenant, but my appetite got the best of me. I enjoyed every bite of my roast beef, mashed potatoes and carrots.

We wrapped up supper and before Lt. Fuller parted ways with me, he handed me a folder, saying, "This will provide you with directions for your first day of class, where to secure your books, and your first semester schedule." I returned to my room that night unpacked and hit the bed. Before I drifted off to sleep, I lay there staring at the ceiling, wondering what might lie ahead for me. I had never imagined that I would go to college, let alone have it completely paid for by the Army. I was nervous and excited, all at the same time. The dorm was strangely quiet that night except for the lonely sound of the wind blowing against my dorm room window.

I woke the next morning to the familiar sound of revelry, playing over speakers mounted in the hallways of my dorm. My goal that day was to secure my textbooks and supplies and figure out the various routes to my classes, scheduled to begin in two days. I dressed in my customary khaki pants, shirt and tie. Lt. Fuller had provided me with the meal schedule of the dining commons and all my classes, which ran Monday through Friday. Saturdays were going to be reserved for weapons training and geographical map studies. I was hungry, so I set out for breakfast. As I left the dorm room, I noticed that there were a few other soldiers moving about the dorm, and others headed in the same direction I was. The sun was just breaking over the horizon as I walked to the dining commons. Snow had fallen overnight, but the sidewalks were shoveled and passable. I reached the dining commons and headed for the chow line. As I held my tray, I struck up a conversation with another soldier with my same rank.

"My name is Allen Voigt. I arrived last night from Buffalo, New York."

The Corporal replied, "My name is John Hall and I am from Palatine, Illinois. I arrived a day before you."

John and I sat together and got to know each other as we worked through our breakfast of scrambled eggs, sausage, toast and coffee. We found out we had similar childhoods, having been the only child and growing up in small towns. I was surprised to discover we shared similar recruitment after completing basic training, although

John had completed basic training at Camp Pickett in Virginia. He had also excelled in basic training and had a similar encounter with Lt. Yates. I was beginning to see a pattern emerging. As I left the dining common, I was glad to have met a new friend and wondered how many of us at the Army War College were recruited for this new kind of military service.

Over the balance of Saturday, my first full day on campus, I spent it walking around, familiarizing myself with the buildings, the rifle range and the bookstore. I secured the required textbooks as outlined by Lt. Fuller. It took me some time, but I found every one of my six classrooms and made a simple map of how to find each one. My class schedule was aggressive, which I was accustomed to in high school, but the course names intimidated me. Outside of English, all the other courses definitely concerned me: German Language and Culture, Advanced Geography, Literature, Psychology and Math. I would be attending three, two-hour classes a day, rotating the classes every other day. The books were thick and it felt like I was carrying bricks, but I was determined to study hard and do my best, partly because I was the only member of my family to attend college up to this point. John Hall and I shared dinner together again that night and found out we had four classes together.

On Sundays, we could leave campus and do whatever we wanted. Sunday came and I decided to attend Memorial Church there on campus. It was comforting being back in church that Sunday morning. I had been raised in a God fearing family and had attended church regularly all my life. Although the worship service was simple, I found it encouraging. I prayed that day that God would have His hand upon me during college and then eventually overseas.

I took a long nap after I got back to my dorm, which was something I had not done in a long time. I decided that there would be other Sundays to venture off campus and explore central Pennsylvania, and I wanted to be well rested for classes the next day.

Monday arrived, my first day of college, military-style. I got up early, ate a good breakfast, and then headed to class. My first class, German Language and Culture, met on the second floor of a building on the backside of the campus. I walked into the classroom just before eight o'clock and took a seat near the middle of the room. The professor and I were the only people in the room. As I took my seat, the professor rose from his desk and walked toward me, and said, *"Guten Morgen Fachmann Voigt. Herzlich willkommen in die Deutsche Sprache und Kultur. Wie sind Sie heute?"*

All I understood was my name. I was too embarrassed not to say anything, so I replied, "Yes, my name is Allen Voigt."

"I know who you are", the professor answered with a smile. "What I said in German was, 'Good morning Corporal Voigt. Welcome to German Language and Culture class. How are you today?'"

I replied, "I am very well but I have to apologize and say up front that I do not know any German. I took French in high school, but barely remember any of it."

With another smile, the professor turned and walked back towards the front of the room. By that time, several other soldiers had joined us and were taking their seats. As class started that cold January morning, I looked around the room and counted six other soldiers. The classroom could hold twenty-five students, so I found it strange that it was not full, but it was not surprising because there were not many soldiers on campus. The professor welcomed us to the class by speaking his introductory comments in German and then translating them into English. After he had spoken several sentences in German, he finally spoke in English, "Welcome to German Language and Culture. My name is Professor Merkle and I will be responsible for teaching each of you the foundation of the German language. By the end of this semester, my goal is to provide you with the building blocks that will allow you to ultimately immerse yourself in the German society, blending in like you were born there."

I was exhausted after my first six-hour day of classes. I sat down for dinner that night in the dining commons with John Hall. We both ate our meals without saying a single word to each other. When I had finished my meal, I pushed my serving tray away from me and finally spoke, telling John, "And I thought basic training was exhausting."

I wanted to go to sleep when I got back to my dorm room, but I had three hours of homework staring me in the face. I wrestled through German vocabulary words, practiced algebra problems and studied maps provided by my Advanced Geography professor. The maps were of Germany. I had not picked my classes, and I thought it strange that I was looking at German maps and learning the German language. Would my first post as a military liaison be in Germany?

As I wrapped up my first week of classes, I looked forward to Saturday and having a break from sitting in class and studying. However, what I actually experienced on Saturday turned out to be more like boot camp at Camp Pine. The day was cut in half, with the morning spent at the rifle range and the afternoon in a map room. The map room was actually a stand-alone building located next to the rifle range. It contained an extensive collection of world maps that showed not only each country's borders, but also specific details on German, Japanese and Russian cities. Over time, my Saturdays became just as important, if not more important, than my Monday through Friday classes.

The importance of my Saturday training became very apparent a few Saturdays later when an Army, half-ton truck pulled up to our firing range, accompanied by black Ford Model A's positioned in front and in back of the truck. After the vehicles stopped, several men with Thompson submachine guns stepped out of each vehicle. A man in a suit exited the rear vehicle and approached Lt. Boone, the commanding officer overseeing the rifle range. They exchanged a few words, and then asked us to put down our 1903 Springfield rifles and assemble near the half-ton truck. Lt. Boone, spoke up and said, "The Springfield Armory is here today with new rifles that they would like us to test-fire."

The man in the suit then addressed us. "My name is Andy Masters and I am proud to be here today. The Army War College has selected each of you to test two of our new weapons, the M1924 Garand and the .276 Pedersen Garand, each having a different caliber. We are asking you to test both of them and let us know which one you like the best." I, along with three other soldiers, volunteered to unload two large crates from the truck and then carried them to the rifle range.

The nine of us on the rifle range that cold Saturday morning were first handed the M1924, a .30-06 caliber rifle. We each fired sixty-four rounds from the gas-operated rifle. The rifle had an eight-shot clip versus the bolt action of the 1903 Springfield rifle. I liked it because it was faster and easier to fire in a true semi-automatic fashion. We then tested the .276 caliber Pedersen rifle, which had a ten-shot clip. The .276 Pedersen was lighter but I did not like it because it did not appear durable enough. Both rifles proved very accurate as we fired one hundred yards down range at a target. Once we completed the test firing, the rifles were collected and loaded back on the truck. Mr. Masters then asked each of us questions about how each rifle performed, and we collectively gave our opinions on each rifle. I was the only one who favored the M1924 model Garand. The three-vehicle caravan soon departed the rifle range the same way it came in.

The first four months of 1927 came and went. I had one month to go in my first semester at the Army War College. May arrived, and it was a welcome relief from the cold winter. The snow had melted, the leaves were in full bloom and flowers dotted the entire campus. I was performing well in all of my classes, except for math. I had always struggled in math, and this class was no exception. The professor was considerate and tutored me all semester. There was an interesting dynamic of professors at the Army War College. They were all veterans of the Great War, but they had retired from active duty and now taught full-time. They offered a unique approach to their teaching in that all of them imparted a military slant into their lectures, homework and tests. This approach would prove invaluable.

During mid-May, my fellow soldiers and I where called into an evening meeting. There were only fifty first-year students enrolled that semester, and all of us were present. This meeting was different in that there were no professors in attendance, only Army officers. The meeting came to order, and a face I had not seen in several months stepped to the front of the room. Lt. Yates was there to speak to us. We stood and saluted him, and then took our seats.

"Men, you all have had a baptism in fire these past four and half months", he said. "I have reviewed your progress to date. For the most part, all of you are doing well. My reason for calling all of you together tonight is to let you know what your activities will be this summer. Most of you will be getting a break from your studies and assigned to various Army camps around the country. Your role at your assigned camp will be that of support, helping to train new recruits in weapons and tactics. However, a few of you will remain here at the Army War College."

I immediately thought to myself, "Staying on campus all summer would have to be a punishment for poor performance in the classroom and on the rifle range."

Lt. Yates continued, "Voigt, Hall and Barton stay behind, the rest of you are dismissed." The three of us received some jabs from our fellow classmates as they left the room. In my mind, I reviewed my progress over the last few months. I knew I was receiving good test grades and performing well at the rifle range. Maybe my map studies were lacking, and I therefore had to stay on campus that summer.

Lt. Yates called us up to the front of the room and asked us to have a seat. He pulled up a chair next to us, paused for a few seconds, and then addressed us. "Voigt, Hall and Barton, you have been asked to stay behind for one specific reason. You three are at the top of this freshman class. You each showed unique abilities during your respective boot camps and have continued to excel through your first year here at the Army War College. You are to stay on campus this summer not as a punishment, but because the Army wants to invest more time in your language studies and weapons training. Bottom line, soldiers, we want to accelerate your training and at the same time provide you with additional tools that will serve you well overseas."

I was relieved but frustrated, because I was ready for a change of venue. I had also hoped to get home to see my family.

Lt. Yates continued, "It is important that the three of you finish this semester strong. Do not let up. Your summer class schedules and assignments are forthcoming. You are dismissed."

As I left the room with Hall and Barton, we exchanged some grumbling about having to stay on campus, but we were excited that we were the top three in our class. When I laid my head on my pillow that night, I pondered the future. There had been a lot of discussion in our classes and on campus about the growing aggression by the Germans and Japanese. There was serious concern that America may one day face them in another global war. If that happened, what would my role be? I eventually drifted off to sleep.

I finished my first year ranked number two in my class, behind John Hall. The only thing that prevented me from finishing number one that semester was my challenging math class.

Summer 1927 was comprised of three activities: more German Language and Culture classes, lots of time in the map room, and extensive practice at the firing range. That summer I really began to get a grip on my German vocabulary and started to write in German. As part of my training, I was given a knife and shown how to use it in combat. I had never killed a man, but that summer I was trained how to sneak up on a man from behind and kill him with a knife. We were taught how to handle and use explosives. I learned how to hide explosive charges in almost anything and how to set a fuse. Summer flew by and I was unable to return home to see my family before the fall semester started. I was soon right back to my normal rotation of six classes, including additional map studies and weapons training.

My last three and a half years at the Army War College were memorable. The original group of fifty soldiers I started school with, had been reduced to thirty-two by graduation. We lost eighteen along the way due to grades or dismissal from the program for unknown reasons. By May 1931, I was preparing to graduate. I could have finished my studies at the end of 1930, but I wanted to take additional classes on interrogation techniques. By the time I graduated on May 18, 1931, I felt I had grown tremendously as a soldier. I was very competent in the German language, able to speak and write it fluently. I was so familiar with the culture of Germany and its rich history, that when I discussed it, I sounded like I was a German citizen. I would be in a better position to translate and exploit captured enemy documents, and my ability to read maps and charts was refined. I could use all forms of military weapons, and use them well. By the time I graduated, I knew virtually every known weapon in use in the world. I could fire, disassemble, repair, clean and reassemble all of them.

Only my parents attended my graduation, as my grandfather Henry had passed away in January 1930. I was sad at his passing and that he was not there to see me graduate. Graduation that day was a simple affair. We were all promoted directly to the rank of 2nd Lieutenant and given a gold bar and a diploma. As graduation ended and we rejoined our families, I noticed an old man slowly walking with a cane in my direction. It was none other than George Walters, the Civil War veteran I had met on the train coming down to Harrisburg four years prior. "Hello, Sir", I said warmly to him.

"Congratulations, Allen, on your graduation today", he replied with a smile.

I did the math in my head, something I had become very good at, and concluded George was now eighty-five years old. He still looked great for his age and could clearly still get around. "Thank you for coming today, George, how have you been?" I asked.

George replied, "I am doing quite well, thank you for asking. Since we parted ways a few years ago at the train station in Harrisburg, I have been following your progress. I have a question to ask you, Allen. During your time here, did you get to Gettysburg?"

I enthusiastically replied, "Yes, Sir, I did on two occasions. I must say, it was very humbling for me to walk the battlefield and pay my respects at the graves of the fallen." That night I joined my parents and George as we shared supper together at a nearby restaurant. It was a special time in that it was the last time I ever saw George.

As June 1931 began, the world was certainly a different place. The United States had experienced a stock market crash during October 1929, and its citizens were experiencing a major, countrywide depression. Herbert Hoover had replaced Calvin Coolidge as President. Germany was restless, looking to emerge from its post Great War suppression. A man by the name of Adolph Hitler was head of the new Nazi Party and hungry to rule the entire country. Japan, too, was restless, and eager to claim territories that would supply it with raw materials to help fuel its industries. This backdrop beckoned me into my next assignment as an Army Military Attaché. Lt. Yates' words spoken to me at Camp Pine over four and a half years earlier were coming to fruition.

I did not leave the Army War College after graduation, since I was awaiting my next assignment. I spent June and July 1931 honing my skills with weapons and explosives. I also spent an incredible amount of time working on hand-to-hand combat techniques. It was during early August 1931 that Lt. Yates called me into his office in the administration building. We spent the better part of a day going over the role of an Army Military Attaché, as well as the dangers and expectations associated with that role. As the clock on the wall neared three o'clock, Lt. Yates shared with me where I would be assigned, Germany. Suddenly, it all made sense. The four years of German studies and the maps I had reviewed and memorized were all pointing to this assignment.

"Berlin is in turmoil, Lt. Voigt, and it will be your job to be America's eyes and ears over there. Your role will report into the United States Embassy in Berlin. This will allow you access to the German government, present you with opportunities for intelligence gathering, and provide you the unique ability to observe military build-ups. Your role will allow you to initiate solo missions throughout the country, missions made clear once you arrive in Germany. That is the good news." Lt. Yates paused for a moment, but did not break eye contact. "The bad news is that after you leave this office, you cannot tell anyone where you are going or what your new assignment will be. The types of issues you will be uncovering and participating in, involves America's national security."

On Monday, August 10, 1931, I made a call to my parent's home in East Aurora, New York. I informed them of my assignment to a new post, but I could not tell them I was going out of the country. It was a hard conversation to have because I had to be honest with them and state I might not see them again. Up to this point in my life, even though we may have been apart, they knew where I was and what I was doing. I told them I would get word to them as much as I could. Late that afternoon I left the Army War College, taking a taxi to the train station in Harrisburg, Pennsylvania. I boarded a train for New York City. The train left at seven o'clock in the evening and I traveled all night to reach New York City's Penn Station. In 1931, it would have been odd to see a man in an Army uniform, so I traveled in street clothes. I arrived at Penn Station on Tuesday morning, August 11, 1931, at eight o'clock in the morning. My instructions were to meet the Navy submarine, the USS Narwhal, at Pier 54. Before I left Penn Station, I stored my small suitcase in a locker at the train station. I wanted to grab some breakfast and take in some sights before I was due to report to Pier 54 at four o'clock that afternoon.

I walked down 8th Avenue and then east on 36th Street. My goal was to end up at the tip of Manhattan in order to get a view of the Statue of Liberty. Not long after walking down 36th Street, I found a local diner named Meme's Kitchen, and they were still serving breakfast. I stepped inside and enjoyed one of the best breakfasts I had ever had. The restaurant's namesake, Meme, was at the diner that morning. She walked over to where I was sitting and asked me how my breakfast was.

I replied as I was chewing my food, "The scrambled eggs and French toast are amazing and I love the grits with cheese in them but

I have never had them before. More restaurants should serve grits, why don't they?"

Meme leaned into me and whispered, "Because these Yankees don't know what good country cooking is like!" Meme then told me that she was originally from Knightdale, North Carolina, and grits were part of every breakfast down South. I thanked her for my breakfast and started out again.

By this time, it was approaching ten o'clock in the morning and I only had six hours to get to Pier 54. I decided to grab a cab and have the cab driver give me a tour of New York City. I asked the driver to show me Times Square, the Empire State Building, and a glimpse of the Statue of Liberty. It was a whirlwind tour, but the cab driver took me all around and even gave me some color commentary along the way. It was amazing looking out over the water and viewing the famous Statue of Liberty.

The cab driver was very perceptive and as I got back in the cab, he asked me, "You were in the military weren't you?" I was a little surprised by the question, especially because I was dressed as a civilian and had made no mention of being in the Army. Before I could answer the cab driver continued, "My name is John and I served in the Great War. You carry yourself like you were in the military, that's all." John seemed honest and I informed him I was currently in the Army. I remembered my strict orders that I was not to mention to anyone that I was in the Army. I figured telling John was harmless.

"I knew it", said John.

I did not elaborate any further and asked John to take me back to Penn Station. He took me back to the train station, pointing out various landmarks and points of interest along the way. We arrived back at Penn Station at two-thirty in the afternoon, which gave me an hour and half to get to Pier 54. As I stepped out of the cab and reached for my wallet, John stopped me and refused to let me pay him. "This is your first time to New York City and you are in the Army, this one is on me." I thanked him for the gesture but still handed him three dollars, thanking him for the tour. We parted ways and I headed back to Penn Station to retrieve my suitcase.

Pier 54 was not far from Penn Station. I headed west down 34th Street and followed the signs to the docks. As inconspicuous as I was, it was humorous that I was to meet a Navy submarine and simply jump on board in broad daylight. I soon found Pier 54 and there she was, the USS Narwhal, with an American flag proudly waving from her stern. Two Navy sailors stood guard at the entrance of the gangplank. I walked up to one of them and simply said one word, "Reciprocity." A word Lt. Yates had instructed me to say to whoever was in charge of guarding the submarine. He had also informed me that the response I was to receive in confirmation was "Perseverance". The sailor responded with that word and motioned for me to proceed down the gangplank to the submarine. There were other sailors performing miscellaneous tasks on the deck of the USS Narwhal, but they paid no attention to me. As I stepped on the deck, I heard, "Welcome to the USS Narwhal 2nd Lt. Voigt." I looked up at the sub's conning tower and the words had come from a man standing partially out of it.

"Thank you, Sir", I responded, as I walked in his direction.

The man soon joined me on the deck of the sub. "My name is Lt. Commander John Brown, Jr., and I am the skipper of the USS Narwhal." Lt. Commander Brown was clearly proud of his sub and he gave me a quick tour of the deck, informing me the USS Narwhal was a brand new submarine, commissioned a little over a year earlier, during May 1930. Lt. Commander Brown did not ask me any questions about why he was being asked to transport me across the Atlantic, or about what I would be doing for the Army when I got to Europe.

I followed Lt. Commander Brown through the small door in the conning tower and down into the submarine. It was dimly lit inside, but it was an active atmosphere, with sailors checking various dials, loading supplies, etc. I was like a kid in a candy store that day. I had never laid eyes on a submarine before, let alone been inside one. I was passed along to another sailor, who showed me my quarters, which consisted of a private room next to Lt. Commander Brown's quarters. I laid my suitcase down and waited for further instructions. The room was small, with several black and white photos on the walls depicting some of the locations the sub had traveled over the last year. It looked like the USS Narwhal had been through the Panama Canal and portions of the Pacific already. As I was looking at the pictures, Lt. Commander Brown poked his head in the room and said, "Let's grab some chow." I was hungry so that sounded like a great idea.

I followed him down the narrow corridor to the small galley where other sailors were already eating supper. They stood to attention, saluting Lt. Commander Brown and he responded in kind, "At ease, gentlemen." They then sat back down and finished their meals. "I try to take my meals here in the main galley with the men in my crew as often as I can." I was introduced to the men in the galley as Allen Voigt, with no mention of my rank or Army involvement. The skipper and I enjoyed a good meal, exchanging some small talk about where the sub had been during its first year. His comments solidified for me that the sub had in fact been through the Panama Canal and in the Pacific Ocean. The sub and crew had been asked to return to the Eastern seaboard of the United States to secure a high priority passenger; transport that passenger to Brugge, Belgium; and then return to its homeport of San Diego, California.

We left the safety of the New York City port sometime that night and headed out to the open water of the Atlantic Ocean. The skipper had told me over dinner that evening that it would take approximately a week to reach the Belgium port. The next morning I heard three knocks on my cabin door and then the door opened. It was the skipper, Lt. Commander Brown. He took a seat on the only chair in the room and shared his concerns about the future security of America. It turned out he was a friend of Lt. Yates and had been asked by him to transport me to Europe. He clearly knew about the role I would be playing as a military attaché. "In some ways you and I are similar," said the skipper. He continued, "My sub's purpose is to act as a solitary vessel, lurking beneath the waves, seeking out intelligence about enemy vessels and opportunities for espionage, and taking out targets of opportunity."

His analogy made a lot of sense to me that morning. Before we headed to the galley for breakfast, he made one more comment that hit me between the eyes. "Rumor has it that Germany will wage war with Europe in the very near future. As a result, I am hearing talk about the United States forming a network of secret operatives that would infiltrate foreign countries, take out various military leaders of interest and basically ensure the safety of America, its armed forces and citizens." I found Lt. Commander Brown to be a person who loved his country very much and would do everything in his power to protect it. I was glad to have met him.

During my third day on the USS Narwhal, the crew fired six torpedoes at icebergs in the North Atlantic. I was able to look at the icebergs through the sub's periscope before the torpedoes fired. Shortly after all six torpedoes fired from the forward torpedo tubes, the sub surfaced. Some of the icebergs broke into thousands of small pieces, others split into huge sections, some larger than a car. I spent a lot of time in the control room that day, learning how the sub navigated under water, how it surfaced and re-submerged.

The entire seven days I was on the sub, the crew was very open to my questions and put up with my stumbling through the small corridors and taking up space in the galley. There was even one instance on day five of our trip across the large expanse of the Atlantic Ocean that we came within a few hundred feet of a German submarine that was heading west as we were heading east. The radioman on the USS Narwhal had picked up the German chatter but could not understand a word of it. Lt. Commander Brown knew about my ability to speak fluent German, and asked that I report to the bridge at once. I made my way to the bridge and joined the radioman and skipper. I simply listened for a few minutes on the ship's overhead speakers. The German sub was identified while we were submerged, nearing the western shores of France. The

German submarine crew gave no indication they knew an American submarine was off its starboard bow. The bulk of the German crew's conversation centered on what the crew would do when it reached its port of call, San Paulo, Brazil. I shared every word I heard from the German crew with Lt. Commander Brown. He did not perceive the sub as a threat as America was not at war with Germany, so we continued to head east.

During the early afternoon of day six, we entered the English Channel. The skipper surfaced the sub and allowed the crew and me to take in some sights, including the famous White Cliffs of Dover and the northern coast of France. The sub's navigator informed me that we would be docking at the port in Brugge, Belgium, around 1100 hours the next morning. That evening at dinner, I thanked the crew for welcoming me as a member of their fraternity.

At breakfast the next morning, I sought out the skipper and thanked him for sharing his insight into what he felt lay ahead for America and its Armed Forces. We docked as scheduled on Tuesday morning, August 18, 1931, at the port in Brugge. I was about to step foot in Europe, thousands of miles away from home. The farthest I had ever been from western New York was when I attended the Army War College. Now I was about to be in a foreign country where I knew no one. I shook Lt. Commander Brown's hand and we parted ways. He wished me Godspeed in my upcoming assignments.

My instructions were to meet up with a representative from the United States Embassy that was located in Berlin, Germany. My contact was to meet me at a small café named the White Rose. The café was located in downtown Brugge. As I left the port and headed into Brugge, I was impressed with the unique architecture of the city. The majority of the buildings were made of stone, and numerous canals ran through the city. Walking the city's streets, I was struck with the cobblestone streets that were such a stark contrast to those I had just walked on in New York City. I stopped to ask an elderly woman sweeping her porch where the White Rose Café was located. I took a chance and asked her for the directions in German, and to my relief she responded in German. She indicated the café was just a few more blocks south. I chatted with her for a few more minutes before parting ways. She told me the city of Brugge had a rich history and dated back hundreds of years. She had lived there all her life.

The morning warmed up as I continued my walk, and I soon came upon the café and entered through its large glass door, facing the street. I had been told my contact would be a Caucasian male in his late thirties, and that he would be wearing a dark suit with a red handkerchief stuffed in the front left pocket of his suit coat. As I walked into the crowded café, with my small suitcase in tow, I scanned the tables. There in the back left corner of the café, a man matching the description of my contact was sitting alone at a table for two. I walked over to the table and took a seat. My instructions were to not reach out my hand and introduce myself, but to act as if I already knew my contact. I was to avoid attracting attention by handling the introductions through mild conversation, drowned out by the surrounding noise of the busy café.

The man in the dark suite spoke first, in fluent German. "My name is John Werth and I am a member of the United States Embassy in Berlin, Germany. Your face matches the photo I was given prior to your arrival. "Would you like a late breakfast, Allen?"

"Yes", I replied enthusiastically.

We then ordered breakfast and coffee. As we waited for our breakfast and throughout the entire meal, we conversed only in German. John shared with me that he had been assigned to the Embassy in Berlin for two years. He was not part of the military, only performing the role of an administrative attaché. He had been directed to meet me and escort me to the Embassy in Berlin. If he knew it, he did not tell me any of the things I would be involved in at the Embassy. John stated he would be assisting me in assimilating to German society, helping me establish a residency and making sure, I knew my way around the large European city.

Just before we got up from our table, John said, "Allen, as you rise from the table and proceed to exit the café, I want you to be very observant of the two gentlemen in the far left corner of the café. They followed you in here and I figure they have probably been observing you since you entered Brugge."

Without even turning around, I replied, "You must be referring to the two men sitting at the table for four. One is wearing a black suit with a red tie and the other is wearing a light brown suit but has his suit coat off and his blue tie is too short, only coming halfway down from his collar." I could tell by the look on John's face that he was very shocked by my knowledge of the two men and the detailed description I provided.

He replied, "Very impressive Allen, they must have really taught you well at the Army War College." John and I got up and walked out of the restaurant. Part of me wanted to walk over to the two men and directly ask them why they were following me. My training kicked in, however, and as instructed, I left without approaching the two men. My objective was to get to Berlin as unassuming and as fast as possible. After John and I walked out into the bright sunlight, he motioned me to follow him down the street to his parked car. We secured my small suitcase and then began our drive toward Berlin, Germany, before the two mysterious men in the café could follow us.

John and I had ample time to talk as the trip took us several hundred miles through Belgium and into eastern Germany. The primary road was a small, two-lane highway, but we made good time and arrived at our destination at eight-o'clock in the evening. The United States Embassy had originally been in the Blücher Palace but just a few months earlier, a fire had damaged it, forcing the employees of the Embassy to take residence in the Tiergarten area of Berlin, just off Bendlerstabe Strasse. John parked the car and we entered the old building from a rear alley in order to avoid onlookers. As we walked up to the third floor, John commented on how the building was under constant surveillance by the Nazi Party, a new political party in Germany.

My assigned room in the Embassy was small but furnished. The streetlight outside barely illuminated the room as I laid my suitcase down on the bed. It contained everything I brought with me from my four years at the Army War College. John had asked me to meet him on the first floor in thirty minutes, where the kitchen staff would work us up a late meal. I unpacked a few shirts and pants and headed downstairs. Before we made it to the kitchen, John gave me a quick tour of the first floor, which contained a reception area, a few small offices and two large banquet rooms. I was then introduced to Susan and Geoffrey, who were still working in the kitchen. They were cleaning up from that evening's meal, but stopped what they were doing and asked me what I would like to eat. I was hesitant to impose, but Susan stepped in and said, "How does a nice liverwurst sandwich and vegetable soup sound?"

I had never had a liverwurst sandwich before, but I did not want to turn down a late meal, so I said, "Sure, that sounds great." Before I knew it, my sandwich and soup were placed in front of me. The liverwurst sandwich was surprisingly good; it was evidently a specialty of Geoffrey's, who had a reputation for great sandwich making. I soon said goodnight to John, Susan and Geoffrey and headed back upstairs to my room on the third floor. The bed welcomed me that night and I slept soundly, mainly due to the welcome change from the cramped submarine.

The next morning I was awakened by the sound of cars, busses and streetcars passing below my bedroom window. I walked over to the large window, opened it and stuck my head outside. The air was cool but the sun was coming up, and it warmed my face. The street down below was busy not only with vehicles, but also with people walking on either side.

It was at that time I heard a knock on my bedroom door. Before I could make it to the door, I heard John on the other side of the door say, "Breakfast is served in the main dining room in thirty minutes."

I showered, dressed and headed down to the dining room. There again were Susan and Geoffrey, preparing the long table with eggs, toast, bacon and pastries. I wondered to myself if the both of them ever slept. I sat down at the table and introduced myself to the three people, already seated. The two women and one man explained their roles as administrative support to the United States Ambassador. They welcomed me to Berlin and stated they had been instructed to support me with anything I needed during my stay. John soon joined us and I listened intently as John shared information about that day's assignments and objectives.

As we wrapped up breakfast, John asked me to join him in an office there on the first floor. We were shortly joined by Frederic Sackett, the United States Ambassador to Germany. He welcomed me to Berlin and asked briefly about my trip across the Atlantic Ocean by submarine. He stated he had never been on a submarine before and expressed his jealousy over my unique opportunity. He immediately then shifted gears and got up to shut the door. He did not sit right back down but proceeded to walk around the room as he talked. "Allen, do you know why you have been assigned to Berlin?"

I answered in a firm voice, "I understand my role to be that of an Army Military Attaché, Sir." He nodded in agreement but responded, "Your role will be much more than that though. Germany is experiencing aggressive change both militarily and socially. Your role while here in Berlin will be two-fold. First, you will report directly to me, and your assignments will be both open and covert in nature. Your Army superiors back in the States will be gauging your activity through my reports, wires and phone calls. Second, your residence will not be here at the Embassy. A small, one-bedroom apartment has been secured for you. Your objective will be to blend into German society as if you are a lifetime Berlin citizen."

I was not really surprised by what I was hearing, as it paralleled what Lt. Yates had told me back at the Army War College. I was about to put all of my extensive training to use in order to protect America's interests. The rest of the morning was spent learning about my first assignment, which was simple but important. My role was to walk the streets of Berlin, and then report on what I heard and saw. I was provided with a large stack of German currency. The funds were to be used for living expenses like clothing, food, cabs, trolleys, etc. My apartment was owned by the United States government, but my name was attached to it. I was also provided with German identification papers that I could present to German authorities if asked; I could also use them to travel throughout the country. My picture was taken, and I was provided with a German version of a driver's license. The name on all my documentation was Fritz Greiner; the name I would use in Germany.

Shortly after lunch, I was provided with my apartment address. One look at a Berlin map in John's office, revealed to me where it was located. Now I knew why I was instructed to memorize the map of Germany and, specifically, the city of Berlin. If I was really going to blend in with the German society, I could not afford to raise suspicion by reading maps on the street corner. I was instructed not to openly take pictures, but to keep any picture taking of key individuals, buildings, or any military activity hidden from view. I thanked John and Ambassador Sackett for their instruction, along with Susan and Geoffrey for their home cooked meals, and then exited out of the rear door of the Embassy. My apartment was approximately three miles east of the Embassy, so I began a crisp walk in that direction. The suitcase I had brought with me from the States was to be delivered later that evening so that I could avoid raising suspicion by walking the three miles to my apartment with a suitcase.

The short walk was thrilling, as I took in the sights of Berlin along the way, careful not to stop and stare but casually observe my surroundings. What stood out to me was the grand architecture of the buildings and the number of statues around the city, as well as the large contingent of pedestrians walking the streets with stern looks on their faces. As I walked the sidewalks, I thought about my parents and what they must have been thinking, not knowing where I was or what I was doing. I knew my first mission had to be a success. I had to follow orders and keep my location and activity a secret, even if I had to carry that burden every day. I soon found my apartment building on the western end of Kronen Strasse. My apartment was on the sixth floor of the eight-story building. I located an elevator in the lobby and took it up to the sixth floor. My assigned apartment was #32 and its two large windows had great views of the Ministry of Justice and the German Chancellery buildings. Clearly, this apartment was not assigned by accident. My apartment was furnished and - to my surprise - there was a closet full of civilian clothes and several pairs of shoes. My dresser drawers were stocked with undergarments and socks. I was tired and hit the bed hard that night.

Chapter 3

FULL COMMITMENT

"The only thing needed for the triumph of evil
is for good men to do nothing."
Sir Edmund Burke

The noise outside my windows woke me. I walked to the windows and pulled the large gray curtain away so that I could see the street. Hundreds of people crowded the streets below. I opened a window so that I could try to hear the conversations taking place. I was careful not to poke my head out the window; instead, I propped myself up against the wall next to the window. I had only been up a minute or two, so I had to work hard to understand German conversations taking place six stories below. A few minutes later, I overheard excited conversations about Adolf Hitler and the fact that he was to pass by in a motorcade on his way to the Chancellery building. The crowd was swelling and the conversations were getting louder by the minute.

The Nazis were gaining both momentum and power in 1931. The German people were eager for an aggressive leader, one that would lead them back to the prominence they had experienced prior to the Great War. The crowd noise generated outside my apartment by now was deafening. I decided not to stay in my room and attempt to listen from my sixth floor window. Instead, I dressed and headed outside, into the crowd. By the time I made it downstairs, the crowd had pressed themselves up against the front doors of the apartment building. I gently opened the right side door and squeezed myself into the crowd. I concluded, based on the direction the crowd was facing, that Hitler's motorcade was coming down the street on my left. I decided to walk to my right, around my apartment building, in order to have longer to observe the passing motorcade. It took me a good ten minutes to work into the crowd and find a suitable place to stand. My six foot, two inch height came in handy, as it allowed me to look over the heads of most of the people in front of me. Initially, I spoke to no one, choosing instead to listen. What I heard over the next few minutes was revealing. The Germans around me seemed to feel that Hitler and the Nazi Party could not seize power fast enough. They also believed Hindenburg was too old to continue to lead Germany. Many felt he was holding the country back from the economic prosperity and the world recognition they thought they deserved as a proud people.

It was time. The crowd got louder, and flags both large and small began to emerge. The flags were all the same: red with an inner white circle that contained a black swastika. Two German soldiers on motorcycles came into view, followed by a military truck full of German soldiers with SS insignias on their left shoulders. The soldiers scanned the crowed in every direction, holding their rifles at the ready. Behind the truck was a convertible motorcar, containing several high-ranking German officers. One in particular stood out to me, as he was very overweight. Adolf Hitler sat alone in the backseat of his own convertible motorcar. He occasionally raised his right hand to acknowledge the crowd.

What came next was frightening. As Hitler's motorcar passed by, practically everyone in the crowd extended their right arms out in front of them, high above their heads. In unison, they all began to chant, "Heil Hitler, Heil Hitler." The crowd continued this chant the entire time Hitler passed by in his motorcar and even for a few seconds after his motorcar passed out of view. As the crowd began to dissipate, the conversations around me revealed that many of the people had never laid eyes on Hitler before and they were extremely excited to see him. As I began the walk back to my apartment, an old man wearing a white shirt and black suspenders stopped me and asked, in German, "Young man, why did you not acknowledge Hitler as he passed by?" His question surprised me, but it made perfect sense, as I was one of only a few people that did not salute Hitler. I paused for a second, pretending not hear him, but before I could answer, he added, "There are some of us who fear Hitler and the direction he is trying to take our beloved country."

I then felt a little more confident about how to construct my reply. I turned in his direction and answered, "I am simply taking it all in and do not have a real opinion on Hitler at this time."

He snapped back, "You had better pick a side, young man! We are in for another war if Hitler comes to power. He is determined to wipe us Jews off the face of the earth."

His comment truly resonated with me. During my time at the Army War College, I had learned what Hitler represented, so I definitely had a strong resentment against him. However, because I did not want to reveal that I was an American, and I did not desire attention in any form, I expressed my neutrality. I did not respond any further to the old man's comment before I entered my apartment building. I was frustrated that I was in this position, but I knew my mission in Berlin was too important and that it might ultimately provide America with the tools to eradicate Hitler for good.

I showered and then organized my apartment; soon I realized it was noon and I had not yet eaten breakfast. I decided to explore the neighborhood and find a place to eat. My new neighborhood was full of interesting shops and family-owned cafes. Beautiful trees lined the streets and colorful flowers bloomed everywhere. It was a beautiful day for a walk. The sky was brilliantly blue with only a few clouds and a mild breeze. I soon found a German cafe' named *Zur Letzten Instanz* that had an outdoor eating area. I located a seat outside that faced the street and settled in for my first meal alone since entering Berlin. I ordered bratwurst and savored every bite. My first day on my own included a lot of walking. I observed the government buildings that seemed to take up several blocks. The Ministry of Justice and

German Chancellery buildings were massive in size and unlike any other buildings I had seen before, even in New York City.

The next several weeks were more of the same. I became more familiar with my surroundings and ventured farther into all areas of Berlin, taking trolley cars wherever they would take me. I picked up a great amount of information from simply listening inconspicuously to the conversations that swirled around me. I armed myself with valuable intelligence. I saw German soldiers everywhere, many of whom were beating Jewish shop owners in front of their stores. My visual observations allowed me to report to the Embassy with information on troop movements throughout the city, manufacturing centers, and, more importantly, the very poor treatment of the Jewish population. By the time I had been in Berlin six months, there was a much larger German military presence, primarily Nazi, in and around the city. My reports back to the Embassy were frequent and detailed.

Christmas 1931 was tough on me, more from the standpoint that my parents had no idea where I was versus just being away from home. I had settled into my new role, knowing it was vital. My assimilation into German society was of utmost importance. Consequently, I was advised not to visit the United States Embassy. Nazis observed all the comings and goings at the Embassy and I could not compromise my identity.

I soon learned that exceptions to this rule occasionally happened. The morning of Thursday, December 24th, I was having breakfast at one of my favorite cafes near my apartment, the Schwarzes Café. My meal arrived, and as I rolled out my cloth napkin, a small piece of paper fell out and into my lap. It was a note from John Werth, instructing me to enjoy my breakfast and then head back to the kitchen. My routine had been redundant since August, so receiving this message was a little out of the ordinary. My communication with the Embassy had always been one-way. My messages, reporting on the increase in military presence and the beating of Jews in the streets, were dropped into mailboxes around the city. I was instructed never to provide a return address and to alternate the ten mailing address provided, each time. Someone connected to the Embassy secured those messages and delivered them to Ambassador Sackett. I finished my breakfast and made my way back to the kitchen, where I opened the door and stepped inside.

I cleared the kitchen and discovered that the only direction I could turn was right. A small office was just in front of me. Standing there in the office was John Werth. We exchanged handshakes, and then John whispered, "You are to join me at the Embassy in order to celebrate Christmas with me, Ambassador Sackett and the rest of the Embassy employees." He informed me that we were to exit the rear of the cafe' and I was to enter the back seat of a black 1931 Ford Victoria Coupe. I did what I was told. The tinted windows ensured that any suspicious Germans watching the comings and goings at the United States Embassy did not see me. Riding through the streets of Berlin that morning, I was happy to know I was not going to spend Christmas alone. As John drove, he told me that Ambassador Sackett appreciated my intelligence reports and emphasized that those reports were helping America paint an accurate picture of the serious developments taking place in Berlin.

That Christmas was indeed memorable. The Embassy was decorated with multiple Christmas trees, and white lights and candles were everywhere. The company was great, and it was extra special having Christmas dinner prepared by Geoffrey and Susan. I spent Christmas Eve, Christmas Day and the following day at the Embassy. As I was preparing to leave that Saturday afternoon, John invited me into Ambassador Sackett's office. The three of us met for over an hour. Ambassador Sackett shared details with me about my next assignment, one that would take me outside of Berlin.

The Germans were rumored to be building a concentration camp outside of Berlin. My orders were simple: find out where it was, why it was being built and who was going to be imprisoned there. News had reached the Embassy, that construction was taking place in northwest Germany, near the town of Oranienburg, that looked like a camp of some sort. I was instructed to secure a job with the camp's constructing crew so that I could avoid suspicion and have more freedom to ask questions, make observations and take pictures. I left the Embassy late that evening. John drove me back and dropped me off a block from my apartment. I walked the balance of the way back, circling a few times, losing anyone that might be following me.

The next day I left Berlin on a train, headed northwest toward Oranienburg, Germany. The trip was relatively short, only a one-hour ride. I took in the sights of the German countryside. I saw only bare trees that late December day but the sky was clear and the sun shone brightly. The views reminded me of central New York, and my thoughts shifted to home and family.

Time passed swiftly, and soon the train pulled into the Oranienburg station. Although much smaller than the one in Berlin, Oranienburg's station was, nevertheless busy with travelers. I departed the train and looked for a taxicab to take me within walking distance of the camp. Cabs were scarce, but I finally hailed one. Speaking German, I asked the driver if he knew of any construction sites that might be hiring, hoping he knew where the camp was being built. The driver responded enthusiastically with a "Yes" and told me that a large camp was under construction northeast of the city. As we rode through the streets of Oranienburg, the driver pointed out every good eating establishment along the way. By the size of his waistline, he clearly enjoyed eating and it was very apparent that he was proud of his city and its eating establishments.

After a short twenty-minute ride, the driver pulled up to a large tract of land that was devoid of any trees. Tree stumps dotted the plot of land, dominated by two buildings, resembling barracks that were in their final stages of construction. I paid the driver, picked up my bag and headed in the direction of the construction. There was a sign posted on the edge of the construction site that read *"Achtung! Bauarbeiten im gange. Wir sind auf der suche nach qualifizierten und unqualifizierten arbeiter. Bei zelt."* "Attention! Construction project underway. We are seeking skilled and non-skilled laborers. Apply at tent."

Although I could pound a nail into a board, I thought a non-skilled position would provide me with more opportunities to make relevant observations and inquiries. I also believed a non-skilled position might allow me to work in many different areas of the camp as it grew. I walked into the tent and found a middle-aged German man sitting behind a small table with stacks of paper piled around him. He asked me my business and I told him I wished to apply for a non-skilled position. He sized me up and asked, "Why would you not apply for a higher paying skilled position?"

"My back is stronger than my hammering skill," I replied. He laughed and asked me to take a seat and fill out a brief application. I completed the application in German and handed it over. He read my application that listed my name, age, current occupation and residence. I had listed my real age, the German name assigned to me, and my apartment address in Berlin but listed my occupation as a waiter. Finally, he looked up from the application. "How did you find us here in Oranienburg?"

I casually told him that I was tired of working indoors and wanted to experience more of Germany. He appeared to be satisfied with that response and asked me if I was ready to start. I, of course, answered with a falsely enthusiastic, "Yes." We left the tent and walked in the direction of a long row of tents that had been partially obstructed by the barrack construction. He assigned me to tent #3, and then instructed me to drop my bag on a cot and follow him. Next, he introduced me to an older-looking man holding a clipboard. "Franz Kappel, this is a Fritz Greiner, a new un-skilled laborer. Use him as you wish." I stood there for a while as Franz shuffled through the papers on his clipboard.

Finally, I decided to speak first. "My back is strong," I informed him, "And I am skilled in organization." He did not even bother to look up at me as he continued to shuffle his paperwork.

Eventually, he announced, "Finally here is someone who is proactive and ready to get his hands dirty."

He handed me a sheet of his paper and instructed me to follow it to the letter. If I completed the list of assignments to his satisfaction, I would be able to keep my position. My jobs over the next few weeks involved shoveling dirt and cement in and out of wheelbarrows as I transported the material to various buildings being built on the property.

January 1932 began bitterly cold. Snow fell frequently, but the construction of the camp did not stop. Most workers at the camp kept to themselves, as much as they could; this was a challenge given the cramped living conditions of our tents. Meals were served outside. The food was always abundant, so I was able to keep my energy level up and remain in good health. It was clear that some form of camp was being built, but what was its purpose? The conversations I had had up to this point with my fellow workers were simply idle chitchat, and no one divulged the real reasons behind the camp construction. Either no one knew, or each was sworn to secrecy. That all changed during mid-February, however.

Multiple copies of the German propaganda newspaper, *Der Angriff*, translated "The Attack," always lay around the camp. That February, the papers were all about Adolf Hitler's election run against the German President, Paul von Hindenburg. With that news, mouths began to open. It soon became clear that the majority of the men at the camp wanted to see Hitler elected, because they believed he could cure all the ills of Germany. Joseph Goebbels was Hitler's propaganda minister and he used this paper as a means to fuel the support for Hitler. Although opinions around the camp varied as to who would be elected, it was abundantly clear that the German people were hungry for a change.

"Who do you want to see elected, Fritz?" asked Franz as we were waiting in line for supper one night.

"I have never cared much for politics. I really do not care who wins." I found it frustrating when I had to make these kinds of

61

responses, as when the Jewish man, on the street corner in Berlin, asked me what I thought about Hitler and the treatment of the Jews. I had a definite opinion and so badly wanted to express it, but I had to keep my cover.

"Hitler will be our future leader of Germany, mark my word, Fritz. He had the vision for this camp and laid all the groundwork."

I answered, "What do you mean by that?"

"Hitler and the Nazi party wish to imprison those who oppose them, and this camp is being constructed by the Nazi party for that purpose. In fact, Hitler himself is planning on visiting this camp as we near its completion," he replied. That was valuable information for me, as it was the reason I had been sent to the camp. Over the next few days, word spread that the camp would initially house political prisoners, and would ultimately hold Jews. I was shocked to know that this activity was to take place, but was even more frustrated by the fact that I had to participate in it, to some degree.

On Monday, March 14, 1932, headlines of *Der Angriff* announced that neither Hitler nor President Hindenburg had won the majority of votes. A second election was held. President Hindenburg won 53% of the vote, a fact that allowed him to remain in power. Many in the camp were upset over the results. I read a late March copy of *Der Angriff* that revealed Hitler had been appointed Vice Chancellor. This appointment still did not satisfy many in the camp, as they wanted to see Hitler in complete control. In July, news spread throughout the camp that the Nazis had won 230 seats out of a possible 608 seats in the Reichstag. This made the Nazi party the largest party in the Reichstag, but they still did not have total control of the government.

I managed to take a few pictures of the camp without anyone noticing. The pictures were mainly of the barracks and surrounding buildings that would house military units and support other functions of the camp. I also took pictures of the interior of a building on the far edge of the camp, that I had had no part in constructing. It appeared that a separate group of workers assembled this particular building. Its interior included a disproportionate number of showers and ovens.

This aroused my curiosity, as there were already enough showering and cooking facilities closer to the main barracks. I snapped as many photos as I could, especially of a large brick chimney that rose from the middle of the building. I walked around the back of the building to take additional exterior shots, so I would not be caught taking pictures. My small, Russian-made camera, given to me by John Werth, could take fifty pictures. I made every picture count. During my entire time at the camp, I hid my camera in my extra pair of boots, alternating my two pairs of boots each day. The film would be developed by the Embassy upon my return to Berlin.

Camp construction had really escalated between March and July. I had been told to return to Berlin by August 1, 1932. Before I approached Franz about quitting my job and moving on, I needed to know what their plans were for the building that housed the showers and ovens. My time was running out at the camp and I needed to report to John Werth and Ambassador Sackett.

Finally, on Wednesday, July 27th, I approached Franz at dinner. Franz sat by himself that night, as he typically did. Most of the men in the camp did not like him due to his position and the fact that he always gave orders but never granted any compliments. Before I sat down on his right, I asked his permission to join him for dinner. His response was immediate. "Of course you can, Fritz, I have wanted to talk to you, anyway. You have been a reliable worker during your time here at the camp. We are nearing the end of our construction, and I was wondering if I could give you a job reference or something."

"Thank you", I replied. "I was planning on giving you my notice anyway, since I wanted to head back to Berlin."

Franz did not say anything at first, so we sat there and ate in silence. Finally he spoke. "You should stay on another few days, as Vice Chancellor Hitler is planning on visiting the camp this Friday to conduct a complete inspection of our work." I agreed to stay at the camp through Saturday, July 30th.

Just before we finished our dinner, I leaned in close to Franz and asked, "What is that large building on the edge of the camp going to be used for?"

Again, Franz took his time, waiting until his last bites of dinner were finished before he responded. "The Nazis are gaining power every day. Soon Germany will be in a much better position when Hitler gains full power. When he does, he will accelerate his plan to build a master race and rid Germany of the Jewish plague."

It was hard, but I kept my composure and did not respond. I thanked Franz for letting me join him and returned to my tent for the evening, pondering what I had seen and heard during my time at the camp. I had much to share with the Embassy upon my return to Berlin.

Friday morning, everyone was asked to assemble outside in front of the newly constructed camp commandant's office. Hitler and his motorcade were expected to arrive at the camp at approximately 10:00 AM, and we were being asked to greet him. Shortly after the appointed time, two large, canvas covered trucks pulled into the camp and stopped in front of us. From the back of the two trucks, more than twenty-five German soldiers with "SS" painted on the side of their helmets, hopped out. They assembled in front of us with their rifles slung behind their right shoulders. One of the soldiers announced that each of us would be searched for weapons and explosives. We individually had to step forward, in order to be patted down. After all of us were searched, we returned to our rows and stood there, facing the soldiers. A few of the soldiers fanned out across the camp, some taking up positions on the roofs and at the entrance to the camp.

At approximately 10:30 AM, we heard the sound of cars off in the distance. Soon after, Hitler's motorcade, including another truck of Nazi soldiers, pulled up in front of us. Franz stepped forward, extended his right arm, and shouted, "Heil Hitler". A few members of the camp also raised their right arms in salute. Those of us, who did not, were subjected to suspecting glances from everyone else.

Hitler's motorcar pulled up right in front of where I stood. Compared to my first visual sighting of him, this encounter was much closer, no less than fifteen feet away from me. An officer who had ridden in the front seat of his motorcar opened Hitler's door. After exiting the vehicle, Hitler took several steps in my direction. Hitler paused for a moment and then began to pace in front of our line, simply observing. He soon returned to where I was standing and stopped, faced me, and said, "What is your name young man?"

I was caught completely off guard, and almost answered in my perfect New York accent, "Allen Voigt." My training kicked in before I could utter my real name, however, and in German, I calmly answered, "Fritz Greiner." Hitler proceeded to ask me where I was from and what I had done to contribute to the building of the camp. I told him I was originally from Austria but had lived most of my life in Berlin. I also told him in detail what my contributions at the camp had been.

"I, too, am from Austria, Fritz." Hitler said in a confiding manner. "It is nice to have someone from my home country, instrumental in the building of this first concentration camp."

I had to get back to Berlin as soon as possible and report on the high visibility Camp Oranienburg was getting with Hitler's arrival. Before Hitler walked away to visit with camp officials, he reached out to shake my hand and thanked me for my contributions. It was very hard for me to say, "Danke", but I managed to get the words out.

Hitler spent approximately two hours at the camp that day, inspecting each building and asking Franz many questions. What stood out to me the most during that entire visit was not that Hitler had spoken to me, but more importantly, that Hitler had spent over thirty minutes of his two-hour visit down at the remote building that contained the showers and ovens.

At 12:45 PM, Hitler and his motorcade left the camp as fast as they had arrived. As they pulled away, Franz walked over to where I was standing and said, "Hitler has a keen eye and I am not surprised in the least that he walked over and talked to you, Fritz. I truly appreciate your good attitude and hard work here these last few months. Our job is practically done, and I know you want to get back to Berlin. I am heading into Oranienburg for lunch with some senior Nazi officials that have monitored our camp construction progress. Would you like to join me? You can catch the late afternoon train to Berlin after we eat."

I agreed to join him and after gathering my limited belongings, a driver drove us the few miles into town. We pulled up to a cafe' named "Gasthaus". As Franz and I walked in, the host greeted us, took my bag and guided us to our table. Three Nazi officers awaited us.

"Welcome, Franz," said one of the officers. "Who is this with you today?"

Franz replied, "This is Fritz Greiner from Berlin. He has been my right-hand man these last few months at the camp and I have asked him to join us today in appreciation for all his hard work."

The officer responded, looking in my direction, "Welcome, Fritz!" Franz and I then sat down in the two remaining seats. I ended up taking one that was in between two of the officers. I was a long way from East Aurora, New York. I was very surprised that Franz had referred to me as his right-hand man, and, even more surprised that he asked me to the lunch meeting.

We ordered our food and, while waiting for it to arrive, we all exchanged some idle conversation about German soccer and our favorite foods. After the food arrived, conversation shifted to the real reason Franz was meeting with the Nazi officers. All three officers started firing questions at Franz, hardly giving him a chance to take a bite of food. I kept my head down and ate at a slow pace, looking up occasionally to gauge the expression on Franz's face as he answered every question. The questions centered on the quality of construction, the number of showers and ovens in the remote building, and when the camp would be completed.

One officer had not asked any questions of Franz up to this point. He now put his fork down and announced, "Franz, you have made Hitler very proud and your construction is ahead of schedule.

Oranienburg is the first of many such camps to be built across Germany. As the first camp, yours is the one that others will be modeled after." I had expected to be asked detailed questions by the officers, but none came.

We finished our lunch, I retrieved my bag, and we all walked out of the cafe'. The officers said goodbye and drove out of sight. Our driver took Franz and me to the train station. Upon arrival, Franz simply extended his hand to me. As we shook hands, he thanked me once again for my hard work and wished me success in my future endeavors. I said goodbye, after which I purchased a ticket for Berlin. As my train headed southwest out the station, I reflected on the six months I had spent at the camp. I had vital news to share with the Embassy and the pictures I had taken had to be developed as soon as possible. The Nazi's were gaining power under Hitler's leadership, and I feared what might happen to Germany as a whole.

My train pulled into the Berlin train station late in the afternoon on Friday July 29, 1932. I took a trolley car back to within walking distance of my apartment, stopping by a local café for some dinner. I asked for my food to go and then walked back to my apartment. I took the elevator up to the sixth floor and slid my key into the lock. The apartment was dark and dusty, but I was happy to have four walls and a comfortable bed to sleep in. My apartment rent had been paid by the Embassy each month during my absence, via an unknown Embassy employee who posed as my brother. I spent the evening enjoying my meal, cleaning my apartment and washing six months of Nazi dirt off my body. My mind was racing and I could not wait to get to the Embassy and outline what was happening at the Oranienburg Camp. Instructions had been left on my nightstand, instructing me where to meet John on Monday morning.

Just after 6:00 AM on Monday morning, John Werth picked me up at the designated spot, a few blocks from my apartment. "Welcome back to Berlin, Allen. We cannot wait to hear what you have to share with us." As we rode through the streets of Berlin that morning, the city, for the most part, was still asleep. I watched as paper boys set out their stacks of newspapers and local cafes were opening their doors for breakfast. John informed me that Geoffrey and Susan had prepared a big breakfast for us. I started to share with John what I had heard and seen but he cut me off in mid-sentence and asked me to wait until Ambassador Sackett could join us. As we neared Bendlerstabe Strasse, in an effort to keep me hidden, John asked me to crawl in the back seat and duck down as far as I could. He reached back to throw a blanket over my body. We soon pulled into the alley behind the Embassy, parked and went in. It had been a long time since I had visited the Embassy, but I was finally back and ready to share my critical information.

As John and I walked back toward the Embassy kitchen, I could smell the ham, eggs and coffee. The kitchen was alive with activity and before I could walk three steps into the kitchen, Geoffrey greeted me with a firm handshake. Susan welcomed me with a hug. "Welcome back Allen, we have missed you," she said.

"It is sure good to be back in your kitchen, Susan. Nothing compares to your home-cooked meals, and I cannot wait to enjoy this breakfast," I truthfully replied.

Only John, Susan, Geoffrey and I shared breakfast that morning. I had expected to be asked questions about where I had been the last six months, but that did not happen.

After finishing breakfast, John and I headed up to Ambassador Sackett's office. He soon joined us and greeted me with a pat on the back and an apology for being late. "I had planned to join you for breakfast, but I received a very early call from your old friend, Lt. Yates. He called to ask me how you were faring and to express his sincere appreciation for your mission these last six months. He cannot wait to hear what you have to share. I will be speaking with him on a secure line later this week after you and I have had a chance to speak. I expect you to be here at the Embassy for a few days, so you can share your vital information and we can get your pictures developed and analyzed."

At that point, I handed my three rolls of film to an Embassy aide. Ambassador Sackett, John and I spent the rest of the day going over every aspect of my time at the Oranienburg Camp. By the end of the day, we had only scratched the surface, and the pictures I had taken were not back yet from the developer. My visit to the Embassy lasted through Thursday of that week. My original room at the Embassy had been prepared for me, along with a change of clothes, so I was able to spend my stay in comfortable surroundings. The pictures were finally ready on Thursday, enhanced and ready for maximum viewing. I explained each picture in detail to John and Ambassador Sackett. I also shared with them Franz's comments about Hitler's plan to rid Germany of the so-called "Jewish plague". I expressed my fear that the showers and ovens were somehow linked to that objective.

John Werth spoke up at that point and said, "You are exactly correct, Allen. Sources within Germany tell us that the showers will be used for killing individuals with cyanide gas produced from "Zyklon B" pellets. We fear the ovens will be used to cremate all those killed by the gas. Your pictures confirm this strong suspicion and provide critical proof as to what is coming."

I was stunned and upset. I shared with John and Ambassador Sackett my deep frustration over the fact that I had contributed to the building of a camp that would eventually participate in the systematic murdering of the Jewish population. John was very firm when he said to me, "Your intelligence gathering at the camp these past six months will save thousands - if not hundreds of thousands - of innocent people. You should feel neither shame nor regret."

Ambassador Sackett added, "Your activity at the camp is just the beginning of what America will ask of you over the next several years. War is coming to Europe and the United States will be forced to intervene." He paused for a minute to let that sink in, then continued, "You are on the front lines and will have to learn how to separate yourself from this assignment and those to come. Your role will save American lives and the lives of those less fortunate here in Europe."

We wrapped up our meetings late that day. Before departing the Embassy, John told me that the information and pictures I had provided would be shared with President Roosevelt, his cabinet and senior military officers back in the United States. Action would be taken to counteract the growing threat taking place in Germany as a direct result of what I had shared. The comments made to me about my recent contribution and future role helped me process what I had been through over the last six months. John drove me back to a drop-off point near my apartment. As I walked home, I wondered what missions laid ahead of me in the coming months.

I spent the rest of 1932 visiting several southern German cities that were rumored to be manufacturing munitions: Stuttgart, Muchen and Ravensburg. My secondary objective was to observe and gauge the Nazi influence throughout the country. I spent a month in each of the three cities, living in boarding houses and securing part time employment in warehouse districts. I stayed alert and was always on my guard as I gathered mounting evidence of articles of war being manufactured. Germany, since the end of the Great War, had not been allowed to produce weapons as part of the Geneva Convention. Germany was truly manufacturing munitions and this provided further proof of Hitler's grand plan to go to war.

In Stuttgart, I witnessed the manufacturing of rifles, bullets and helmets in great quantities. For a few weeks, I swept the floors in a large warehouse situated just outside the Stuttgart city limits. In early November 1932, I heard a warehouse supervisor berate a shop floor worker that was responsible for test firing Mauser rifles.

The warehouse supervisor continued, "Can anyone here successfully test fire this new Mauser rifle?"

The shop floor was silent. I took a chance and spoke up, in German, "I can."

The warehouse supervisor did not even bother to ask me about my qualifications, responding simply, "Outstanding. Give me your results within two days."

In those two days, I fired fifty rounds each through ten Mauser rifles, five hundred rounds in total. I was very impressed with the firepower of the rifle; I knew it would give the American 1903 Springfield a run for its money. I reported my results to the floor supervisor late on the second day of test firing. I was honest with my feedback, and told him that the rifle was accurate and reliable. He offered me the job full-time, but I gave him a plausible excuse that was in line with my cover story. I was only in Stuttgart for a few weeks visiting my aunt and uncle and my job at the warehouse was only to make some traveling money. He was clearly disappointed but thanked me for my hard work.

In December, I visited Ravensburg, Germany. I was due to report back to Berlin by Christmas, so my time in this region of Germany was limited. It was during this time that I received a coded message from John Werth. I was staying at the Hotel Residez during my time in the city. On the morning of Thursday, December 15th, I received a white envelope under my hotel door. After reaching over and picking it up, I opened the sealed envelope and read, "Hotel Gasthof Gyrenbad, December 17th, J.W." I immediately knew it was from John Werth at the Embassy. How did he know where I was staying? Did he personally deliver the message? Was someone monitoring all my movements?"

I put the message back inside the envelope and placed it in the left front pocket of my pants. I went down to speak to the hotel clerk on the first floor and asked him where the Hotel Gasthof Gyrenbad was. The clerk did not even hesitate to think for a second and replied, "Zurich, Switzerland". I then asked the clerk for the best route, how long it would take to get there, and details about the hotel. He informed me the hotel was very historic and that the distance was just over one hundred and ten kilometers by train. I thanked the clerk for his help and as I turned to head back up to my third floor room, the clerk said, "You must be from the northern part of Germany. I recognize your accent."

With surprise, I replied, "Why, Yes, I was born in Berlin." All those years spent learning the German language had really paid off.

As I threw what little clothing I had with me into my small suitcase, I heard some conversation outside my hotel window, which faced a small alley below. What caught my ear was the word "concentration camp." I cautiously approached the partially opened window, a window I had propped open the previous evening to let in some of the cool winter air. I stopped far enough back from the window in order not to be detected. The conversation became more aggressive as words like "cleansing" and "purging" were shouted. I had to get close so I could see who was making these comments. I inched closer to the open window, eased my head up and looked out. I saw a German soldier with a Nazi swastika armband around his right upper arm. He had a cigarette in his left hand, and screaming at the shop owner sweeping the area behind his store. The German soldier then said to the shop owner, "You Jews are ruining Germany and when Hitler comes to power, we will wipe all you Jews off the face of the earth!" The shop owner said nothing, as he kept sweeping. The conversation ended when the German soldier flicked his cigarette butt at the shop owner's head, turned and walked into the back door of my hotel.

I decided to delay my departure to Zurich. I placed my suitcase on the bed and walked downstairs in an attempt to find the shop owner. As I walked off the last step leading down to the hotel lobby, the German soldier passed me going up the stairs. I was upset and decided to bump him hard with my left shoulder. He spun partially around and said, "Watch where you are going!" I did not even give him the credit by turning around and responding. I kept on going and walked out the back door of the hotel. I took a right out into the alley and tried to determine which building housed the shop owner's store. To my excitement, it was a cafe' - I was hungry.

I walked into the café and found a small table near the back. I was soon greeted by a young woman who provided me with a menu and asked if I wanted a cup of coffee. I nodded in the affirmative and asked her, "May I have your eggs and ham special I saw on the sign out front?" She smiled and walked back into the kitchen. I soon heard conversation coming from the kitchen. The young woman was talking, evidently trying to alleviate the evident frustration of the café owner. They both soon walked over to my table, as the young woman delivered my hot cup of coffee. I listened and waited for the right opportunity to share my opinion on the cafe' owner's encounter with the German officer. I took a sip of coffee and laid the cup on the table, and proceeded to ask the cafe' owner to join me.

I introduced myself and shared with him that I had witnessed his recent encounter with the German officer in the alley only a few minutes earlier. My goal was to redeem myself from the first encounter I had with a German Jewish citizen back in Berlin. My lack of honesty during that first encounter outside my apartment, when I first laid eyes on Adolf Hitler, and asked if I had picked a side, haunted me. I knew my reason for answering as I did, simply to keep my cover, but on this occasion, I was not going to hide my true feelings, regardless of the outcome. I wanted to let that café owner know how I felt and what was coming, regardless of how secretive I had to be about my identity. After letting the café owner know some of what I had heard and seen, he paused and then replied in a sincere, calm voice, "My name is Jacob Petersen and I have lived here in Ravensburg all my life. My father owned this shop before me and his father before him. I fought for Germany during the Great War and I love this country. One German soldier will not shake my Jewish foundation."

Jacob and I continued to talk as my breakfast was delivered. "This is my daughter, Elsie", Jacob said with pride when she delivered my breakfast. I thanked her for my hot breakfast. As I ate, I let Jacob know that I was upset over how he had been treated and how the Jews overall were being treated throughout Germany. I so badly wanted to share with him my information about the gas chambers and ovens that I had seen, but I was sworn to secrecy. After I finished my breakfast, I asked Jacob if I could speak to him privately. He agreed and we walked back into the kitchen. His daughter happened to walk back in the kitchen about the same time. "If you have something to tell me, Fritz, you can tell me in front of my daughter, as we have no secrets in our family."

I hesitated for a moment and proceeded to warn Jacob and Elsie about the coming Hitler atrocities. I shared what I could in a very urgent tone. "If Hitler assumes the overall leadership of Germany, the Jewish citizens are in real danger. Things will get worse for you and your family, Jacob. I beg you to take your family and move out of Germany."

Jacob looked at me and said clearly, "I refuse to be intimidated by Hitler or any German soldier. We will never leave Ravensburg as long as I am alive." I respected his position but found it disconcerting. I looked at Elsie; she bowed her head and looked away. Before I left the kitchen to return to my hotel and retrieve my suitcase, I thanked Jacob and Elsie for my breakfast and their hospitality.

I walked out the back of the cafe'. Just as I reached the back door of my hotel, Elsie ran up to me and said, "Thank you for coming for breakfast and sharing your concern for my family and me. I, too, am scared of what might happen if Hitler comes to power. I hope that if more people tell my father what you told him today, he might listen." She turned and walked away but not before looking back again and waving good-bye. I walked in the back door of the Hotel Residez, gathered my belongings and checked out of the hotel.

I made my way to the Ravensburg train station and purchased a one-way ticket to Zurich. I soon boarded and took my seat. The afternoon trip to Zurich was to take a little over three hours. It was ten days before Christmas 1932. It had been fourteen months since I had spoken to my parents and seventeen months since they had seen me graduate from the Army War College. I was far from home and traveling to yet another country in Europe. The views outside my train window were unlike any I had ever seen before. The train, shortly after leaving Ravensburg, Germany, crossed over Lake Bodensee, a very large fresh water lake that bordered Germany and

Switzerland. The Swiss Alps soon came into view and I could not believe my eyes. They were the highest mountains I had ever seen, certainly much larger than the mountains in upstate New York. The train continued to travel southwest toward Zurich and before long, we arrived at our destination. The station was comparable in size to the one in Berlin. People were everywhere. I picked up my suitcase and stepped off the train and into a sea of people. I made my way out of the station and hailed the first cab I saw. "Hotel Gasthof Gyrenbad," I said in German to the cab driver.

As we pulled away from the station, the driver asked in German, "Is this your first time in Zurich?"

I replied, "Yes." No other words were exchanged between us as we traveled to the hotel. We soon arrived. I paid the driver and walked up the stairs into the hotel and over to the front desk.

The hotel clerk welcomed me to the historic Hotel Gasthof Gyrenbad. He shared with me that the hotel had been built in the 1600s and that the staff was going to make my stay very comfortable. He gave me the keys to room #424 along with a sealed envelope, and I made my way to the stairs leading up to my room. My room was very similar to the other hotel rooms I had stayed in over the last six months in southern Germany, with one exception. Instead of seeing other buildings and alleys, my view in this room was of the snow capped Swiss Alps. A light snow fell outside and I could feel the cold air seeping in around the edges of my fourth floor window. I sat down at a small desk near the window and opened up the envelope that had been handed to me by the desk clerk. It read, "Meet me downstairs for supper, in the main dining hall, at 6:00 PM. J.Y." I considered who JY might be and the only person that came to mind was Lt. Yates. It occurred to me that during the entire time I had known Lt. Yates, I never found out his first name. It had been just over a year since I had seen Lt. Yates. The clock on the desk said it was already 5:18 PM. I took a quick shower and changed clothes before heading downstairs for dinner.

I made my way down to the main dining room. As I met the maitre d' I scanned the dining room for Lt. Yates, but I did not see him. I glanced at my watch, 5:59 PM. Just after the maitre d' seated me Lt. Yates arrived. He saw me and headed in my direction, dressed in street clothes. I rose from my seat and reached out my hand to shake his, debating in my mind whether I should greet him in German or English. That concern was erased as he greeted me in English with, "It is great to see you Allen, how are you?"

I replied, "Very well Sir, thank you." We took our seats and proceeded to catch up on the last year. It was so nice to be carrying on a conversation in English. Just before our dinner arrived, I had asked Lt. Yates, "Why are we allowed to talk in English instead of in German?"

He responded, "Switzerland is a true friend of the United States, and this particular hotel acts as a safe house for our military."

I then had to admit to Lt. Yates that I still did not know his first name.

A smile tugged at the corner of his mouth before he answered, "My first name is Joe."

Our dinner arrived. I shared stories about my time in Germany and he shared news about what was happening back in the United States. As we wrapped up our dinner, Lt. Yates shared with me he had recently been promoted to the rank of Captain. It was well deserved.

A little later, we were both convinced, by our very efficient maitre d', to each have a piece of chocolate cake and a cup of hot coffee. I had taken one bite of dessert when, Captain Yates, handed me a small box. Inside was a single silver bar, a First Lieutenant's bar. My heart stopped for a split second and I looked up at Captain Yates.

"Congratulations, 1st Lt. Voigt. You are officially promoted in recognition of all your hard work over the last year."

The promotion came as a big surprise to me. I placed the box in my coat pocket. We wrapped up dinner and as we were getting up from the table, Captain Yates asked me to follow him to a small meeting room not far from the front lobby.

We entered the room and there, waiting for us, was John Werth. I walked over and shook his hand as he said, "Congratulations 1st Lt. Voigt." The three of us sat down at a table. Then the real purpose of our meeting became clear. On the table was a detailed map of Germany, but what stood out to me were all the red dots scattered across it.

"These red dots represent areas of severe hostile treatment of the German Jews. Hitler and the Nazis are rapidly gaining popularity and the propaganda they are spreading throughout the country is winning over the populace," John told me. I thought back to the day before when Elsie's father, Jacob, had his encounter with the German officer.

John continued, "President Roosevelt is aware of your activity in Germany and wants me to express his gratitude." I was shocked that our newly elected President knew who I was. He continued on, "Your contributions have allowed the United States to extricate critical German Jews from various cities around the country. Many across Europe are concerned that Hitler will rise to Chancellor any day now and spread his political manipulations and violence across Europe."

Our conversation shifted as Captain Yates shared in detail with me how the Japanese were increasing their presence in China. He recounted stories of Japanese brutality and of the thousands of Chinese citizens, which had been murdered, including women and children. "Allen, there are military attachés like yourself over there but the sheer number of square miles to be covered is daunting. You and your unique skills are sorely needed in the Pacific region, but that will come in time. You and John will be leaving Zurich tomorrow and heading directly back to Berlin." He announced.

We parted company and I headed back up to my room. The entire evening had been a blur. My promotion, the fact that President Roosevelt knew of my activity, the news about Hitler, and the disturbing news of Japan's atrocities in China was somewhat overwhelming to me. As I tried to go to sleep that night, Captain Yates' comment about the Japanese kept running through my mind. I thought to myself, "Where would my role take me over the next few years?" The only noise I heard was the cold wind blowing outside my window. As I drifted off to sleep, my mind found its way back to my parents in East Aurora and how our home might be decorated for Christmas.

The next morning, I met John downstairs for breakfast. He said we would be taking the 4:00 PM train back to Berlin. We did not exchange many words as we ate; John was clearly distracted with his thoughts. After I finished my breakfast, I put down my fork, wiped my mouth with my napkin and asked John what was on his mind.

Before answering, John paused for a moment, and then said, "The rise of Adolf Hitler in Germany, specifically in Berlin, greatly concerns me. My family is in clear danger if Germany goes to war. I am considering resigning my post and returning to America with my family."

I thought to myself, "John has a right to be concerned. His family does come first." John finished his breakfast and asked me if I wanted to spend the day alone touring the city of Zurich. I took full advantage of that opportunity and told John I would meet him at the train station by 3:30 PM. We parted ways; I made my way up to my room, packed and checked out of the hotel. I then went outside and found a cab.

I really had no idea where to start my tour of Zurich so I took a gamble and asked the first cab driver I found, in German, what I should see first. He asked me how much time I had. I looked at my watch and told him I had six hours before I had to be at the train station.

The cab driver replied, "I suggest you see the Opera House, National Museum, St. Peter's Church and my favorite chocolate shop. I will give you a flat rate of twenty-five Swiss Francs."

Just a few minutes earlier, when checking out of the hotel, I had received a lesson from the hotel clerk on how many German Marks equaled a Swiss Franc. All I had on me was German Marks. I did a quick conversion in my head and replied, "Excellent, let's get started. By the way, what is your name?"

"My name is Werner Egloff and I am Zurich's number one cab driver." He announced.

I smiled and we headed off. As the cab pulled away from the hotel, I asked Werner if he had been born in Zurich and he replied, "Yes, I love my city and I cannot wait to show it to you."

As Werner drove through the streets of Zurich, all I could do was marvel at the architecture of the buildings, the beautiful bodies of water, and the beauty of the Swiss Alps that surrounded us. Werner was very eager to point out the historic aspects of the city, including the church where he and his wife were married.

We soon pulled up to the famous Swiss Opera House and found a place to park on the street. The Opera House was closed, but that did not stop Werner. He knocked on a side door and soon an elderly man opened it.

"Hello, my old friend, I have a guest with me today. His name is Fritz and I want to show him the Opera House that you take such good care of." Werner informed him.

Werner looked at me and said, "This is Stefan and he is responsible for caring for the building."

As we stepped inside, I shook Stefan's hand and thanked him for allowing us in. I had never been in an opera house before, so I was not sure what to expect. As we walked onto the stage, I took in the spectacular view. All I could see were seats and balconies. Stefan explained to me in detail how the stage worked. He took the time to lower and raise the series of curtains, open some trap doors and show me the orchestra pit where the instruments were played during the shows. The three of us walked up into a far balcony so I could experience the perspective of someone watching the opera. Before Werner and I left, Stefan took us back to a large room that contained all the costumes, hats, swords, and other paraphernalia that the opera company used for its plays. As we went to leave, I thanked Stefan for his hospitality.

Our next stop was St. Peter's Church. It was clearly visible, long before we came upon it. The most prominent feature of the church was its large clock tower. I had never seen a church building this large before. It seemed to go on forever as Werner drove by it in an attempt to find a parking spot. It was Friday afternoon, so the church was not conducting a service. We had free access to the church. Unlike the Opera House, the church door was unlocked. Werner and I walked in the front door. The windows were massive and a large balcony wrapped around the inside of the church. We walked all the way through the congregation seating area and up to the area where the homilies were conducted. As I looked out on the congregation seating area, I thought to myself how long it had been since I had been in a church, let alone one this large. Neither Werner nor I said much as we walked around the church. I reflected on how good God had been to me, keeping me safe. I offered up a prayer on behalf of my parents who I was sure were worried about me, and wondering where I was.

"It is time, Fritz, for me to take you to my home for lunch so you can meet my wife Elena," said Werner.

I felt comfortable enough to join him, and by this time, I had worked up a good appetite. As we headed back to the cab, I took a second to look back at the church and wondered when I would have another opportunity to set foot in a church in the near future.

Werner drove for approximately twenty minutes on our way to his home. The short trip allowed me to gain even a better perspective of Zurich and its architecture.

"We are here, Fritz", Werner announced as we pulled up to his modest home.

Elena met us at the front door, and I was introduced. At first, I felt awkward being in a stranger's home, but Werner and Elena immediately put me at ease. She had already been preparing a large lunch for Werner, so there was plenty of food to go around. The smell of food cooking in the kitchen made me think of home and the meals my mother cooked. Werner said a short prayer as he, Elena and I sat down to eat. This was my first home cooked meal in months. I missed Susan and Geoffrey's Embassy meals. I had not had a meal cooked by my mother in years. I was somewhat hesitant, lest I eat too much, as Elena had not expected me for lunch that day, but that did not stop her from pushing more food in my direction. We had a great time conversing in German.

I glanced at my watch. It was not yet 1:30 PM, and I had just over two hours to get to the train station. Werner saw me glance at my watch.

"Fritz, you have plenty of time before you have to be at the train station, so let me take you to the National Museum and my favorite chocolate shop," he cheerfully informed me.

I thanked Elena for her generosity and the wonderful meal. Werner and I were back in his cab, headed in the direction of Zurich's famous museum. When we pulled up to the museum, I would have thought we were in the wrong place had it not been for the National Museum sign. All I saw was a large castle, not what I had envisioned. Werner ran me through the main exhibits that explained the history of Switzerland and its people. I had always had a passion for history, starting way back in that one-room schoolhouse in Boston, New York. The tour of the museum was short, but I enjoyed the personal guided tour, by my new friend, Werner Egloff.

"It is time for some Swiss chocolate, Fritz. We do not have much time left." We headed back to his cab. "The Swiss make the best chocolate in the world and I cannot wait for you to taste some," Werner continued. "The chocolate shop we are going to has just recently opened, but I promise you Fritz, this is the best chocolate in all of Switzerland and it will be world-famous someday."

Our last stop on my Zurich city tour was the Teuscher Chocolate Shop. It was already 2:45 PM, so I only had forty-five minutes to meet John Werth at the train station. Werner and I walked in and the smell of chocolate almost knocked me off my feet. Back in the states, I had occasionally enjoyed a Hershey Bar but I had never seen this much chocolate in one place. Over in a far corner of the shop there was a large machine mixing an enormous vat of chocolate. In another area of the shop stood a group of workers, cutting the cooled chocolate into bars and dipping cherries and strawberries into chocolate.

I was dying to taste some of this chocolate when I was stopped dead in my tracks. A group of nurses had just walked into the chocolate shop, and one nurse in particular drew all of my attention. I was so smitten that Werner noticed and walked up to me. "You appear to like the nurses more than the chocolate, Fritz."

I could not even muster a response as I watched this one particular nurse and her friends walk up to a shop worker and ask how much a box of chocolate was, in clear English. They were American nurses - what were they doing in Zurich? I glanced at my watch, it was 3:10 PM and Werner and I had to get going. I had to know this nurse's name before I left. I got up the courage to walk up to the group of nurses, but then I froze. I could not even get the word "hello" out of my mouth. I had attracted the group of nurses' attention by this time and had to say something.

"Alice, they have your favorite cherries dipped in chocolate," said one of the nurses in the direction of the nurse I was intently observing. Now I knew her name but time was running out. I walked closer to her and said "Alice, may I speak to you for a moment?"

She turned and looked at me and hesitantly responded by saying, "I do not know you. How do you know my name?"

I responded, "I overheard your friend say your name and would like to introduce myself."

By this time, all of her friends had turned in my direction. One of them blurted out, "Are you an American?"

I than realized that I had spoken in English, broken my cover and attracted the attention of the entire group of nurses. With a sense of desperation, I motioned for Alice to step aside with me. She followed me a few steps away from the counter, where I felt comfortable enough to speak to her without being overheard. "My name is Allen Voigt. I am a First Lieutenant in the United States Army and here in Switzerland on assignment. I wasn't supposed to let anyone know that, but I couldn't leave this shop without letting you know something about me." Alice simply stared at me as I struggled to put my thoughts into words. I put my head down, then looked up at her, and said, "Alice, I have never seen a woman as beautiful as you. I wish we had more time to get to know each other. Can we see each other again?"

Alice looked at me and said, "Thank you, Allen. I do not know what to say. We are here in Zurich for only a few months, helping a local hospital with their sterilization techniques. From here we are due to report to a hospital in Paris, France." She paused for a moment, and said, "I would like it very much if you contacted me again, but I do not have anything to give you that would help you find me. I am so sorry."

My shoulders slumped. I knew my chances of seeing Alice again were a million to one, but I was glad I had gotten up the nerve to speak to her. Before we parted ways, I asked Alice to keep my identity secret and she solemnly agreed. Before I walked out of the shop with Werner, I bought a box of chocolate-covered cherries as a present for Alice. When I gave it to her, she smiled and whispered, "Thank you". I could not tear my eyes away from her all the way to the door. I made a memorable exit, by tripping as I missed the step out onto the busy street.

As Werner and I walked back to the car, he was smiling from ear to ear. I did not know if he was smiling because he heard me speak in English or because of my obvious obsession with Alice. We jumped in the cab without saying a word. Werner drove fast as my time in Zurich was running out. As he was driving, it hit me like a ton of bricks; I had not even asked Alice what her last name was. I thought to myself, "How would I ever expect to find her again?"

As we pulled up to the train station, I thanked Werner for his hospitality, for his welcoming me into his home, and for the one-of-a-kind tour of his city. When I tried to pay him his fare of twenty-five

Swiss Francs, Werner looked at me and said "Your obsession with that nurse in the chocolate shop was fun to watch and worth twenty-five francs. You owe me nothing, Fritz."

With great relief, I realized that Werner had not overheard me mention my name in English. "Please let me pay you, if not for anything but for the meal your wife made me," I implored.

Werner would not hear of it. After parking his cab, he handed over my suitcase, shook my hand, and motioned me in the direction of the ticket booth. I thanked him profusely for everything and waved goodbye.

I found John Werth standing by the ticket booth; he had already purchased both our tickets. As we walked in the direction of the train platform, John asked me how I spent my afternoon. I just smiled and said, "It was fantastic." Our train was already boarding, so we jumped on board and found our seats.

Chapter 4

PERSEVERANCE

"He conquers who endures."
Persius

There was very little discussion between John and me as we traveled back to Berlin. I wanted to tell John all about the beautiful woman I had met in the chocolate store, but I was afraid to bring it up as I had compromised my German cover. I decided not bring it up at all, and if asked, I would just talk about touring the city of Zurich all day. As John slept in the seat next to me, with his head propped up against the window, I reflected on the day. My thoughts primarily involved Alice, and I wondered if I would ever see her again. I was twenty-four years old, and had never been knocked off my feet by a woman like that before. Although I had dated some girls in high school, I had never gotten that serious with anyone. I kept my thoughts to myself the rest of the trip back to Berlin. I soon drifted off to sleep.

Awakened by the announcement from the train's conductor that we would be arriving in Berlin in thirty minutes, I rubbed my eyes and looked out the window. I saw the lights of Berlin off in the distance. I glanced at my watch; it was 3:00 AM, December 19, 1932. By the time the train pulled into the station, John had moved to another train car in order to avoid drawing attention to the two of us together. I walked off the train into the cold, early morning air, pulling my coat collar up around my neck. The wind was blowing hard and snow was falling heavily. I had not seen my Berlin apartment since early August. I selected the first cab I could find and gave the driver my address. I finally got to bed around 4:15 AM.

Later that morning, after grabbing a few hours of sleep, I walked downstairs to buy a newspaper in order to read up on recent events in Berlin. I put the paper under my arm and headed out to find some breakfast. Between the conversations taking place around me and what I was reading in the morning paper, change was indeed coming to Germany. It was clear that the population was favoring Hitler and the Nazi party. The paper had articles about President Hindenburg and his poor health. Other articles shed light on Hitler's window of opportunity to gain more control of the country.

Christmas was around the corner and it looked like it would be a lonely one for me. Ambassador Sackett, John Werth, Geoffrey, Susan and the majority of the Embassy staff were going to be out of the country or spending time with their families. There was one bright spot, however. On Christmas Eve, I received word that John had mailed a letter to my parents in New York. The letter, drafted by the U.S. Army, informed my parents that I was alive and well, serving my country in a foreign post in Europe. I was pleased that they now would know that I was alive and have at least an idea where I was. I spent Christmas 1932 in my apartment, listening to local Christmas music on the radio. I thought of home and that beautiful nurse I had met in Zurich. I wondered where Alice was and how she was spending Christmas.

Berlin was a flurry of activity in January 1933. I received instruction from the Embassy to work my way into some form of employment within the Reichstag, the heart of the German center of government. The idea was for me to get closer to the changes that were consistently taking place within the government. I first scanned the daily newspapers for classified advertisements listing any jobs within the Reichstag. During the 2nd week in January, I stumbled upon what I was looking for. I was in the lobby of my apartment, just returning from the local market with some groceries. I overheard a man complaining to another neighbor that one of his favorite employees at the Reichstag had recently passed away and he was not sure how he was going to fill the position. I took advantage of this overheard conversation and approached the man. I had seen him come and go in the apartment building, since I had become a resident, so I hoped he would recognize me.

I simply walked up to the man and offered my service. "My name is Fritz Greiner and I live here in this building. I am very sorry for the loss of your employee. I am looking for work and would be able to start immediately."

My aggressive offer surprised the man. He paused for a minute and asked, "Do you speak English? This job requires some limited English translation."

Without hesitation, I responded, "Yes, I speak English fluently, practically with no German accent."

The man replied, "My name is Albert Koch and I work in the defense ministry. I am in need of a runner, someone who can cover the expansive grounds of the Reichstag, delivering messages, paperwork, and the like. Let me hear your English, Fritz. Say something for me."

I paused, thinking what to say and soon responded, in perfect English, "Germany is a vast country, and opportunities abound for young entrepreneurs like me."

Albert smiled and replied, "Meet me here at 6:00 AM tomorrow and we will walk together to the Reichstag." We shook hands and I continued up to my apartment with my groceries.

The next morning I dressed and was in the lobby at 5:45 AM. To my surprise, Albert was already there reading a paper. "Good morning Sir, I am ready to begin my employment at the Reichstag." Albert folded his paper, tucked it under his arm, and replied, "Not before a hearty breakfast. We will grab some on the way."

The walk to the Reichstag was about a mile and a half. We ate a quick breakfast at a diner right next to the Reichstag. Albert and I chatted about politics, mostly. I was surprised that he did not mention Hitler one time during our breakfast conversation. We finished up and walked over to the Reichstag. It was an impressive building from my apartment window, but was even more so up close. The building was incredibly ornate. The floors were primarily made of marble, cut into intricate patterns. Large paintings hung in the hallways. Albert's office was simple, however, with only enough room for the two desks that currently resided there.

After filling out some employment paperwork, the balance of my first day working in the Reichstag consisted of Albert going over a detailed map of the building with me. He explained to me my duties, which were simple in nature but, in my mind, would provide opportunities to see and hear things that would be vital to United States intelligence. My job was simply to deliver and pick up written correspondence. Albert's office served as a repository center for all things correspondence at the Reichstag.

Monday morning, January 30th, rumors circulated throughout the Reichstag that Hitler would be appointed Chancellor. Sure enough, at noon that same day, Hitler was sworn in as Chancellor. The ceremony took place at the Hindenburg's presidential palace. Cheers rang out throughout the Reichstag when the news arrived. I was in one of the main halls when I heard the news. As people all around me were clapping, some singing and still others standing in place with their right arms extended, shouting "Heil, Hitler", I felt a chill run up the back of my neck. I made it back to Albert's office, and he was sitting at his desk with his head in his hands, a stark contrast to other employees I had just seen. I said nothing as I laid a stack of papers on his desk. Hitler was now second in command, leaving only President Hindenburg remaining. I had read many news articles over the last year about many high-ranking government officials aligning themselves with Hitler.

I spent the next four weeks running paperwork between offices. I would often pass by Hermann Goering, Joseph Goebbels or Reinhard Heydrich in the hallway. On one occasion, I personally handed a sealed set of documents to Martin Bormann himself.

During my time at the Reichstag, I photographed a high percentage of the documents I handled, before the designated recipients received them. Albert often left his office for long periods, giving me time to photograph documents and unfettered access to his stationary and stamps. Each night, after I returned to my apartment, I removed the film from my camera and sealed the rolls in a metal container.

Each morning, when I left to walk to the Reichstag, I bought a newspaper in the lobby of my apartment. I would discreetly place the mental container, holding the film, in the rolled up copy of the newspaper. After walking approximately a half-mile in the direction of the Reichstag, I placed the rolled up newspaper in a designated trash can on the street. The designated trash can differed from day to day; I knew which one to place the newspaper in by looking for a white chalk line on the side of the trash can. Someone working for John Werth, assigned to the local Berlin waste management department, then emptied the trash can and secured the canister. The canister containing the film was delivered to the Embassy, and then mailed to Washington, D.C. for development and interpretation.

In those first four weeks, I provided eleven rolls of film. Sensitive information on the film included detail about the Nazi Party's goal of taking full control of the country, along with details on armament buildup and news about something called a V-1 rocket. At the time, I had no idea how vital that information would be to the United States' efforts to support its allies in Europe.

Late in the evening on Monday, February 27, 1933, I heard the sound of sirens blaring outside. There was a significant amount of light coming into my apartment window, so I looked out the window. I was shocked to see that the Reichstag was on fire. Flames were leaping out of some of the front windows and portions of the roof. Even though my view of the building was partially blocked by another building, I could tell the Reichstag was in serious trouble. I threw on a warm coat and headed outside to get a better view. It was bitterly cold outside. People were also coming out of surrounding buildings, all headed in the direction of the burning Reichstag. As I walked closer, simply trying to get myself in position to see the entire building, I could actually feel the heat of the flames. The fire by now was really whipping up, primarily coming out of the top of the building. As I watched the fire, I wondered if the fire was an accident or purposely set. I stood there watching the fire as long as I could. Fire trucks and emergency personnel began to arrive on the scene and I decided to get out of the bitter cold and back to my warm apartment for the remainder of the evening. It was hard to fall asleep with the sounds of crowds below and the wail of sirens off in the distance, but I somehow managed to catch a few hours of sleep.

I awoke the next morning to the sound of knocking on my door. I picked up my handgun and peered through the hole in the door. To my surprise, I saw that it was Geoffrey from the Embassy. I opened the door and let him in.

"I have been asked to escort you to the Embassy Allen", he told me.

"I assume this has to do with the Reichstag fire last night, correct?" I replied.

Geoffrey answered, "I honestly do not know, but John Werth asked that I retrieve you immediately. Pack some clothes, you may not be returning."

I had acquired enough civilian clothes by this time to fill three suitcases. Sensing my hesitation, Geoffrey directed me further. "Pack only three outfits, your personal items and leave the rest. Do not leave anything here that could tie you back to the Embassy or the United States Army."

It did not take me long to pack what little I had. We soon made our way down to the lobby and out to Geoffrey's car.

"Hop in the front seat," he instructed me. I threw my suitcase in the back seat and took my place in the front seat. I had always ridden in the back seat of John's vehicle, hunkered down out of sight. Geoffrey jumped in the car and off we went in the direction of the Embassy. "Not enough time to keep you out of sight," he explained. "The good news is that Susan is back at the Embassy preparing a big breakfast for us."

When I walked in the back door of the Embassy, John Werth greeted me. He shook my hand as he said, "Thank you, Allen, for your excellent work at the Reichstag these past few weeks."

We walked together down the long hallway towards the kitchen. Susan did not disappoint as she had prepared a delicious breakfast spread for us. As John and I ate, he shared with me that word was already spreading throughout Berlin that the Reichstag fire had been set deliberately. The Berlin newspapers that day were full of accusations by Hitler and the Nazi party that the fire was set by the Communists. Hitler, in his recent speeches, had denounced the rival Communist Party. John informed me that my job at the Reichstag was over now, and my services would be needed elsewhere. In the course of our discussions that morning, John told me that some of the photographs I had taken of the Reichstag documents described new tank and aircraft designs with planned manufacturing dates of 1938. My next assignment was to gain access into the research and design facilities for these new designs and find out what I could. It was clear that Germany was looking to reclaim its former prominence on the world stage.

In March 1933, Hitler passed the "Enabling Act", which allowed him and his Nazi Party to unleash dictatorial-type powers against anyone who challenged them. He would soon disband all political parties other than the Nazi Party. Hitler would replace state governors with his chosen Nazi officials, and even go a step further by getting rid of labor unions and making strikes illegal.

During my week at the Embassy, I was told that Ambassador Sackett was resigning his post. I said good-bye to him on March 24, 1933, his last day in Berlin. A new ambassador had not been named yet.

After things cooled down, I was able to return to my apartment. Over the next few weeks, I watched as Hitler corralled the newspapers, schools, and authors under the hand of the Nazi Party, simply through intimidation. I also witnessed the worsening treatment of the German Jewish population. Textbooks published by Jewish authors, along with any other books blacklisted by the Nazi Party, burned in large piles, right in the middle of the street. During 1933, as things continued to worsen, Hitler shocked the world by withdrawing from the League of Nations. At that point, I knew it was crucial that I find out as much as I could about Hitler's plan to re-arm the military.

The Embassy directed me to German manufacturing facilities all over Germany, as far south as Berndorf, Austria. My goal was to cover as much ground as I could during the remainder of 1933 and into 1934. The forged paperwork that had allowed me to previously gain employment throughout Germany, still gave me the opportunity to present myself for employment at any German manufacturing or design facility. I took odd jobs at as many facilities as I could, observing and photographing in secret. Typically, I worked at one location for a month and then moved on to a new one. I reported to the Embassy every sixty days with what I discovered. I was shocked at the level of production taking place throughout the country. Panzer and Tiger tanks, along with Me109, Me163, Ju87 and Ju88 planes were being built at a rapid pace.

Days drifted into weeks and weeks into months. The amount of information I reported to the Embassy in Berlin resulted in their having to bring in extra staff to handle all of the picture development and document processing. I was finally told during late July that I had secured what the United States military was seeking. I traveled back to Berlin and ordered to take a month off before my next assignment. On Friday, August 3, 1934, I picked up the morning paper and read that President Hindenburg had died the day before. The next week, Hitler abolished the role of President and combined the office of chancellor and president. The German military collectively swore an oath of loyalty to him. The last step Hitler took during August 1934 was to assume the role of Fuhrer and Reich Chancellor. War was imminent but no one knew when it would begin. By that time, I had grown frustrated with my perceived limited role in the United States Army. I had been trained in explosives and taught how to kill, but had not used those skills since I hit the ground in Europe.

During early September 1934, I asked for a meeting at the Embassy with John Werth and Captain Yates. We spent the whole day together. I expressed my desire to John and Captain Yates to see more action. I let them know I was weary of seeing the Jewish population humiliated day after day, and not being allowed to intervene when I saw innocent men and women beaten in the streets. Both men reminded me that my efforts over the last three years had and would save countless lives. They also stated that my contributions had allowed the United States military and government to secure valuable information that enabled proactive, rather than reactive, military planning. As the day wore on, I could not tell if I was gaining traction with Captain Yates in regards to my request.

I continued to express my frustration to John and Captain Yates as dinnertime approached. The three of us ate dinner together in the Embassy dining room. I did not have much to say to either man. Instead, I listened while they discussed some of the activities taking place back in the States. Their topics included President Roosevelt's administration and Captain Yates' desire to see more funds appropriated to the U.S. Army. Since our meal did not wrap up until 10:00 PM, John asked that I remain at the Embassy that night. His plan was for us to take up our conversations again in the morning. I was tired and decided to go to bed. As I laid my head on my pillow that night, I was extremely frustrated and even questioned staying in the Army much longer.

The next morning, I got an early start to my day. I did not want to miss the great breakfast Geoffrey and Susan always prepared for me when I was a guest at the Embassy. They did not disappoint me that morning, and it was a pleasure catching up with both of them. John joined me and as we finished our last cup of coffee, Captain Yates walked in for one of Susan's famous cinnamon rolls. The three of us soon made our way up to the office of the newly appointed ambassador to Berlin, Mr. William Dodd. I had not yet met the ambassador, so I hoped he was there that day. The three of us sat down and were soon joined by Ambassador Dodd. He did not say a word as he entered his office and took a seat in the chair behind his desk.

Unbeknownst to me, John and Captain Yates had stayed up late the night before reviewing with Ambassador Dodd my activity over the last three years and how that lined up with the U.S. Army's needs across the world in light of recent events.

Ambassador Dodd spoke first. "Allen, you have performed above and beyond the call of duty, young man. The information you have secured for both the United States military and the office of the White House is priceless."

He paused, which allowed me to interject, "Thank you, Sir."

He continued, "Captain Yates and John have sung your praises both to me and to senior officials back in the States. America owes you a debt of gratitude for a job well done."

It was at that point Captain Yates spoke up. "Allen, we have considered your desire to see more action. In all honesty, you really cannot secure any more information that others cannot secure for us, simply due to the inroads you have made. Your role as a military attaché is ending. As you know, America is currently not at war but I think we all agree Germany is looking to pick a fight. If they do, America will rise to the occasion. The question now is what to do with you." He paused for a moment, as if he needed time to think. Finally, he continued. "The first thing we need to do is promote you to the rank of Captain."

Captain Yates reached into his pocket and then handed me the silver bars. I had not worn a Unites States Army uniform since I left the Army War College. Although I was eager to display my new rank, that would have to wait.

"Thank you, Sir", I replied in a firm voice. I placed the silver bars in my shirt pocket.

Ambassador Dodd spoke up again. "Allen, you have caught the eye of President Roosevelt. He is fully aware of your three-year mission here in Germany. Even before you expressed a desire to see more action, the office of the White House contacted me and asked if

I could give you up." I simply sat there, stunned. He continued, "You will be reassigned to Fort Meade in Maryland, but your primary role will be to work out of the White House."

I felt overwhelmed by that point in the conversation. Ambassador Dodd rose from his chair and walked over to me.

I stood and said, "Sir, I do not know what to say, I am truly honored."

I thanked Ambassador Dodd and Captain Yates for their vote of confidence and spent that second night at the Embassy. In the morning, John Werth greeted me at breakfast. "Congratulations on your next assignment stateside. I have to admit I am jealous, but I am also excited for you."

I smiled and thanked him, than ate my breakfast. As I left the Embassy kitchen for the last time, Geoffrey and Susan hugged me good-bye and wished me safe travels. They thanked me for always being considerate. John asked me to grab my suitcase and meet him at the back door of the Embassy by 8:00 AM. My flight out of Berlin would take me to London, where I would board a luxury liner for New York City. It had been so long since I had seen my parents, and I was excited to be heading back to the United States. In order to keep my cover as long as possible, I was to travel under my assumed German name and documentation all the way back to New York City. Upon entering the port of New York, I would present my American military identification.

John and I said very little on the way to the Berlin airport. The leaves were off the trees and the sky was gray as we drove past the burned Reichstag. The number of stores I saw with the required Star of David painted crudely on the windows was appalling. The Jewish population throughout the country was now taking the full brunt of Hitler and the Nazi Party's wrath. As John and I continued on to the airport, I witnessed a Jewish shop owner beaten on the street by two armed Nazi soldiers. My heart sank for the man, who did nothing to fight back, other than grab the soldier's boot as the beating continued.

We reached the small airport and without much fanfare, I said goodbye to John, thanking him for his friendship. I boarded the small twin-engine plane and found a seat. I had never been on an airplane before. I was scared to death but did my best not to show it. I was one of only seven passengers heading to London that day. After the small plane lifted off the runway, I surveyed the landscape and the buildings of Berlin. A storm was gathering, and Hitler was going to bring the German people into a war, a war that would most likely involve America.

The engines of the plane drowned out any discernible conversations between me and the other six passengers. As we crossed the English Channel, I saw small fishing boats dotting the channel. The White Cliffs of Dover came into view and the plane soon began to descend for the airfield. We landed and taxied up to a small building where new passengers were waiting. After I exited the plane, I saw a man holding a piece of paper out in front of him with the initials "A.V." written on it. I concluded that the paper referred to me, so I introduced myself for the first time in a long time as Allen Voigt.

"Welcome to England, Allen. My name is Greg Jones," he said as we shook hands, "and I am assigned to the United States Embassy here in London."

I followed Greg to his car and we continued on to the piers. Greg informed me that he had been in London for just over a year, but was originally from Normal, Illinois.

"We are both a long way from home, but I think you win the award for being the furthest," I responded.

My ship, which was due to leave Southampton later that evening, was the RMS Mauretania. There was no time for me to tour London. I was finally returning to America after a three-year absence. In that time, I had not corresponded with my parents. The only news they had received about me was the letter that the U.S. Army had sent them the previous Christmas. Greg dropped me at the Southampton pier where the RMS Mauretania was docked. As we exited the car, Greg handed me my updated passport that showed my real name.

He also handed me the required documents that would allow me to board the large ocean liner. We shook hands and I headed toward the ship. I had never laid eyes on a ship that large before. My 1931 crossing of the Atlantic Ocean was underneath it; I was excited to be traveling on top of it this time.

I found my room aboard the large ship and wasted no time in dropping off my suitcase. I soon made my way up to the top deck. It was now late afternoon and the sun was finally trying to break through the gray clouds. A westerly breeze blew in the direction of home. I remained on deck for a long time, watching the ship's lines loosed from the dock; the gangway removed and soon heard the ship's engines come to life. The ships exhaust funnels belted out smoke and a large whistle blew loudly, heard along the entire length of the ship. I watched as the tugboats guided the large ship out of its moorings and in the direction of the deep water of the Atlantic Ocean. As the sun set in front of us, I returned to the lower decks of the ship and to my room, but not before taking in some dinner at one of the dining rooms.

The RMS Mauretania was due to arrive in New York City on Sunday, the 16th. On our third day at sea, the Captain announced over the ship's speakers that we were near the area where the RMS Titanic had hit an iceberg and sunk twenty-two years earlier. It was a somber moment for all of us. I was only four years old when the RMS Titanic sank, so all I knew about it was from word of mouth. There was a moment of silence throughout the ship for several minutes. A large floral memorial wreath was gently placed in the water. I watched it as long as I could as our ship continued to steam west.

We arrived as scheduled in New York City. The large ship docked and the gangway was extended to the dock. I could not grab my bags fast enough. I practically ran down the gangway and finally stepped foot on American soil again. I was due to report to Fort Meade by Monday, October 1st and to the White House by Tuesday, October 9th. Captain Yates had given me permission to return home to Buffalo, New York for the interim. I could now share limited information with my parents, like where I had been the last three years and my upcoming assignment.

Before I headed for the station and the train that would take me home to Buffalo, I found a taxi and headed straight for Meme's Kitchen. I had not had those cheese grits in three years and I was long overdue. Meme was not there that morning, but I enjoyed my breakfast of cheese grits, French toast and bacon.

I caught the last train out of Penn Station to Buffalo with little time to spare. It would be a six hour train ride west, with many stops. I settled into my seat and read the New York Times from cover to cover.

It was close to eight o'clock in the evening when my train pulled into the East Aurora train station. Since my parents had no idea I was coming home that night, my transportation options were limited. The temperature was in the low fifties, which made it a great night to walk the short mile and a half home. I picked up my suitcase and headed in the direction of home. I had not seen 345 South Street since Christmas 1929. Walking the streets that night, I reflected on all I had seen and done the last five years. As I walked down Center Street and made a left on South Street, I barely kept myself from running the rest of the way.

I arrived home at 8:45 PM. Since it was Sunday night, I hoped my parents were still awake. I saw a light on in the living room and walked up the porch steps. I laid my belongings down and knocked on the door. I was surprised to hear a dog barking inside the house that I did not recognize. The porch light lit up, the door opened, and there stood my father, decked out in his bathrobe and slippers. I saw the surprise look on his face as he reached out to hug me. No sooner had he placed his arms around me, when Mom shouted from the kitchen, asking who was at the front door.

"It is Allen, come quick!" my father said.

My Mom soon came into view, running toward me. We had a tearful reunion for a few minutes. I realized the dog that I heard barking was desperately trying to get my attention.

"Allen, this is Bessie. She is a Labrador retriever, and we got her soon after Porgy died about a year ago," my Mom informed me. She continued to tell me that they found Porgy one morning in her bed, dead, assuming she died of old age. I was sad not to have been there to bury my dog but the emotion of being home, after such a long time, helped compensate the sadness I had over losing Porgy.

We proceeded to the family room, but not until my Dad picked up my suitcase and placed it near the stairs leading up to my old bedroom.

My parents and I stayed up until three o'clock in the morning talking about the last three years. As instructed, I only shared with my parents some of the countries and places I had visited. In no way did I share with them any details about my activities for the Embassy and U.S. Army. I had purchased a few things for my parents while overseas and had packed them carefully in my suitcase. I now unpacked them and happily gave them to my mom and dad. My mother loved the lace tablecloth and napkins I had bought for her in Belgium and my father especially liked the three knives I had custom-made for him in Berlin.

The next morning came early, awakened by Bessie licking my face. Over breakfast, I shared with my parents the news of my new assignment at the White House. My parents' jaws dropped when I informed them that I would be working indirectly for the President of the United States. I really knew very few details as to what my duties at the White House would entail, but it was a proud moment for my parents. I spent the next few days enjoying being home and catching up on what my parents had been doing over the last few years.

The day of my departure for Fort Meade, Saturday, September 29th, came much too early. It was too hard for my mom to see me off again at the train station, so we hugged goodbye and I promised her that I would keep in touch as much as I could. My father took me to the train station and very little was said between us. I knew it was also hard for him to say goodbye to me after such a short time together. He shook my hand and hugged me, and then he told me he was proud of me.

"I am glad you will be stateside this time, and I hope you can make it home for Christmas," said my Father. We hugged goodbye.

The train ride from Buffalo to Maryland was to take about nine hours, covering six hundred miles. I would miss my parents, but I was extremely excited to begin my next assignment. With very little fanfare, I arrived at Fort Meade early Saturday evening. I reported to the Commandant's Office as instructed. I received paperwork that outlined in more detail my living quarters, my upcoming White House assignment, and the rules on my limited personal interaction during my time there. My living quarters were definitely an upgrade from Camp Pine, as I was assigned my own apartment. The next few days were filled with getting to know my way around the large Army base and the surrounding area. An Army Jeep provided me granted me the freedom to come and go as necessary. It was Sunday, and I was due to report to the White House on Tuesday. I needed to make sure I knew the best route to take, so I made three practice runs that day.

The challenge for me was that I never knew where my superior officer, newly promoted, Major Yates, was. The paperwork I received upon my arrival at Fort Meade was sealed in a confidential envelope. I was a solitary soldier, asked to perform unique assignments for my country. At times, I fought feelings of loneliness because I had never really made any close friends in the Army. My new role was to commute back and forth from the White House to Fort Meade, Monday through Friday. I would find out more once I arrived at the White House.

Tuesday morning came early. I awoke at 5:00 AM, prepared my newly pressed Army uniform, pinned on my Captain bars, and headed out for downtown Washington, D.C. I was so nervous I could not eat any breakfast. I arrived at the front gate of the White House at 6:45 AM and showed my credentials to the Army Private guarding the gate. He saluted me and motioned for me to pull up to a designated parking lot off to the right. My initial contact at the

White House was to be The Secretary of War, George Dern. A Navy Ensign met me in the parking lot and escorted me into a small office just inside the White House. After presenting my identification to another Navy ensign seated at a small desk, I took a seat and waited. At 7:15 AM, Secretary Dern greeted me. We shook hands and he asked me to follow him. As we were walking down a hallway, he turned to me and asked if I was hungry.

"Yes, Sir, I did not eat before arriving this morning as my nervous stomach did not agree with me," I said.

"A little nervousness is to be expected, Captain Voigt," he responded.

By this time, I was over my initial concern over arriving on time and felt like eating. We enjoyed a light breakfast in a small room just off the White House kitchen and exchanged light conversation. As I ate, I noticed a White House orderly pushing President Roosevelt down the hallway in a wooden wheelchair. I had not known that the President could not walk. I finished my breakfast and followed Secretary Dern out into the hallway.

"I am taking you to meet the President," Secretary Dern announced. My heart skipped a beat, and then we continued down the hallway to the Oval Office.

President Roosevelt was seated in a chair next to a large couch when we entered the room. We walked over to where the President was sitting and stood directly in front of him.

"Mr. President," said Secretary Dern, "I would like to introduce to you Captain Allen Voigt. He has just returned from Berlin, Germany, at your request."

I stepped forward and shook the President's hand. He apologized for not rising to greet me and invited us to take a seat on the couch. "I understand we are both from New York State," he remarked.

"Yes, Sir", I responded. "I was born in Buffalo and I understand you are from Hyde Park."

After thanking me for making the long trip from Berlin, the President spent the next two hours asking me a multitude of questions. All were questions that he most likely already had the answers to, but he evidently wanted to obtain feedback directly from me. He was fascinated that I had seen Hitler on not one but two occasions. As we entered our third hour of discussion, the Secretary of the Navy, Claude Swanson, joined us. President Roosevelt had been in office since March 1933, Dern and Swanson had been with him since the beginning.

The President continued, "Allen, I am sure you are wondering why I asked you to work out of the White House. Your excellent work in Berlin and other cities within Germany provided all of us with a wealth of information. We know now that we face an enemy of profound evil in Hitler. Yet another enemy is brewing in the Pacific region of the world. Japan is now in China, and we do not know where they will strike next. Your ability to infiltrate a country and relay information is of vital importance to us. Secretary Dern is in favor of a higher degree of efficiency within our armed forces. He wants a fighting force that can expand very fast when faced with a crisis across the globe."

Secretary Dern then outlined to me his five-year plan to provide the Army with new planes, ships, tanks and weapons. He also explained how he would implement a secret fighting force that could send a individual soldier behind enemy lines, performing a wide range of tasks - tasks designed to save American lives, create havoc for the enemy, and set the stage for a quicker end to conflicts.

He finished his comments by saying, "Captain Voigt, your accomplishments in Berlin and Germany paved the way for us, and we would like you to help us reach these military milestones as well. You will work out of the White House and report to me."

At that point, I understood why I had been called to the White House. President Roosevelt then addressed me.

"Allen, your service to America thus far has been exemplary. Our great country will eventually be drawn into another war, and when it is, we need to be ready. I am looking to you to help us get there."

My reply was to the collective group. "I am honored to be chosen for this assignment, and I give you my word that I will continue to pour everything I have into the service of my country. You have the right man for the job. Thank you for the opportunity, Sirs."

With that, the meeting in the Oval Office was adjourned and I was handed off to someone I knew very well, Major Yates. He had been waiting outside the oval office.

"Welcome to the White House, Allen. I trust you had a good trip from Berlin?" he inquired.

"It was a trip of first time experiences, never having flown on an airplane or traveled on an ocean liner." I answered.

He then invited me to follow him to an area of the White House reserved for Army and Navy personnel. Over lunch, we discussed what my job objectives would be for the next two years. They included alternating weeks between Fort Meade and the White House. At the White House, I was to provide Secretary Dern with a very detailed account of my time in Germany, specifically what I had seen, heard and experienced. At Fort Meade, I was to support Secretary Dern's military enhancements. In addition, my superiors wanted me to spend my evenings over the next year, learning the Japanese language at George Washington University. I took my instruction like a good soldier, but internally, I groaned at the thought of having to learn yet another new language, especially one as hard as Japanese.

The balance of 1934 and all of 1935, I worked hard on the military initiatives set by Secretary Dern. My Japanese language studies were slowly coming along. The bulk of my military initiatives centered on being the eyes and ears for Secretary Dern during my time at Fort Meade. Although I was excited to be working for the Roosevelt administration, I still had a deep desire to apply my learned skills in a wider capacity. I wanted to help prevent America from having to enter another world war, or if that failed, at least play a significant role in allowing me to save American lives. I wanted so much to see active combat like my father had. I kept my frustrations in check, however, and worked diligently on my assignments.

In early 1936, I traveled home to Buffalo to see my folks several times, visits we all enjoyed. By late summer of that year, I knew the Japanese language. My classes then focused on learning the Japanese culture. I also learned about the continued expansion of the Japanese into China, Manchuria and beyond from members of the military that had first-hand knowledge of Japan's territorial expansion. I spent most evenings reading German newspapers. My goal was to keep my German language abilities fresh, and keep up with what Hitler and the Nazis were doing. My meetings at the White House were full of intelligence gathering as new information was coming out of Berlin. In March, the Jews in Germany lost their right to vote. Months later, the Nazis blacklisted over 2,000 books, written by Jewish authors. I frequently shared accounts of my time in Germany, and the reports I had sent back during that time were now correlating with current events.

August 1936 was eventful for many reasons. The Olympics were held that year in Berlin, Germany, and one of the planes I had seen manufactured in secret during my time there, was displayed at the games. It was a Messerschmitt ME-109, a single-engine fighter armed to the teeth. On August 27th, Secretary Dern passed away and was replaced by Secretary Harry Woodring. My work with Secretary Woodring would turn out to be a lot different.

On November 4, 1936, I was invited to the White House to see President Roosevelt reelected. In that election, he carried forty-six out of the forty-eight states. The following week I joined the President on a South American trip. My assignment was for me to be his eyes and ears from a military standpoint. I accepted the invitation.

We left Washington D.C. on Saturday, November 21st and did not return until December 12th. We traveled to the island of Trinidad; Rio de Janeiro, Brazil; Buenos Aires, Argentina and Montevideo, Uruguay. I was fascinated by the mountains, which reminded me of the time I spent in Switzerland. After we returned home to the United States, the President asked if I thought South America would be an ally to the United States if another world war began. I told

President Roosevelt that I was concerned about the Nazi sympathy I had recently witnessed in Argentina. We agreed that none of the countries we visited had militaries of any significance and could not hurt us from that standpoint.

1937 was a blur with the exception of a tragic event that took place on Thursday, May 6th. During my time in Germany, I had befriended an older German couple through my association with Geoffrey and Susan. The couple was Otto and Elsie Ernst. They were kind to me in so many ways, but mainly for providing me several home-cooked meals during visits I had made to Hamburg, Germany. They never knew my identity when I was in Berlin, but they treated me like the son they never had. Word came to me that they were coming to the United States. I received permission to travel to Lakehurst, New Jersey to see them fly in on a famous dirigible balloon, the Hindenburg. My superiors wanted me to solicit information from them on the recent Nazi activity in and around Hamburg. My plan was to act surprised when I saw them and simply state that I was in the United States visiting and had come to see the Hindenburg, but nothing turned out as planned.

I was in a large crowd of people as the Hindenburg descended toward its designated landing area there in Lakehurst. It was just about seven o'clock in the evening when the Hindenburg's rear section suddenly burst into flames. The crowd and I watched in horror as the large balloon engulfed in fire. Although we were far enough away that we were not in any real danger, we still felt the tremendous heat emanated as the entire dirigible rapidly burned and collapsed to the ground. I immediately left the crowd and ran in the direction of the accident to see if I could help in any way. Several people had jumped from the passenger compartment and had broken their legs. Those of us who rushed to offer assistance picked up survivors and carried them further away from the burning flames. None of us on the scene knew how many passengers had actually survived the crash because of the utter chaos around us. It was hard to tell whether the people we were helping were survivors of the Hindenburg, innocent bystanders, or personnel originally assigned to secure the Hindenburg's ropes as it descended.

The fire, caused by the hydrogen gas that kept the Hindenburg aloft all the way from Germany, burned for over two hours. The heat was so intense that all the hair on my arms singed off. When I walked among the survivors, I was amazed to see both Otto and Elsie Ernst. Other volunteers surrounded them, but I managed to work my way up to them. I immediately knew that Otto was worse off. His face was severely burned and he was in shock. Elsie recognized me however, so I gave her a supporting hug. Nothing was said between us. Soon, they were carried away by ambulance to a local hospital. I later learned that Otto died of his injuries and that Elsie had his body carried back to Germany on a steamship.

I spent the next two and a half years working more closely with Secretary Swanson of the Navy than I did with Secretary Woodring. My primary objective was to improve the communication lines between the Navy and the Army. I visited several of the shipyards in Baltimore, Maryland, and Philadelphia, Pennsylvania. The goal was to act as a liaison and show the Navy personnel logistically how each branch of the service could support each other in the event that America was thrust into war. Although I did not find these years to be the most exciting years of my career in the Army, I was able to overcome something I had always struggled with – loneliness. I was able to make a few friends during this time and I enjoyed their friendships.

By 1939, my relationship with Secretary Woodring had become very strained. America was now witnessing what I had earlier feared from Hitler and the Nazi Party. In March, Germany invaded Czechoslovakia, in September, Poland. The quickness and ferocity of the German advance was almost unbelievable, but it did not surprise the White House. Thanks to my eyewitness accounts of Germany's rearmament, the White House knew of Germany's capabilities. I learned that the United States had warned the countries of Europe as to the pending military might of Adolf Hitler. President Roosevelt wanted to send military support to American's allies in the form of tanks, guns and ammunition. Secretary Woodring supported many of Secretary Dern's initiatives, like helping to increase the strength of the Army and the National Guard, but he was against the idea of supplying our Allies with arms. Secretary Swanson died in July 1939, and my duties with the Navy suddenly slowed.

My strain with Secretary Woodring was minor compared to the frustration the White House had with him. When Germany invaded Denmark, Norway and France during early 1940, the response of the White House was to equip Britain with fighting equipment. This approach reached a fever pitch when Britain was faced with rescuing over 300,000 of its soldiers from the beaches of Dunkirk, France. All of the strain with Secretary Woodring came to a head in June when he publicly disagreed with the approach that the White House had taken regarding supplying Britain with war materials. Woodring was asked to resign and he left the office of Secretary of War on June 20th.

With all the changes taking place within the White House administration, my duties drifted. I spent the latter half of 1940 working with National Guard units, helping train them on weapons and hand-to-hand combat techniques. One National Guard unit that I really enjoyed working with was the one back in my hometown. Typically, I worked with each National Guard unit for only a few days, but because this particular unit was in my hometown, my superiors arranged for me to spend the entire month of December in Buffalo.

Christmas that year was special because I spent it with my parents during my ten days at home. My parents continually asked me questions about the White House and President Roosevelt. During that visit home, I visited my Grandfather Henry's grave at Maplewood Cemetery in nearby Patchin, New York. As I knelt at his grave, I apologized to him for not being there when he died and for not attending his funeral. I told him I hoped I was making him proud.

The start of 1941 saw me back at Fort Meade. The war in Europe continued to escalate, and Britain was bombed every night. I wondered if, and when America was going to enter the fight against Germany. Germany had recently formed a pact with Italy and Japan. If America joined the fight, I wanted to play a part in it. I was becoming more and more frustrated that I was not using the skills I had been taught. I knew I could lend my talents to my country's aid in a greater way.

In April, I received a surprise visitor at my Fort Meade apartment. The news he delivered was exactly what I had been waiting for.

Chapter 5

MOUTH OF HELL

"If you are going to go through hell, keep going."
Sir Winston Churchill

That April 1941 knock on my door caught me by surprise. No one ever knocked at my door, simply due to the solitary nature of my assignments. It was nine o'clock in the evening and I was interested to see who on the Fort Meade base was looking for me at that hour. I opened the door, and there stood Major Yates. Since October 1934, I had not spent considerable time with him. He periodically attended some of the high-level meetings I had with the Secretaries of War and Navy, but his attendance was not consistent. In fact, this was the first time he had visited me on the base.

I invited him in and over the next two hours, Major Yates explained the roles the United States Army had for me, in the event of war with Germany and Japan. By this time, I had become fluent in the Japanese language and had worked hard to keep the German language fresh by forcing myself to read German newspapers. Major Yates told me that Japan had become even more aggressive in the Pacific region, and the White House was concerned that the Japanese might try to draw America into a war with them. The effects of the alliance of Germany, Japan and Italy during September 1940 had resulted in mind-numbing fear across the globe that another world war could occur imminently. However, Americans felt safe due to the protection afforded them by the oceans on its eastern and western borders. Nevertheless, the White House was concerned about the islands of Hawaii, where a large isolated Navy base was located.

Before Major Yates left that night, he dropped a name to me. "Allen, you've caught the attention of General William Donovan. He is a veteran of the Great War and a Medal of Honor recipient. He covered the same ground in France that your father did. The General is currently in Great Britain assessing the country's ability to withstand Germany's nightly bombings, and their ability to liberate Europe. He is lobbying the White House to form an elite group that will go behind enemy lines and perform covert activities. Your recent actions in Germany and the White House, along with your fluency in German and Japanese languages, make you the ideal candidate for initiating the program."

Major Yates wrapped up his visit with instructions for me to leave Fort Meade within the week and travel to the island of Oahu in the Hawaiian island chain. My role was to work with the Army and Navy as a White House liaison. The immediate need would be to assess our country's ability to fight the Japanese in the Pacific and to report any threats to our security that might exist on the island. With such a large population of Japanese on the island, my ability to speak and understand their language would come in very handy. Major Yates then left but not before wishing me Godspeed and safe travels.

Over the next few days, I attended meetings at the White House with the new Secretary of War, Henry Stimson, and the recently appointed Secretary of the Navy, Frank Knox. Although I had not met either man prior to the meetings, I immediately liked them both simply because they had, in a short amount of time, learned about my activity. Fully aware of my new assignment, Stimson and Knox made it clear that I had all of their backing and support.

I was not able to visit my parents before leaving for Hawaii, but I spoke with them on the phone before departing on April 14th. I boarded a train in Washington, D.C. for a five-day trip to San Francisco, California, with stops in Kansas and Colorado. I traveled in my full Army uniform and spent the majority of my time studying the maps of Hawaii and the South Pacific. I did, however take the time to enjoy the tremendous view outside my train window as we traveled through the Rocky Mountains. Like the Swiss Alps, the Rocky Mountains still had snow on their peaks. I had been east and now I was traveling west, adding to the total number of miles I had covered in my relatively short Army career.

By the time my train pulled into the San Francisco train station, I had only one day left before my ship departed for Hawaii. I checked in at the Presidio Army Base and confirmed the name of the ship I would be traveling on, the Battleship California (BB-44). I wrapped up my only day in San Francisco with quick visits to take in the Golden Gate Bridge and Ghirardelli Square.

I boarded the Battleship California on April 20th. I was not the only member of the Army boarding that day, as there were over one hundred newly inducted Army Privates heading to Schofield Barracks on Oahu. There was a friendly rivalry between the Army and Navy and it played itself out regularly onboard the ship as we headed west. The Battleship California had spent most of its time in the Pacific, but had recently returned to California for rudder repairs. The ship had only come to San Francisco to pick up my fellow Army soldiers and me. The weather was kind to us, so I spent a good bit of time over the next six days up on the top deck. My thoughts ranged from America's pending involvement in a world war to wondering where Alice was and if I would ever see her again. I had tried to find her several times over the last few years, but none of my contacts could help me locate her. On the evening of April 26th, we anchored at Ford Island, located right in the middle of Pearl Harbor, on the western end of Oahu. We anchored alongside several other battleships. I left the ship on the 27th, and as I walked along the docks on battleship row, I was blown away by the size of the ships. I thought to myself, "What country would dare pick a fight with us?"

I soon found the Schofield Barracks. The barracks were sectioned off for enlisted men and officers. The designated officer's quarters accommodated two officers each. My quarters appeared to be empty, so I had it to myself.

Over the next few weeks, I covered a large portion of the island, conducting surveillance on the beaches where a foreign enemy could potentially come ashore. I surveyed existing maps, made notes, and reported my findings back to Washington and the offices of Secretary Stimson and Knox. By mid-May 1941, I still had not received a roommate, so I established my own routine and did not worry about interruptions. After I surveyed the beaches, the rest of May and all of June I spent inspecting the submarine pens, fuel tanks, and ship docks for gaps in security and possible attacks from the sea or air. I also interviewed the majority of the submarine and ship Captains. My objective with the interviews was to gather their concerns with security, the speed of navigating subs and ships out of the harbor in the event of an attack, and what level of armament each vessel needed in case they were attacked from the sky by aircraft.

By early July, the series of reports I sent back to Washington had become increasingly aggressive with my level of concerns. My findings showed that our subs, ships, barracks and fuel reserves were sitting ducks, in the event we were attacked from the air. My reports resulted in a series of phone calls with Secretaries Stimson and Knox. I am sure my findings were relayed to President Roosevelt, but nothing ever came of it. I went so far as to reach out to Major Yates via phone and letter. He did all he could to reiterate my concerns to those in higher positions, but he, too, had no success with the offices of the Army or Navy. All of the Navy Captains that I spoke with shared my concerns.

I felt extremely frustrated, but knew I had done my best to carry out my mission as instructed. I therefore proceeded to the next step of surveillance. In July and August, I visited tourist destinations, restaurants and hotels frequented by Japanese visitors and/or Japanese island residents. I simply listened to conversations in Japanese taking place all around me. My goal was to gather any derogatory conversations about the United States, and to pick up any discussions of espionage. I heard nothing alarming during that entire time.

By September, I had completed my Oahu Island surveillance assignments and arranged to return to Washington, D.C. The feedback I received was to sit tight and wait for further instructions. With that news, I decided to circle back with all the sub and ship Captains I had met and arrange for time on their vessels as they conducted training exercises around the Hawaiian Islands. The time I shared with Navy personnel was invaluable and I found all of them to be very gracious with my questions about ship defense and maneuvering.

The second week in October, I was notified that both Secretary Stimson and Knox were going to visit Pearl Harbor and wanted to meet with me as part of their visit. Their visit lasted four days, and during that time, I had three meetings with them. I showed them aerial maps of Pearl Harbor and brought in various battleship Captains to share their concerns over an attack by air. By the end of the meeting, Secretaries Stimson and Knox reassured me that my findings on Pearl Harbor security were being taking very seriously and that preventive measures would be taken.

As the last meeting with them adjourned and Secretary Stimson began to leave the room, he leaned into me and said, "Great job Voigt, nice work here. Soon you will receive correspondence from General Donovan."

With that, he left the room. I felt a little better that my security findings were taken seriously. I also thought back to the comments Major Yates had shared with me in Washington about General Donovan's desire to create a covert fighting unit.

Several days went by, when late one evening toward the end of October I received a knock at my door. Upon opening it, I found a two star general standing on the stoop. I saluted him. He reached out to shake my hand, informing me, "Captain Voigt, I am William Donovan. May I come in?"

I always kept my room neat and orderly, but it was a little intimidating having an Army General visit. I offered the General my only chair, and I sat on the edge of my bed. I did not say or do much over the next two hours apart from giving an occasional "Yes, Sir" or nodding my head in agreement.

"America," Donovan stated, "is not prepared to wage war, Captain Voigt. The Army and Navy are not prepared from a manpower standpoint, and do not have the required number of tanks, ships and planes to wage war."

He then shared his plans to create a department called the Office of Strategic Services. The OSS would train certain groups of the Army and troops of friendly nations in the Pacific. Our conversations continued for some time into the night as General Donovan told me that he spent the better part of 1940 and early 1941 in Britain as an emissary on behalf of President Roosevelt and Secretary Knox. He described how he assessed and studied the British intelligence services, and worked on a parallel model for creating an American intelligence service.

General Donovan continued to talk. "What caught my attention, Captain Voigt, was your activity in Germany and most recently, your reports back to the White House regarding the vulnerability of Pearl Harbor. I have been very vocal myself regarding the pending outbreak of another world war," he stated gravely. "Like your father, I fought in what I now call World War I. I am confident we will soon be at war with both Germany and Japan."

He paused and then looked me in the eye. "Allen, I need you to get ready for what is coming. You are trained to kill, to operate covertly, and to gather intelligence. I will be calling on your services in the very near future. You come highly recommended by Major Yates, so I am confident you will not fail me or the United States."

With that, General Donovan rose, shook my hand goodnight and departed. As I shut the door behind him, astonished by what had just happened. All my training and persistence were finally going to pay off. The question was when. I laid my head on my pillow that night and wondered when I would hear from General Donovan again. The next day I asked some of the senior Army officers around Pearl Harbor about the General. I found out that he was also from New York. I asked about the Purple Hearts and Distinguished Service Cross medals I saw on his uniform the night before. Like the Medal of Honor, he secured these awards also during the Great War. After the war, he had worked in the Coolidge administration and lost a run for the Governor of New York. His visit with me became even more monumental in my mind, in light of the information I gathered about him.

With no clear-cut orders, I spent the month of November getting my body and mind into peak physical shape. I had worked very hard to keep fit since exiting basic training, but the years in Germany and now my time in Hawaii had prevented me from physically training. I ran extensively for the next four weeks, covering the majority of the island of Oahu. I also spent extensive time at the Army gun range working on my marksmanship. I took the time to train some newly inducted Army recruits on the basics of hand-to-hand combat, knife handling and explosives. It was rewarding to teach, but the activities also afforded me the opportunity to brush up on my training.

Early on the morning of Sunday, December 7, 1941, I decided to get a run in before it got too hot. I was running down near Battleship Row when I suddenly saw a plane dive out of the clouds toward the battleships anchored nearby. As the plane banked and leveled off over the row of battleships, it dropped what looked like a bomb. I could not believe what I was witnessing. I watched in horror, as the bomb hit and detonated on the battleship USS Oklahoma. The concussion from the explosion knocked me hard to the ground. More and more single-engine planes were screaming out of the clouds. The acrid scent of smoke filled the air. Trying to get up, I managed to lift my head off the ground and make out the markings on the undersides of the planes, Japanese! The red circle was easily identifiable. I considered my options, of which there were very few, and decided to run in the direction of the USS Oklahoma to help in any way I could. By this point, high-level Japanese planes were dropping larger bombs all over Battleship Row.

My brain simply could not comprehend what I saw right in front of me. Everything was happening so fast. Ships were bombarded; sailors were being knocked off ship decks and falling into the water. The water offered no relief however, as it caught fire from all of the leaking fuel and oil that gushed from the gaping holes in the anchored ships. I finally managed to get close to the USS Oklahoma, but it had taken on too much water and started to roll on its side. Japanese planes filled the sky. I ran up to a two-ton Army truck that had pulled up next to the docks and found some rifle boxes in the back. I broke one open, grabbed a 1903 Springfield rifle, an ammo box and positioned myself near a large palm tree. I loaded the rifle and scanned the air for any low-flying Japanese planes. I did not have to wait long. A green colored, Japanese Zero fighter plane, flew by so low that I could see the pilot's face and the brightly colored bandana tied around his head. I squeezed off every round in the rifle, firing in the direction of the pilot's cockpit. I saw the pilot's cockpit window splinter and blood splatter fill the canopy as the Japanese pilot's head slumped forward. His plane suddenly took a hard turn to the right and crashed into the water, barely missing a destroyer anchored nearby. Sailors on the deck of the destroyer raised their arms in celebration and shouted in my direction. I felt no regret for killing the Japanese pilot. This is what I was trained to do.

Men doused with fuel and oil screamed in agony as they caught fire. The USS Oklahoma was almost completely capsized by now, and sailors from the great battleship jumped by the hundreds into the water. Surrounded by utter chaos, I looked to the sky for another low-flying plane but saw none. I slung the rifle over my shoulder and began working my way further down Battleship Row. A multitude of ships, of all kinds, were either listing or sinking fast, after being hit with high-level bombs or torpedoes.

Through the hell that surrounded me, I managed to come across the Captain of the USS Dobbin. I had befriended him during my evaluation period. He was not aboard his ship when the sudden attack began and was now attempting to reach it and his men. Suddenly, we heard the drone of another airplane approaching. We both looked up and watched helplessly as a bomb descended, headed in the direction of the Battleship Arizona. The sailors on the deck were watching other Japanese planes as they buzzed around them. Although some were firing deck mounted anti-aircraft guns at the passing planes, the majority of sailors scurried around, attempting to avoid Japanese strafing.

Detonation was not immediate after the bomb hit the forward deck of the Battleship Arizona. Seconds later, I felt the sudden release of heat from the massive explosion that soon detonated from inside the battleship. The flames were so intense and they seemed to reach hundreds of feet into the sky. The battleship heaved partially up out of the water, and then crashed back down. When the monstrous fireball subsided, sailors whom I had seen, just seconds before on the ship's deck were no longer there, and the deck was engulfed in flames. The combined heat of the initial explosion and the burning battleship was unbearable. Sailors were on fire and jumping off what remained of the ship's deck. Debris of all kind was falling from the sky, all around me and into the surrounding water. Instinct took over and I worked myself closer to the water and jumped in. The jump into the water was close to thirty feet. I hit the water with considerable force, and upon sinking several feet, was shocked at the water's hot temperature. When I came up for air, I bumped up against what I assumed was floating debris. Upon opening my eyes, however, I found three dead American sailors floating face down in the water around me. When I saw what the explosions and fires had done to the sailors, a sick feeling formed deep in the pit of my stomach. Anger soon overrode any other emotions.

I had barely gotten myself oriented when a Japanese plane strafed the water around me. A few sailors remained alive and worked to stay afloat, but they struggled due to their injuries. Bullets pierced the water all around us, but none hit us. I swam toward the nearest wounded sailor and motioned that I was there to help him get ashore. The combined noise of massive explosions, droning Japanese planes and the rapid-fire of the deck guns was deafening. Using a cross-chest carry, I pulled the sailor along. Even though I sucked in oily water all the way to the nearest shoreline, I still made it and hoisted his body onto the shore. After making sure he was still breathing, I slipped back into the water to retrieve another sailor. I soon pulled a second sailor to shore and by that time, Army medics were arriving to treat the sailors.

Exhausted, I sat on the shoreline and just stared at the Battleship Arizona, which had begun to settle into the bottom of the harbor, still burning fiercely. It was then that one of the sailors that I had brought to shore asked me if I was a sailor on the Arizona. I told him I was not, whereupon he stated that he and the other sailor were from the Arizona. He asked me my name and then thanked me repeatedly for my help. He was carried away a short time later.

Rising to my feet, I noticed a Japanese bomber hit by naval gunfire. It was falling from the sky in flames, in the direction of the water between the Arizona and its sister ships. I watched as the two-pilot bomber crashed into the water and began to sink. Both Jap pilots pushed back their canopies and slipped into the water. One pilot actually pulled a pistol from underneath his life vest and began to fire some rounds at sailors on a nearby ship. The ship's deck guns could not turn down far enough to fire on the pilots. In what seemed like slow motion, I witnessed a sailor dive off a nearby battleship in the direction of the two Jap pilots in the water.

The Jap pilot was still firing, while the other pilot was struggling to stay afloat; it was obvious he did not know how to swim. The sailor, who had dived off the ship, came up for air about twenty yards from the struggling pilot. Hidden by the flames of the water still burning in some areas, the sailor went back underwater and swam behind the thrashing pilot. My eyes still burned from the oily, salty water, but I was still able to see the sailor come up from behind and beneath, grab the pilot's legs, and drag him under the water. The pilot, grasping for air, aggressively fought the sailor, as he was pulled deeper. Soon the dead pilot's body floated to the top of the burning water and drifted away.

The other pilot firing his pistol had now noticed the sailor in the water. He loaded a second clip into his pistol and turned in the direction of the swimming sailor. The pilot fired sporadically at the sailor. Some of the sailors by this point had found rifles on board their ship and were firing at the brazen Japanese soldier. One sailor on the deck of a nearby ship managed to hit the Jap pilot in the head. I watched as the back half of the pilot's head blew away. The pilot sank beneath the oily water.

Destruction was everywhere and my worst fears had been realized. I found myself becoming upset over the fact that the White House had not taken my early findings more seriously. Japanese planes were still circling and inflicting damage. I found some medics assisting more wounded sailors than they could handle. I spent the next few hours lending aid. I picked up the wounded and the dead and loaded them into the back of trucks that transported them to the hospital or makeshift morgues.

By twelve o'clock, there were no more Japanese planes circling overhead or attacking. By four o'clock in the afternoon, I looked bedraggled and exhausted, so much so that an Army medic suggested I be checked out at the hospital. The white t-shirt that I put on when I headed out for my jog that morning was covered in blood, oil and dirt. My arms and legs were littered with cuts and burns, some severe enough that I felt I needed to heed the medic's advice in order to get treatment. I hopped into the back of one of the last Army trucks headed to the hospital.

When the truck pulled into the front of the hospital late that afternoon, I jumped off the back and helped transport the wounded into the overflowing hospital. When I entered the hospital, the sharp scent of antiseptic made my nose tingle and my eyes water. Upon entering the hospital further, however, I immediately felt the sense of urgency that prevailed all around me. I could barely take in my surroundings; it was unfathomable what I was seeing. The floors and beds were covered with soldiers, sailors and civilians. Makeshift cots had been erected, as well; they, too, were all occupied. Other soldiers had not been lucky enough to secure a bed. They were left to slump against the walls, where they waited to receive care.

We eventually brought the last sailor in from the back of the truck and laid him in the only available space, which was in a hallway already full of men. I chose to stay with him until he was seen. The sailor's lower left leg was shredded. He was administered morphine before being transported to the hospital, but it was wearing off. Even experiencing severe pain, he kept it to himself, as he knew others had more severe injuries that demanded immediate attention. I decided my injuries could wait to be treated. I tried to engage him in conversation to distract him from his pain. I found out his name was Don Rasmussen and he was from Garland, Texas.

Don's turn finally came and they took him into surgery down the long hallway, behind a set of double swinging doors. It was seven o'clock in the evening, just about twelve hours since the surprise Japanese attack started. I saw that many people still waited to be seen and were much worse off than I was, so I decided to leave the busy hospital and procure some antiseptic and bandages from the small infirmary at the barracks.

Walking towards the front lobby of the hospital, I heard a familiar voice behind me call out, "Allen, is that you?"

I turned and there, just a few feet away from me, stood Alice. We last saw each other nine years ago in the chocolate shop in Zurich, Switzerland. I stood there speechless and just stared at her. She, as I, was covered with other people's blood, but she still looked beautiful.

After what must have been thirty seconds or more, I managed a response. "Yes, it's me, Allen Voigt."

I slowly walked closer, but she must have grown impatient, because she quickly closed the distance between us. She then gave me the biggest hug I had ever received.

She whispered in my ear, "Allen, I have thought about you every day since you introduced yourself to me in Zurich. I have tried so hard to track you down but the Army couldn't tell me anything."

I once again found myself unable to utter a single word. We were still holding each other when I finally found my voice. "You have been in my thoughts since Zurich, too, Alice. I also tried to find you. Do you know how many nurses have the name Alice? I never even asked you for your last name."

Alice loosened her embrace, and then slipped her hand into mine and said, "Davison, My name is Alice Marie Davison and I am from Jacksonville, Florida." Before I could say anything, she continued, "We need to tend to your cuts and burns - follow me."

I followed her to an area just off the main hallway, joining several other sailors and soldiers who had minor injuries. Alice took me as her own patient and tended to the worst cuts and burns. "There is no need to treat the rest of your wounds until you have gotten a good shower and removed all this dirt, oil and blood off your body."

She gave me a bag full of supplies and walked with me out of the hospital. Whispering in my ear, she said, "Today has been a terrible day, but seeing you has lifted my spirits more than you can imagine. When can I see you again?"

"I'm based here, housed in the Schofield Barracks, if they are intact after today." I replied.

She gave me the number to the apartment building where she and her fellow nurses lived and told me to call her very soon.

"I have to get back to the hospital and help the others. I hope you call me sooner than later," she told me before turning away.

I promised to call her and hugged her goodbye. I watched her every step as she walked back into the hospital, admiring her long legs!

Returning to the barracks, I was filled with a wide range of emotions: anger for what had been perpetrated by the Japanese that day, sorrow for the loss of life, and frustration over what I thought could have possibly been avoided. At the same time, however, I was ecstatic that I had reunited with Alice!

The rest of December 1941 and the first few weeks of January 1942, I volunteered my time and energy to help with the massive cleanup in and around Pearl Harbor. The most frustrating aspect of the work was the fact that only a few men from the capsized USS Oklahoma could be rescued. We heard several sailors tapping from inside the ship, at the capsized bottom of the hull, in an effort to be rescued. Nothing could be done to rescue them. The sheer carnage left in the wake of the attack was enormous. Thousands were dead, five battleships were either destroyed or left to sink in the harbor, and almost one hundred planes were destroyed along with numerous hangers and buildings. The clean up would take a lot longer than the Army wanted me to remain in Hawaii.

A notice arrived for me saying General Donovan wanted me back in Washington for meetings with him, President Roosevelt and Secretaries Knox and Stimson during the second week of January 1942. My trip back east had been arranged specifically by General Donovan; this time I was taking a submarine back. The USS Tautog (SS-199) was assigned to deliver me to Oakland, California, where I was to hop on an Army Air Corps plane back to Fort Meade. It was Wednesday, January 21, 1942, and the USS Tautog was due to depart from Pearl Harbor at nine o'clock that morning. Since the attack, I saw Alice twice, both times because I visited the hospital specifically to see her. I went in hopes of grabbing a quick lunch or a cup of coffee. However, due to her active duties at the hospital, we just hung out in the halls of the hospital and talked. I vowed to myself that I would not leave Hawaii without seeing Alice one last time and hopefully securing her stateside address and phone number.

My orders were not to share any information with anyone about my trip back east, my final destination, or even my mode of transportation. I had two hours to make the dock where the USS Tautog was tied up. I caught a cab to the hospital where Alice was working, taking a chance that she was working the morning shift and would be able to step away to say goodbye and scribble down her address and phone number.

When the cab driver pulled up to the hospital, the sun was rising and only a few clouds drifted across the blue sky. I stepped out of the cab and the sun hit my face; I took a moment to enjoy it, since I would be spending the next week in a cramped, dark submarine. When I entered the hospital lobby, I saw what appeared to be all hell breaking loose. A passing Marine informed me that a suspecting Japanese man had walked into the lobby with a large bag that caught the attention of a passing nurse. Before she could summon any military personnel to investigate, however, the Japanese man disappeared. When I walked in, everyone was running around and searching frantically for the mystery man, concerned about sabotage.

I was immediately concerned, and hurried to find Alice in the hospital so I could protect her. I looked in the lobby, several patients' rooms and down countless hallways, but there was no sign of her. I began to think maybe she was not working that day, and I would not be able to see her before leaving Hawaii. About the time, as I had concluded she was not working that morning, around the corner she came. She stopped me dead in my tracks and suddenly I found myself very nervous.

She looked at me and with a smile asked, "Allen, what are you doing here this morning?"

I could not take my eyes off her. I eventually pulled her aside as others were walking by. I pulled her close and kissed her for the very first time. It was definitely a risk, but it paid off when she responded by kissing me back.

We eventually parted, whereupon I told her, "I am leaving in the morning for the states. My transportation leaves in approximately one hour."

Alice responded, "You can't leave me, we haven't had enough time together. When will I see you again? Please don't go!"

After a pause to gather my thoughts, I informed her, "The Army doesn't wait, unfortunately, and we are actively at war with Japan and now Germany. I am departing on a sub that will take me to Oakland, California. From there, I'll take an Army transport plane to Washington, D.C., where I will become part of a secret military branch of the Army."

We looked into each other's eyes for the longest time before Alice pleaded, "Please come back to me, Allen."

After I promised to come back, I pulled her close and held her. We then walked hand in hand to the front lobby of the hospital. I had totally broken protocol by telling Alice where I was going and what my role would be. I did not care at this point. She had a right to know. We had had been apart too much.

Suddenly, the mysterious looking Japanese man appeared again in the lobby. With one hand, he reached into his tattered bag and pulled out two grenades. He looked around wildly and yelled "Death to Americans!" as loud as he could. Without a second's hesitation, I ran at the man and tackled him to the floor. I dislodged the grenades and tossed them aside. I then reached down to my leg and pulled out my knife, whereupon I thrust it as hard as I could into the man's upper chest. He struggled for a few seconds, but his arms eventually dropped to the ground. He died there in the lobby of the hospital, his blood drained out onto the cement floor. I rose to my feet, covered in his blood. I had never killed a man with my bare hands before. I had trained for years how to kill a man but this was the first time I had to put my training into practice. My right hand trembled as it held my knife. I quickly gathered my senses and relaxed my breathing, slowing my heart rate.

Several people had gathered around us, but they kept their distance, with looks of shock on their faces. I peered back in the direction of Alice, who stood with her hands covering her mouth. I walked slowly towards her; she pulled me to her. She did not care about getting blood on her clean white uniform.

"Thank you for saving my life," she whispered into my ear.

The people around us then began to clap; some walked up, patted me on the back, and thanked me for saving their lives.

The time grew late and my time of departure was near. With blood all over the front of us, Alice and I left the hospital, leaving the chaos in the lobby behind. The USS Tautog was moored approximately three miles from the hospital. Alice was determined to accompany me all the way to the sub and I was not disappointed. Regardless of the protocol and confidential nature of my departure, we hailed a cab, whereupon we received an inquiring stare from the cab driver as we slid into the back seat.

"Pier #3 please," I instructed the cab driver.

Alice and I did not say a word to each other but held hands during the short trip. When the cab pulled up to the pier, we saw my assigned sub tied up at the end. I asked the cab driver to wait for Alice and to take her to the hospital in a few minutes; I handed him a sizable fare for both trips. Alice and I got out of the cab and walked hand-in-hand down the pier to the USS Tautog.

We saw several sailors milling about as we approached the gangplank; they were loading last minute supplies and diesel fuel. We garnered a lot of attention not only for our blood-covered clothes, but also because it was not every day that a beautiful nurse visited the Navy's submarine pens.

It suddenly occurred to me that with all the events of the last hour, I had not yet asked Alice for her address back in the states.

"What's your address, Alice?" I asked.

Without speaking, Alice reached into the right front pocket of her nursing uniform and pulled out a small pencil and notepad. She scribbled on the pad, folded it twice and handed it to me, saying, "Don't read this until you are underwater and on your way."

I noticed the sub's Captain walking down the gangplank in our direction. He spoke first, "You must be Captain Voigt, judging from the looks of your uniform."

I had worn a basic uniform that morning but by the time I reached the sub, it was not very presentable thanks to the blood and dirt. I replied, "Yes, I am Captain Voigt."

"Your actions at the hospital this morning have been radioed all over the island. My name is Captain Joseph Willingham, Jr., and I am the senior officer on the sub. Who is the lovely lady with you, Captain?"

I smiled, noticing by now all the sailors peering down at us from the deck of the sub and replied, "This is Alice. She is an Army nurse working at the hospital here on the island."

Captain Willingham reached out and shook her hand. "You are one lucky soldier to have caught the eye of this beautiful woman," he told me.

Turning to Alice he said, "Nice to have met you, Alice. I will take good care of your man."

"Voigt, I will see you on board in five minutes." With that, he turned and walked back up the gangplank.

The next few minutes were extremely hard for me. I held Alice close and we did not speak. Soon it was time for me to leave as sailors all around us were loosening the mooring lines. Just before letting Alice from my grip, I whispered into her ear and said, "I promise to find you Alice, don't forget me. I love you."

Tears flowed down her cheeks as she smiled and replied, "I know you will Allen, I love you."

I turned and walked up the gangplank. Just before I entered the sub's hatch and descended the ladder, I turned and looked back. Alice was still standing in the same spot, waving goodbye to me. I waved goodbye and descended into the sub.

An officer greeted me and escorted me to my quarters, complete with my own bathroom and shower. On the bed in my quarters were some fresh clothes - a clean Army uniform! Before I headed for the shower, I sat on the edge of the bed and opened the scrap of paper that Alice had written on, it read, "Allen, I believe I have fallen in love with you. Please be safe and come back to me. My parents' address is 173 Shady Crest Lane Jacksonville, Florida." I sat there and for several minutes just stared at her note.

I cleaned up and by the time I finished, we were well on our way, headed east. I had dinner that evening with Captain Willingham. He informed me that the USS Tautog had spent the last few weeks around the Marshall Islands in the Pacific, where they hunted Japanese shipping. They were due to repeat the exercise when they received instructions to get me to Oakland, California as fast as possible.

"You must be very important to the Army," Captain Willingham stated as we sipped on hot coffee after our meal.

"I'm no one special, just being asked to report back to Washington, D.C. for a meeting," I insisted.

I was under strict orders from General Donovan not to discuss any aspects of my meetings with him or about the new special operations group he was forming. Captain Willingham, even with his rank, knew his place, as he did not ask me any detailed questions. He knew I was important and that is all that mattered.

I closed my eyes that night thinking of Alice. However, thoughts of her could not keep me from thinking about future missions and my role in them. We sailed uninterrupted for seven days, surfacing only a few times to charge the sub's batteries and catch some fresh air. Even though we were actively at war, a few of the sub's crew went swimming when we surfaced. I was too afraid of sharks and decided to keep my feet on the sub, even in spite of the ribbing I received from several of the sailors.

We sailed under the cover of darkness into the Naval Yard at Oakland, California on Wednesday evening, January 28, 1942. The outer hatches of the sub were opened in order to let in some cool night air, but we were asked to remain on board until the morning. The next morning, I thanked Captain Willingham for his hospitality and left the sub. I had not been stateside for almost a year; the first thing I did was phone my parents, letting them know I was stateside and would eventually try to get home for a few days. They were glad to hear from me and to learn I was safe.

I had to catch a C-47 Army plane out of the Army airfield located nearby. I ate some breakfast at the local PX and headed out to the makeshift hangar to look for my flight. Three C-47 planes sat on the runway that morning, so I knew I was in the right place. I checked the board in the hangar and saw the flight number leaving for Washington, D.C., with several stops in between. Boarding the aircraft, I was surprised to see Major Yates walking into the hanger. I saluted him.

"Hello, Allen, it's good to see you!" He replied.

"Hello, Major Yates. It is good to see you, too. I assume you're headed to the same meeting I am with General Donovan?" I made note to speak quietly and continued, "How many of us are joining this special military unit?"

Major Yates just smiled, patted me on the back, and said, "All in due time, Allen, all in due time. By the way, I am now a Lt. Colonel. The promotion came through a few weeks ago."

As we both boarded the small plane, I congratulated Lt. Colonel Yates on his promotion. The plane would make stops in Denver, Chicago and Pittsburgh, before our arrival at Fort Meade. I was eager to learn more from Lt. Colonel Yates about General Donovan's plans for me and this newly created Army unit. We sat across from each other, near the back of the plane away from all of the other passengers; letting the roar of the two engines drown out our conversation.

Lt. Colonel Yates proceeded to say, "Allen, I have had the privilege over the last few months of sharing my thoughts and opinions on how the newly formed unit should best be formed, trained and utilized during this Second World War that America is now facing. I consider you the tip of the spear, Allen. No one else in the present day Army has experienced what you have, nor contributed in the ways you have. The information you gathered in Germany has proven invaluable as America looks to supply Great Britain with arms and supplies. The identification of Hitler's plans for the Jews has allowed us to extract hundreds of key Jewish personnel from Germany and the surrounding countries. Your actions on December 7th of last year and your most recent takedown of the Japanese threat in the hospital showed immediate courage and action to the threat at hand."

I had no idea that my actions were monitored so closely. Lt. Colonel Yates continued, "These attributes are what will be required of the OSS members on a day-to-day basis. General Donovan has already laid the groundwork with President Roosevelt, and we expect the unit to be activated in early June. Your role will be to collect and analyze key information required by the various units of the United States Armed forces. You and your counterparts will conduct secret operations, in most cases solo, that will not be assigned to the regular Army enlistees. As I said earlier, Allen, this is not much different from what you have already done for the United States Army. The only real difference is that your targets will be of much higher profile."

As I sat and listened to Lt. Colonel Yates, I became more and more excited that I was finally going to make more of an impact in keeping America, its citizens, and fellow armed service men and women safe. For the rest of our trip, we shared personal background on each other. I shared with Lt. Colonel Yates my news about Alice. He was happy for me and shared with me how he had met the woman who eventually became his wife years ago.

As the day wore on, the sound of the C-47's engines was almost hypnotic. Looking out the window to my left, I examined the houses and roads below us. I knew they were sacrificing also by sending men and women off to war, having to ration food, rubber tires and gas. We were all doing our part.

We made a quick stop in Denver. I ate a quick lunch in the nearby hangar and settled back into my seat. We soon took off and I drifted off to sleep. I had not been asleep long when a sailor who had bandages on both his head and neck awakened me. I had not noticed that several new armed forces personnel had joined our flight to Chicago. Now, one of them was trying to get my attention. Once I was able to focus on him, the sailor asked, "Sir, were you at Pearl Harbor?"

I replied in the affirmative and he stated, "You're Allen Voigt! You are the man that rescued me from the oily water that morning! I was blown off the deck of the Arizona. You pulled me and one other sailor to shore. I've been trying to find you for months so that I could shake your hand and thank you for saving me!"

I was stunned that this sailor and I had reconnected and were now on the same flight. I asked him to take a seat beside me and we talked the rest of the flight to Chicago and then to Pittsburg. His name was Henry Frye and he was heading home to continue his recovery. He had suffered a major concussion and had multiple lacerations. Although he had been given the opportunity to leave the Navy, he had elected to stay in and get back in the fight against the Japanese. He was rightly upset over what they had done to America on that day, as well as the loss of his ship and so many of his fellow sailors. His mom and dad lived in Latrobe, not far from Pittsburg. He asked me where I was from and where I was going. I told him some of my history, but did not give him any details regarding my future assignment. I introduced him to Lt. Colonel Yates, after which Henry took his seat back in the front of the plane for landing.

When we touched down in Pittsburg to refuel, Lt. Colonel Yates leaned over and said, "Allen, Henry is just a small sample of the hundreds of American lives you can expect to save during this war."

We did not stay on the ground in Pittsburg long. We soon lifted off again on our final leg to Fort Meade outside of Washington, D.C. I must have dozed off to sleep, because the next thing I remember was being jolted awake when we landed. My original lodging at Fort Meade was waiting for me. I was back in the states and ready to begin my next assignment. We were fully engaged in World War II and the mouth of hell had been opened wide. The barbaric acts of the Japanese and Germans were well documented. Evil was spreading across the globe and it was up to America and its armed forces to stop it.

Chapter 6

NO QUARTER

"In every battle there comes a time when both sides consider
themselves beaten, then he who continues the attack wins."
Ulysses S. Grant

I had now been in the Army for almost sixteen years and was
considerably older than most of the men signing up for military
service in early 1942. My years of service had flown by, but I had
seen more direct action in the last two months than I had seen in all
of my previous years in the service. The Japanese and Germans were
advancing on all fronts across Europe and the Pacific. America was
rapidly trying to catch Japan and Germany in regards to the sheer
volume of men, ships, planes and armament that both countries were
throwing into the fight.

Though I was approaching my mid-thirties, I kept my body
in shape and was better prepared than most of the teenagers that
were enlisting by the thousands each day. I had a few days before
my meeting with General Donovan, so I used that time at the rifle
range there at Fort Meade. After my third day at the range, the
quartermaster stated I had fired over 1,000 rounds, more than all
of the soldiers combined who had used the ranges during the entire
month of January 1942. I was edgy and ready to take the fight to the
Japanese and Germans. I wanted to stalk the enemy and destroy them
where they slept. The extent of death and carnage I had witnessed at
Pearl Harbor burned fresh in my mind. I had seen what the Germans

had planned for the Jews, and it sickened me. My years of training and hard work were ready to be tested.

My new assignment began on the first Tuesday in February 1942. I expected to have a solo meeting with General Donovan. When I walked into the room there at Fort Meade, there were five other men sitting in the room, all approximately my age. General Donovan was not there yet, so I took a seat up near the front of the room. No one seemed to be in the mood for small talk that morning, and the room was warm, even though there were a few inches of snow on the ground outside. My stomach began to rumble and I regretted not securing breakfast before the meeting. At 5:50 AM, General Donovan and Lt. Colonel Yates walked in the room. Right behind them was an aide with hot coffee and doughnuts! I hurried to the breakfast table, where I poured myself a large cup of coffee and helped myself to two doughnuts. In an attempt to finish my breakfast before the meeting started, I inhaled my two doughnuts and burned my mouth trying to wash them down with the hot coffee.

Lt. Colonel Yates spoke first. "Men, each of you have been handpicked to be on the ground floor of an elite Army unit called the OSS. Your training and time in the field have predetermined your selections, for what will be very dangerous assignments. I personally know each of you but you do not know each other."

At this, the other men and I looked around the room, taking each other's measure.

Lt. Colonel Yates continued, "Over the next few months, each of you will learn to rely on only yourself and no one else. Your individual missions over the balance of this Second World War could save thousands of American lives. Your service to this great country has been noticed. We are now asking you to take that service to the next level and commit to the tasks we assign you." Lt. Colonel Yates then took his seat and General Donovan rose from his and began to speak.

"Men, I am honored to lead you in this new endeavor. My time in the trenches during World War I, led me to believe that there had to be a better way to take our fight to the enemy. Too many young men died senselessly in World War I and the war lasted longer than it should have. For the last eighteen months, I have lobbied the White House to allow me to assemble an elite fighting unit that could secretly, but aggressively, take the fight to our enemy, before they know what hits them. Your missions will be behind enemy lines and will involve a very high degree of risk, but they also carry an extremely high rate of return if they succeed. You will be assigned to capture or kill very high-level enemy targets. Your missions may often feel senseless to you but rest assured, they are very critical to America's ultimate victory in this ugly war."

The rest of the morning, we were briefed on our itinerary for the next ninety days. We would spend the next three months doing a variety of things. We would be jumping out of airplanes, covertly working our way through urban areas and densely populated forests, practicing hand-to-hand combat techniques and testing our accuracy with small arms and explosives.

The meeting ended, and Lt. Colonel Yates asked me to remain in the room. I took a seat by him, after which General Donovan came and sat next to me. The room was empty except for the three of us.

Lt. Colonel Yates spoke first, "Allen, you have never met any of the other men who were in the room today and that is for a reason. They, like you, are positioned around the globe, conducting similar missions, designed to gather information, report on activities in various countries, and conduct espionage. These men also went through the Army War College several years after your graduation. Your missions in Germany and Hawaii were above anything else that those other soldiers have faced. None of those men experienced meeting Hitler. Not one of them was at Pearl Harbor on that fateful day last December. You have been the first one in the group to encounter the enemy and kill them. Reports of your exploits in Hawaii have made it all the way to President Roosevelt's desk."

As Lt. Colonel Yates talked, my mind flashed back to my time in Germany and all of the things I had seen Hitler and the Nazi Party doing in preparation for this Second World War.

General Donovan addressed me next. "Son, you are regarded as a prime soldier for the OSS. Your German and Japanese linguistics are a perfect match and you have seen action on both fronts of this war. After these initial ninety days of extreme training, you will be set loose to do what you have been trained to do, to kill the enemy and save American lives."

I thanked both of my senior officers for their extreme confidence in me. We all stood in unison. I shook their hands and saluted them. I walked out of the meeting room that morning with my heart racing. I was more than ready to seek out and destroy the enemy.

The other OSS inductees and I were put through aggressive conditioning programs for the next few weeks. We moved into our second month of training, at which point we were retrained on how to survive in extreme surroundings. We traveled into northern Canada, where we went through isolated five-day survival trips in the snow, wind and ice. We then were transported to Columbia, South America. We learned how to navigate individually through the jungle, how to eat off the land, and how to lay quiet for upwards of twelve hours at a time. To wrap up our grueling time in Columbia, we spent our last training mission navigating twenty-five miles of jungle by ourselves, only allowed to carry one sidearm and a knife. Our movements were restricted to nighttime only. The climate of the jungle hit me the hardest, specifically, the extreme heat and humidity. During the day, the temperature hovered close to one hundred and ten degrees but the nights cooled off to the low seventies. I had experienced extreme cold in upstate New York and Canada but never faced heat and humidity like this before. The insects I saw crawling over me and in my clothing was discomforting, to say the least. I knew I would soon be facing challenges on a greater scale.

I was the first OSS candidate soldier to complete the twenty-five mile exercise and make it out of the jungle. The second soldier to finish walked out of the jungle a full four hours after me. Nearing the end of the day, news spread among us that one soldier had not returned. I volunteered to find him and bring him out. The other soldiers looked at me with crazy looks in their eyes. They all had their hands on their knees and were full of cuts and bruises. That picture caused my mind to flash back to Camp Pine and SGT Nolan. Inwardly I smiled. Already having my handgun and my knife, I secured two canteens of water, a first-aid kit, a hammock and disappeared into the thick jungle. None of us OSS soldiers had interacted very much during the entire training thus far. This was driven by our strong sense of competitiveness, combined with our even stronger sense of determination – everyone wanted to get into the real fight against the Germans and Japanese.

The sun was setting in the West and although the temperature was dropping fast, I stuck to my mission. I knew it was not going to be easy. I exited our encampment and pushed back the thick jungle branches directly in front of me. I also knew from my recent incursion into the jungle that the search could take over three and a half days to cover the required twenty-five miles. During the last incursion, I slipped on the wet jungle floor multiple times, nearly hitting my head on rocks and trees. I foraged for food, and not being allowed to start a fire, my eating options were very limited, mainly bugs and fruit. It was very different from the good food I had enjoyed at Meme's Kitchen back in New York City.

I did not know the soldier's name. Stealth was the primary attribute that the Army drilled into us. The ability to sneak up on the enemy unnoticed and eliminate them, regardless of the terrain or climate, was the objective. This was more or less an exercise for me, allowing me to rehearse those skills. The missing soldier was most likely lost, miles away from our rally point, or, worse, he may be unconscious, bitten by a deadly snake or even mauled to death by a large animal. My eyes adjusted to the dark jungle and I was ready to find him. I walked deeper and deeper back into the jungle, scanning side to side for any trace of broken limbs, boot tracks and remnants of clothing that might have been snagged on a branch or rock. My compass allowed me to keep my direction in check, but I had no real idea how far I had walked.

It was 2330 hours and I had struggled through the dense jungle for close to three hours, without seeing anything abnormal. I sat on a large rock situated on the side of a steep ravine, sipped some cool water out of my canteen, and just listened for any noise that might give me a clue as to the soldier's location. Sitting there, I heard the same animal noises up in the trees I had heard the three previous nights. The moon was full that night, which allowed me to navigate fairly clearly, avoiding rocks, branches, and any large snakes that may have been crossing my path. The moon also reflected off the eyes of several animals that appeared to be staring at me from the dense brush and down from the trees above.

After listening for over an hour and hearing nothing abnormal, I decided to head due west this time, hoping to intercept the missing soldier. The last thing my superiors told me before I disappeared into the jungle that evening was, that if the missing soldier had managed to find his way to the rally point, they would fire three successive shots to let me know he had returned. I would then double time it back to camp. I walked for several more hours, alternating my direction each half hour. I looked down at my watch and saw that it was 0430 hours. I had not slept for close to twenty-four hours and the sun was due to begin its slow creep through the dense jungle in about one hour. I desperately wanted to lay my head down and sleep, but the missing soldier had to be found. I also knew that if I did not sleep at least for a few hours, my search might result in finding the missing soldier but not having the strength to carry him out, if necessary. I decided to suspend my hammock between two trees. The previous three days, sleeping during the day and traveling at night, allowed me to grow somewhat accustomed to this reversed sleep pattern, but what I had not grown used to was, the immense amount of noise the jungle made, especially at night.

I had just crawled into my hammock, approximately four feet off the jungle floor, when my ears caught the soft rustle of dried leaves not far from where I was lying suspended. The sound was barely detectable over the noises all around me. Nevertheless, I listened intently so I could determine the location of the noise. I concluded that the noise was in front of me but slightly off to my left. As quietly as I could, I slipped out of my hammock and slowly eased my boots onto the jungle floor. I pulled my handgun out of its holster and ducked behind one of the trees that supported my hammock. The sound of footsteps was coming closer, but I still could not see anything. The usual noises in the jungle went eerily silent, leaving me to wonder if there was a wild boar or panther sniffing me out as a meal.

A person finally emerged from the dense jungle, coming towards me. The native Columbian Indian headed my way and had a large spear in his left hand and a dead boar across his shoulders. I did not want to receive a spear through the gut, so I put my pistol away and walked toward the intimidating native with my hands held high. When I walked out from behind the large tree, the native stopped, looked at me, and said, "I was wondering how long it was going to take you to walk out from behind that tree, American. I smelled you from several yards away."

My jaw dropped and before I could even utter a word in response, the native continued, "My name is Pablo. I was taught to speak English as a child from American missionaries."

My new friend Pablo had not let go of his spear yet, but I felt less threatened, so I finally responded, "My name is Allen and I am an American soldier. I'm looking for a fellow soldier who may be lost here in the jungle."

Pablo nodded. "Yes, I saw him earlier this morning sleeping between two trees. It appeared he had wounded his left leg, but he was alive when I saw him."

Pablo pointed in the direction of where he last saw the wounded soldier and estimated it would take me upwards of two hours to find him, assuming he had not moved. I thanked Pablo, gathered my weapon and hammock and headed off in the direction he had indicated.

As I walked further into the jungle, the foliage became much thicker and I found it hard to see more than ten feet in any direction. By late morning, I had walked for about ninety minutes. Suddenly, I heard a shot from what I knew was a .45 caliber handgun. I dropped to the ground as fast as I could and laid flat, hoping I was not the target of that bullet. I then heard a second shot. I waited a few minutes before I rose to my feet, but did not hear any more shots. I then headed off in the direction from which the shots came. At that point, I decided to talk as I walked, hoping the missing soldier would hear me coming and recognize me as someone coming to his aid versus a threat. I began to repeat, "My name is Captain Voigt and I am a member of the United States Army. I am here to help a wounded American soldier." I must have repeated the same two sentences at least thirty times over the span of the next twenty minutes.

I had just finished saying the word "Army" when I heard a faint voice to my left utter the words, "Captain Voigt, over here."

I looked to my right and barely visible through the thick foliage was the missing American soldier. He was reclining against a tree with his handgun in his right hand. I knelt down on one knee and asked him his name and the nature of his injury.

With a sense of relief, he responded, "My name is SGT Hendricks. I believe my left leg is broken below the knee. How did you find me?"

I told him we would save that discussion for later. I gave him my extra canteen of water and checked out his left leg for a possible compound fracture. His leg was clearly broken; however, it was not a compound fracture. I stabilized his leg with some strong tree branches and got him to his feet. It was close to 1400 hours and the sun would be setting in approximately five hours. It would take every bit of five hours, or maybe more, to make it out of the jungle on two good feet, let alone with someone who could not walk well.

I fabricated a makeshift sled out of branches and vines and asked SGT Hendricks to lie in it. The idea was for me to pull it, having it harnessed around my upper body and shoulders. It would not be easy, but it was my best option. As we headed out of the jungle, I asked

SGT Hendricks about the two shots I had heard over the space of several minutes that morning. He shared with me that he had been warding off a large panther that had been circling him. Each time he fired his gun the panther took off into the recesses of the jungle, only to return a few minutes later.

I used my compass in order to make the best time possible through the jungle. After pulling the makeshift sled with SGT Hendricks in it for over two hours, I had to stop so that we could make repairs to the sled. The rough jungle floor, filled with rocks and sticks, was cutting the vines holding the sled together. It was strenuous work, but we had to make repairs about every ninety minutes as we slogged through the jungle. Very little conversation took place between us, partly because the noise from the sled scrapping the ground prevented it. By 1800 hours, I had been pulling and repairing the sled for four hours off and on. By my estimation, we were only three to four hours from exiting the jungle and regrouping with our team. It had been close to twenty-four hours since I had entered the jungle the night before. I was tired, not having slept at all. We decided the best thing for us to do would be to push forward until we exited the jungle. It took us four more hours, but we finally cleared the jungle. The medics in our group immediately took responsibility for SGT Hendricks.

The next morning, our rag tag group of soldiers boarded two trucks and left the Columbian jungle. We boarded a C-47 airplane out of Bogotá that afternoon. I found the most comfortable spot I could on the cramped plane, closed my eyes and slept.

I was startled awake when our plane hit the runway hard in the Florida Keys. We had stopped to refuel, and while I had the chance, I got out of the cramped quarters of the plane and stretched my legs near the small airport hangar. The airport bustled that early evening as various types of military aircraft took off and landed. The civilian who refueled our plane told us that since we had declared war on Germany during early December 1941, German subs had been spotted off the Georgia coast and had been seen in the Gulf of

Mexico, near Panama City, Florida. Military planes and Navy blimps were now scouting the shorelines in an effort to keep merchant ships and shore targets safe from German torpedoes.

We finally landed back at Fort Meade, late in the evening of that same day. It was Thursday, February 19, 1942, and I was eager to get back in the fight. I had been in training the vast majority of my time in the Army and my patience had worn thin. American men were dying in the Pacific. Meanwhile, I sat on the runway at Fort Meade, unable to do anything about it.

I spent the balance of February 1942 at Fort Meade. I kept my body in shape and read about the war developments in newspapers. I saw the Universal Newsreels that showed all the Japanese victories and atrocities in the Pacific. My heart broke for the city of London and all the German bombing it had suffered. Because of their inability to defeat the Soviet Union, the Germans had decided not to invade Great Britain. They were also busy in other areas such as North Africa and Italy. The world's security had changed dramatically since I joined the Army.

During early March 1942, I received orders to visit the White House and meet President Roosevelt and Secretary of War Henry Stimson. An Army car delivered me to the White House, and as it was pulling up to the front door, there waiting for me was Lt. Colonel Yates. I had not seen him in some time. We shook hands and entered the White House together. As we walked down the main hall, General Donovan walked out of a side door and greeted us.

The three of us proceeded to the outer door of the Oval Office. The door opened and out walked Harry Hopkins. I had seen him on various newsreels and in the newspapers but never laid eyes on him during all my previous trips to the White House. He had become one of President Roosevelt's most trusted advisors. It was now our turn to enter the Oval Office. President Roosevelt was in his wheelchair near the fireplace as we walked in. Most of the country never saw President Roosevelt in his wheelchair because the White House worked very hard to conceal his health challenges, primarily his struggle with polio.

"Allen, it is good to see you again, how long has it been?" President Roosevelt asked.

"It is good to see you, Sir. I believe it has been close to a year since I have been to the White House," I replied.

We all took our seats and exchanged small talk as the White House staff brought in some hot coffee and warm bagels.

Before I could even claim one bagel, General Donovan, looked me in the eye and said, "Allen, are you ready to take out more of the enemy?"

I shot back a firm reply, "Yes, Sir, tell me where and when and I am there."

President Roosevelt then spoke in a calm voice, one that occasionally caught with emotion, as he expressed his continued grief over the loss of American lives at Pearl Harbor and the months that followed as the Japanese continued to roll over us in the Pacific.

"Gentlemen," he gravely informed us, "we are faced with two vicious enemies in Germany and Japan, and they are bent on destroying us. It is time to take the fight to them. I am telling you here and now that that is exactly what we are going to do, starting now."

Someone knocked at the door and an Army Air Corps Lt. Colonel was ushered in. I recognized him but could not place him.

"Jimmy, come over here and join us," said President Roosevelt.

I then realized it was Lt. Colonel William Doolittle. He sat down next to me on the couch. As he sat, he reached out to shake my hand and said, "Allen, I am a friend of Lt. Colonel Yates. He told me what you have accomplished throughout your career in the United States Army. A job well done, Captain."

I was astonished that he knew of me. I shook his hand firmly and simply responded, "Thank you, Sir."

President Roosevelt, over the next half-hour, shared with us the mission that Lt. Colonel Doolittle and seventy-nine other men would be taking the following month against the Japanese. Held to the strictest confidence, I was told not to repeat anything to anyone, period. The next half-hour, General Donovan outlined what my mission would be. I was disappointed to find out that I would not be part of the team that would be leading the attack on the Japanese home islands.

General Donovan continued to outline my mission. "Allen, you are the best officer in the newly formed OSS. Your field experience, time already spent in Germany, and your command of their language makes you the perfect fit."

"We need you to infiltrate occupied Europe and confirm the extent of the brutal activities against the Jewish population of Germany and the countries Germany has invaded." General Donovan continued. "Since your reports came back about that very first concentration camp north of Berlin, numerous others camps have been built, and they are now holding Jews. We fear Germany is killing the Jews at a rapid rate. Your mission is to infiltrate the large concentration camp called Auschwitz. The camp is located in southern Poland, deep in occupied Europe. Your knowledge of southern Germany and Austria should allow you to navigate easier than any other soldier we could send." As he wrapped up, he paused and finished his overview by stating to me, "And by the way Allen, kill as many German officers as you can before you leave the camp."

We concluded our meeting and left the oval office. Lt. Colonel Yates and I walked out of the White House together and shared a cab back to Fort Meade. As we rode back, Lt. Colonel Yates told me pointblank that I would be constantly on the move from now until an American victory was secured. My assignments would take me all over the globe and there would be plenty of killing ahead.

Two days later, I was on a DC-3 Army Air Corps plane that departed Fort Meade. I flew over the Atlantic this time for two main reasons. The shipping lanes between New York City and London were full of German submarines and my instructions were to get to southern Poland as fast as possible. My flight took me up the northeast coast of the United States, over Nova Scotia, Newfoundland, Greenland, Iceland, with a final stop in Ireland. The flight would take us four full days, but it was still shorter and safer than going by ship. Our multiple stops for refueling in these far northern countries taught me how cold the temperature could really get. The DC-3 was cold enough, but every time we stopped to refuel, I ran from the plane to the nearest hangar and looked for a hot cup of coffee. My Army overcoat was not keeping me very warm.

On the flight, there were four other Army officers. They shared with me why they were heading to Europe. Their mission was to scout for locations throughout Britain that could serve as Army training camps and Army Air Corps bases. Staging military personnel, supplies and equipment was going to be a major undertaking, if Europe was ever going to be liberated.

When the four officers asked why I was flying to Europe, I simply replied, "I am not at liberty to share my mission." They did not press me for any more information. The flight wore on and I eventually drifted asleep, using my Army overcoat as a blanket.

I was jolted awake when our plane landed in Dublin, Ireland I parted ways with the other four Army officers. From there I took another flight to London. My flight that time was on a British Avro Lancaster bomber. I had never seen a British bomber up close, and this one was impressive. Its four massive engines, along with its mounted machine guns and dark paint, made it one intimidating aircraft. The crew greeted me and soon we were off. The flight to London took three hours. During the flight, I learned about the bomber and it capabilities, thanks to the seven-member crew. The highlight of the flight was when we flew over a rural part of Northern England and the crew let me fire twin .50 caliber machine guns out of the rear of the aircraft.

It was early morning when the heavy bomber landed at an airstrip northwest of London. I thanked the bomber crew for the lift, and from inside the hangar, I called for a cab to pick me up. My instructions were to get to the coastal city of Dover and arrange for passage across the English Channel. Ideally on a small boat that would go undetected by German submarines or aircraft. By the time my cab delivered me to the port city of Dover, it was close to dinnertime and the sun was setting.

In order to shed my Army clothes and blend in, I asked the cab driver to drop me at a predetermined men's clothing shop. When I walked in the shop, the tailor was about to close for the night. When he noticed my Army uniform, he invited me in and locked the door behind us. He spent over an hour with me, helping me secure the proper clothing. He did not ask any questions when I told him I needed three outfits. He also agreed to keep my Army uniform, boots and overcoat in storage until I returned. The shop owner did tell me, that he had a son serving in a British Royal Tank regiment in North Africa. I secured the three best outfits that would help me assimilate back into German society. The shop owner also provided me with two pairs of shoes, undergarments and socks. I put on one outfit and placed the other two outfits, along with all the other items, in a small brown suitcase, given to me by the shop owner. As we parted ways, he directed me to a local inn where I was to meet David Quinn, the proprietor. We shook hands and I was on my way. The inn was only a mile away, right near the port, allowing me to make the quick walk.

I soon arrived at the inn and met the proprietor, Mr. Quinn. I purchased a room for one night. During dinner in the small dining room, he came over to my table and took a seat. I asked him a few questions that confirmed his authenticity. He verified that he knew his role, which was to provide me passage across the English Channel to Dunkirk. He slid a small piece of paper across the table towards me and walked away. It instructed me to be at dock #7 by 5:00 AM in the morning, where I would meet a man by the name of Ron Ashmore.

I met Ron promptly at 5:00 AM the next morning. He was a middle-aged man and carried himself well. We each confirmed our identities and I boarded Ron's twenty-five foot sailboat. He handed me a cup of hot coffee from his thermos and untied the lines holding the sailboat to the dock.

"It will take us approximately seven hours to sail to Dunkirk but we should arrive safely, evading German subs in the area," Ron informed me. "We could make better time with a powerboat, but that would attract much more attention from not only ships, but also from German shore batteries."

As we sailed toward the northern coast of France, Ron described how he and his sailboat had made two trips back in late May and early June 1940 to help rescue British soldiers from Dunkirk as they were escaping the German invasion of France. I also learned Ron was a veteran of World War I and had fought in France with the British Army. I explained to him that my father had fought in the war, and that his service is what encouraged me to join the Army after high school.

Shortly after 2:00 PM, we saw the coast of France off in the distance. There were still remnants of the morning fog still lingering, allowing Ron to navigate toward the shore undetected. As we neared the shore, Ron broke out some sandwiches he had prepared earlier.

"Allen, I do not know your exact mission but Godspeed and return safely." Ron said as the sailboat ran up on the beach at Dunkirk.

I shook Ron's hand and thanked him for delivering me across the English Channel. I secured my suitcase and jumped overboard, hitting the soft sand. I helped Ron turn his sailboat around, waved goodbye and with a brisk wind behind him, Ron headed back toward the English coast.

I worked my way up the sand dune toward the nearest road. Without much difficulty, I found a road and saw a series of buildings off to my immediate left. I removed the sand from my shoes and walked in the direction of the nearest building. After about a ten-minute walk, I was encouraged to find that the first building I came too was a small train station depot. I walked inside and read the destinations listed in French and German. A train was due to depart Dunkirk for Brussels, Belgium shortly. I purchased a ticket from a frail, elderly man behind the counter. I took a seat on a small bench in front of the train depot while I waited for my train to arrive. A young boy on his bicycle rode by and waved to me and I returned the favor. With the entire country of France now occupied by the Germans, it had to be hard on the French citizens. Outside of a few Nazi flags, I saw no real evidence of a German occupation. I soon heard a train off in the distance. The smoke from the coal-burning locomotive was the next thing I saw, followed by the train itself. I soon boarded the train and found a seat in the first car.

The trip to Belgium would only take two hours. Soon after we pulled out of Dunkirk, I began to see more evidence of the German occupation. As the train ran parallel to the beach, I saw massive pillboxes and large eighty-eight millimeter guns being installed every five hundred feet. The Germans were preparing for the Allies to liberate occupied Europe, but since they did not know where they would land, they had to shore up their defenses in the most likely locations. The train turned southwest towards Belgium, and I soon saw German tanks and anti-aircraft defenses along the roadsides. The war I had seen brewing during my time in Germany was now front and center. I knew my mission was critical and as the train rolled on, I rehearsed in my mind the German language I had learned but not spoken frequently in over a year.

The train later pulled into Brussels. My goal was to make it to southern Poland and the Auschwitz camp by the next morning. I immediately looked for a train that would take me as close as possible. As I walked through the large train station, a woman off to my right caught my eye, as she looked like Alice. I had not seen her for over six months and I thought to myself, "How could she be here in Belgium?" When the woman got closer, I immediately knew she was not Alice and I kept on walking.

I found a train that would take me all the way to Katowice, Poland, which was less than forty kilometers from the concentration camp. The train was leaving in twenty minutes, so I purchased a ticket and headed for track #6 where my train was to depart. After boarding, I found a seat near the rear of the train where it would be a little quieter. As the conductor walked by me, I asked him how far it was to Katowice. He informed me it would take us eighteen hours to get there. I placed my suitcase in the compartment above my seat and settled in for the long ride.

The train slowly pulled out of Brussels, and I began to rehearse the mission in my mind. My goal was to somehow work my way into the Auschwitz concentration camp, visibly confirm the rumors of Jewish extermination, take as many pictures as possible, and secure any pertinent paperwork I could get my hands on. If the opportunity presented itself, I was ordered to kill as many German officers as possible, elude capture, and then make my way back to England. All the training I had been through, prepared me for this mission. I was ready and willing to do whatever it took to help my country end the German atrocities against the Jews and all the occupied countries it had invaded since the war began.

Looking out my window as the train rolled through southwest Belgium, I saw so many buildings, damaged by German tanks or bombs. When we crossed into Germany, the evidence of war changed considerably. I laid my head against the window, softening it with my rolled up coat. I looked at my watch; it was three o'clock in the afternoon. I soon drifted off to sleep.

When I awoke, we were in Cologne, Germany. It was dark outside, and my watch showed it was nine o'clock in the evening. The conductor said we would be in Cologne for two hours as the train took on more coal. I felt refreshed, having slept for six hours, even though I had a little discomfort in my neck from the awkward way I had positioned my head on the train. I was hungry, so I went looking for something to eat. I found a small café just inside the station and ordered up some bratwurst and sauerkraut, a meal I had come to enjoy during my time in Germany. During my previous assignment in Germany, I had never traveled to Cologne. After dinner, I had an hour to spare, so I left the train station and ventured out into the city. I walked about a mile away from the station and saw the massive Rhine River flowing right through the city. The city lights were on and the German people were milling around, even though it was a late, cold February night. When my time was up, I headed back to the station and boarded my train for Poland.

The train rolled on through the night, making only one more stop in Dresden, Germany. Around sunrise, the conductor notified us that we were one hour out of Katowice, Poland, which was the termination point of the trip. My adrenaline picked up, as I got closer and closer to my destination. I was not sure how I was going to get from Katowice to Auschwitz, but I would figure that out. The train stopped at eight o'clock in the morning. I stepped off the train into a hard, cold wind blowing and snow falling steadily. My coat was not going to keep me warm, that was immediately evident. I stepped inside the small train station in an effort to escape the cold and figure out the best way to get to Auschwitz. The train had left the station and was heading back to Brussels, Belgium. With the train gone, I was able to make out a row of storefronts across the tracks. Almost by divine intervention, I thought I recognized a man I knew, walking into a café. The man I recognized was Franz Kappel - the man that had put me to work, years ago at the Oranienburg concentration camp in northwest Germany. I figured this was my one shot to find a way into Auschwitz.

I hurried down the train station stairs, across the tracks and street, and walked into the warm café, looking for Franz. My objective was not to walk directly up to him, but to be seen by him and gauge his reaction. I took a table with close proximity to Franz and ordered breakfast. It was good to be out of the cold and even better to get some hot breakfast in me. I had not eaten since Cologne and I was starving. Before my breakfast even arrived at the table, I could hear my German name shouted across the café.

"Fritz Greiner, come over here and join me for breakfast!" Franz shouted.

I turned, acting surprised, and walked over and sat down at Franz's table. I let the waiter know I would be taking my breakfast with Franz.

"What are you doing here in Katowice, Fritz?" Franz asked me.

"To be very honest, Franz, I am looking for work. I know that there is a new concentration camp being built nearby and I was hoping to find some work."

Franz scratched his chin and replied, "Well Fritz that is very interesting. I am actually heading to that large concentration camp this morning after breakfast. It's called Auschwitz, and I was instrumental in its construction for the past two years," he said proudly. "I cannot tell you how many times I wondered what you were doing, because I needed reliable workers."

Our breakfast arrived and we exchanged pleasantries over eggs, sausage and coffee. I quickly had to fabricate things that I had supposedly been doing since I last saw Franz.

Out of nowhere, Franz asked me, "Why have you not joined the German Army? You should be fighting somewhere in Russia."

I was not prepared for this question, but it made logical sense as I was a supposedly a young, able-bodied German. I explained, "I have a bad heart. It is called a heart murmur; my heart often skips a beat. I was diagnosed with it shortly after I left Oranienburg."

Franz shook his head and replied, "That is terrible, Fritz, I am so sorry. Germany needs men like you. You must be able to work though, right?"

"Yes I can work, but it has to be limited to light construction." I replied.

We finished our breakfast quietly and I could see Franz mulling over a few things in his head. I could tell the look on Franz's face was a mix of sympathy and belief in my concocted story about my inability to be sworn into the German Army. After a few minutes Franz finally spoke.

"Fritz, I want you to come with me this morning to Auschwitz and act as my assistant for the next few weeks. I have to audit the camp, and the construction of the second phase is nearing completion. We need to look for any areas within this second phase that might not meet Nazi standards. The job will require you to come behind me and make the necessary corrections. Does this meet your approval?"

I paused and answered "Yes, Sir."

My way into Auschwitz was now secured. I took one more sip of hot coffee and then followed Franz out to his car. I threw my suitcase in the back seat and we set off from Katowice. Our ride took just under an hour to reach the camp. The snow had severely affected the roads; consequently, Franz had to drive very slowly in order to prevent us from sliding into a ditch.

When we came upon the camp, I found its sheer size intimidating. It looked like a small city in the middle of nowhere. What immediately caught my eye was a large sign in German over the main entrance that read "Arbeit Macht Frei," "Work Makes Free."

Franz pulled into a side entrance of the camp and parked near a series of buildings that looked much nicer than most of the other buildings in the camp. He parked and asked me to grab my suitcase and follow him. We walked into what looked like the camp Commandant's office, and then took our seats next to a female secretary who was hastily typing away on her typewriter. Franz informed her that we were here to see Camp Commandant Rudolf Hoss.

Soon the Commandant's door opened and out walked Rudolf Hoss. He appeared to be in his early forties, and despite his relatively short height, had a commanding presence. Franz reached out his hand and shook Rudolf's hand. I was than introduced to the Commandant. I reached out my right hand and firmly shook the hand of a man who was already responsible for thousands of deaths at Auschwitz. Inside I burned with anger as I remembered all the Jewish abuse I had witnessed throughout Germany during my time there in the late 1930s.

We all took a seat inside Rudolf's office. For a half-hour, Franz outlined to the Commandant what I would be doing at the camp to assist him. As Franz continued to talk, he reviewed with the Commandant the details of the final construction phase of the adjoining camp called Auschwitz II-Birkenau. As the two men talked, the details of, and reasons for the second phase of construction, became clear. The second phase of the camp was much larger than the first, evidently because Auschwitz was overrun; they had to do something to ease the congestion of Jews.

As Franz and Rudolf talked, I worked extremely hard not to show my anger and desire to kill both of them where they sat. What I heard next horrified me and solidified for me why I was now here. The United States needed an eyewitness to the German systematic extermination of the Jewish race. I learned that this second phase included a larger extermination camp. The construction of this camp had begun back in October 1941. Over 2,000 Jews were arriving every day.

Rudolf and Franz laughed as they discussed how other categories of prisoners like gypsies, mentally retarded, and Soviet and Polish prisoners of war were also arriving. The trains that delivered the Jews and other prisoners literally rolled right into the camp. The prisoners were unloaded from the cattle cars where they had spent the last several days imprisoned. They had been crammed in side by side and had to stand up for the entire trip without food or water. The Nazis were unloading the prisoners off the train. They forced them to remove all their clothing, and directed them to large rooms where they were told they would shower. Once all the prisoners were inside, airtight doors were closed. The Nazis then dropped Zyklon-B tablets into pipes located inside the walls. As the tablets hit the water, they released cyanide gas that eventually filled the entire room. The occupants of the room would breathe in the poisonous gas and die within seconds.

Once the gas chamber had grown silent from the screams of its occupants, the Nazis forced other prisoners to remove the bodies and place them in a large crematorium where the bodies burned. The conversation between Franz and Rudolph revealed that Franz had already built one crematorium and was now planning to construct four more by the summer of 1943. They were literally burning the bodies as fast as they could. The loose conversation and occasional chuckles that Franz and Rudolph shared during that entire exchange sickened me. Everything I had witnessed in the first concentration camp construction, years earlier, had now been set in motion and I could do nothing about it. I felt helpless and very alone at that moment.

Franz finished updating Rudolph and we all left the Commandant's office. We walked a little further into the camp and they showed me my temporary residence. It was a small room with a wood burning stove in the middle. A bathroom was shared by four other adjoining rooms, one of which Franz occupied.

From the adjoining room I heard Franz call out, "Fritz, it's time for you and I to tour the second camp and look for any inconsistencies in the construction. I will call for a car to deliver us since it is two miles away."

Driving through the first phase of Auschwitz, I saw hundreds of prisoners wearing gray and white striped uniforms with a yellow star sewn on the left side of the shirt. There was snow everywhere and none of prisoners wore coats. There were mostly men, but I saw a few women and young boys, also. The car passed over the train tracks used to roll in the trains filled with the next batch of prisoners. In fact, off to my far left I saw a train that had recently arrived and was still pumping out smoke from its coal-burning engine. I saw the Jews unloading off the train's cars. A long line had formed and camp personnel were splitting the newly arrived Jews into two lines. Some directed left, while others right. Families divided, women and children were screaming.

Off in the distance I saw grayish-colored smoke coming out of the chimney of a large white building. As the car drew near, a terrible smell penetrated the car.

Franz sensed my reaction to the smell and laughingly said to me, "Fritz that is the smell of burning Jews!"

Our car continued through the camp and the smell began to dissipate, but new horrors greeted me. When our car pulled into Auschwitz II-Birkenau, I saw a mound of naked bodies stacked twice as high as our car.

"Fritz," Franz told me gravely, "these piles mean that there are fewer Jews in the world now that they are dead. They have been gassed and soon any trace of them will be destroyed when they are tossed into the crematorium."

The car stopped. My body quivered with the effort it took me not to grab my knife and thrust it into Franz's chest. I could not fathom what I saw in front of me and could not believe what I heard coming out of Franz's mouth.

We exited the car and I followed Franz toward the additional crematoriums under construction. Franz inspected the masonry work, checking for any cracks in the workmanship. We then inspected some of the newly constructed barracks that would house more Jews when they arrived. We counted bunks, some as high as four levels, and checked flooring, plumbing, and other areas. To wrap up the day, Franz and I walked through a brand new gas chamber, very similar to the one I had photographed in northern Germany, several years earlier. This gas chamber was much larger than the one I photographed, and it looked just like a shower facility found in a gymnasium locker room or military barracks. The only difference was that cyanide gas came out of the showerheads instead of water.

I laid my head on my pillow that night and all I thought about was how I could exit the camp and get back to Washington, D.C., and report what was going on here at Auschwitz. I knew the Army wanted me to take pictures, to research as much as I could, and to disrupt the camp's operation. I was also personally determined to help as many Jews escape as possible.

I spent the next two weeks following Franz around both camp sections of Auschwitz taking notes of construction irregularities. Daily, I watched a train pull into the camp and more Jews get off. The camp's crematorium never stopped; there was always smoke billowing out of the tall chimneys. During my third and fourth weeks at the camp, Franz asked me to go back to all the places at which I had noted construction irregularities so that I could supervise the corrections. I was assigned three male Jewish prisoners, and our job was to fix one irregularity at a time and then move to the next one. The names of my Jewish prisoners were Efraim, Amit and Yosef. I came to know these three men very well over the two weeks I spent with them. One thing they immediately noticed in me was that I was kind to them, never raising my voice or hitting them. Each man was very proud of his name and shared with me its Biblical meaning. Efraim told me he was named after the grandson of the Bible character Joseph. Amit said his name meant friendly and faithful. Yosef told me he was named after one of Jacob's sons, another Bible character.

I bonded with these men and the more time I spent with them, the more I felt pressed to tell them who I was and why I was there. However, I knew that if word got out to the Nazis operating the camp, I would be killed. The news about Auschwitz would never make it back to the United States. I began to put as much food as I could get my hands on, in my toolbox and coat pockets, subsequently giving it to the three Jewish men in my care. I strongly advised them to eat the food out of sight of Nazi guards.

I had to take some photographs, so I used the excuse that it was for repair record keeping in the Commandant's office. Even so, I made sure that the photographs were taken in the early morning hours when fewer guards patrolled the camp's grounds. I photographed the outside and inside of the crematorium and gas chambers. With the gas chamber hiding my body and camera, I photographed a large pile of Jews that had recently been gassed. By the fourth week, I had completely filled both of my rolls of film, so I hid the rolls and threw the camera into the back of a crematorium oven.

The time for me to leave the camp drew near. I had concluded that my goal over my last few days was to get Efraim, Amit and Yosef out of Auschwitz, and to kill Franz. During my third and fourth weeks at the camp, I had secretly sabotaged the crematoriums and gas chambers in such a manner that there would be no blowback on the Jewish prisoners. I poured cement into several pipes in the gas chambers, cutting off a full flow of cyanide gas. I also destroyed cans of cyanide pellets by burying them under a foot of cement that was being poured for barrack foundations. With the crematoriums, I worked to prevent coal shipments from coming into the camp by telling drivers delivering the coal that we had plenty of it stored in other areas and that regardless of their orders, they could take the next day off. A few drivers opted to deliver every other day but the vast majority of coal deliveries kept coming.

It was also during those last two weeks that I secretly left my room during the night and killed German guards. I staggered my hours and worked my way up behind the guards patrolling the perimeter of the camp. I slit their throats as I pulled them to the ground. I would carry the dead Germans on my back approximately a mile away from the camp and bury them in a shallow grave. I would then return to the camp and take out a few more guards, killing upwards of three or four each night. After the first three nights, soldiers grew nervous and wondered aloud what was happening. Word began to circulate that some of the German soldiers had grown sick of the brutality at the camp and had deserted. I knew better but even with the sheer number of German soldiers I had killed, it made me wonder if it really was making a difference. I told myself it was.

During my last week at the camp, I approached Franz and asked if I could take my three Jewish prisoners and a truck into Katowice for lumber, nails and miscellaneous supplies. He asked why I needed to take the three prisoners with me and I used the excuse that a German should not carry the lumber. He relented and we set the date. I notified Efraim, Amit and Yosef that we would be going into town the next morning. They were visibly surprised and somewhat elated that they would have a chance to leave the camp for a few hours. I had convinced Franz that I would not need any guards to accompany us because I had come to know the men and their temperament. I told him that they did not have the mental capacity to do anything other than follow orders. It was Wednesday evening and we were leaving the following morning. I knew tonight was my last chance to kill Franz and prevent the camp from having their competent construction superintendent. Those last few hours I spent at the camp, I took the time to process all the things I had seen, heard and conducted over the last four weeks at Auschwitz. I looked at my watch; it was 2:38 AM. I knew Franz would be fast asleep by now. I turned out my light and waited thirty minutes. My timeline was short. Efraim, Amit, Yosef, and I were scheduled to leave the camp at 5:00 AM. My plan was to kill Franz in his sleep, and then gather my belongings and head for the truck.

Just after 3:00 AM, I silently worked my way to Franz's room. He was fast asleep, lying on his right side. To prevent the floorboards from creaking as I approached his bed, I lay flat on the floor and slowly belly-crawled toward the bed, thereby distributing my weight. When I neared the edge of the bed, I slowly stood up on the side facing Franz's back. I took out my knife and with one swift motion stuck the knife up into the base of Franz's skull. I rammed the knife all the way in, until the blade handle met his skull. I twisted the knife left and right a few times before removing it. The knife's motion left very little blood. I left Franz on his side and walked out of the room. I was breathing heavily, but relieved it was over. I walked back to my room and lay on my bed. I listened for any movement outside the building, but there was none. I shut my eyes but could not sleep. All the killing I had done over the last few weeks suddenly hit me. All these men had families, someone that loved them. They were now dead, all by my hands. I saw every man's face in my mind as I lay on my bed. At 4:30 AM, I got up and sat on the edge of the bed. I ran my hands through my hair and gathered my faculties. I had been trained to kill and I was doing plenty of it. The Germans were killing thousands of Jews a week in barbarous ways. I knew the killing I was doing was justified but it did not make it any easier.

It was time to secure Efraim, Amit and Yosef from their prison barracks and head for the truck I had arranged to deliver us to Katowice. I knew Franz lay dead in the next room, and would not be discovered until later. Before I picked up the film containing all the pictures I had taken, I literally put on all four sets of my clothes that I brought with me to Auschwitz. I would give the three top layers of clothing to Efraim, Amit and Yosef. I also took an extra pair of shoes, confiscated Franz's two pairs of shoes from his room and threw them all into a bag. I left my suitcase in my room, not wanting to raise suspicion. I met the German soldier guarding Efraim, Amit and Yosef's barracks and asked that they be released to me; they soon came out. In spite of the extra food that they had received from me over the last two weeks, they were still emaciated.

The four of us crammed into the cab of the truck. I started the truck and we headed toward the main entrance of Auschwitz. The two German guards patrolling the main gate stopped us and I rolled the window down and gave them my German name. I also provided the names of my three German prisoners. They checked their records and released us. As we pulled out of Auschwitz, Efraim, Amit and Yosef looked back at the camp nervously. We soon reached the main road and were well on our way. At that point, I told the men that I was going to help them escape. After a lot of discussion, in which the men asked me why I was so willing to help them escape, the truck got quiet.

The sun was barely starting to come up in the east. I knew my timing had to be right if I was going to make a 7:00 AM train from Katowice back to Brussels and, then to Dunkirk, Belgium.

As we neared the outskirts of Katowice, Yosef spoke up. "Fritz, we are eternally grateful for how you have treated us over the last few weeks and how you are now supporting our escape."

After a slight pause, I responded for the first time in English, "You three gentleman will never see me again, but the Jew's current plight has been carried back to the United States. I can promise you that we will do everything in our power to bring this human tragedy to a swift end."

Again, my travel companions looked bewildered, as they now knew for the first time that I was an American. I could not give them my real name, in case they were captured and forced to give up my name under duress.

Just as we hit the outskirts of Katowice, I pulled the truck off the main road and parked behind some large trees. I turned off the engine and got out of the truck. I motioned the three men to follow me a short distance from the truck so as not to be seen from any passing vehicles on the road. Once we were out of sight, I started removing layers of clothing and handing the shirts, pants and socks out to the three men as fast as I could. I instructed them to change out of their striped prison clothing and lay the tattered outfits collectively in a pile. I handed out the three pairs of shoes, and fortunately, all three men found a pair that fit comfortably. Once everyone had changed, I lit the prison uniforms on fire with a lighter I located in the truck. While the uniforms burned, I instructed Efraim, Amit and Yosef that I would be securing train tickets for all of us and that I would accompany them all the way to England. At first, they were worried as to why I would take them so far. They understood once I explained to them that Germany had now occupied most of Europe and that their risk of recapture was very high.

I concluded, "My goal is to get you back to England where you can tell your stories."

I drove the truck a little farther back into the woods and asked the men to follow me as we walked the last mile into Katowice. My only concern over traveling with the three men was the fact they were very thin and did not look healthy. It was a risk I had to take. The mile proved to be very hard for Amit; however, with sheer determination, he kept moving forward. When we got to the train station, I purchased four tickets. The train was already in place and the steam engine was running. We boarded the train; it was 6:47 AM. We secured our seats together in the second-to-last train car, alternating our seats so as not to draw unwanted attention.

As I took my seat, I looked out the window of the train and saw a truck full of German soldiers pull up. The officer in the front passenger side of the truck got out and spoke to the conductor who was still taking tickets and boarding passengers. My heart sank. We had come this far and now were in real danger of being caught. I was sure by this time that Franz's body had been found. The camp most likely had not connected that killing to me yet. The officer followed the conductor onto the train and the other soldiers were now exiting the truck. They all lined up outside of the train, covering every possible exit.

By now, my three Jewish companions had noticed the activity outside the train car. They were nervously looking at each other and back at me. I motioned for them to look down and pretend they were sleeping. I waited for the German officer and conductor to work their way through our train car. To my surprise, they looked through the first two train cars but stopped there. No sooner had the German soldiers pulled up, and then they returned to the truck and departed the train station. I breathed a sigh of relief. The train soon left the Katowice station and lumbered northwest in the direction of Germany.

Hours later when we stopped at the Dresden train station, I instructed Efraim, Amit and Yosef to remain on board while I left the train for a few minutes. I found a public phone and placed a call back to England, asking for the inn where I had met David Quinn.

To avoid attention from others in the crowded train station and to avoid anyone tapping the telephone line, I spoke a simple phrase in German when David answered the line, saying, "The bird is flying back via the same route and expects to cross the English Channel in twenty-four hours; the nest has yielded three eggs."

That was the code phrase to notify David that I was on my way back to Dunkirk with three Jews, and that we would need a ride back across the English Channel. The idea was for Ron Ashmore to immediately leave and head for the same beach where he had dropped me off a month earlier.

The train left Dresden, and Efraim, Amit, Yosef and I ate our lunches separately, with very little conversation. For the rest of the journey, the three men stared out of their windows. I could not begin to imagine what they were thinking. Shortly before 1:00 AM the following morning, our train lumbered into the Dunkirk train station. There were only a few passengers left on the train, and the street outside of the station was quiet. I told Efraim, Amit and Yosef to follow me. We left the train and walked down the steps, several yards away from the small station. I told the men that we would be walking down to the nearby beach and continuing our journey via boat. The men nodded and followed me out onto the beach. We walked to the approximate spot where Ron had dropped me off, sat down on the sand and waited. The wind was blowing hard from west to east and it was bitterly cold. I stared out into the darkness of the channel and looked for any sign of Ron and his boat.

After about one hour of waiting, a small light appeared out in the channel. There was no sound of an engine, and my gut told me it was Ron. As the light drew closer to the beach, I made out Ron's boat and saw its sails flapping in the wind. I motioned Efraim, Amit and Yosef to follow me out into the water. Ron waved and I responded by waving my arms back and forth. Ron did not take his boat all the way onto the sand but motioned us to walk a little further out into the surf. He motioned us out until the water was up to our waists, and Ron quickly lowered a rope. I helped the three rescued Jewish men onboard. I followed them up and into Ron's boat, thanking him for assisting us. Before Ron turned his boat around, he opened up a thermos, pouring each of us a hot cup of coffee and handed out some homemade sandwiches. As Ron directed his boat back in the direction of Dover, England, I updated him on our guests' identities.

"Allen, I cannot begin to imagine what you had to do in order to get these men to safety, but let me take it from here; a job well done," commented Ron.

After a few hours, Ron gently pulled his boat into the Dover port and tied it to the pier. The ride back to Dover was much faster this time, due to the shift in the winds, which were now blowing northerly. I thanked Ron, then helped Efraim, Amit and Yosef up to the inn, and secured their lodging.

David Quinn met me in the lobby and I provided him the names of my three companions. David replied, "Allen, I will take good care of these men and will make sure their story gets out. I will be taking them directly to London in the morning and securing a meeting with Winston Churchill. From there, the men will be cared for and their needs will be met."

I felt a great sense of relief now that I had gotten the men to safety and knew that their lives were out of jeopardy.

David continued, "You are due to depart back to the United States. I have arranged for a car to take you to an airfield just north of Dover. There you will meet an American bomber crew that will transport you back to Fort Meade. Your transportation will be on a Boeing B-17. The name on the plane is the *Lucky Seven* and the crew is expecting you."

I shook David's hand and hugged Efraim, Amit and Yosef. I said goodbye and left the inn. A car was waiting for me out front. I was exhausted, and fell asleep, trusting the driver to take me to the airfield. The next thing I heard was the roar of a bomber's radial engines. I looked out the window of the car and saw a large B-17 off to my right. *Lucky Seven* was displayed on the fuselage. I exited the car, thanking the driver, thinking to myself, I had never even learned his name.

The Lucky Seven's co-pilot shook my hand and asked, "Are you Allen Voigt?"

"Yes." I replied.

"My name is Andy McMasters and we have been assigned to carry you back to the States. You must be a very important person. We are part of an advanced flying group attached to the Eighth Air Corps. We have only been in England for three weeks and were just assigned to deliver you back to the states." I boarded the plane and assigned a seat near the middle, right next to a .50 caliber machine gun. The flight home took two days with stops in Ireland, Greenland and Newfoundland before we arrived back at Fort Meade. I thanked the crew and found my way back to my Fort Meade residence. I had left my key under a rock near the front door. I opened the door, found my bed and promptly lay down. Exhausted, I immediately fell into a deep sleep.

Chapter 7

RIDE THE LIGHTNING

"All war is deception."
Sun Tzu

I woke up the next day full of adrenaline and ready to get my Auschwitz film to the White House for developing. I arrived early at the White House on that spring morning in 1942. My instructions were to hand deliver the two rolls of film to General Donovan, who was to debrief me.

A White House staffer received me and escorted me to a private room not far from the Oval Office. As I passed the Oval Office, I saw President Roosevelt meeting with some of his staffers. General Donovan soon joined me in the hallway.

In a low but serious tone, he said, "Welcome home, Allen. You have done your country a great service."

I saluted the General and thanked him, then handed him the film that I had kept on my person for the last several days. We found an open office and spent the next three hours together as I outlined in intricate detail, every aspect of the two camps at Auschwitz, as well as my activities, what photos I had taken and the escape of the three Jewish prisoners. During our conversation, a female White House staffer came into the room and took the two rolls of film from General Donovan. Near the end of our three-hour conversation, the staffer returned and placed a large white envelope, marked "classified," on the table between General Donovan and me.

Once she left the room, General Donovan opened the envelope and pulled out fifty glossy 8.5 x 11 black and white photos. The resolution was very clear and details were extremely sharp. It took another full hour, as I explained to the General what each photograph was and how it corresponded inside the camp complex.

"Allen, you have exceeded my expectations - not only with the mission itself, but also with the photographs," General Donovan told me. "You also orchestrated the escape of three Jewish prisoners. Those three men that you rescued have already been before the British Prime Minister and told their story. Their stories have been transcribed and provided to President Roosevelt. These pictures will be added to those transcripts, providing a complete picture of the German war crimes."

General Donovan then looked directly at me and stated, "Allen, because of your exploits at Auschwitz, the rumors of the Nazi brutality against the Jews have been confirmed and the story is now made public. America will now accelerate their actions to bring this mass murdering to a rapid close and hold those war criminals accountable."

We closed our meeting, and the General instructed me to expect another mission in the coming days. I left the White House that day encouraged that I was able to get the story of Nazi concentration camps out, but extremely frustrated that I could not do anything else about it. My heart bled for the remaining Jews still under German occupation and even worse, the thousands killed each day.

On April 11th, I found a small white envelope inside my front door. Upon opening the envelope, it contained mission details from General Donovan. This mission was going to be very different from my recent Auschwitz mission. This new assignment would take me back to the Pacific campaign, assessing our military position and conducting a rescue mission. My directions were to leave the next morning and catch a flight to San Francisco. I would receive additional instructions upon my arrival in California.

My flight to San Francisco left the following morning at 6:00 AM. Our C-47 lifted off just as the sun was coming up behind us.

The heat of the sun warmed the plane's fuselage as we flew west. I was one of only three passengers on board, so very little conversation took place between us as we flew west for several hours. My mine raced, trying to figure out what type of rescue mission I would soon be undertaking. Our wheels touched down in St. Louis, Missouri to refuel. I looked at my watch, which read 11:30am. I exited the plane and stretched my legs. As I walked around our plane, my eye caught a large four-engine bomber that did not look familiar to me. The plane had no paint scheme. Its metal skin was reflecting the morning sun like nothing I had ever seen before. I asked our pilot how much time we had before departing. He replied, "Thirty minutes." I walked over to the large silver bomber.

Even before I got within fifty yards of the plane, two burly military policemen greeted me. The larger of the two MPs spoke up and said to me, "Sir, you cannot go beyond this point. This plane is off-limits."

I paused, smiled, and took a chance with leveraging a significant contact I had recently met. I looked at the MPs and replied, "My name is Allen Voigt and I am a personal friend of Colonel Jimmy Doolittle."

The two MPs looked at each other and began to laugh at my comment. I continued on, saying, "You both will have to explain to your superior officers why I was not allowed past this point. I welcome you to call Fort Meade and ask for the Provost office and give them my name."

The laughing stopped and one MP turned and went in the direction of the hangar. He soon returned and said, "Captain Voigt, we apologize for our error. You are welcome to proceed in the direction of the B-29."

I now had a name for the massive bomber.

Approaching the plane, I was amazed and intimidated by its size. It was slightly larger than the B-17 and British Avro Lancaster bombers I had ridden on previously. As I walked around the plane, one of the plane's pilots approached me. We talked for a few minutes.

The pilot informed me that the B-29 was a new Boeing airplane, manufactured up in Seattle, Washington. This particular plane was one of the first five to come off the assembly line three months earlier. This plane's mission was to fly to the east coast and back to Seattle in under three days. The objective was for the pilots and crew to check the plane's stress capabilities at various altitudes. The pilot let me crawl up into the large cockpit and he explained to me that the aircraft was pressurized to fly at 30,000 feet, allowing it to avoid anti-aircraft fire.

I had to get back to my assigned C-47 because it had already restarted its engines. As I walked away from the B-29, I heard the pilot yell, "Just be sure you're not on the ground when we start to rain hell down on the Japanese."

I climbed aboard the C-47 and we were back in the air heading west. A few more folks had joined us in St. Louis. One of those new passengers left his seat and walked back toward me. I could tell from his uniform that he was an Army Major. He sat across the aisle from me and introduced himself.

"I'm Major McCoy. It's s a pleasure to meet you, Captain Voigt."

I saluted him and shook his hand. We were the only two passengers in the rear of the aircraft as Major McCoy outlined for me what my particular mission would be once we landed in San Francisco. He told me that the Japanese had overrun our military in the Philippines. The civilian population was placed in camps and most of our military personnel had escaped to the island of Corregidor, off the Bataan peninsula. Our remaining Army personnel were isolated and no one knew how much longer they could hold off the Japanese. My mission was to assess the situation by sneaking onto the island and then report back on what I saw. I felt like there was more to the mission but that was all the details I had for now.

Our C-47 landed in San Francisco as the sun starting to set. I looked out the window of the aircraft and saw familiar surroundings, having been there about a year earlier on my first trip, traveling to Hawaii. Major McCoy and I hurried off the plane. We had a tight window in which to catch a Navy sub, assigned to take us all the way to the Philippines. After a brisk walk of about thirty minutes, we saw a row of subs tied up at the docks. We were to report to the USS Spearfish, but all the subs looked alike. In the darkness, we saw a lone Navy officer standing by the gangplank of the last docked sub. He greeted us, as we got closer.

"Welcome to the USS Spearfish, gentlemen. I am Communications Officer Richard Waugh," he informed us. "I assume you are Major McCoy and Captain Voigt?"

Major McCoy confirmed our identities. We then shook hands with the CO and followed him down the gangplank and onto the USS Spearfish. The cramped corridors of the sub were all too familiar to me, but Major McCoy had a hard time with the cramped space, which was understandable since it turned out to be his first time on a submarine.

The USS Spearfish soon got underway. As the sub maneuvered out of San Francisco Bay and underneath the Bay Bridge and Golden Gate Bridge, many of us remained topside and watched as the remaining rays of sun dipped under the horizon. The sky was streaked with brilliant orange, blue, red and yellow. It was an amazing sight.

We were directed back into the sub and soon the sub dove into the depths of the Pacific Ocean and into waters unknown. After a light dinner, I took advantage of what would be a long ride and got some much-needed sleep.

The next morning I awoke just after 5:00 AM and made my way up to the communications section of the sub where Major McCoy showed me detailed maps of the Island of Corregidor and told me about the expected Japanese troop levels. He also had aerial maps that showed the dense jungle foliage, along with various streams and known Japanese positions. In the middle of all these preparations, Major McCoy gave me some unexpected news.

"Allen, your mission will be to assess the true situation on Corregidor and the status of our troops. More importantly, though, we have American nurses on Corregidor, and we need you to help get them out. I can't begin to imagine what the Japanese could do to them."

I immediately wondered if one of the nurses on Corregidor could be Alice. I immediately questioned Major McCoy, "Sir, do you happen to know how many nurses are holding out on Corregidor and do you have their names?"

"Yes, Allen. There are an estimated twenty-six Army nurses among the large population of Army personnel, Filipino troops and civilians. One of them is, in fact, Alice, your friend."

I took a deep breath, let it out, and concentrated on what he said next. "You were chosen for this mission, Allen, because of your brave actions during the Japanese attack on Pearl Harbor, not because of your affiliation with Alice."

I then sat down on a nearby chair and tried to take it all in. I knew the Japanese were focusing their efforts on the Bataan Peninsula and the island of Corregidor. I could not imagine what Alice was going through.

I spent the next several hours studying the maps and aerial photographs while sharpening my Army knife. I made sure it was razor sharp. I would be given a .45 caliber handgun, a 1903 Springfield rifle, and explosive ordnance once we reached Hawaii.

After two more days at sea, we reached the Hawaiian island of Oahu. Most of us were topside now and eager to see what progress had been made on the cleanup of the numerous sunken and partially damaged ships in the harbor. The awful events that took place on December 7th came back to me. News soon spread throughout the boat that I had been there the day of the attack. As the USS Spearfish carefully maneuvered around the wreckage, several sailors questioned me about what it was like on that day. I downplayed my actions and instead pointed out where the USS Arizona and various other ships were that had been sunk or damaged that day. The USS Spearfish soon arrived at the submarine pens at Pearl Harbor. I related to the men the amazing fact that the submarine pens and fuel tanks went undamaged during the attack.

I was ready to grab my remaining gear and get on with the mission. We would be at Pearl Harbor for thirteen days in order for the Army to continue to assess the situation on Corregidor and to evaluate the Army's chances of breaking out. It was an agonizing thirteen days. I looked up a few friends that were still on the island, but I used the bulk of my time working my body into better shape. I ran ten miles every other day and the days in between, I swam two miles. I made sure to keep close to the shore, looking out for hungry sharks.

I was instructed to check in with Major McCoy every three days. During those times, we reviewed new intelligence and updated aerial maps. The maps showed the Japanese were gaining additional ground every day. Our armed forces on the island of Corregidor were trapped, with nowhere to go.

I was eager to get going and Major McCoy had to work hard to keep me calm and focused. He knew my personal connection to Alice, but continued to remind me of the overall picture. What had started out as a mission to gather intelligence and assess the threat posed by the Japanese had now evolved into a rescue mission for American' nurses.

April 26, 1942, finally arrived. I was instructed to return to the USS Spearfish and be ready to depart that evening.

Major McCoy met me as I climbed aboard. "Are you ready, Allen, to take the fight back to the Japanese?" he said.

I responded, "I'm ready to ride the lightning and bring the thunder down on them."

He smiled and motioned me into the sub. It took five full days and nights to reach the western side of the Philippines and within sight of the Corregidor fortress. We were on high alert and very mindful of enemy subs. This was the closet I had been to the Japanese, outside of my encounters with them at Pearl Harbor. The sheer number of enemy ships, sailors and army personnel we saw through the sub's periscope, as we maneuvered closer to Corregidor, was staggering.

The USS Spearfish had somehow managed to avoid the multiple Japanese subnets and mines staggered around the various bays and inlets throughout the Philippine island chain. It was now May 2nd, and I was called to the control room to join Major McCoy. We peered through the sub's periscope, raised slightly about the waterline. It was dark outside but lights were visible on the southern end of Corregidor. Every few seconds, I saw tiny pinpricks of light scattered in the dense jungle. They were most likely from Japanese campfires. The small fires surrounded the tip of Corregidor, where the American soldiers, nurses, and Philippine scouts were making their last stand. Reports we had received told us our military force was running out of food and water. The only way they had been able to hold off the Japanese this long was due to the Malinta Tunnel that had been built into the mountains of Corregidor. The tunnel had barracks, food stores and a hospital.

It was time for me to go. A young Navy ensign opened the main hatch of the Spearfish and I started up the ladder. Cool salt water dripped in all over my face as I looked up the hatch at the dark sky. The night was on my side. It was a moonless night and there was a lot of cloud cover, darkening out even the brightest stars. I climbed out the hatch and checked my weapons and supplies one final time. I had to travel light, but I wanted to pack enough firepower so that I would be ready if I encountered a large contingent of Japanese soldiers. My handgun was on my side with a full clip of ammunition. I had ten additional clips of ammunition tucked away in a small backpack, along with three hand grenades. In my large Army issued pants pockets I had a few medical supplies. My knife and canteens were secured to my belt.

A small black raft was lowered over the side of the submarine, and I descended the ladder that led to it. I had one oar and it was approximately one and a half miles to shore. I looked at my watch; it was 1:38 AM. I had thirty hours to reach the nurses and make it back to the sub before sunrise on the following day. A small map showed me where the Malinta Tunnel was, but unfortunately, no one there knew I was coming. Not only did I have to find the tunnel, I had to avoid being shot by my fellow soldiers, and escape capture by all the Japanese soldiers surrounding the tunnel.

The tide rolling in allowed me to make good time to the beach. My raft rolled up unto the shore and I pulled it onto the beach and up into the dense jungle, covering it with a few dead palm branches. I looked at my watch; it was 2:11 AM. The distance from the beach to the cliff base was only about thirty yards. After that, the Corregidor cliffs rose upwards for several hundred feet. Because of my training, I would scale the steep cliffs up, but if I was to rescue the Army nurses, I had to find a way out of the jungle that would allow me to bring the nurses back down to the beach.

I looked down both sides of the beach; to my left was a small outcropping of trees and rocks. I walked over to that section of beach and was relieved to see that it provided a steep but gradual slope out of the jungle and back onto the beach. I could use this route to bring the nurse back down.

To keep on time, the cliffs were my only way up. There was no way a contingent of soldiers would expect someone to attempt to make the ascent, as the cliffs were too steep. Time was not on my side. I had to go and this was my best way up into the jungle. My mind was made up.

Before I began to climb, I stopped to listen for any Japanese conversations. I heard only monkeys screeching off in the distance. I felt like I was back in South America. At that moment, I was thankful I had gone through that training; I was now putting it to good use. I started my ascent, making sure I secured good footing with each step. The last thing I wanted to do was loosen a section of rocks and have them go tumbling down, making noise and giving away my position. I knew the Japanese were everywhere and it would only be a matter of time before I would come across them.

After climbing one hundred yards or so, I was nearing the top of the steep cliffs. I looked back over my left shoulder and could make out the vast ocean below. There was no sign of the Spearfish, as it had already descended below the ocean waves. Before working my way up the remaining thirty yards, I stopped to listen again for any conversation. I could not hear anything. After completing my climb, I saw a small campfire burning off to my right. I knew it had to be a group of Japanese soldiers. I slowly worked my way towards the fire. I could make out three Japanese soldiers lying near it. I wanted to bypass this group of soldiers, which would have been easy, but I knew that if I wanted to make it back out of the jungle with a group of nurses, I had to eliminate any threats to my return mission. My only way to ensure a safe exit was to kill the three soldiers.

As quietly as possible, I crept closer and decided to take out the soldier furthest from the fire. I inched toward him; the noise of the crackling fire covered any noise my approach made. As I reached the first soldier, I saw he was lying on this right side, a perfect position for me. His rifle was lying next to him, between him and the fire. I knelt on my right knee, directly behind the Japanese soldier. With my right hand, I slid my knife from its sleeve, and with my left hand, I reached for the front of the Japanese soldier's face. With one swift motion, I gripped the front of his face with my left hand and rammed the six inches of steel into the base of the soldier's skull, ramming it in an upwards motion deep into his brain. He twitched for a brief second but other than that, there was no sound or reaction.

I then worked my way around to the next Japanese soldier. His sleeping position was not as favorable. He was lying on his back. With no hesitation, I came at him from his right side, placed my knee over his throat and with my left hand, covered his mouth. With my right hand, I thrust my knife deep into the right side of his chest. Before the Japanese soldier passed into his afterlife, he managed to thrash his legs about and it startled the last remaining soldier awake. This last soldier rose into a sitting position and turned in my direction. He quickly assessed what was happening and reached for his rifle. I pulled the knife out of the chest of the dead Japanese soldier I had just killed and with one motion, threw it as hard as I could in the direction of the remaining Japanese soldier. The knife landed squarely in the right side of his chest. He immediately fell forwards and landed right into the fire. Before he died, I saw him reach his hands up to his chest in a futile effort to extract the knife. His hands fell back to his sides and he died without making a single sound.

I sat there and gathered myself. It was a horrific sight and I just sat there, staring at the burning soldier. The Pearl Harbor attack had hardened me in many ways. I felt no regret, no remorse. It was payback.

I realized his burning body might give off a distinct smell that could alert other soldiers in the area. I grasped his feet and pulled him out of the fire. With a blanket lying nearby, I snuffed out the fire burning on his body in various places. I also retrieved my knife. It was then almost 3:30 AM, which gave me only twenty-seven hours to find the nurses, make it back down to the beach and out to the USS Spearfish. The only way the crew of the Spearfish would know I was back on the beach was when they raised their periscope and saw me signal, using Morse code with the small flash light I had secured on the raft.

By the light of the campfire, I looked at my map. I gauged the direction I needed to go if I had any chance of finding the Army nurses and gathering as much intelligence as I could from the U.S. Army holding such a tenuous position. Before leaving the three dead Japanese soldiers, I threw large sticks and dead palm tree leaves on the burning campfire. My intent was to have the fire burning bright as I made my extraction a few hours later, giving me some sense of direction to the beach below.

I went deeper into the jungle, avoiding any additional Japanese soldiers. I saw other campfires burning off in the distance but successfully skirted around them as I moved closer to the Army's position. I assumed everyone would be hiding in the tunnels, behind the large steel doors securing the entrance. The pictures I had been given of the area gave me some clues as to where I was going. I finally found the doors to the cave and worked my way as close to the entrance as I could. There one was in sight. I knew there had to be a door or hatch at the rear of the tunnels. I felt I had a better chance of alerting those inside if I attempted a rear entry versus simply knocking on the front steel doors.

Just at that moment, the large steel doors opened ever so slightly. I peered through the darkness and made out the face of a U.S. Army soldier wearing a World War I doughboy style helmet. He emerged through the small slit in the doors and closed the doors behind him. He had a rifle in his right hand and he began to walk in my direction. I figured I had one opportunity to get his attention that would not startle him. When he was about three feet from me, just on the edge of the dense jungle vegetation, I whispered in his direction, "I would love a cheeseburger right about now."

The young soldier stopped immediately in his tracks and pointed the rifle in my direction. I continued to say, "A cold Coke would seal the deal for me but I have to first rescue some Army nurses."

The soldier lowered his rifle and I emerged from behind a large palm tree.

"At ease, soldier. My name is Captain Voigt and I have just come up from the beach," I informed him. "I am here to assess your situation, gather as much intelligence as I can, and rescue the Army nurses here with you."

I could tell by the look in his eyes that he was shocked to see me standing there in the jungle. He tried to salute me but I motioned the soldier to sit down with me. I asked him what he was doing outside of the tunnels. He explained that he was a lone scout ordered to assess the number of Japanese soldiers in the area. I saved him the time by telling him about the three soldiers I had killed earlier. I then gave him an estimated count of sixty-five additional soldiers in the area, based on the number of fires I had counted as I worked my way toward the cave. I figured if there were at least three soldiers at each fire, there would be at least sixty-five to seventy Japanese soldiers within one square mile of where we were.

When I asked his name, the soldier replied, "I'm Corporal Robert Trent, a member of the 12th Infantry Division. Our unit was here in the Philippines to train and lead the large number of Filipino scouts assigned to us."

He gave me the estimated number of soldiers, scouts and nurses hiding out in the large tunnels behind the steel doors. He told me that at last count, there were over five thousand people inside the vast network of tunnels. That count was much higher than the intelligence provided me before I left the sub.

"How many Army nurses would you estimate are with you?" I asked.

"I would put that figure close to eighty-five, Sir".

This number was also higher than I had been told. Corporal Trent went on and explained that the highest-ranking member of the Army in the tunnel network was General Wainwright.

I then asked Corporal Trent how we would reenter the tunnel network.

"I simply have to knock three times, pause, knock two times, pause, and knock five times." He replied.

Rather simple, I thought.

Time continued to be my enemy, so I suggested to Corporal Trent that we go back into the security of the tunnels. We walked up to the large steel doors and with a succession of knocks, completed the re-entrance sequence. Just as the large steel doors began to open, a shot rang out and a bullet ricocheted off the steel door just above my head. Successive shots bounced around my feet near the door. I fired off all eight rounds in my handgun in the direction of the gunfire. By that time, Corporal Trent and I had wedged ourselves inside. The large doors slammed behind us and I heard subsequent shots bouncing off the steel doors behind us.

I looked around and all I saw was a large group of soldiers staring at me. Although there was a series of electric lights running down each side of the large tunnel, it was still very hard to see. An older man emerged from the darkness and walked up to me. "Captain, I am General Wainwright and in command of our forces here on Corregidor. How did you manage to get to us?"

I saluted and shook the General's hand. I fully introduced myself and provided him with a detailed summary of my activities thus far: arriving by sub, working my way up the cliff, and encountering a small patrol of Japanese soldiers. Before I could even tell him why I was there, he said he had already concluded the reason and asked me to follow him.

The General and I walked past the large contingent of soldiers to a side tunnel that led to a series of small rooms. We entered one and the General motioned for me to sit down on his footlocker in the corner. A small light bulb dimly illuminated the makeshift room.

General Wainwright lowered his voice and gravely stated, "Captain Voigt, I am not going to sugarcoat this conversation with a lot of fluff and stuff. We as an Army group are in a crisis. We are rats cornered in a maze of tunnels; food and water are running out. We have over five thousand personnel huddled in these tunnels. We have close to one hundred female nurses and a large contingent of Filipino scouts. We are not a combat ready fighting force. We have fought hard for the last several months to keep the Japanese from taking the Philippine Islands, but their land and air forces have been overwhelming. General MacArthur has left for Australia and we are on our own."

General Wainwright than paused and hung his head low. I felt like I had to say something but the words escaped me. At that moment, we felt a loud explosion above us. The single light in the room flickered and dirt from the room's ceiling fell like heavy dust.

"That one was close, Sir," I said, rising to my feet.

"That is just one of many shells the Japanese have rained down on us over the last two weeks. The shells are coming more frequently now because the Japanese know we are running out of food and water."

I then asked the General what other information I could take back with me. He rose and walked over to his makeshift desk. He picked up three sheets of paper and handed them to me. "Captain Voigt, these pages contain the exploits of several soldiers and Filipino scouts who performed above the call of duty during these last few weeks. I want you to take this list back with you as a record of that. My real fear is that the Japanese will kill us in the event we surrender. Surrender is not in their code, but we as a group do not have a choice. This list will at least provide those family members back home with a record of what happened here."

I took the list from the General, folded it twice and placed it in my large pant pocket. "General, I have been charged with trying to extricate as many nurses as I can. One particular nurse I am very fond of and I was hoping she is here. Her name is Alice Davison."

General Wainwright paused, smiled and said, "Alice is in fact here, she is one of the wounded men's favorite nurses."

The General did not elaborate any further but I knew what he meant. Her raw beauty and drop-dead figure are what caught my eye all those years ago in Switzerland. I could not wait to see her and help get her out of this hellhole called Corregidor. Another bomb landed outside the compound; the ceiling shifted and more dirt and dust fell around the General and me. General Wainwright than led me out of his office and back out to the main corridor, where most of the occupants of the cave were huddled. We walked past hundreds of men, deeper into the tunnel. We soon came to the hospital ward. There were hundreds of cots set up in every available spot. Several nurses were running around, helping the men with their wounds, checking IVs, and passing out cups of water.

The General led me over to an older nurse, who I took to be the senior nurse. She was responsible for the nurses and men under her care. General Wainwright made the introduction. "Captain Voigt, this is Lt. Baker and she is the head nurse."

I shook her hand and then the General explained to her my assignment; which was to take as many nurses out of the tunnels as possible before the Japanese overran it or the group had to surrender. Lt. Baker expressed her concern over the fact that the men under her care would not receive the attention they needed if the nurses left. The General and Lt. Baker came to an agreement that I would lead a small group of nurses out and a handful of Army and Navy nurses would remain on Corregidor. My heart sank because I had not seen Alice yet and I was not sure if the small number of nurses that I would be evacuating would include Alice.

I stood in the dimly lit tunnels wondering how I was going to get a handful of nurses through a dense jungle, down a steep embankment, and into a waiting submarine, all while evading Japanese soldiers who were rapidly advancing on our location. At that moment, two arms grabbed me from behind and held on to me tightly. I turned my head and saw that it was Alice. I swung her around and pulled her close. We kissed passionately, not caring at all about everyone watching us, including General Wainwright.

"What are you doing here, Allen? How did you even get here?" she asked.

I briefly explained my mission to her, skipping over the Japanese soldiers I had neutralized along the way. We did not let go of each other for the next few minutes. My window of time was rapidly eroding, as more Japanese rounds fell overhead. It was mid-morning, May 3rd, and I felt the best way to avoid detection by the Japanese was to wait until dusk. Alice had patients to treat so she left my side, motivated by the evil eye from Lt. Baker. For the next few hours, I talked with several Philippine scouts. They had fought alongside the United States Army when the Japanese attacked. They knew the area, had maps, and outlined the best route for me to take that night.

Food was very scare in the tunnels and I felt guilty eating it but the men were determined I shared in what was left. I was handed several letters that had been written by various soldiers in the tunnels. They asked me to mail them to their loved ones as soon as I could. Some included small personal affects that the men knew their loved ones would value in the event that they were later killed.

Other than looking at my watch, which now showed it was 8:00 PM, I had no idea if the sun had set. Lt. Baker then approached me. "Allen, the nurses that will be going with you are ready and assembled in the rear entrance of the cave. There are a total of seven nurses and they have all changed into dark clothing."

I then walked with Lt. Baker back into the very rear of the cave. General Wainwright was also there. He wished me success and asked me if I had the list of soldiers' names, he had given me, safely secured. I assured him the list was safe and it would be delivered to senior Army officials as he had requested.

I looked around for Alice, but did not see her. I figured she was still changing her clothes. I rehearsed the exiting sequence and route with a Philippine scout one more time. It was almost 9:00 PM and it was time to go. The USS Spearfish would wait until 6:00 AM on May 4th. If we were not on the beach by that time, they would have to leave. I still did not see Alice with the group of nurses. Lt. Baker then pulled me aside and told me that Alice had elected to stay with the wounded. She could not see me off because she did not want to make it any harder for the both of us. Lt. Baker handed me a letter from Alice. I placed it in the right front pocket of my jacket and held my emotions in check. I greatly respected Alice's decision, but I so much wanted her to go with me so I could ensure her safety. I could not begin to imagine what might happen to her now.

I gathered the seven nurses around me that were going with me to the USS Spearfish. I informed them of what they could expect and the danger involved. What complicated the matter even more was that all seven nurses still wanted to stay with the wounded on Corregidor. The nurse's declining health and age were the basis for the selection. I needed to get back to the USS Spearfish promptly. The trip to the tunnel network was perilous enough; the trip back would be even more so, under the very nose of the Japanese.

I did not have a lot to tell the nurses but started with sharing our designed route and the need for them to be quiet along the way. I taught them hand signals that I would use to tell them to stop, proceed forward and duck down. I informed them I had a raft hidden on the beach, and it would take four trips to get them to the sub.

I concluded with saying, "The faster we could get back to the beach, the better."

One nurse spoke up. "We have all heard about you, Allen. Alice told us what you did at Pearl Harbor. We have not been trained on how to navigate a jungle or fire a gun, but we will follow your direction and feel completely safe with you."

I swallowed hard and simply said, "Thank you." I took a deep breath, looked around at all of the women's faces, and then said, "It is time for us to go now."

General Wainwright led our group to the rear of the tunnel. There I saw a small metal door, not more than five feet high and four feet across.

General Wainwright spoke, "Captain Voigt, you and the nurses in your care will need to crawl on your hands and knees through this man-made tunnel in order to reach the jungle on the outside. The fifty-yard tunnel will exit you out in a very dense section of the jungle. There is a door on that side of the tunnel also. Simply turn the crank handle counter-clockwise and push the door open. Good luck."

I took the lead and entered the small tunnel entrance first. There was no light in the tunnel system and the further I crawled, the tighter the tunnel got. The small flashlight I was given was flickering, the batteries were about to give out. I turned my head slightly to see the nurses behind me. The tunnel was damp and musty, and I hoped the nurses could make it through safely.

The flickering flashlight soon revealed a metal door in front of me. We had finally reached the rear of the tunnel. I laid the flashlight down and before opening the door, I withdrew my pistol and chambered a round. I wanted to be ready to shoot my way out of the door if we encountered any Japanese soldiers. With my pistol in my right hand, I turned the door handle with my left hand. It took some muscle, but I pried the door open, greeted by the familiar sounds of the jungle at night. I paused for ten seconds, listening for any surrounding Japanese conversation. I heard nothing, so I opened the door completely. I crawled out, not using my flashlight, and surveyed the area directly around the tunnel door. I saw no campfires and smelled no smoke, so I felt confident we could all get out.

Helping all of the nurses out of the tunnel and into the humid jungle did not yet give me a sense of relief. With no verbal communication between us, I led our group toward the beach. I estimated the beach to be just under three miles away, and due south from our current position. The jungle was unusually quiet as we walked in a single file. I worked hard in the darkness to find a route that would be easier for the nurses, as none of them had any prior experience walking through dense underbrush. Finally, we had walked far enough that I could see the Pacific Ocean off to our right and Manila Bay off to our left. The moon had broken through the clouds, which helped illuminate the water and the path in front of us.

With just over a half-mile left before we had to descend to the beach below, I heard one of the nurses behind me say in a soft whisper, "I cannot go any further. Please let me sit for awhile." I stopped and turned. I asked who spoke in a low voice. Before anyone spoke up, it became obvious to me that it was the very last nurse in our ragtag line, as she was the only one sitting down.

I walked back in her direction and as I got closer, a shot rang out. I immediately motioned for all the nurses to lay flat on their stomachs. I put my finger to my mouth in a gesture to ask them not to make any noise. I was on one knee at this point and had pulled my pistol out of its holster. I concluded the shot had come from off to our right and behind us. I waited and listened for voices. The jungle was quiet. My fear was that we were dealing with a Japanese sniper in a tree and he was just waiting for us to rise up and continue walking.

Just then, I heard a low voice off to our right. "President Roosevelt is in his third term and is from Hyde Park, New York."

I knew there were Japanese soldiers that had gone to school in the United States and could speak perfect English without an accent;

but the more I thought about it, I believed it had to be someone from the sailors from the USS Spearfish.

I responded, "Do you like submarines?"

The voice replied, "Only if they are named after a fish."

I knew now it was someone from the USS Spearfish. "Show yourself." I demanded. Two figures, dressed all in black, emerged from the jungle off to our immediate right.

The figures were two sailors from the USS Spearfish. The sub's Captain had concluded that with the number of Navy nurses under my care, I would need some help transporting them back to the sub. All the recent conversation and the shot fired, had me concerned that we may have alerted the Japanese. The shot fired was simply a way to get my attention in a way that caused the least distraction. At least that is what the sailors thought. Little did they know how close I was to firing back in their direction.

With the support of the two sailors, we as a collective group made good time down to the beach. There on the beach were two additional rafts. Combined with the raft I had used the evening before. We only had to make one trip to the waiting USS Spearfish. We assisted all the nurses into the sub. I was the last one standing on the deck of the sub. Before climbing down into the sub, I looked back in the direction of Corregidor. All I could think about was Alice, alone and about to be overrun by the Japanese Army. What would be her fate? It took all my willpower to make myself climb down into the sub and seal the hatch shut. I wanted to jump into the sea and swim back to the beach and rescue her.

The sub's hatch closed behind me and I climbed down into the sub. As I walked through the galley, the nurses who had been rescued were provided with something to eat and were sipping that famous Navy coffee.

One nurse touched my arm and said "Allen, we are all eternally grateful for what you did on our behalf. I can tell by the look on your face that you are concerned about Alice. She will be okay, she is strong and God will protect her."

I thanked her by simply touching her arm in response nodding my head. I found my cabin and threw the equipment I had carried with me into Corregidor over in the corner, forgetting I had a few hand grenades and a loaded handgun in the mix.

I collapsed on my cot, my body begging for sleep. I struggled to calm my heart and mind the uncertainty of whether I would ever see Alice again was consuming me. The note from Alice, given to me in the cave system on Corregidor, was heavy in my pocket. I pulled it out and read three simple sentences. "Allen, I had to stay, the men here need me. I love you more than words can say. We will be together again."

The words were hard to read but I understood why Alice had to remain on the island. A strange peace came over me after reading the words and I eventually drifted off into a deep sleep.

The next thing I knew, I was thrown from my cot and onto the floor. I looked at my watch; I had been asleep for six hours. The sub was rocking and when I opened my cabin door, there was a flurry of activity outside, with Navy personnel running up and down the small hallway. I stopped one sailor by the arm as he ran by and asked him what was going on.

He hollered at me, "We are being pursued by a Jap destroyer. They have been tracking us for two hours and now they are dropping depth charges."

"What can I do?" I asked.

"Nothing but hold on," he replied and continued down the hallway.

I went up to the bridge where the Captain was busy shouting orders, ordering the sub to change its depth every few minutes and subsequently turn left and right, every quarter nautical mile.

Communications Officer Waugh and Major McCoy were both on the bridge already when I arrived. Major McCoy, like me, could not offer a lot to support the current situation, simply because we were not Navy men. By this time in the war, I had ridden on a few subs. The reality was I did not know how to handle submarine dive planes, launch torpedoes or operate a conning tower. I was standing there helpless when another depth charge from the Jap destroyer exploded right above the sub. The concussions from the depth charges rocked the sub. This blast knocked me clear off my feet. I stood back up, looked around, and saw I was not the only one knocked off their feet by the blast.

The chatter taking place around the bridge was that the sub could not rise because the Jap destroyer was waiting on the surface. If the sub could manage to raise enough to fire its torpedoes, we might have a fighting chance. I looked over at the sub's depth gauge; it displayed 325 feet. I did not know a lot about subs but I knew we were at a critical depth. The sub was not built to sustain pressure at that depth for too long.

A few minutes passed. Seawater was leaking in from many of the sub's valves due to the outside water pressure. Other valves were bursting. No additional depth charges had fallen. After consulting with his officers, the sub Captain elected to make a dangerous move by raising the sub to take a few torpedo shots at the Japanese destroyer. Once the sub shot a torpedo, the approximate location of the sub would be discovered, putting it in danger of the destroyer's 120mm deck guns. Even slightly submerged, a destroyer's deck gun rounds could penetrate upwards of fifty feet into the water and still have significant impact.

Chief Officer Waugh shouted in my direction. "Captain Voigt, please proceed forward to the torpedo room and assist the men there. A depth charge knocked out one of our Navy loaders. The remaining men need your help. We are going to try to get one or two shots at the Jap destroyer."

I immediately headed in the direction of the forward torpedo room.

As I worked my way through two watertight doors, I noted the amount of water leaking in and filling the floor of the sub. My feet were completely underwater by the time I reached the forward torpedo room. There were only two men standing in the room. The unconscious Navy man was lying near the hatch, clearly positioned there by the other two men so the he would avoid further injury.

"What can I do to help you?" I shouted out in the direction of the two men.

One of the men shouted back, pointing off to my right. "Grab that chain – it's attached to the hooks that pick up the rear of the torpedo. We need to get a torpedo in the firing hatch before the sub gets to firing depth."

I pulled the chain and worked the large hooks into position. One of the sailors opened the hatch to the right torpedo tube. "We are rising rapidly, men; we are now at two hundred feet. Be ready to fire the torpedo on my command!" shouted the sub's Captain over the torpedo room's intercom.

I did my part by attaching the hooks to the torpedo, and with the assistance of the other two men, we lifted the large black and red torpedo from its rack and worked it into the firing tube.

"One hundred and twenty-five feet now men," came the shout over the intercom. The firing hatch was shut.

"Let's fill that other firing hatch before we get to firing depth!" shouted the sailor to my left.

The three of us now worked over to our left side and began to repeat the same action. The seawater seeping in was now halfway up my shin and did not appear to be slowing. The other two men did not seem alarmed about the water at all. I assumed it was due to their training and time spent in the sub.

As we moved the torpedo into position, I asked the two men their names and hometowns. Somewhat of a strange time to ask but I had to relieve a little bit of the tension I was feeling by that time.

"My name is Kevin Munley and I am from Endwell, New York!" shouted the sailor to my left.

"Steve Biles from Greensburg, Indiana!" shouted the other sailor, who was opening the second firing hatch.

"Seventy-five feet now men, get ready," came the message over the intercom. Steve now reached for and turned the valves that flooded both torpedo tubes. He explained to me that this would allow the pressure inside the tubes to equalize to the pressure outside the sub, allowing the torpedo to keep its direction once fired. We waited now for the sub's Captain to issue the firing command. I waited anxiously with Steve and Kevin in the torpedo room.

"Fifty feet now, we will fire at twenty-five feet, get ready!" was the update over the intercom.

The time between fifty feet and twenty-five feet seemed like an eternity. We had very little time to get the torpedo fired. "Fire one!" was the order over the intercom.

Kevin pounded the button on the right torpedo's firing control box. The release of the right torpedo rocked the sub slightly, but the torpedo launched successfully. We waited for over a minute, waiting to hear an explosion, hoping the torpedo hit its mark.

"We missed men, the torpedo went completely under the Jap destroyer," shouted the sub commander over the intercom. "We are now breaking the surface, men, and will be visible to the Jap destroyer. We have one more chance to level the playing field!"

I could feel the pressure inside the torpedo room change as the sub broke the surface. "Fire!" was the command over the intercom. Kevin hit the firing button for the second torpedo but nothing happened. Kevin hit the button several times but the torpedo still did not launch.

"Why has the torpedo not fired?" shouted the sub's Captain over the crackling intercom.

Steve picked up the torpedo room intercom mic, "Captain, the left firing mechanism appears to have shorted out due to the water coming in. We will get another torpedo into the right torpedo tube, Sir."

All I could picture was the Jap destroyer's Captain looking down on our sub, smiling as they positioned their deck guns and additional depth charges in our direction. The three of us worked aggressively and began to lift another torpedo into place.

Suddenly a round from the Jap destroyer's gun exploded outside the right side of the sub, not far from the torpedo tube. The concussion of the blast must have affected the outside torpedo hatch, because water came pouring in through the right hatch. The volume of water was so great that the third torpedo could not be loaded into the tube. Steve shut the hatch of the torpedo tube to keep any additional water from leaking in.

Kevin got on the intercom, "Captain, torpedo tube one is damaged, we cannot fire another torpedo."

Before he set the intercom mic down, I took it from him and said loudly, "This is Captain Voigt. Open the main hatch of the sub."

I knew some of the Army equipment onboard the sub included a bazooka and a few rounds.

I continued, "Get me close enough to that Jap destroyer and I will do the rest."

Initially, there was only silence on the other end of the mic.

"Do it," eventually came the response from the sub's Captain.

I ran back toward the control room, jumping over the still unconscious man lying there. I ran through the control room as fast as I could, not even acknowledging anyone. The distance was short but for the safety of the crew, I had to hurry. As I cleared the control room, I could see the nurses I had rescued all huddled together in the galley area with the look of sheer terror on their faces.

I knew right where the bazooka was stored, along with its three rounds of ammunition. I had seen it by accident when I initially looked to store some of my equipment on the sub back in Hawaii. I originally thought it was odd that a bazooka was on a sub but I was now very thankful it was there. I grabbed the bazooka and all three rounds of ammo. I cradled the large bazooka and the rounds in my arms and worked my way back toward the central hatch near the control room. Pure adrenaline drove me forward. Rounds from the Jap destroyer continued to fall all around the sub.

I made it to the hatch, and laid the three rounds down near its base. I needed a volunteer to load each of the rounds. Without even saying a word, Major McCoy came over and picked up the three bazooka rounds, knowing what had to be done. A sailor had already climbed the ladder leading up to the main hatch and had opened it. Water dripped down into the hole as I looked up and saw the dark sky. It was night when I expected it to be day. This was an unexpected advantage, and it made sense as to why the sub's Captain elected to raise the sub when he did.

The ladder and hatch were too small for me to carry the bazooka up with me. I asked the sailor who had opened the hatch to climb back up and let me hand him up the bazooka. I soon exited the sub and immediately looked for the location of the Jap destroyer. It was off to my immediate right, illuminated by the destroyer's small control tower. By now, the USS Spearfish was rapidly approaching the Jap destroyer. The bazooka had a short range. The furthest I had ever attempted a shot with a bazooka back in basic training, was twenty-five yards. Even at that range, the round could penetrate upwards of five inches of steel. I estimated we were forty yards from the Jap destroyer.

Major McCoy had now joined me. I had shifted to one knee and felt Major McCoy insert the first round into the back of the bazooka. Our sub was closing fast and I estimated the distance between the Jap destroyer and me was still about thirty-five yards. I knew the closer we got, the destroyer's 120mm gun would have a hard time turning down in our direction. Rounds from the destroyer landed just off to my left, hitting the water and having it cover me from head to toe. The rounds hit close enough to the sub to knock Major McCoy and me off our feet. I somehow managed to keep the bazooka in my hands. I had had enough by that point with the depth charges, the foot of water in the sub, and being rocked by the destroyer's deck gun. While I had felt helpless up to that point, with the bazooka I felt I could finally inflict some payback on the Japanese. I swung around, planted my right knee, and fired. The bazooka round flew fast and true and by sheer luck, found its mark. The round flew far enough to hit the destroyer's control tower and then exploded. The Japanese destroyer Commander was most likely in that room when the round hit. He never knew what hit him.

Major McCoy chambered another round into the bazooka. I felt it slam into position and I fired again, this time hitting the rear smokestack, blowing it in half. The last bazooka round was inserted by Major McCoy. I fired this one in the direction of the second smokestack but missed, firing too high. I was not done yet. I threw the bazooka down and jumped to my feet. I ran to the USS Spearfish's 40mm deck gun, screaming for rounds to be passed up to me from down below. I rapidly prepared the deck gun for firing and three sailors quickly delivered the 40mm rounds. I slammed the first five rounds into the 40mm gun's clip and chambered the first round. I swung the gun in the direction of the stricken destroyer. Although it was dark, the moon provided all the illumination I needed.

I fired all five rounds at the destroyer's rear propeller, aiming just above the water line. I opened up a nice hole with the first five rounds. A sailor loaded another five rounds and I fired them back into the hole I had just opened up. Those five rounds found their mark, stalling the momentum of the ship. By then we were receiving small arms fire from the destroyer's deck and rounds were hitting all around me, bouncing off the sub's hull. The last five rounds we had were loaded into the deck gun's clip. I fired these back in the direction of the control tower, it exploded and started to burn.

We had inflicted enough damage. I ordered everyone below. I descended back into the sub and sealed the hatch. The sub commander ordered the sub to submerge to one hundred feet and turn ninety degrees starboard.

I sat down on the control room's floor with my arms on my knees, breathing heavily from the intense action.

The sub's Captain came over to me. "Captain Voigt, you personally saved this sub and all its crew. What you did up there was an act of solitary vigilance."

It hit me then that all this time I had not even found out the sub Captain's name.

"Sir, I was just acting upon my years of training. I hate the Japs for what they did at Pearl Harbor and I was sick and tired of the shelling. By the way, what is your name?"

He replied, "Captain Dempsey, Charles Dempsey. I heard about your actions at Pearl Harbor and I am not surprised by what you did today. Thank you."

Captain Dempsey instructed the sub to immediately head back to Pearl Harbor for repairs. I asked a sailor how long it would take us to get back to Pearl Harbor.

He replied, "At twenty knots and a little current, it will take us six to seven days."

I had not showered in three days and was exhausted and hungry. I went back to the galley. A few sailors slapped me on the back. A few nurses prepared a hot meal of toast and eggs for me; it was like eating steak and mashed potatoes. I devoured every bite. My smell must have overpowered everyone around me but no one said a word. I finished my meal, took a long shower and put on some fresh clothes. I sat back down in my cabin and took it all in, the rescue of the nurses, seeing Alice, the attack by the Jap destroyer and the fight to save the sub. The war was viscous and brutal. Mentally I was drained. I bowed my head and asked God to give me the strength to continue the fight and for Him to protect Alice and keep her safe. The war was not going to end anytime soon.

Chapter 8

AS DAYLIGHT DIES

"Courage - a perfect sensibility of the measure of
danger and a mental willingness to endure it.
William Tecumseh Sherman

The USS Spearfish finally arrived at Pearl Harbor on Tuesday, May
12, 1942. As we entered the harbor, a lot of us had gone topside and
were taking in the fresh air. As I stood on the deck of the sub, I
turned my face to the sky and felt the hot rays of the sun beat down
on me. It was late morning, but the sun was high in the sky and it felt
good to be out of the sub after a week of travel from the Philippines.
We had traveled over 5,000 nautical miles and the last thing I wanted
to do was get back in that sub.

The Japanese attack on December 7, 1941, had really taken its
toll on the United States Navy. Twisted metal and partially sunken
ships remained in the harbor, but progress was being made on the
USS Oklahoma. I looked on as the Navy installed large winches on
Ford Island in order to secure large cables that would later upright
the ship. I watched as divers entered the water around the ship and
welders removed various pieces of machinery on the ship, all in an
attempt to lighten it.

As the USS Spearfish maneuvered closer to the submarine pen,
where repairs could be made to the damaged right torpedo tube,
Captain Dempsey joined me up on the top deck of the sub. He spoke
first.

"Captain Voigt, thank you for what you did for us."

"Thank you for delivering us safely back to Pearl Harbor." I replied.

The Captain continued, "I heard that you are fond of an Army nurse and that she is still a prisoner on Corregidor. She will be fine, and you will see her again when this ugly war is over."

"Thank you Captain Dempsey. I will get Alice back, even if I have to fight the entire Japanese Army to get her back," I replied.

The sub docked at its designated location at the submarine pens. Walking off the sub, the realization hit me that I had no assigned lodging and no instructions on where my next assignment would be.

Major McCoy joined me and we walked together, carrying our limited belongings with us in Navy sea bags.

"Hungry?" the Major asked me.

"Yes, I know a great spot," I replied.

I knew of a great diner nearby that was not far from where I had lived during late 1941. I had eaten there a few times and the food was good. Major McCoy and I soon ended up at the diner, Harry's Café, on Waimanu Street in Honolulu.

Harry's Café was very crowded, as it was now approaching lunchtime. We found a seat in the back of the restaurant and sat down to order. Surrounded by Army, Navy and Marine personnel from all over the island, we were among company. The island of Oahu's population grew overnight in light of the Pearl Harbor attack. The island inhabitants were more alert now than ever. Military sentries stood on every street corner. Anti-aircraft gun emplacements were positioned all around the harbor in anticipation of another attack.

Major McCoy and I ordered a late breakfast and reviewed the last two weeks of activity. He had exchanged some correspondence with General Donovan while we traveled from Corregidor back to Hawaii.

"Allen, your accomplishments in the Philippines have reached the desk of General Donovan. He is very pleased and is currently planning your next mission."

I downplayed my activity. "Major, I'm just doing what I was trained to do. I am eager to fight the Germans and the Japanese, anywhere, anytime. I had so many years of training and espionage activity in Germany; I am itching for a fight."

Major McCoy then put his fork down and pushed his breakfast plate away from him. His demeanor changed suddenly.

"Allen, while we were traveling back from the Philippines, General Wainwright surrendered on Corregidor. They were the last United States armed forces still holding out in the Philippines."

I know he had to see the reaction on my face as I suddenly stood from my chair, slammed my right fist on the table and walked out of the restaurant. A sudden rush of fear overtook me as I contemplated what might have happened to Alice. Never had I felt as helpless as I did at that moment.

Major McCoy soon joined me outside Harry's Café and put his arm around me. "Allen, General Wainwright surrendered on May 6th, not long after we left the area. You knew this was inevitable and Alice made the decision to stay. She will be alright, you have to believe that."

"You're right, but that doesn't make it any easier. Just thinking of what might happen to her, her fellow nurses, and the rest of the Army personnel, makes me extremely anxious." I replied.

Major McCoy went back into the restaurant to settle our bill. I decided to take a long walk along Waikiki Beach and clear my head. I found a palm tree, took my boots and socks off and left them by the tree. I rolled up my Army pants and walked in the surf along the beach, not even paying any attention to the sun worshippers lying nearby or the countless folks splashing around in the water. I walked and walked, paying no attention to the sun that beat down on me. I knew I had walked several miles because I could barely make out the hotels along the beach where I had started. My mind raced, thinking of every possible scenario that could happen to Alice and the others. Surely, they had been taken prisoner. What was next? The Japanese did not feel any obligation to treat their prisoners humanely.

Major McCoy must have been a tracker in his previous life. He suddenly ran toward me in a full sprint, coming down the beach.

"Allen, there you are. I checked in at Army headquarters and they have some updates for us on the Corregidor group. Do not worry; I have your boots and socks in my Jeep. By the way, when was the last time you washed those socks?"

I ran up the beach to the street with Major McCoy. After knocking off what sand I could from my feet, I hopped in the Jeep with him, put my socks and shoes on, and rolled my pants legs down. Neither one of us said a word as Captain McCoy drove through the crowded streets of downtown Honolulu.

We pulled into the Army headquarters, which I was very familiar with, as I had spent some time there in 1941. Major McCoy and I hurried up the stairs and bolted through the front door. Lt. Colonel Yates and General Donovan greeted us inside. I saluted both men.

"Allen, it's good to see you," General Donovan stated as we shook hands. He led us to a private room, where Lt. Colonel Yates motioned us over to a long table covered with maps.

Lt. Colonel Yates spoke next. "Allen, you did a great job defending the USS Spearfish and its crew by taking on that Japanese destroyer. Our sources tell us that destroyer was the Natsuzuki. It had to be towed back to Tokyo for repairs because it was dead in the water. You have to be the first person in military history to solely take out an enemy destroyer."

I simply nodded my head in response.

Looking down at the maps on the table, I realized that they were the same maps I had studied before I hit Corregidor beach. General Donovan cleared several of the smaller maps off the table and pulled the largest one into the center. He then gave us an update on the activity in and around Corregidor.

"The Japanese Navy and Army have overrun the Philippine islands. They have a complete blockade around the larger islands and they are unloading thousands of Japanese soldiers by the hour," he said, pointing out locations on the map.

"General Wainwright, his soldiers and the Filipino scouts with him, were taken back to the Bataan peninsula as prisoners of the Japanese. Our island sources tell us the Japanese are forcing them to march north in the direction of several large prison camps photographed by our Army Air Corps. Our soldiers are reportedly on a forced march with no food or water. Many have been killed and even beheaded after simply falling down."

As General Donovan spoke, I noted that one group on Corregidor had not been mentioned, the remaining nurses. The news about beheadings and a forced march infuriated and sickened me. It was not the time to bring up the nurses, but in light of my recent mission and Alice, I interrupted General Donovan, anyway.

"General Donovan, Sir, what is the fate of the nurses that remained with General Wainwright on Corregidor? I was surprised that so many of them elected to remain, even with the opportunity to escape."

He responded with a firm look on this face. "Captain Voigt, we do not know."

That response did nothing to ease my mind. Fear gripped me, as the fate of Alice was unknown. General Donovan continued to outline the grip the Japanese had on the United States military. As I listened, I thought to myself, "This war is just beginning."

General Donovan painted a very bleak picture for the United States military. The Navy lagged behind in overall ship production. The Army had fewer personnel than either Japan or Germany. Both Army and Navy recruitment were up since the Pearl Harbor attack, but still way behind in terms of overall recruiting and combat readiness.

During a lull in General Donovan's update, Lt. Colonel Yates addressed me. "Allen, what you are about to hear is classified but we know we can trust you with the information. The survival of America is at stake. We are including you into these conversations because of your role with the OSS and your consistency in accomplishing missions over the last eight years."

General Donovan then spoke again. "The United States has elected to take the fight back to the Japanese in two ways. First, we will outpace them in sheer war production when it comes to ships, planes, tanks, and so on. Second, we are going to adopt an island hopping campaign. We are devising a plan to invade the island of Guadalcanal this fall with Marines. The Japanese have a tight grip on the entire Pacific. There is a key airfield on Guadalcanal and we are concerned that the country of Australia is in danger. Admirals Nimitz and Halsey will lead the Navy and Marine island-hopping and General MacArthur will lead the Army initiatives."

"Germany has now invaded most of Europe and encroaching into North Africa." He continued, "Due to your activity in Germany prior to the war and most recently at Auschwitz, we know that Germany is actively imprisoning and exterminating Jews. A careful secondary review of the pictures you took around southern Germany back in the late thirties alerts us that Germany is rapidly working toward nuclear technology. The rockets they developed are crippling England. The United States has decided a Germany first approach. We are planning an invasion for some time in mid-1944 on the northwestern coast of France."

General Donovan let that sink in for a minute, and then informed me, "The OSS is going to play a vital role on both fronts of the war. That is where you come in, Allen. Until this bloody war is over, you will not rest, but you will help kill a lot of the enemy and save American lives."

An Army aide suddenly rushed into the room. He approached the table, handed General Donovan a sheet of paper and spoke.

"General, we have just learned that the nurses with General Wainwright on Corregidor are safe and all accounted for. They were, in fact, captured by the Japanese, but were not taken with the Army personnel that were forced to march north."

I felt relieved as the aide continued on, "They were transferred to the Santo Tomas Internment Camp near Manila. Our sources tell us they are already helping the sick and wounded there in the camp."

I did not say a word, but I felt as if a huge weight had lifted off my shoulders. Major McCoy gave me an encouraging pat on the back. The aide left the room as quickly as he had entered it.

The meeting was over. I was surprised I did not receive my next mission assignment but knew General Donovan and Lt. Colonel Yates probably needed some time to assess both Japanese and German developments. Major McCoy and I walked out of the Army headquarters together, after which he drove me over to the same barracks I had occupied back in 1941.

He handed me the keys to my quarters and said, "Allen, you must be relieved over the fact Alice is safe. I knew she would be okay."

I smiled in response.

As the Army Jeep pulled up to my quarters, Major McCoy informed me, "You will find a few clean uniforms, shoes, socks and many other comforts of home in your quarters. This is where you and I part ways Captain Voigt. It has been a privilege to work with you and watch first hand, your contributions to the war effort."

I stepped out of the Jeep, saluted and shook Major McCoy's hand, thanking him for his support. I opened my door and headed straight for bed. After slipping off my boots and socks, I fell onto the bed and immediately fell asleep.

I woke up Wednesday morning to the sound of birds chirping outside on a nearby tree. It was peaceful not having to hear gunfire or the sound of a submarine's diesel engines. The smell of war was not in the air that morning. I showered and put on a fresh uniform, not having put on a new one in weeks. I hailed a cab and headed over to Harry's Café, where I hoped to redeem myself and apologize personally to the owner, Harry Nagahara, for not finishing my meal the day before. I soon found an open seat and settled in for a hot breakfast.

While I ate, my thoughts ran wild as usual. Chief among them was the thought that I should have done more to convince Alice and the other nurses at Corregidor to escape with me. If they had come with me, they would not be prisoners of the Japanese now. As

I pushed my scrambled eggs around on my plate, however, I knew in my heart that Alice and the others had stayed because of their military training and dedication. They remained behind and did what they were trained to do, care for others. I had to think that many of the soldiers currently on a forced march north might somehow manage to survive the march, due in part to the excellent nursing care they had received prior to their surrender.

I finished my breakfast and when I went to pay for my meal, Harry came up to the register and waived his hand, motioning me to put my cash away.

"Captain Voigt, I know who you are, you are a local celebrity around here, whether you know it or not. Your exploits at Pearl Harbor were talked about here at Harry's for months. This breakfast is on me."

I thanked Harry, shaking his hand as I left.

I left the restaurant frustrated, not yet knowing my next assignment. After everything I had learned from General Donovan about the Japanese and German advances, and about how unprepared we were as a nation to combat their advances, I thought to myself, "Here I am on the beautiful island of Oahu, and do not have a hand in the fight."

I opted to walk back to my barracks, letting the long walk calm me down. After walking about a mile, a group of Army nurses ran up to me.

One of them shouted, "Allen, we have heard from Alice! She is okay and wanted us to tell you that she misses you. Alice said to tell you she will survive and that she will see you again."

I recognized several of the nurses as being from the group that I rescued from Corregidor. I asked them how they had heard from Alice. They said that the camp where she was being held had civilians working there. They came and went from the camp each day. They were able to smuggle messages out and telegraph them back to the United States.

I thanked the nurses for the message and several of them thanked me again for rescuing them. I continued the long walk back to my barracks with a renewed sense of commitment to hold on and a stronger sense of determination to do my part to end this global war.

As if things could not get any worse for the United States Navy, the news hit Pearl Harbor that a few days earlier, two of our Navy aircraft carriers were heavily damaged in a battle against the Japanese Navy in the Coral Sea. The USS Lexington had sunk and the USS Yorktown was shot up pretty bad. On May 27th, while I was running, I saw the massive USS Yorktown limp into Pearl Harbor for repairs. I was extremely frustrated at that point. It was late May 1942 and I was yet again stuck in Pearl Harbor while the war raged on around the globe.

I sometimes wished I were a member of a traditional Army unit. I wanted action and Pearl Harbor was not offering it. I had received no additional updates on Alice or the fate of the soldiers captured by the Japanese and forced to march north. By this point in the war, the Germans had progressed eastward against the Soviets and south to invade North Africa.

The United States was now getting into the offensive fight, which became very apparent when the news hit Pearl Harbor that the battle of Midway had commenced. By June 7th, we had heard that the USS Yorktown had been sunk. However, the United States Navy had inflicted even greater damage on the Japanese by sinking four of their aircraft carriers and one cruiser. There was a buzz around the island that we were now taking the fight back to the Japanese.

I anticipated receiving orders any day, but nothing came. I kept up my daily routine of running, weight lifting and practicing at the rifle and pistol ranges. June came and went. July was pretty much the same until late in the month when I was asked to report to Army headquarters. It was July 25th and United States military activity was heating up everywhere. I had no idea where I was going to be assigned or what my role would be. I walked into the Army headquarters around mid-morning of the 25th. Lt. Colonel Yates greeted me right away. There was no sign of General Donovan or Major McCoy this time. After some brief small talk, Lt. Colonel Yates asked me to accompany him to a nearby office. He shut the door behind us and asked me to have a seat. I had been in this position before, behind closed doors as classified information was shared.

Lt. Colonel Yates took a seat in front of me, across from a large wooden desk. From the desk, he pulled out a set of files and a folded piece of paper that looked like a map. Lt. Colonel Yates then began to explain what my next assignment would be.

"Allen, as we communicated to you a few weeks ago, the United States is going to land armed forces on the Solomon Islands, in the far southwest Pacific Ocean. We are going to land on the island of Guadalcanal. Not many people have heard about that island, but the Japanese have invaded it and taken control of a key airfield," he informed me. "That entire area around Guadalcanal is swarming with Japanese. They control both the sea-lanes and air. The mission to take back Guadalcanal from the Japanese is called Operation Watchtower. You will be working closely with the 1st Marine Division."

I replied to Lt. Colonel Yates with a slight grin on my face. "Lt. Colonel, I guess this Army Captain will have to show those Marines a thing or two on how to kill Jap soldiers in a jungle environment."

Lt. Colonel Yates smiled and continued. "Allen, the Marines are a proud bunch and they are not keen on Army personnel telling them how to fight and they do not like being shown up on the battlefield. Your role will be to insert at night, a few days before the Marines land on Guadalcanal. You will need to find out where the Japanese are positioned, assess their troop strength and the types of weapons they have on the island. The mission will not be an easy one. The news coming out of the Philippines and China are not good. The Japanese are torturing their captives and beheading some of their military prisoners. You have clearance to kill as many Japanese officers as you can find, carry out sabotage behind enemy lines and obtain as much intelligence as you can. You will leave in the morning with the 1st Marine Division. You will be sailing west for several days. Your objective and military background was shared with Marine General Alexander Vandegrift. He originally was not very pleased with the idea of an Army Captain joining his 1ˢᵗ Marine Division. However, General Donovan shed some light on what you have contributed prior to and during this war. That changed General Vadegrift's mood and he was then agreeable to you joining his Marines."

I thanked Lt. Colonel Yates for the opportunity to get back in the fight. We shook hands and I left Army Headquarters. I spent the rest of the day preparing for my mission. I cleaned the two handguns I had secured from the local armory. This type of insurgency behind enemy lines would not require a heavy rifle. I packed my sea bag with a few changes of clothes and boots. I cleaned and sharpened my knife. I had very few personal belongings with me, mainly because of the nature of my work. I did pack a small black and white picture I had of Alice, away in my small New Testament. The very same New Testament I received when I joined the Army back in 1926, and now well worn. I tried to read the New Testament as much as I could, as it gave me peace in the midst of the war I was now involved in.

I had been in the Army for sixteen years. I looked and acted much older than the majority of service men entering the armed forces at this stage in the war. In fact, I was now thirty-four years of age, almost twice the age of the men enlisting.

The next morning I headed down to the docks to get to the ship that would carry me to Guadalcanal. To my surprise, when I got to the ship that morning, there was already a flurry of activity taking place. Sherman tanks, 110mm and 155mm Howitzer cannons, Jeeps and crates of all sizes were being loaded into the ship's cargo holds and many other ships docked nearby.

My Army uniform made me stick out in a crowd of Marines. As I was watching the intricate loading of the ships, a group of seven or eight Marines approached me. They were preparing to board the same ship as I was assigned.

"Are you lost, Army Dog?" One of the Marines shouted in my direction.

I turned toward him, smiled, and said, "I've killed more Japs in the last year than all of you jarheads combined."

That reply did not sit well with the Marines. One of the Marines lunged forward and snatched the front of my Army uniform. With one swift motion, I dropped my right shoulder, holding my sea bag, letting it fall to the ground. With my right hand, I pulled out my knife and put it to the Marine's throat. I could have easily killed the Marine in the same motion but he was not my true enemy that morning. The remaining Marines backed away; surprised by the swift action I took in response to the Marine grabbing me. I held the knife to the Marine's throat for a few seconds and then released it, putting it back in its sheath on my belt.

Collectively, we then heard the loud voice of someone up on the top deck of the ship. "Marines, do you know who you just failed at intimidating? His name is Captain Voigt and he a member of the Army. We are not the only branch of the military that has to fight this dirty war."

I turned and saw that the man speaking was, in fact, General Vadegrift of the 1st Marine Division. Since learning of my new assignment the day before, I had done my homework on the General by asking Lt. Colonel Yates about him. General Vadegrift had been a member of the Marine Corps a long time, having joined the Corp in late 1908. He was well respected in the military community, even among the Army and Navy.

I removed my cap in respect to the General and raised it in his direction. He nodded in response. I placed my cap back on my head, picked up my sea bag and walked up the gangplank and onto the ship. The General greeted me, and I saluted him and shook his hand.

He spoke first. "Thank you, Captain Voigt, for not killing my Marine. He can hold his own, but I think you put the fear of God in him."

I smiled and replied, "Sir, it is a gut reaction to the years of training I have received. I hope the young Marine did not wet his pants."

The General patted me on the shoulder.

One of the General's aides showed me to my quarters. I was a little taken back by the nice accommodations; away from the bulk of Marines hunkered down below. I was sure the tale of my little encounter with the young Marine was making its way around the ship by then.

Our ship and the others following it soon exited the protected cove of Pearl Harbor and headed out into open water. The trip would take us southwest and into Japanese territory. We had a few destroyers that escorted us on both sides of the convoy, and I was sure that there were a few of our subs patrolling just underneath the waterline, as well.

I was due to report to General Vadegrift's office on board the ship by 10:00 AM. I stowed away my gear and made my way up to the top deck. There were plenty of Marines up on top, many of them only on their second voyage on a ship. Most of the Marines on board were probably coming out of Camp Pendleton near San Diego, CA. I decided to tempt fate, working my way in between all the Marines, seeking out the Marine whose throat had met my knife. I was feeling a little bad and wanted to encourage the new Marine and possibly teach him a few techniques on how to attack the Japanese with a knife.

As I walked the deck, I felt like I was walking through an enemy encampment. The ship was now gaining speed and the morning breeze felt good as it whipped my hair.

"Captain Voigt!" was the shout from behind me. I turned and saw the Marine who earlier had an encounter with my knife.

"Captain Voigt, when I called you out earlier, I had no idea who you were. I've been asking around about you, and found out you are a good man to have on board."

I went over to the Marine and reached out my hand in a conciliatory handshake. I asked him his name and hometown.

"Name's Sander Phillips. I'm from Mobile, Alabama." He answered with a smile.

We talked for a long time, and mid-way through our conversation, I noticed a large crowd had gathered around us. There was a lot of whooping and hollering as the Marines got excited over the stories I shared with them about killing Japs. I had to speak in general terms, of course, but the ending was still the same – I killed them.

Before the conversations ended, Sander and some of the other Marines asked me to show them my unique knife techniques. They had all learned how to handle a knife in boot camp but they wanted to hear real life examples. I looked at my watch and realized I was very late to my meeting with General Vandegrift. Even so, I was glad I had met Sander and many of his fellow Marines.

I had not taken five steps when General Vandegrift walked into my path. "Captain Voigt, I observed your conversation with the Marines. Thank you for spending time with them and encouraging them about what they are heading out to face. Let's proceed into my office and talk about your mission."

The General led me into a cramped office containing only a small desk and two chairs. Maps littered the table, something of a familiar sight to me.

"Captain Voigt, your mission, as you know by now, will be a solo mission behind enemy lines. The Japanese are on Guadalcanal and we Marines need to know where they are. The tree canopy is thick on the island and our air patrols cannot see through it. More times than not, they are shot out of the sky by the already famous Japanese Zero fighter plane."

I pulled what looked like a map of the island close to me. I looked at the map for a minute and asked, "General, is this the island of Guadalcanal?"

He confirmed that it was. We talked about where the Marines wanted to come ashore and he concluded that the Japanese most likely used the same beaches.

The General informed me I would be dropped off on a sparsely populated remote island, seven hundred and fifty miles northeast of Guadalcanal, called Pleasant Island. There would be an Army

Douglas DC-2 plane waiting for me, and I would be flown to the island at night, a few days before the planned Marine's incursion onto the island. I was to parachute into the jungle and begin my hunt for the Japanese. With the dense tree canopy, a parachute drop was risky enough, let alone a night drop. I could end up caught on a tree and become a target for Japanese troops. I could also clear the trees but end up landing right in the middle of a Japanese battalion.

I would covertly hunt for the Japanese, only at night. All that jungle training I had received down in South America would come in handy. Once I found the main contingent of Japanese soldiers, and assessed their strength and armament, I would work my way back to a designated beach where a raft would be waiting for me behind some trees. I was to paddle out two miles and a Navy destroyer would pluck me out of the water. The mission sounded like pure insanity, but those were my orders and I was trained to follow orders, regardless of the risk or personal feelings.

The Marines and I continued steaming southwest for three more days and nights. On the morning of Friday, August 1st, our troop transport laid anchor off the coast of Pleasant Island.

A knock sounded on my cabin door. Upon opening it, I found General Vandegrift standing there in the hallway. "Captain Voigt, time to go. We can't risk being anchored here off Pleasant Island very long as these southwest Pacific Ocean waters are patrolled heavily by Japanese submarines."

I replied, "Yes, Sir." I turned, picked up my small backpack and followed the General up to the top deck of the ship. The sun hit my face and I relished its rays, as I knew the next couple of cold nights I would be hunting Japanese soldiers in thick jungle growth on the island of Guadalcanal.

My backpack contents were simple: k-rations, knife, matches, badges, rope and a camouflaged poncho. I had my handgun, five extra ammunition clips and two canteens of water.

I was directed to the left side of the ship where a rope ladder was waiting for me. Peering over the side of ship, I saw a small boat at the base of ladder. Even though the ship was anchored, the sea was choppy, and I felt the effect of the waves as I stood there, ready to climb over the side of the ship and down the ladder.

General Vandegrit put his left hand on my right shoulder and said, "The 1ˢᵗ Marine Division is counting on you to locate those Japs. You do that, and we'll do the rest, basically kill them all."

I turned and replied, "General, you have my word. I will find the Japs and with your permission, take a few out for you."

The General laughed and shook my hand. With that, I was clambering over the side of the ship. By then a large group of Marines had gathered on the deck of the ship.

I firmly gripped the rope ladder with both hands and slowly worked my way down the ladder. The motion of the waves caused the ladder to sway left and right several feet and occasionally forced the ladder to separate from the side of the ship and slam back into its side. I clung to the rope firmly and held on for the ride. I had climbed down a few feet when I looked back up to the top of the ladder. There must have been ten or eleven Marines peering down at me. I continued my way down, feeling I was gaining no momentum. All of a sudden, I heard a familiar voice. It was Sander Phillips.

He hollered down to me, "Captain Voigt, kill some Japs for me!" I somehow managed to free my right hand and raised it up over my head and gave a firm thumbs up gesture. Sander and his fellow Marines yelled out in support.

I finally worked my way down the remaining rungs in the rope ladder and jumped into the waiting boat below. I stowed my backpack and took a seat in the small motor boat. The young Army Corporal operating the boat looked half my age, but he saluted me and introduced himself as Jack Boyd from Miami, FL. I settled in for the ride to shore. Corporal Boyd steered the small boat around the east side of Pleasant Island. I soon saw a small dock and some makeshift buildings just off the beach. We made it to the dock and the young Corporal secured the front and back of the boat to the dock. Corporal Boyd and I then walked up the dock to a parked Army Jeep.

I threw my backpack into the back of the Jeep and hopped into the passenger seat. Corporal Boyd cranked it up and off we went, taking a small road through a patch of palm trees. We traveled on the dirt road for approximately one mile until the dense palm trees disappeared and a large clearing opened up. I saw a small runway and a few buildings built around the edges of the jungle. Backed in under some palm trees was an Army DC-2 plane camouflaged, the plane that would take me over Guadalcanal.

Corporal Boyd pulled the Jeep up to a small wooden building and parked. The structure was on stilts, roughly four feet off the jungle floor. I followed the young Corporal up the stairs and into the building, where I heard a familiar voice. I looked over at a man sitting at a small table, talking on a shortwave radio. He had a headset on, talking aggressively to someone on the other end of the line. I walked further into the small building and the man at the table turned in my direction. I immediately matched that familiar voice with the man's face. It was Tom Beckett. I had not seen Tom in sixteen years. He threw down his headset, rose from his chair and greeted me with a big bear hug.

"Allen, how long has it been my friend?" Tom blurted out.

I replied, "Sixteen years, Tom. Can you believe that? The last time we saw each other was when we graduated from Camp Pine in 1926."

Tom replied, "I didn't know you were coming here, Allen, until late last night. I have been in Army intelligence since the war started. I am also a Captain and in charge of getting you to Guadalcanal in one piece."

I smiled and said, "Tom, I am sure glad the details of this mission are in your hands. Who is flying the plane that takes me over the island?"

Tom laughed and replied, "That would be yours truly. After exiting basic training, I took flying lessons courtesy of the Army.

I have been flying for fifteen years. Corporal Boyd and I flew in here three weeks ago, not knowing why. That reason became very clear last night when I found out you were coming and the details surrounding your mission. You are one crazy soldier, Allen."

I smiled and asked, "Anywhere on this little island to grab a bite to eat?"

Corporal Boyd instantly commented, "Yes, Sir. The locals cook for us."

"Lead the way," I replied.

Tom said he would join us in a little while and returned to his desk and short wave radio. As I left the small building, I heard the voice on the other end of the radio say, "Tonight is our only window of time over the next four days. The visibility over the island will be poor after tonight. The last thing we need to happen is to drop Captain Voigt into the middle of a Japanese battalion."

I thought to myself that the mission had to be one of the craziest things I would attempt during my sixteen years in the Army. Regardless, that was my mission and I was ready and willing to do my part in the coming invasion of Guadalcanal.

Corporal Boyd and I walked across to the other side of the small airfield, an area where some local island inhabitants were cooking over an open fire. Whatever they were cooking really smelled good. I had worked up a large appetite and did not know when I would get another chance to eat again before my jump.

As we approached the locals cooking, Corporal Boyd looked at me and said, "Let me do all the talking."

What happened next was exactly the opposite. Corporal Boyd never said a word, he only pointed at what looked like chicken breasts cooking over the fire. The woman smiled at us as she placed two chicken breasts on each of our plates. We worked our way past the makeshift grill and procured some grilled vegetables that I did not recognize.

I was surprised to find an Army water container nearby and some cups. I laid my plate of hot food on the top of the container and filled up a large cup of water. I then walked over to a large palm tree and sat down underneath it, resting my back against it. Corporal Boyd soon joined me.

We ate for a bit until Corporal Boyd spoke up. "Captain Voigt, have you participated in any other missions, like the one you are about to take, during your time in the Army?"

"Corporal, all I can say is there have been a few," I replied.

He was quick with a response. "Tell me about them."

I looked in his direction, smiled and just shook my head from side to side and said, "Nope."

He kept coming at me, though, asking me, "Have you killed any Japs?"

I answered him again, "Yep, and a few Germans, too."

His mouth dropped open and his eyes got big. Before he could ask me another question, I simply raised my hand up and waived it, signaling no more questions. He looked very disappointed and sat back against the palm tree, finishing his lunch.

There was a nice island breeze hitting my face and blowing my hair as I took my last few bites of chicken and mystery vegetables. I thought of Alice and my parents, wondering what they were doing, but knowing they were certain to be worried about me.

The thoughts of Alice and home were interrupted, when all of a sudden two F4U Corsairs flew over our heads and circled the airfield. I rose to my feet in awe of the single engine fighter with curved wings. I had heard about the new fighter but had never seen one until then. The two fighter planes completed their wide arc and landed right after each other on the small runway. The planes taxied off the runway and into a shaded area and turned off their radial engines. I walked in the direction of the planes, hoping to get a close-up look at them. Both planes were painted light blue. The sun really bounced off the paint, almost blinding me.

When I walked closer to the planes, one of the pilots walked toward me and asked me, "Is this Pleasant Island?"

I answered, "I sure hope so, because that is where I am supposed to be."

The pilot laughed and as he approached me, reached out his hand to shake mine and said, "I'm Major Boyington. We just flew in from the escort carrier, USS Long Island. We are scheduled to escort some Army DC-2 plane to an unknown destination."

I saluted him and shook his hand saying, "It looks like both of us have been in the service for our country for a few years. My name's Captain Voigt, a United States Army veteran of sixteen years."

He laughed and replied, "No need to salute me, Mr. Army."

The other pilot had by then joined us, and upon hearing my name, he blurted out, "I know you!" as he looked at me with a big look of excitement on his face.

The young pilot continued, "You were that guy who shot down that Japanese plane at Pearl Harbor with only a rifle. I was stationed at Wheeler Field and heard all about it. You are a legend back at Pearl Harbor."

I simply smiled and tried to change the subject by asking the two pilots for a look around their planes. The young pilot introduced himself as Lt. Jeremy Savage and that he was from a small town in middle Georgia named Macon. Lt. Savage showed me around his plane, pointing out the .50 caliber machine guns in the wings and the slope of the wings. He even let me climb up on the wing and peer inside the cockpit. I was amazed by the number of gauges and levers.

As I worked my way off the curved wing of the Corsair, I heard my name shouted across the airfield. "Voigt, get over here! It's time to work out the mission details."

The voice was that of Tom Beckett. He was standing in the doorway of the small building that housed the short wave radio. Major Boyington was standing in the doorway with Tom. I hurried off the large wing and followed Pilot Savage to the building where Tom and the Major were waiting.

As we walked across the airfield, my mind raced as I thought about my pending night drop; a drop I had not made in a long time.

I would soon be the only American soldier on the entire island of Guadalcanal. Talk about being outnumbered! However, I was very confident in my training and knew it had provided me the tools needed to conduct the mission. Pilot Savage and I reached the building and I was the first to enter. A small table I had not noticed earlier was in the middle of the room, covered with maps. Tom was back at the radio, but Major Boyington was sitting at the table studying one of the maps.

When I took my seat at the table, Tom turned in my direction and said, "Voigt, do you remember SGT Nolan from Camp Pine?"

I replied, "How can I ever forget him, Tom?"

Tom replied, "I recently found out he passed away in upstate New York from a heart attack. Rumor is, he tried to get the Army to let him fight overseas, but he was turned away due to his age. He sure was a tough old man, but you have to respect his training methods and getting us prepared for this war."

I paused for a minute and replied, "You're right, Tom. I may have cursed SGT Nolan during that first couple of weeks at basic training, but looking back on it now, he knew what he was doing."

Soon, we were all seated at a small table in the middle of the room. I assumed that Major Boyington would lead the mission planning session, simply due to his rank, but that was not the case. Tom led off the meeting by sharing specifics about the maps on the table. As he talked about the map showing the island of Guadalcanal, I saw a red 'X' drawn on the southern end of the island. I concluded that was most likely my designated drop zone. Tom confirmed for us that the name of the invasion of Guadalcanal was called "Operation Watchtower." The invasion date was set for Thursday, August 7, 1942; the 1st Marine Division would storm the island.

Tom outlined a complete walk-through of the pending invasion. He informed us about the number of Marines involved, transport ships, supporting Navy ships and also estimated number of days to take the island, he finally got to why I was there and the details of my mission.

"Allen tonight you will parachute onto the island of Guadalcanal. The number of ships that will be steaming this way in the next seventy-two hours will erase any secrecy left in this mission. Major Boyington and Lt. Savage will escort you and me over the island. You are scheduled to jump at 0200 hours at an elevation of 15,000 feet. Navy planes have flown over the island over the last two weeks at various altitudes. There has been no sign of Japanese troop movements on the island. We know they are there because the Australian army has island-watchers and they witnessed the Japanese disembarking earlier this year."

He continued, "After exiting the plane, I will follow the Corsairs to an awaiting aircraft carrier approximately one hundred and fifty miles northeast of the island. You will be on your own for three days. Your mission is to scout the Japanese defense positions. The location of the enemy will be vital to a successful 1st Marine Division landing on August 7th. On the third day, you need to make it to the southeast corner of the island. Wait until dark and then scan the horizon for a red light near the waterline that flashes every fifteen seconds. The light will emanate from a partially submerged Navy submarine, scheduled to extract you. You can find a raft or you will have to swim out to the sub no later than 0400 hours, which will be on the morning of the fourth day. After that, the submarine is ordered to leave the area. Your Japanese positioning update has to reach the submarine and you are the only source of Jap positioning that the Marines have."

I understood what was expected of me and I had been trained well. Marine lives depended on my successful three-day mission and communication back to Navy personnel.

The four of us continued to talk for another hour as Major Boyington and Lt. Savage went over the flight plan and explained that if we were attacked from the air, they would both spin off and fight any threat from Japanese fighter planes. In the event ground forces or naval gunfire fired upon us, we would simply climb to a higher flight elevation. If we were too close to my jump point and an attack became too intense, Tom would keep our plane on course and

I would need to prepare to jump at any moment, regardless of where we were over the island.

Before leaving the building, I secured my backpack, which would contain the only supplies I would have over the next seventy-two hours. I had two canteens of water, seven clips of ammunition for my handgun, bandages, antiseptic ointment, three grenades, a few packs of K-rations and D-rations and binoculars.

As I was completing the inventory of my backpack, Major Boyington walked over to the corner of the room where I was and put his hand on my back. "Captain Voigt, when was the last time you actually jumped out of an airplane?"

I turned and said, "It's been a few years."

Major Boyington replied, "What makes this jump interesting for you is the canopy tree line. When I was helping the Chinese, as a member of the Flying Tigers, I had to bail out after a Japanese Zero had shot up my engine. My parachute opened fine and I had a few thousand feet to fall; unfortunately, all I saw below me were trees. As the ground rushed up to me, I was hoping I would fall between some trees, allowing me to hit the ground safely, without being suspended on branches and bait for Japanese soldiers below. When my feet hit the tree line, I was not very lucky, however. I crashed through some large branches, finally snagging my parachute on some of them. I was left dangling about thirty feet above the ground. Thankfully, it was close to 1600 hours, so there was plenty of daylight left for me to see if anyone was approaching, but, more importantly, I could see to cut myself out of my parachute. Cutting yourself out of a parachute is not easy, but let me give you some advice I did not receive before my hang-up. In the event you are snagged on some trees and too high in the tree to simply cut your cords and fall, try to get some momentum and swing toward the tree and grab a hold of it. You can then cut yourself out of your harness and work yourself down to the ground safely."

I smiled and replied, "Major Boyington, unlike northern China, the island of Guadalcanal has palm trees and I should avoid being caught on any branches. Unfortunately, I will be jumping at night, though, and my visibility will be poor. Don't get me wrong, where I'm jumping, I'm glad it's dark, but if anything goes wrong with my jump, I'll be in lots of trouble."

We both laughed. I threw my backpack over my right shoulder, checked my Colt 45 and walked out of the building. By that time in the day, daylight was beginning to die in the western skyline. I knew the time was getting close for me to board the Army DC-2 and prepare to jump onto an island filled with Japanese soldier's intent on killing Americans.

I walked toward the plane. There was a cool breeze blowing, enough for me to pull up the collar on my shirt, hoping to stay warm. Corporal Boyd soon met me, carrying my parachute and said, "I packed your chute myself, Sir."

"How many chutes have you packed in your lifetime?" I replied.

He smiled and replied. "Seven, but that includes the four I had to pack in basic training."

I swallowed hard and took the chute from the young Corporal.

By that time, Tom had come over to the plane carrying his own parachute and said, "Allen, wheels up in thirty minutes. We have about a three hour flight to the island, leaving a very small window of time to get there."

I threw my backpack onto the plane through the open door. I found a nearby palm tree and sat down with my back pressed up against the trunk of the tree so I could collect my thoughts before stepping into that small plane.

The cool wind I had felt earlier returned and blew against my face and hair, giving me a chance to close my eyes and take my mind to another place, even if it meant for only a few minutes. I tuned out the talking between Tom and Corporal Boyd. I thought of Alice and wondered where she might be at that very moment. I was tired of being apart from her for so long. We both knew our roles in the military and were committed to them, but that did not make it any easier. Sitting there, I realized I had not written or spoken to my parents back in New York for over six months. I assumed they knew I was still alive simply due to the fact they had not received a Western Union telegram announcing my death. Regardless, I felt bad for not reaching out to them more often. I had been away from home for years but thought back to what my father had told me at the train station when I joined the Army in 1926, "Learn all you can, fight as hard as you can and come home to your Mom and me."

I must have dozed off for a minute or two because I was suddenly jolted awake by the noise of the DC-2's two plane engines cranking up. It was time to go. I hopped to my feet, dusted off my pants and walked over to the waiting plane.

Tom was at the controls and checking all the gauges. Corporal Boyd was checking the tires and looking for any leaks that might be noticeable on the outside of the engines. The noise of those two engines was incredible as I crawled up into the waiting plane and worked my way into one of the two seats behind the cockpit.

Tom turned back in my direction and said, "Here we go, the moment of truth."

The DC-2 had been positioned between several palm trees so Tom had to be very careful while he maneuvered out onto the runway. He revved the engines slightly and the plane began to move forward and to the left. As I looked out the left side of the plane's window, I noticed the proximity of the plane's left wing to the surrounding trees was very close. Tom managed to miss all of them and we soon hit the open grass surrounding the runway. I looked out to my right and saw Major Boyington and Lt. Savage in their F4U Corsairs, with the engines running and their plane's single propellers turning rapidly, kicking up the surrounding dirt on the makeshift runway. Even though the sun had set a few hours earlier, the light of the moon illuminated everything.

Major Boyington had his cockpit window open and he waved Tom to precede first down the runway. Tom worked the DC-2 unto the runway and stopped the plane for a moment. He looked back at me again.

"Allen, we might not get much of a chance to converse after we take off. There is no telling what we might encounter when we fly southwest in the direction of the island. So many Marine lives are counting on you to find them a safe entrance onto the beach. They need to offload supplies and be ready to fight. Godspeed my friend."

Tom then turned and revved the DC-2's engines to full power and let go of the brakes. The plane lurched forward. We gained speed and blew by the two Corsairs, which were waiting to take off after us. Tom worked to lift the plane off the dirt runway. There was a large clump of palm trees ahead of us, getting closer by the second. Tom managed to get the plane off in plenty of time, leaving at least a few yards between the tree line and us.

It was not long after the plane lifted off, that we cleared Pleasant Island and were flying over open water. Tom and I were soon joined by Major Boyington and Lt. Savage, as their Corsairs flew up on each side of our plane. The moon's brightness allowed me to see both pilots clearly through the small windows in the plane. For the first hour of our flight, the Corsairs flew next to us. It gave us a sense of security knowing they were there and ready to combat any attack from the air.

Tom had been correct; there was no conversation between us during the fight so far. I could only imagine the concentration it took to pilot the plane, and avoiding drifting into one of the Corsairs in mid-flight.

We had flown about ninety minutes when the Corsairs split off from us and banked hard right and hard left. Over the DC-2's radio crackled Major Boyington. "Tom, we are going to dive down to the waterline to check out what we think are Japanese destroyers below. We will be back, continue on your course."

Tom replied over the plane's radio, "Roger that, we are approximately one hour from reaching the island."

Clouds then covered the moon, and it became very dark. It felt like we were flying into a black hole. Tom's cockpit navigation equipment showed us flying due west. I started to visualize jumping out of the plane and landing safely on the jungle floor. I would pull out my handgun as I neared the ground. In the event there were Japanese soldiers waiting to shoot me. I would rain lead down on them first.

We flew for another forty-five minutes with no visible air support. Suddenly a large explosion went off about one hundred yards to the right of our plane. The entire plane shook violently. It was anti-aircraft fire.

Tom shouted back in my direction, "Allen, we're over Guadalcanal and taking fire from the island. I need you to jump now!"

I had my parachute on since boarding the plane. I reached for my backpack and strapped it to my body. Another anti-aircraft explosion went off nearby. It was time to jump. I opened the right side door of the plane. Our exact location over the island was a mystery. I crept to the edge of the door, gave Tom a nod goodbye and jumped.

Chapter 9

RETRIBUTION

"We sleep safely at night because rough men stand ready
to visit violence on those who would harm us."
Winston Churchill

My body tumbled end over end after I exited the plane, thousands of feet above the island of Guadalcanal. As my body cartwheeled, I caught a glimpse of Tom and the DC-2 he was piloting, when he banked the plane hard left, in an effort to clear the island. Although I was not sure of my altitude when I jumped from the plane, I did know that I had to get my parachute opened before I slammed into the ground. I reached for the ripcord to release my parachute, but the force of my freefall made it very hard for me to grab it.

While trying to grab the ripcord, a loud explosion went off somewhere above and behind my right shoulder. The sound was deafening, leaving me unable to hear the rush of the wind, or anything else, for that matter.

Despite my rapid descent, uncontrollable cartwheeling, and concussion from the blast, I somehow managed to find the ripcord and pull it. The parachute fully deployed and corrected my body position so my feet were now beneath me. The opening of the chute slowed my descent, and I was finally able to determine my position in relation to the ground.

The simple fact that the Japs had seen the plane and fired upon it, meant they could probably see my large parachute descending to the ground. My ears were affected by the concussion of the blast, but my eyes were fine. I caught a flash of light, followed by an explosion, out in front of me. The illumination from the explosion revealed Tom and his plane. The tail of the plane was gone and the plane was banking hard to the left, plummeting rapidly toward the jungle floor. Tom evidently had not been able to clear the island before being hit by Japanese anti-aircraft fire. The descent of Tom's plane outpaced mine; I had a front-row seat to the horrific event. The plane hit the tree line and skirted the tops of the palm trees before disappearing into the jungle below. I waited for an explosion but never saw one.

I tried to direct my descent, in order to ideally land in between some trees. As I fell, I just hoped my parachute did not snag on a tree. Managing to clear the trees, the ground quickly met my feet. The force of hitting the ground caused me to roll to my left. After lying on the jungle floor for a second, I instinctively knew I was not safe, so I sat up. I did not appear to have broken any bones in the fall. I checked my side and felt my handgun and the three clips of ammunition on my belt. I still had my backpack. I was very fortunate.

I rose to my feet and scanned 360 degrees, looking for any Japs with rifles pointed at me. While it was difficult to see in the darkness, I could tell I was in the clear for a little while, at least. I detached the parachute, stepped out of it, and then gathered it up from the jungle floor and carried it over to some nearby palm trees. I then laid it on the ground and covered it with dead palm branches in an effort to hide it from any passing Jap soldiers.

I then leaned against a palm tree and weighed my options. In my mind, what was originally supposed to be a mission to locate Japanese soldiers in advance of the 1st Marine Division's assault on the beaches of Guadalcanal had now turned into a search and rescue mission for Tom Beckett. I figured by finding Tom, I would find the Japs. My friend Tom, whom I had entered basic training with, was either dead or severely injured in his downed plane; scores of Japanese soldiers must now be descending on his location. I had to find him and rescue him if he was alive.

I looked down at my watch, the same one I had acquired after exiting basic training so many years ago. The time read 3:15 AM, which meant the sun would be up in less than three hours. To have a chance of finding Tom before the Japs did, I had to search throughout the night. It was difficult to determine from the air exactly where Tom had crashed his plane. My best guess was that it was due north from where I had landed.

I pulled out my compass, which told me I was already facing north. I looked briefly over my backpack's inventory and confirmed that all my supplies were still inside. I then took a quick sip from one of my canteens and attached my backpack securely to my shoulders and back. Lastly, I took out my handgun, chambered a round, and started walking in a northern direction as quietly as I could.

As I walked, I felt like every step was echoing across the island. The jungle vegetation was very thick, and dead palm branches and leaves littered the ground. The darkness would help me spot any possible fire from Tom's wreckage. I also looked for debris from the plane or trees that might have been broken by the plane's descent. I glanced again at my watch; it was now 4:05 AM and I had yet to find anything that led me to Tom and his downed plane.

Soon I came to a clearing with a perfect view of the beach on the north side of the island. The moon illuminated the entire area and reflected off the water below. I used my new vantage point to scan thoroughly for any signs of Tom's plane. I could not stand there long, due to the risk of being seen, so I worked my way back into the thick cover of the tree line and continued walking north. I walked for another thirty minutes and finally came to a large creek that appeared to run to the ocean. The moon gave me a little light, but it was still hard to find a suitable crossing. I had no choice but to wade across. While I had no idea the creek depth, I hoped it would not be any higher than my waistline. I took off my web belt holding my handgun, grenades and a canteen of water. I wrapped the belt across my chest and right shoulder, then took my backpack off and held it high above my head.

Before stepping into the slow-moving creek, I peered into the darkness as best I could and looked across the creek for any sign of Japs. I saw nothing suspicious, so I stepped into the creek. The water was cold, but tolerable. I had about thirty yards to cross to the other side. As I worked my way across, the water crept up my body, inch by inch. By the time I was halfway across, the water was a good two inches above my belt line. My pace had slowed due to the depth of the creek. I continued to move forward.

I soon felt the bank on the other side of the creek rise slightly. After working through the water for another ten yards, I finally emerged completely out of the water and was on the other side of the creek. I walked to a large tree and sat down. I removed my boots and socks, rung my socks out and hung them on a low hanging branch. I did not remove my pants or shirt; they would have to dry on my body, and I wanted to avoid mosquito bites anyway. There was no way I could build a fire in order to dry out my socks and shoes; they would have to dry as best they could in the night air.

I was relieved that I had not run across any Japs yet, but frustrated that I had not found Tom. I felt my eyes getting heavy from lack of sleep. I had not slept since the night before. There was no way I could sleep now. I had to find Tom and any sign of the Japanese. I looked at my watch; it was 5:05 AM. I opted to stay where I was until daybreak. I listened intently for any sounds. I tried very hard to tune out the noise of the creek running toward the ocean, but it was too overpowering.

By 5:45 AM, the sunrise was near and I had to find cover and, more importantly, any sign of Tom or his plane. My socks were not completely dry, but I put them back on my feet, anyway. My boots were still water-logged but back on my feet they went, and I made sure to pull the laces tight. I rose to my feet and walked due north, following the creek line. I soon found where the creek emptied out into the ocean. The sun was breaking over the horizon. To my pleasant surprise, a large tree had fallen across the creek and formed a perfect bridge for me to cross back over into the dense jungle.

Within minutes, I was back under the thick tree canopy and working south this time. As I walked, I opened a D-ration and two Hershey candy bars. I washed them down with some water from my canteen. I checked my compass and adjusted my direction slightly to make sure I was still walking due south. Not long after placing my canteen back in my backpack, I thought I heard voices, Japanese voices, specifically. I stopped walking and dropped down to one knee. I pulled out my binoculars and scanned the area to my left, right and directly in front of me. The dense Guadalcanal jungle made it very hard to discern Japanese soldiers from the trees. I did not hear the voices again, so I continued my journey south quietly at a very slow, steady pace.

I walked another ten minutes and then paused to look through my binoculars. This time my eyes caught something ahead of me, a bright reflection bouncing off the early morning sun's rays that were piercing through the trees. I shifted my position slightly, hoping to minimize the sun's reflection off whatever was laying there on the jungle floor. With the binoculars, I was able to see that the object reflecting the sun's rays was a badly damaged plane. The aircraft was clearly an American-built DC-2, Tom's plane. I crept closer, hugging the jungle floor with my knees and elbows. The voices I had heard earlier were gone, and there were no signs of the Japanese Army. I finally worked my way to the plane. Instead of whispering Tom's name, I chose to go around to the front of the plane and see if Tom was still in the cockpit. The plane had landed hard, shearing off all its landing gear, and leaving the plane flat on its belly. The co-pilot's window was shattered, but Tom's side was intact. I peered in the broken window but there was no sign of Tom.

Where was he? I worked my way around to the side of the plane, carefully pulling back a few palm branches that had wrapped around the fuselage in the crash. The entire rear section of the plane was gone, and the very same door I had jumped out of hours earlier, was mangled and barely hanging on its hinges. I placed my backpack on the ground and, with minimal effort, was able to push the door open far enough for me to wedge myself into the plane. A quick scan of the middle section of the plane yielded no signs of Tom.

I then thought perhaps he had jumped from the plane before it crashed, but judging by the view I had of the plane going down, he would not have been able to jump. The angle of the dive and the low altitude would not have allowed him to get out of the plane in time. He had to have gone down with the plane. He was not ejected upon impact, as his pilot window was intact.

I took a closer look in the cockpit and saw a fair amount of blood on Tom's seat. I also saw a blood trail on the instrument panel. Suddenly it became clear to me: the Japanese voices that I heard earlier, the fact that Tom was missing, and the blood in the cockpit – all pointed to Tom's capture by the Japanese. They had to have heard the crash and were then able to track where the plane had landed.

I remembered the conversation I had with Major Yates back in Switzerland about how the Japanese Army savagely mistreated the Chinese civilians and prisoners of war. Tom did not have a fighting chance if I did not get to him in time. I carefully backed out of the plane and began to search for clues indicating which direction the Japs had headed. I searched around the front of the plane, and what I found surprised me. I had expected to find shell casings and boot prints that might point me in the right direction, but what I discovered was something entirely different.

Lying on the ground were United States minted pennies, every few feet, extending out from the front of the plane; most likely dropped by Tom as he walked away from the plane. This told me he was alive and had enough thought to drop the pennies. I now had a lead on how to find him. I also noticed a fair amount of blood on the ground extending along the same line as the pennies dropped. Tom was wounded from the crash, but the blood could also be the result of wounds inflicted by his captors.

I secured my backpack, took a count of how may bullets and grenades I had and headed out in search of Tom. My watch read 7:25 AM. As I walked away from the plane, I continued to scan the ground for the dropped pennies. I must have walked about thirty feet from the downed plane before I found there were no more pennies on the ground. The direction I had gone in during those brief thirty feet was northwest. I crouched down to one knee and scanned the ground for any signs of recent disturbance. There was no way to determine how many Japs had Tom, but regardless, there should be some sign of foot traffic on the jungle floor. I located two sets of drag marks, most likely caused by Tom's boots. The drag marks were sporadic, mainly caused by the rough terrain.

The jungle floor was a combination of dirt, grass, fallen branches, small gnarly bushes and other vegetation. I looked hard at the ground in order to follow the drag marks, but at the same time, I tried to stay aware of any Japs that might be hiding out in pillboxes or simply encamped nearby. The drag marks meant Tom was passed out from his injuries or had been knocked out by the end of a Japanese rifle butt. Either way, it did not look good for Tom.

In two and a half days, the Marines would be storming the beaches of Guadalcanal. They were counting on me to determine which beachhead was the safest. I would not leave Tom behind to face a certain death by the Japanese. The limited time I had already been on the island, looking for Tom, showed me that the Japs were not populating the south or northeast corners of the island. Those beaches and surrounding area were clear. As I looked to rescue Tom, I would most certainly locate the Japanese and best determine how they were fortified. The Japs knew the Americans were coming but did not know when. Our Navy had been decimated at Pearl Harbor and the Army was just now ramping up in both personnel and equipment. I was sure the Japs figured they had lots of time before we would beat down their door.

By 9:15 AM, I had walked deep into the jungle, still keeping my northwest direction. The drag marks suddenly stopped and there was a small pool of blood in the area where the trail ran cold. I had nothing left with which to follow Tom and his captors. I sat down on a nearby log and drank from my last full canteen. I had emptied the first one shortly after jumping. Fresh water would be a priority for me soon. I took out the only map I had of the island and reviewed it. The island of Guadalcanal was narrow and long, running northwest to southeast. I estimated I had landed near the southern end of the island but by now was positioned somewhere in the middle of the island. I decided to continue in a westerly direction because I concluded that if I had a prisoner, I would take him to a command post located deep inside the island versus near the beaches.

I was putting my map away in my backpack when I suddenly heard yelling in Japanese, coming from in front of me, due west. The words I heard alarmed me because they solidified that the Japs definitely had Tom prisoner. I clearly understood the words yelled across the jungle. The one-sided conversation was a mixture of Japanese and English.

"Walk faster, you American scum! We will beat you to death if you stop and bury you where you fall!"

I fell to the ground and flattened my body hard against the jungle floor. I estimated I was less than one hundred yards away from Tom. I listened hard for any movement before I got up to one knee. Once I felt comfortable that the Japs and Tom were again walking in a westerly direction, I rose slowly to my feet. The group was now approximately eighty yards away. There were six Japanese soldiers surrounding Tom. His clothes were tattered and bloody but he was on his feet. Tom was noticeably dragging his right leg, which forced him to walk at a very slow pace.

The sun was now high in the sky and the humidity on the island of Guadalcanal was steamy at best. The time I spent in South America had prepared me for this type of environment, but that was a while ago. If anything, I knew how to walk quietly through the jungle landscape without being detected. I also knew how to forage for food and how to find safe drinking water.

Without risking alerting the six Japs that had Tom, or the rest of the Jap army stationed on Guadalcanal, I chose to keep my distance for the time being and follow a good distance behind. This approach served two purposes. First, it would allow me to rescue Tom under the cover of darkness when the time was right. Second, it would permit me to locate where the large contingent of Japs were encamped.

Tom was really struggling to keep pace with the Jap soldiers. Each time Tom stopped or fell, a Jap hit him in the back or the side of his head with his rifle butt in an attempt to drive him forward.

After following Tom and his captors for over two hours, we came upon a large valley sparsely populated with trees. All around the valley stood small wooden buildings and tents. I finally had located the large contingent of Jap troops. I estimated that we were at least ten miles in from the beaches I had seen earlier that morning. The island was very large at approximately ninety miles long and twenty-five miles across.

Based on what I saw, there was enough lodging in that valley to support a Japanese Army of at least five to eight thousand men. The information Tom had shared with me earlier was that the Japanese had landed on Guadalcanal in May 1942. Over the last ninety days, based on the looks of it, they must have been busy setting up camp. This had to be a staging area, because no army in its right mind would have all its troops exposed like that, being subject to potential strafing or bombing runs by American planes. The Japs knew they had hit us hard at Pearl Harbor and because of that, they knew they had time on their side and in their minds; America would not be coming after them anytime soon.

I positioned myself low to the ground, amongst a large section of brush. I carefully concealed myself in the event there were Japs walking by or scanning the ridgeline where I was positioned. I pulled out my binoculars and tracked Tom's movements as one particular Jap soldier pushed him down the hill. He stuck out because he was a little taller than the rest of the soldiers. I decided I would kill him first.

I was fortunate Tom was not been taken too deep into the camp. Consequently, I was able to keep my binoculars trained on him the entire time. He was moved into a small wooden building, most likely a senior officer's quarters. I figured this was probably where they were taking him for questioning.

I was exhausted but could not afford to doze off for one second in the event Tom was relocated. I would never be able to find him if that were the case. I kept my binoculars trained on the building. I was too far away too hear any talking, yelling or screaming coming from the building. I was close enough, though, to hear any potential gunshots.

I never moved my body position once over the next five hours. I only had two or three ounces of water left in my reserve canteen. What I did have was plenty of ammo and grenades in the event I had to use them.

The sun had begun to set in the west, directly in front of me. The glare rendered my binoculars almost useless, but I could not move and risk being spotted. I had to keep my concealed position.

Suddenly, I heard Jap soldiers conversing, and it sounded like they were very close to me. They stirred up the dirt nearby and some of it drifted in my direction, covering a portion of the binoculars. The Jap soldiers were within two feet of where I was laying on the ground. The only thing working to my advantage was that the brush concealing me was thick.

I could not tell how many Japs were standing practically on top of me. They seemed at ease, conversing and smoking cigarettes. What I gathered from their conversation was that Tom did not have long to live.

"That American pilot is tough, I will give him that. Why was he flying solo over the island, knowing we were here and likely to shoot him down?" asked one soldier.

"Our forward anti-aircraft cannons were definitely positioned correctly. If any more American planes try to fly over the island, they will meet the same fate," a second soldier stated definitively.

A third Jap complained, "I know the Captain is trying to extract information from him, but so far he has not been able to get anything out of him. If this pilot does not talk soon and reveal why he was over the island, the Captain is going to bury him up to his neck and let the jungle animals eat him."

"I bet he was flying over the island to take pictures of our location and troop strength. Those Americans do not have a chance of winning this war. We defeated the Chinese, took the Philippines in less than a week and destroyed the American Navy at Pearl Harbor," claimed another Jap soldier.

I then heard the Jap soldiers walking away and decided they were most likely on a night patrol. They knew the Americans would come eventually, and I am sure they had patrols all over the island and planes flying miles out to sea in search of encroaching American ships.

By the time the Jap soldiers were out of earshot, it was dark. I took one more look through my binoculars but it was hard to see anything in the dimly lit night. The thick jungle foliage obstructed the moon.

I knew if I somehow were able to free Tom from his captors, we would be hunted down by hundreds of Japanese troops and would not have an exit strategy for getting off the island. I had been on the island not yet twenty-four hours. The sub would not reach the southeast coast of the island for another forty-eight hours. My only chance of getting Tom and me off the island was to wait one more night. My plan was to secure Tom the next evening, after midnight. We would move as fast as we could to the extraction site, conceal ourselves just off the beach as best we could, and wait until nightfall. We would then watch for the red light from the sub to appear and swim out to it.

Rescuing Tom and getting him to the extraction site was going to be hard enough, but if he was hurt as badly as it looked before he entered the building, he was most likely going to be in even worse shape by the time we tried to escape. By that point, he may have endured torture by the Japs, or he may not even be conscious or ambulatory. Regardless, I had to get him off this island.

I rolled the dice and opted to use that night to scout more of the island. I decided to travel light. I took out three additional clips of ammo from my backpack and made sure my knife was attached to my belt. I picked up the empty canteens, hoping to find some fresh water.

I covered my backpack with leaves and dead branches and then stood up. My legs were sore from lying on the ground for so long. I scanned all around me and did not see anyone in my vicinity, so I left my secure spot and worked my way back into the darkness of the jungle. After looking at my compass, I decided to walk in a large circle to be sure I could find my way back to the valley. I started out walking northwest with the idea of eventually moving to my right throughout the night, changing directions approximately every five miles. It was hard to determine distance in the jungle, but my training told me my walking pace and time traveled could help me gauge, with some accuracy, how far I had traveled. Moving through this deep jungle, while trying to avoid Jap patrols was going to be a challenge.

I figured I had a good seven to eight hours to work my way back to where I had hidden my backpack. I would then have to reposition myself before the sun broke the horizon. Carefully, I walked through the jungle, making as little noise as possible. I had walked about three miles when I heard what sounded like rushing water. I continued in the direction of the sound and found a small waterfall. The water was running over some large rocks, flowing down a hill into a running stream. I was pleasantly surprised to find this source of water and figured it was probably going to be my only chance to fill my canteens. I surveyed the area as best I could before approaching the waterfall. The noise of the rushing water erased any chance I had of hearing a Jap trying to sneak up behind me. I walked up to the waterfall, and let it run over my head. It was refreshing and it was good to clean my face, as I had not showered since I was on the ship with the Marines. I then cupped my hands and drank my fill of fresh water.

I filled both canteens and secured them to my belt. I left the waterfall and decided it was time to turn to the right, keeping a circular movement. I looked at my watch; it was 12:47 AM.

As I walked, I heard what sounded like an aircraft landing. According to the maps of Guadalcanal, I had seen back on Pleasant Island, there was an airfield on the northwest side of the island. I had to be close to that airfield. The Japs had active control of the airfield already, and that would pose a problem for the Marines and the Navy.

I made my way closer to the sound of aircraft and saw some lights piercing the darkness. Soon the airfield was right in front of me. I knelt down next to a large tree and counted three Japanese Zero fighter planes parked near the runway. Another one landed as I was observing. The good news, I guess, was that there were not a lot of Japanese aircraft parked at the airfield; the bad news was that the Japanese controlled the airfield. I watched the pilot of the recently landed plane, position his plane over by the other three Zeros. He soon exited his plane and walked over to a nearby building. He entered and shut the door behind him. The building was likely used for housing a radio room and spare aircraft parts.

With the four Japanese aircraft sitting idle, less than fifty yards away from my location, I chose to take full advantage of my opportunity. I made my way around the runway to the backside of the four fighter planes and approached the first one. It would be hard to inflict major damage to the planes with only my knife, but I wanted to do as much damage as possible. Even if the most I could do was to delay the planes from taking off in the next forty-eight hours, that would still give Tom and me a fighting chance at avoiding any aircraft when we made our trek to the extraction site. The Japanese were carelessly confident and no guards were around.

I punctured all the tires on each of the four planes. I also cut each of the planes' fuel lines and a few hydraulic cables. I made it back into the jungle and headed toward the valley where Tom was imprisoned. It was now 2:17 AM. I had less than four hours to get back.

Over the next three and half hours, as I worked my way through the jungle, I came across evidence of prior encampments by Jap soldiers. The evidence consisted of burned-out campfires surrounded by scatterings of empty bowls and uneaten rice on the jungle floor.

Less than three miles from where I started, I came across a clearing that had a Japanese Type 11, 75mm anti-aircraft cannon. "Was it the anti-aircraft cannon that shot down Tom's plane?" I was surprised there were no Jap soldiers guarding the large weapon. "Where were they?"

Once I got closer to the gun, however, I spotted a Jap sleeping on the ground. I carefully walked up to him and pulled out my knife. I then collapsed my full weight on top of him and rammed my knife into his heart, all the way up to the knife's handle. I covered his mouth with my left hand, to muffle any screams.

I could not risk leaving him and have him be discovered the next morning in a pool of blood. I pulled his body off into the jungle about thirty yards and covered his body with brush. While placing the last bit of brush on his body, I sensed someone behind me. My instinct told me to duck down and turn, so I did. My instincts proved correct. I felt a rush of air as a samurai sword sliced through the air where my head had been. I rushed the Japanese soldier wielding the sword and tackled him to the ground. The sudden tackle forced him to drop his sword. He tried to grab it, but it had landed a few feet from him. My right hand held the knife, dripping with blood from the Jap I had just killed. I was not going to let go of that knife, so with my left arm and knees, I tried to pin the Jap to the ground. Unsuccessful, we wrestled in the darkness. I attempted to stab him, but missed each time.

The Jap soldier managed to push me away for a brief moment. He jumped to his feet and immediately reached for his sidearm. I could not risk him firing a shot; not wanting to alarm any Japs nearby, let alone be shot myself. I drew back my knife and with all my strength, rammed it into the Jap soldier's right side, enough to halt his progression. He instantly dropped his sidearm and with his right hand, reached for the knife in his side. I was not done, however.

I picked up the samurai sword that was lying on the ground and administered the fatal blow to his upper right chest. I rammed the blade all the way through his body. I watched his eyes go dim, and he fell to the ground. I was exhausted. I collapsed to my knees, thanking God for sparing my life.

I took a moment to catch my breath and assessed the situation. I had to hide this Jap, as well, but time was not on my side. I pulled my knife from the Jap's side and extracted the samurai sword from his chest. I decided to cover his body right where he lay, with his sword next to him. The sword would have been a nice extra weapon to carry with me but I decided to leave it lying next to the dead Jap. I covered his body and sword but confiscated his sidearm, placing it inside my right boot. Jap blood covered my clothes.

The last thing I did before leaving the site was to place several large rocks down into the firing tube. I filled it completely; the last rock I put in was larger than the rest, and I forced it down into the chamber, wedging it in place. The next Jap that fired that cannon would get the surprise of his life, as the 75mm shell exploded in the chamber. My watch read 4:36 AM, which meant I had less than ninety minutes before the sun would begin to illuminate the entire jungle. I had to increase my pace if I was to get back to where Tom was imprisoned, and then return to my hidden vantage point and the rest of my supplies. I had to double-time it, not a preferred approach on an island overrun with enemy troops.

If my calculations were accurate, I would arrive in the exact spot that I had left about five hours earlier, if I walked northwest. Jap patrols would be out in force in a few hours. I did not know if Tom had been moved. The sub, designated to pick me up, may not have been able to reach Guadalcanal. The odds were against me, but I kept to the mission, as this was what I had been trained to do and this particular mission was critical.

In just under ninety minutes, I was back in the general vicinity of where the main concentration of Jap troops was located. There was no sign of troop movement, but I remained on high alert because my ability to conceal myself was rapidly fading as the sun was breaking through the darkness behind me.

I soon found the brush in which I had hid the day before. My concealed backpack contained bandages and my remaining D-rations, supplies that would now prove vital to Tom. I carefully worked my way back into the brush, and then removed my canteens, handgun and Japanese pistol, laying them on the ground near me. I saw no movement from the building that imprisoned Tom.

I had not slept in almost three days. If I had any chance of rescuing Tom - and there was a good chance I could - I had to get some sleep. I had slept in some strange places over the years, but nothing compared with this; lying in thick jungle bush, on an island in the middle of the South Pacific, with thousands of Jap troops a mere one hundred yards from where I was. Regardless, I had to sleep. Before I closed my eyes, I covered myself with some branches and leaves, trying my best to conceal myself. I took one last look at my watch, which read 6:05 AM.

While I slept, the flotilla of American Navy ships was bearing down on the island. I had less than twenty-four hours before the scheduled rendezvous with the Navy sub was to take place. I would relay to the sub's Captain the best location for the Marine landing. He would then radio the lead Navy ship, giving it time to alter its course, if necessary. The Marines were eager to hear from me, but they in no way had to have my information in order to land. They had already surveyed the three possible landing zones around the island and rehearsed each landing location long before I parachuted onto the island. My information would simply allow them to land rapidly, hopefully, with limited enemy engagement and no American loss of life.

My eyes opened to the sound of vehicle movement. I looked up and saw blue sky, with a few clouds rolling left to right ever so slowly. Why did I hear vehicles? I turned to my side and listened intently. The sound I heard was bulldozers. I snatched up my backpack and pulled out my binoculars. I edged forward, allowing myself a clear vantage point of the valley below. The Jap army was clearing a road less than fifty yards from where I was lying. They must have had the heavy equipment parked somewhere in the camp where I did not see it the day before.

I looked at my watch; it was already 2:18 PM on the third day. I had slept for over six hours. My body needed the rest, but I found myself feeling guilty. Tom was imprisoned and I had slept soundly on the ground. I had slept so hard but my strength was now renewed.

There could be no risk of the Japs discovering me so I had to stay exactly where I was. I ate a D-ration and a candy bar, washing them down with a little water from my canteen. I had enough cover and room to move my legs and roll from side to side to avoid cramps. For the rest of the afternoon all I did was keep my eyes trained on the building where I hoped Tom was still located. I also surveyed as much of the camp as I could, trying to get a read on the number of men, types of equipment, and so on.

One important development that I noted was the large quantity of tanks, mortars and howitzer cannons in one corner of the camp. From my position, I counted at least fifteen Jap tanks. There were stockpiles of ammo canisters everywhere. It looked as if the Japs were preparing for a large American invasion. Little did they know that there was already an American on the island and ready to administer a little retribution for their attack on Pearl Harbor. At 6:00 PM, I finally had proof that Tom was still alive, but that confirmation was coupled with concern and even some uncertainty about our situation. Tom was shirtless, bloodied, and being dragged out of the building by two Jap soldiers. I watched him pushed to the ground and kicked repeatedly. A senior ranking Jap officer was screaming at him in broken English, telling him to kneel in front of him. From what I had witnessed thus far, Tom barely had enough strength to pull himself up. The Jap officer continued to scream at Tom, while he attempted to pull himself up. He finally managed to get to a kneeling position, at which point the Jap officer pushed him back down with his large black boot. The officer screamed again for Tom to rise. Tom managed to get to his knees a second time, and the Jap officer just pushed him down again with his boot.

The screaming from the Jap officer, Tom struggling to rise to his knees, and the subsequent pushing by the Jap officer, continued for over an hour. Now 7:00 PM, Tom was on his knees, with his hands tied behind his back. He was forced to sit like that for over an hour. By that time, the sun had set completely. A light from a nearby building illuminated the area around Tom. The Jap officer pulled his samurai sword from its sheath on his right hip and raised it above Tom's head, where he held it for what seemed like minutes.

Several times the Jap officer cut a swath through the air with the sword only to stop within an inch of the back of Tom's head. Tom stayed motionless. After three false attempts from the Jap officer's sword, Tom pulled his head up, turned in the direction of the Jap officer and screamed, loudly enough for me to hear. "Do it, you Jap coward!" Tom then lowered his head and stayed very still.

The Jap officer was furious and instructed two other Jap soldiers to raise Tom to his feet. He told them to secure Tom by his arms and legs to two large posts. Tom was left in that X position as the Jap officer and his fellow soldiers reentered the nearby building. A few other Jap soldiers returned from patrol, walked by Tom and spit on him.

I assessed my options for rescuing Tom. My best option was the one I had mulled over the day before. I would wait until after midnight and then work my way down to Tom, secure him, kill a few Japs and head for the coast. The sub would be waiting; at least I hoped it was. The fact that Tom never reported his landing or reported back to his superiors, could have been interpreted by them that I never parachuted and that Tom and I had simply crashed and died. Going for the sub was our only viable means of escape.

Midnight came. I surveyed the area all around me and listened for any movement; it was all clear. I prayed to God, asking Him to make my motions swift and sure and to give me the required strength to rescue Tom. I secured my backpack and inventoried my grenade count, ammunition, knife and remaining food rations. I secured my last remaining canteen of water to my side, after which I removed my handgun from its holster, chambered a round, and rose to my feet.

I saw no one, other than Tom, anywhere within fifty yards in front of me. I left the secured area where I had been for over fifteen hours and slowly moved in Tom's direction. With relative ease, I was able to approach him. I heard all of the Japs in the surrounding buildings laughing and hollering, probably drunk with sake.

Tom's head was down and he appeared to be unconscious, not surprising from the beatings and torture he had received over the last thirty-six hours. I holstered my handgun, took out my knife and cut away the rope holding Tom's arms and legs. As he fell, I caught him and put him over my back. Carrying Tom, I headed toward the nearest patch of dark jungle. We had not been detected as we cleared a few trees and approximately one hundred yards into the jungle. I was not going to leave just yet. Those Japs had ticked me off and I was going to get a little retribution for Tom.

I gently laid Tom down on the ground and positioned his head and back up against a palm tree, facing back in the direction of the camp. He finally woke up and immediately recognized me and said, "Allen, what are you doing here? How did you find me?"

I gave Tom some fresh water from my canteen and replied, "It wasn't easy, but I came upon your crashed plane and saw the Japs had carried you off. We are one hundred yards from where you were a prisoner. It's probably not the best idea, but I'm going to leave you here and head back to the Jap camp for a little payback."

All Tom did was raise his head and say, "Especially the officer!"

Time was not on our side as we had a very small window to make it to the sub. I left Tom my handgun and an extra clip of ammo for protection and said, "Tom, shoot first and ask questions later. You and I are the only two Americans on this island. When I come back, and I will be back, all I will say as I approach you is the word 'Freedom'."

As I headed back to the Jap camp, all I kept thinking to myself was, "Is this a good idea?"

I had somehow lost the Jap handgun I had secured earlier but I had my knife and three hand grenades. If overwhelmed by Japs, I would simply pull my grenade pins and take most of them with me in the subsequent explosion.

I paused as I cleared the jungle and reentered the clearing of the camp. Surprised that I did not see even one Jap milling around the camp, I walked right up to the building where Tom had been kept earlier in the day. I peered into the single window on the right side of the building. All I could see were a small lantern in the corner of the room and two Japs lying on cots in the far corner. I carefully worked my way around to the front door of the small building and turned the handle. It was unlocked. I quietly entered the room, leaving the door slightly open behind me. The Jap officer was on the far cot. I knew this because his samurai sword and uniform were hanging nearby on a hook. I would kill him first.

The wood floor creaked slightly with every step I took. I stopped every step, looking for any signs of movement from the two men lying in front of me. I decided to change weapons and borrow the Jap officer's samurai sword, mainly for speed of killing and because it was clearly longer than my knife. As I approached the sword hanging on the hook, the Jap officer suddenly moved and turned over. The officer's samurai sword was hanging in such a way that I could simply grab its handle and pull it out of its sheath in one swift motion.

I paused, checked the position of both men lying there, and with one quick motion pulled the samurai sword out of its sheath with both my hands. I then turned it sideways and rammed the weapon into the right side of the officer's chest, pushing it into him all the way, until the sword came out of his body on the other side. The officer's eyes opened, and although he saw me, the force of the sword's blade ripping apart his heart, left him unable to make a sound.

In my peripheral vision, I saw the other Jap that lay to my left, rise up when he sensed something was happening. I pulled the sword out of the now dead Jap officer, turned, and with one quick movement decapitated the soldier. He did not have a chance to shout or scream. The only noise made was that of his head hitting the wooden floor with a thud and rolling a few feet away. His body immediately fell back down to his cot. Blood pumped from his neck.

It was time to go. I wiped the Jap blood off the sword as best I could on the officer's blanket, and returned it to its sheath. The sheath had a red cord on it that allowed me to carry the sword on my shoulder. This time, the sword was coming with me. I picked up a clean Jap blanket for Tom that was on a nearby table.

Not knowing if my actions stirred any other Jap movement outside, I approached the partially opened door with slight hesitation. I listened first, but heard nothing. I then pushed my body partially out the door and looked in both directions. The camp was dark with the exception of a few dim lights shining from nearby buildings or tents. I moved out of the building, heading back in the direction of the jungle. I managed not to alert any Japs and made it back in the direction of where I had left Tom about thirty minutes before.

When I arrived, I saw that Tom was still leaning against the palm tree and his eyes were shut. My handgun was in his right hand. I moved closer and whispered "Freedom".

Tom's eyes opened and he turned in my direction and said, "Allen, glad you're back."

I knelt near Tom and said, "It's time to move. Can you walk?"

Tom spoke through his parched lips, "If it means getting off this God forsaken island, I can walk."

I helped him to his feet and handed him the Jap blanket I had secured.

"Tom, you hold on to my handgun because I'm going to need both my hands to get you out of here," I shared.

I looked at my watch; it was now 1:45 AM. We had just over four hours before the sub designated to pick us up would leave the area. With one of Tom's arm around me, we headed out. For the next ninety minutes, we did our best to maneuver through the jungle, continuing in a southeast direction. We did not want to encounter any Jap patrols, but we could not afford to slow down and precede any more quietly because our window of time was quickly closing.

At 4:15 AM, we saw the beach below us. We had about a half-mile to walk to the beach, but it was a steep grade. I kept Tom behind me as we made our way down. The rocks and thick vegetation actually gave us some footing and something to hold. Tom had no shoes, and the walk by now had ripped his feet open. I told him to stop. I bent down, pulled him over my shoulders and carried him down the rest of the way. It took us another twenty minutes to make it to the beach. We hit the soft sand and continued to the waterline. Tom sat down and let the salt water cover his feet. Even though it must have been incredibly painful, he kept his feet in the water, as it was the best way to clean his wounds. We both scanned the horizon for any sign of a flashing red light. We saw nothing. My heart sank. The time was 4:40 AM; we had twenty minutes left. We knew we were on the right section of beach because of the maps we had diligently studied back on Pleasant Island.

I pulled out my binoculars and scanned the water in a one hundred and eighty degree sweep. Still we saw nothing that resembled a red light. I suddenly heard dead branches cracking behind us, back in the direction of the jungle. By now, Tom had given me back my handgun. I pulled it out, knelt down on one knee and pointed the gun back in the direction of the jungle. The cracking sound got closer. I still could not see who or what was coming toward us. I placed my gun in my left hand and with right hand peered through my binoculars in the direction of the movement. What I saw blew my mind. There stood two young Navy sailors. I put my binoculars down and walked over in their direction.

As I approached them I simply said, "Go Navy! I am Captain Voigt."

One of the sailors replied, "Yes, Sir. We know who you are. We are here to take you to the sub. We saw you and the other man clearing the jungle just a few minutes ago. We were hiding in the shadows, hoping it was you. There is a raft to take us out to the sub. We did not know what condition you would be in, so the Navy asked for two volunteers. We were the first two to volunteer. We were told you might not even make it back."

The sailor and I walked back up to the waterline and stood with Tom and the other sailor. We all scanned for a red light. A few minutes passed and then Tom shouted, "There it is!"

We all saw it at that point. A red light flashed on and off every three seconds. The two sailors ran back to the edge of the jungle and removed a small raft that they had hidden under some dead branches. They carried it out into the surf.

One of the sailors shouted, "Climb aboard."

I helped Tom into the raft, and then I threw my backpack and samurai sword into it and climbed in. The other two sailors followed suit. They took the two oars lying on the floor of the raft, put them in position, and began to row with all their might. The red light looked hundreds of yards away as the raft bobbed up and down in the water. We must have been closer to the sub than I first estimated. Suddenly, less than fifty yards in front of us, the sub rose up beyond periscope depth to a point where half of the hull was exposed on the waterline.

The sailors rowed up to the sub. A large hatch near the conning tower opened up, and three sailors climbed out to assist us. One of them threw us a rope, which the sailors in our raft used to navigate us over to a small ladder attached to the sub.

Tom was asked to go first. With all his might, he pulled himself up and held onto the ladder. One of the sailors and I helped him get out of the raft and then halfway up the ladder. The sailors on the sub took over from there and helped him onto the sub. I secured my backpack and samurai sword and followed behind Tom, working my way up the ladder. The two sailors that had rescued us then climbed aboard and let the raft simply drift away.

We hastily made our way into the sub. The last sailor down the hatch closed it and turned the handle, securing the seal tight. Because we had entered the sub from the forward compartment, we had to work our way back toward the control room, where we would meet the sub's Captain. As we walked back in the direction of the control room, I felt like I had been in this sub before. I then heard a familiar voice shouting in our direction. It was Captain Dempsey. I was back on the USS Spearfish!

We arrived at the control room and Captain Dempsey gave me a big bear hug and said, "When I heard the Navy was covertly looking for a sub to pick you up on Guadalcanal, I immediately volunteered our sub for the mission. The necessary repairs were made back at Pearl Harbor and we are back out hunting Jap subs. It took us three days to get to you, but here we are, Allen!"

I shook my head in disbelief. I removed the samurai sword from my back and handed it to Captain Dempsey. "Captain, please accept this sword as my appreciation for rescuing me twice from islands full of Japs."

Captain Dempsey took the sword in both his hands, looking at it for the longest time and said, "Allen I have never seen one of these before. I see a little blood on it, is that yours?"

I smiled and replied, "Not mine; the Jap that bled on this sword will not need it back."

The USS Spearfish soon disappeared below the waves and into the blackness of the ocean. Tom was taken to sickbay and his wounds were treated. As the sub traveled southeast, away from Guadalcanal, I spent the next hour with Captain Dempsey and a Marine Captain by the name Stowell, pouring over a map of Guadalcanal and pointing out the location of the Jap positions. I related the types of military equipment and ammunition I had seen. I pointed to the northeast corner of the island as the best landing spot for the Marines. I told Captain Stowell that although the beaches were narrow, the jungle opened up, which would allow men and machines to pour onto the island.

I finished up with both men by saying, "The Japs will be very shocked in the morning when they find that Lt. Beckett is gone, and several Jap officers are dead. The big surprise will be the landing of the Marines."

It was the early morning of August 6th. The Marines would be landing in just over twenty-four hours. To myself, I wished them a good landing and hoped that my time on the island would prove helpful in some way.

I checked on Tom. He already felt better; the morphine helped ease the pain. A young Navy doctor told me Tom had two broken ribs and had some deep bruising on his back, but otherwise he would be fine.

I found some edible food in the sub's galley. Afterwards, I went to the rear of the sub where there were several cots. I found an empty one, crawled onto it, and soon fell asleep.

The USS Spearfish would sail for three days and nights in the direction of Brisbane, Australia.

Chapter 10

MY LAST SERENADE

"War means fighting, fighting means killing."
Nathan Bedford Forrest

The USS Spearfish had to maneuver for several days in the Coral Sea. Japanese subs were everywhere and as a result, we had to avoid them as we traveled south towards Australia. We docked in the port of Brisbane, Australia, on Wednesday morning, August 12, 1942. News of the Marine invasion of Guadalcanal filled the Australian newspapers. We had finally taken the fight back to the Japanese. Several Navy ships were anchored nearby. A crowd of Australians greeted us on the dock as we exited the sub. They cheered, clapped and shouted, "Thank you, America!" The Japanese had been bombing northern Australia, specifically the city of Darwin, for months. The Australians, like the Americans, were a resilient people.

A round of applause was the last thing I expected as I walked off the sub that morning. Tom was doing better but he was still having a hard time walking. He did manage to get off the sub unassisted, though.

Commander Dempsey stayed with his sub, but an Army Jeep, driven by none other than Major McCoy, picked up Tom and me. Our reunion was a pleasant surprise. We exchanged some small talk, but for the most part, the three of us did not speak as Major McCoy drove the Jeep through the streets of Brisbane. The number of buildings, the cleanliness of the streets, and the abundance of shops and businesses astonished me. I felt like I was back in New York City.

After taking a hard right, Major McCoy drove down a side street to a four-story building displaying a simple banner that read, "United States Army HQ."

Major McCoy parked the Jeep in front of the building and we all piled out. He led us up a series of stairs to the third floor. Tom was last up the stairs, as he refused any help offered by the Major and me.

We entered a spacious room that buzzed with activity. Maps and tables were everywhere. Army and Navy personnel, both men and women, scurried around as they answered phones, typed reports, and went about their other duties.

The Major led us to an enclosed office in the far corner of the floor. The office had glass windows, allowing us to see the flurry of activity out on the floor. The office also had large windows facing the outside world that gave us a view of the harbor, a few miles west of us.

Major McCoy spent the next hour or so filling us in on the Marines' successful landing on Guadalcanal, unopposed. The information that I had provided had helped reduce the loss of American lives and it help secure a safe beachhead. It had been worth it all.

After their successful landing on Guadalcanal, the Marines had begun moving inland, having already secured the airfield I had seen just a few days before. On August 8th, the Japanese bombed the Marines at Henderson Field in an attempt to take back the airfield. That same day, the Allies had successfully recaptured the small islands of Tulagi and Gavutu, just off the coast of Guadalcanal. On the very day of our arrival, they renamed the airfield, Henderson Field in memory of a Marine Major who had lost his life at the Battle of Midway during June 1942.

On the opposite side of the globe, the Germans were fighting Allied forces in North Africa and the Soviet Union near the city of Leningrad. More news was being published about the German atrocities against the Jews in the concentration camps - the very same camps I had described to President Roosevelt in the late 1930s. For the rest of the day, Tom and I were briefed on what the American military was up against across the globe.

Late in the day, I said goodbye to Tom. He was soon headed back to Pearl Harbor for continued recovery. I was assigned a small apartment near the United States Army HQ building. I reported to the HQ building each day. The intent was for me, yet again, to share with senior military personnel, all of the insights and intelligence I gathered during my time in Germany. My command of the German and Japanese languages was helpful for translation purposes and radio monitoring.

The weeks passed and I found myself getting restless. I wanted to get back in the fight. November came and I heard about the Marines fighting the Japanese on the island of Tarawa. Over 1,600 service men died over the three-day battle for the island. The Japanese were proving to be a formidable enemy.

I spent Thanksgiving and Christmas in Brisbane, becoming more and more frustrated over my length of stay in the city. One bright spot over that 1942 holiday season was that my superiors in the OSS were able to get a message to my parents in East Aurora, New York, letting them know I was alive and in good health in Australia.

There was also a very dark spot, however. I was able to confirm that Alice was still a prisoner of war in Manila, Philippines. My heart longed for her and I asked my superiors repeatedly to stage a rescue mission, but my requests were denied. I was able to get a letter to her that I had written during my lengthy time in Brisbane. I received confirmation that the letter was successfully smuggled into the country and hand-delivered to her. I was not able to receive a letter in response, but knowing Alice had received my letter was a relief. I had poured my heart out to her in that letter. She would clearly know my long-term intentions after reading it.

I would spend New Year's 1943 and all of January and February in Brisbane. In mid-February, I received news that the Marines had successfully secured the island of Guadalcanal. Over 7,000 Marines, Navy and Army personnel had died in the seven-month battle, fought on land and sea. The United States military had killed over 30,000 Japs during the seven-month campaign.

During early March 1943, I finally got word that I would be leaving Brisbane. I received direct orders from General Donovan that I was to report to Army HQ in London, England, by early April. My route and modes of transportation had been arranged. I would take a ship from Brisbane, Australia back to Pearl Harbor, Hawaii. I would eventually make my way to New York and from there to Liverpool, England and on to London.

I left Brisbane on Thursday, March 11, 1943. My trip east took over three and a half weeks, but I met many proud American military personnel along the way. I arrived in London on Wednesday, April 7th. Two familiar faces met me: General Donovan and Lt. Colonel Yates. I spent the rest of April getting up to speed on the preliminary invasion plans for Europe. The mission, Operation Overlord, was being planned and orchestrated by an Army General, Dwight Eisenhower. I had heard of the General but had never met him.

I learned during my initial time in London that the American objective was to free Europe from the Nazis first. The Pacific campaign was secondary. My part in all of this became clear during early May 1943. I had been handpicked by General Donovan to lead exploratory missions into France and Belgium in order to conduct espionage, learn what the Germans were planning, and survey the beaches of France for suitable landing areas for the pending invasion.

For the last half of 1943 and the first few months of 1944, other OSS agents and I ran over thirty missions into occupied France and Belgium. The mission was the same each time. I parachuted in and ferried out by boat, back across the English Channel. The missions were dangerous but perfect for me. Thanks to my fluency in German, I was able to infiltrate several German HQ offices. I had even secured a German officer's uniform by killing him on a dark side street in Paris, France.

The information I obtained was invaluable to the planning of Operation Overlord. The Germans, under the watchful eye of

General Rommel, were securing the entire coast of France with pillboxes, anti-aircraft guns, and hundreds of tanks. German troop movements clearly showed that they expected an Allied invasion.

According to the information I obtained during my time spent in the German HQ offices, the Germans were not faring well in Eastern Europe against the Soviet Union. They were losing thousands of men each day. The Allied forces were bombing Germany night and day. In March 1944, I watched as hundreds of American B-17 bombers flew overhead on their way to Germany. The sheer number of planes blocked out the sun. I thought back to all that time I had spent in Germany. When I recalled the people I had met and the places I had visited, the one thing that stuck out in my mind was the arrogance of the German people and their inhumane treatment of the Jews. Germany was now reaping what they had sown.

It was now mid-May 1944. Following my return, from yet another trip to France, I attended two weeks of closed-door meetings. Our location was a secret. Generals Donovan and Eisenhower both attended the entire two weeks. The final planning phases were underway for Operation Overlord. The date of the invasion was set for Monday, June 5, 1944. The information I had provided to General Eisenhower and his staff showed that the Normandy Beaches, located between the French cities of Cherbourg and Le Havre, were undoubtedly the best beaches for an Allied invasion. I had seen pillboxes and gun emplacements along the beaches, but that location appeared to be the best place to land men and heavy equipment. Thanks to my time spent in the German HQ offices, we knew that German troop movements leaned toward the beaches closer to Calais, France, as that is where they assumed the Allied forces would land. The Normandy Beaches, based on my observations, could be taken in under two days.

On June 2nd, I met with Lt. Colonel Yates. I had not seen him in some time and we spent a few minutes catching up. Then we got to the purpose of the meeting. My next assignment would be to jump with the 101st Airborne into occupied France on the eve of the invasion. My role would be to assist the airborne troops as much as I could with navigation and interpretation, when German soldiers were captured. As Lt. Colonel Yates spoke, in the back of my mind, I questioned the legitimacy of my upcoming role. The 101st already had interpreters, and I knew they had studied the same maps that I had over the last year. They did not need my assistance.

The conversation continued and the real purpose of my jump became clear. I was hitching a ride back into occupied France. Upon the initial landing, I would offer navigation and translation services but would soon spin off and hunt down a very high-ranking German officer in the 12th SS Panzer Division, General Rudolf Fritz. The information I had given General Donovan and Lt. Colonel Yates during my recent missions to France was that the 12th SS Panzer Division was one of the main German Panzer divisions in and around Normandy. We expected the Germans to be confused initially after the Normandy landings, and it was my responsibility to cause even more chaos by taking out one of their key officers. Once my mission was complete, I would hook back up with the 101st near Caen, France. I allowed the 101st to be the tip of the spear, doing my best to stay alive.

I spent the weekend at Upottery Airfield with the 101st Airborne. Only a few of the senior offices knew my mission. The unlisted soldiers were told I was there to assist with navigation and German language interpretation. My short time with the 101st was special. None of the 101st had seen active combat yet, and for many of them, this jump was going to be their first into active combat. The 101st had been charged with taking out gun emplacements that could potentially rain fire down on the invasion beaches, and bridges, thereby preventing German tanks and equipment from reaching the invasion area.

I spent a few hours with the senior officers sharing a little bit about my time in Germany and in the Pacific. I could not reveal too much, but the officers I spoke with were amazed by the number of places I had been. They asked me questions about the Germans, but for some reason they were more interested in how the Japanese fought.

It was Sunday, June 4th, and we were called to the ready room to pack our parachutes, gear and prepare for our jump later that evening. At 3:00 PM, the news broke that the jump would be postponed forty-eight hours. Operation Overlord was pushed to Tuesday, June 6th, due to bad weather. We all understood, but were frustrated nonetheless. I spent the next day resting in my temporary quarters, assuming sleep might be hard to find over the next few days.

In the late hours of Monday, June 5th, we rechecked our parachutes, gear, and then proceeded onto the runway, where a large contingent of C-47 transport planes awaited us. I boarded a C-47 with twenty-five soldiers from the 101st and took my seat. I had not jumped from an airplane since diving out two years earlier over Guadalcanal. I was hoping this jump would be smoother than that night's jump.

There I sat on a C-47 in my French civilian clothes. The 101st members, on the other hand, had shaved their heads in a Mohawk style, leaving a thick strip of hair down the middle of their heads. They had painted their faces and had every piece of combat equipment they could carry. The men were an intimidating looking bunch. The men enjoyed kidding me about my appearance, and since it helped distract them from being nervous on this, their first mission, I let them say whatever they wanted and took it in stride.

I had my parachute, my handgun and my knife – the very same weapons I had used to kill the enemy and keep myself alive throughout all my years of military service. We had been provided with clickers that would allow us to distinguish Americans from Germans in the dark. If we heard a click, we were to respond in kind with two clicks.

Two hours after sunset, our C-47 lumbered out onto the runway, taking its place with the others. Shortly after takeoff, I looked out of the plane as best I could, astounded by how many planes were in the air with us. There were other C-47s towing gliders filled with airborne troops not only from the 101st, but also from the 82nd. We all flew out over the English Channel, leaving the coast of England behind. I looked at my watch and it was just after midnight, the early hours of Tuesday, June 6th. We had cleared the channel and were approaching the Normandy coast.

Flak from German anti-aircraft guns started popping all around us. The flashes lit up the sky and the concussion from the explosions shook our plane violently. I watched with a feeling of helplessness as several of the C-47s were blown out of the sky and crashed in the Normandy countryside.

The flak got so bad that the decision was made to jump immediately, rather than waiting for our designated drop zone, and not risk being shot down. I was fifth in line to jump. I attached my cable to the jump line and approached the exit. I watched as the men who jumped before me disappeared in an instant behind the plane. Then it was my turn and there was no time to take in the sights, as men lined up behind me. I jumped into the darkness; the cable pulled my chute automatically, and I quickly orientated myself. I looked around and could not believe what I saw: hundreds of parachutes floating to the ground. I then saw a C-47 explode off in the distance, lighting up the entire sky. My heart sank for the men that were aboard that plane, and my hatred for the enemy grew even greater.

I landed hard. I hit the ground with my legs but immediately started rolling end over end. Finally, my momentum stopped and I sat up. I had survived the jump, and I still had my handgun and knife. I removed my parachute and came to my feet. No one else was around. How had that happened? I could not wait for anyone else. I had to find my target and kill him.

I spent the next five hours walking east. Thanks to my numerous trips into France, I soon determined my location in proximity to the 12th SS Panzer Division headquarters. I estimated I had walked roughly twelve miles and was very close to my objective. My plan of attack was very simple but extremely risky. Once I laid eyes on Rudolph Fritz, I would wait for the perfect opportunity to kill him privately.

The sun finally rose. I secured my handgun and knife under my clothing and walked right into the town of Argences, a small town southeast of Caen. The 12th SS Panzer Division had been camped out there for months leading up to June, and I hoped they were still there. I knew they would soon be on the move once news of the large-scale Allied invasion reached them.

Walking into the small town, I saw some dogs running around aimlessly in the street and a few old men shuffling about. I looked like an average French citizen. The problem was I did not speak French fluently. I had picked up a few words, but if forced into a lengthy conversation, I would be in trouble.

I made my way to the rear of town and saw that the German tanks were still there, all lined up in formation. I counted fifteen tanks, none of which had its motor running. I knew where the officer's quarters were, as I had impersonated a German soldier a few times in my quest to secure information.

I was standing next to a two-story building when a voice behind me asked, in German, "What are you looking at?"

I did not have to turn around to know he was a German soldier. I turned and saw a German tank commander standing there, half-dressed in his army uniform, with shaving cream all over his face.

I replied in German, "I am merely looking at your tanks, Sir. I am impressed with both their number and their size."

The German officer, who was about my height and build, laughed and continued shaving his face with the straight razor that was in his right hand. Through his shaving cream he boastfully stated, "The Americans will be slaughtered when they invade."

Just then, the alarms sounded and I knew exactly what that meant. The news had traveled to the small town of Argences that the Allies were invading. The German officer rushed back into his quarters and I followed him. Thanks to the noise of the alarm going off, he did not hear me when I came up behind him. Keeping clear of the straight razor in his hand, I pushed him from behind, forcing him to turn in my direction. I quickly stabbed him in the heart with my knife. As he stared at me, with his eyes glazing over, I pulled my knife out of his chest. He fell to the ground and died immediately. I raced to shut the officer's door. I removed the officer's pants and put them on over my civilian clothes. I found a clean shirt in his closet and hastily put that on over my clothes. His jacket was hanging nearby, so I donned it as fast as I could, as well. He was actually a little rounder than I was, so his clothes fit perfectly over mine. Lastly, I removed my shoes and replaced them with the officer's black boots. I found a map of the coastal area of France that lay on a nearby table, folded it, and placed it in the right front pocket of the dead German officer's coat I was now wearing.

The alarm continued to sound throughout the headquarters area. I had very little time in which to find my target, Rudolf Fritz, before he jumped in a nearby tank. I left the dead officer lying there on the floor. I exited the officer's quarters. All I had to go on was the memory of a grainy black and white picture of Fritz, shown to me a few days prior.

The Panzer headquarters was alive with activity by then. Soldiers darted here and there, and tanks rumbled to life. I did not see my target, so I went back to a building that I knew had previously housed senior ranking German officers. The three-story brick building had a large Nazi flag flying from it. I walked right in and headed up the stairs in hopes of finding Rudolf Fritz. By a stroke of luck, I spotted him immediately when he walked out of a bedroom door.

I spoke in German and said, "General, I have news about the Allied invasion. May I speak to you in private, Sir?"

He nodded and walked back into the room, motioning me to follow him. I pulled out the folded map I had placed in my newly acquired jacket and laid it on a coffee table. I asked him to come over as I pointed to a particular area on the map. He pulled out his reading glasses and put them on, then bent over the table and looked at the map. With quick action, I pulled out my knife with my left hand, the hand he could not see, and rammed it into the base of his skull with an upward motion. He immediately fell onto the table, and the force of his body falling, broke the table in half. He made a lot of noise doing it.

I abandoned Fritz's quarters and went back downstairs. I then walked away from the building at a steady pace. Germans were everywhere, hopping into tanks and trucks. I walked into what looked like a French bakery and went back to the bakery's storage area. The Germans had complete control of the town and none of their actions were questioned. I removed the German uniform I has been wearing over my civilian clothes and threw it into a nearby trash can. I then noticed a pair of brown shoes sitting on a nearby shelf; I picked them up and put them on. They were a size too large, but with the officer's socks on, the shoes fit better. I headed out a back door and into a nearby alley. The town was clearly awake now as French civilians were running around. They knew what was coming.

I took a bicycle that was propped up against a nearby building and hopped on it. I had not ridden a bike since I was a kid. I rode right out of town, heading for Caen. I had an approximate sixteen-mile bike ride ahead of me. As I rode, I looked back and saw no one following me. After a few miles, some trucks, full of German soldiers, rushed by me on their way west toward the beaches.

The invasion by then would have been in full force. The Allies would have landed on five designated beaches around the Normandy area code named Utah, Omaha, Sword, Juno and Gold. The Americans were taking the beaches of Utah and Omaha.

An American P-51 Mustang, a single fighter aircraft, swooped out of the sky and strafed the road in front of me, hitting a German truck that had recently passed me. The truck careered off the road to the right and flipped over into a deep ditch. A few German soldiers stumbled out but soon fell to the ground, shot up pretty badly. The P-51 veered off to the left and out of sight. The Allies, it seemed, controlled the skies.

I peddled that bike for hours, constantly delayed by all the trucks slowly passing by, while the entire time, trying to avoid large holes in the road caused by months of Allied bombardment. I finally peddled into Caen, ditched my bike, found a haberdasher store and walked in. The owner greeted me in French and I replied in kind, using limited words. He continued to speak in French, using words I did not understand. He pronounced the word "American" more than once and was smiling the entire time. I felt I had a friend. I broke out in perfect English, taking him by surprise. He started to speak slowly in broken English. I informed him I was an American and needed to remain in his store for a while, waiting for American soldiers that would be coming. He understood and took me back upstairs to his residence. He introduced me to his wife and two young sons. The family took me in and fed me breakfast. We talked for several hours and they explained the brutality of the German occupation, an occupation that had lasted four years. They had prayed for this day to come; a day when the Americans would drive out the Germans.

Every other hour, I went downstairs into the haberdasher's store and looked out the window for Allied troops; none came. There were plenty of German soldiers running around, though. I had to wait it out. The only conclusion I had was that the Allied advance had stalled. The haberdasher allowed me to stay with him and his family for three more days. I was fed and had a bed to sleep in, the comforts of home.

On the morning of Saturday, June 10th, I elected to walk outside and attempt to find out from the Germans, what was going on from their vantage point. I walked right up to a Panzer tank and asked the tank commander, who was propped out of the turret, if he was with the 12th SS Panzer Division.

He replied, "No, we are the 7th SS Panzer Division. The 12th is still stuck in Argences!"

I immediately knew that the goal of my mission, to cause chaos by killing General Fritz, had succeeded. The 12th was in disarray. I spoke with the tank commander about the Allied invasion. He stated that the Allies had successfully landed in the Normandy region and were rapidly moving toward Caen. He also informed me that his Panzer division would beat the Allies back to the beaches. I was surprised he shared that much with me, who he assumed was a French citizen who also spoke German.

I thought to myself, "Good luck with that, you Kraut."

I considered leaving the security of the haberdasher's store and heading for the coast. The words of Lt. Colonel Yates rang in my ears, "Stay alive".

The thought of being caught between the German and Allied armies was not appealing, to say the least. I had jumped out of planes, spent days in hot jungles, and killed numerous Japs and Krauts, but maneuvering between thousands of troops was not something I wanted to try. I stayed put.

Over the next few days, the town of Caen was rocked with aerial bombardment, tank battles, and hand-to-hand combat in the streets. The haberdasher's home was pelted with stray bullets and a portion of his roof was blown away. I was determined to protect him and his family at all costs. As challenging as it was with a portion of his roof blown away, I convinced him and his family to stay upstairs, away from street battles and random bullets below.

On Sunday, June 11th, British soldiers entered the haberdasher's home in search of German resistance. The haberdasher greeted them and allowed me to take it from there. I informed the group of British soldiers that I was with the American military branch, called the OSS and needed to get to the 101st Airborne as soon as possible. They accepted my explanation immediately and asked me to follow them. I said my goodbyes to the haberdasher and his family and walked out the door, never to see them again.

The British troops took me to the town of Caen and straight to the 101st headquarters. I spent the day with the 101st, connecting with the right members that knew of my mission and would arrange my transportation back to England. It was a full week before I was escorted back to Omaha Beach, boarding an LST for England. I was amazed by the enormity of the equipment and troops being unloaded onto the beach. Supplies and munitions were stored everywhere.

Temporary harbors were set up off the beaches; some had already been damaged by recent storms.

By June 20, I was back in England. I met again with Lt. Colonel Yates and General Donovan. They expressed their appreciation for my most recent mission into France and I was updated on the success of Operation Overlord. To my relief, the beaches I had identified were, in fact, the right ones. The good news of the Allied beach landings and movement inland was short-lived, however, as I was immediately briefed on my next assignment.

Over the next two days, they gave me more detail on my next mission. I would be heading back to the Pacific campaign to kill a Japanese General. He had been assigned to defend some godforsaken island in the Pacific called Iwo Jima. The next day, June 23rd, I prepared to leave England and officially left on June 24th. For the whole month of July, I traveled back to the Pacific theater of war and the waiting Japanese. I hitched rides with thousands of other soldiers and sailors, heading to war against the Japanese.

America and its allies had made a lot of progress fighting the Japanese during the last two and half years I had been in Europe. The island hopping strategy was working but casualties continued to mount. Since the battle of Guadalcanal, the Marines, with the support of the Army and Navy, had worked their way up to the Mariana Islands and were close to flushing out the Japanese from the Philippines. My assignment was to report to the island of Saipan, the largest island in the Marianas.

During June 1944, the Marines and the Army's 27th Infantry Division had landed on Saipan and driven out the Japanese Army. Thousands of Americans died during that month-long campaign. The island was vital for the Army Air Corps to use as a staging area for bombers, specifically the newest American bomber, the B-29. We were close enough now to Japan to use the new long-range bomber to bomb the Japanese into submission.

While traveling back to the Pacific, I met young American military personnel heading off to war for the first time. I was now thirty-six years old, twice the age of the men traveling with me. The vast majority of these men were very young or infants when I entered the Army back in 1926. I sure felt old around them. I was asked questions about my lengthy service in the Army. I answered the questions as best I could, in light of my position in the OSS.

I secured a ride on a brand new B-29 from Seattle, Washington, to Honolulu, Hawaii. After a few days back in Hawaii, I continued on to the island of Saipan on that same B-29 named Enola Gay. The Enola Gay touched down on Saipan on August 3, 1944. I was assigned to the Army Air Corps officer's quarters near Obyan Beach, on the very southern tip of the island. As beautiful as the beach was, the amount of devastation on the island was staggering. The Marines and the Army's 27th Infantry had landed on the island from its mid western shores and immediately flushed out the Japanese from the southern and central sections of the island. They then pushed north and completed the job. Everywhere I looked, I saw burned-out tanks, trucks and buildings. The smell of rotting Japanese corpses filled the air. The Navy Seabees were pushing the Japanese bodies into mass graves as fast as they could.

I spent the next four and a half months on Saipan. I worked to keep my body in shape and my skills sharp, by joining the Army soldiers on the island, helping to flush out the remaining Japanese on the island who had hidden in caves.

I received direction in late December from my OSS superiors to begin training for a nighttime encroachment onto a beach from the sea. I was introduced to the Navy's Frogmen, officially called Underwater Demolition Teams. They taught me the best method for swimming in the ocean and how to use a new underwater device called an aqualung. It allowed me to swim underwater for long distances and various depths. This was a completely new experience for me, and practicing it helped to pass the time. Within a few weeks, I was able to leave the safety of a Navy vessel three miles offshore and successfully reach a beach in less than one hour.

Christmas and New Years rolled around again. I missed Alice, my parents, and the snow of New York. I had spent so many holidays away from friends and family. I wondered to myself when this war was going to be over.

The brass soon showed up on Saipan. The final planning phases of the invasion of Iwo Jima were underway. Due to my rank, position in the OSS, and ultimate mission on the island, they gave me the details of the invasion, which was set for February 19, 1945. I was to wait in reserve off the island in a submarine until the approximate position of the Japanese General was determined.

The Marines that were going to invade Iwo Jima left primarily from Hawaii. I left Saipan, along with the UDT team I had trained with, on Tuesday, February 13th. We boarded a Navy submarine, the USS Redfin, during the early morning hours of the 13th. The sailors on the USS Redfin were not quite sure what to think of the frogmen and me when we boarded the sub with all our diving equipment.

Our travel to Iwo Jima took four days. We surfaced off the island to find ourselves surrounded by a multitude of other Navy vessels of all shapes and sizes. The Navy was shelling the island from the large Navy battleships nearby. Each time a shell was fired, the entire sub shook. It was a sound like I had never heard before. The Marine and Navy single engine fighters were flying all over the island, strafing and dropping ordnance at will on the Japanese holding the island.

On the late afternoon of February 18th, the Navy frogmen left the sub and surveyed the beaches around the southern end of Iwo Jima, the designated landing spot for the Marines. They removed various mines and obstacles, clearing a path for the landing craft. They returned later that evening to the USS Redfin.

The invasion of Iwo Jima commenced on February 19th, just as planned. It was amazing to watch the landing craft advance onto the beach. Even from my vantage point on the USS Redfin, I could make out the sand on the beaches, black as coal. The sounds of explosions and small weapons fire from the beach resonated around me. I had never witnessed anything like this during my career in the Army.

The courage it took for those Marines to take those beaches was beyond my comprehension.

The next day the USS Redfin, and me as its guest, sank beneath the waves and began its assigned scouting mission around Iwo Jima. The sub patrolled the perimeter of the entire island seven times, in order to make sure there were no other Japanese Navy ships dropping off reinforcements on the backside of the island. Fortunately, there was none. The sub took ultimately took a defensive position on the southern side of the island, giving us a front row seat to one of the bloodiest battles the Marines ever fought.

I was getting extremely frustrated. Americans were dying on the island by the hundreds every day. I had not seen active engagement against the enemy for months. I had continued to train hard and I was ready to reengage and do my part to help secure this godforsaken island in the middle of the Pacific Ocean. Here I was stuck on a submarine.

My time finally came on the evening of Wednesday, March 22nd. The battle was still raging on Iwo Jima, now four and a half weeks old. The Marines were killing thousands of Japs a day but it was estimated the Japanese Army had over twenty thousand soldiers on the island. They were dug in like ticks, taking defensive positions in a vast network of caves and tunnels.

The idea was that if we cut off the head of the snake, the body would die. I was simply shown a picture of the Japanese General commanding the troops on Iwo Jima and his expected location, the eastern corner of the island. I was not provided with the name of the General, just a picture. I had six hours to find my target, eliminate him and return to the USS Redfin. The sub maneuvered to the eastern side of the island and partially surfaced. Using my aqualung equipment, I exited the sub through a rear hatch.

It was so dark in the water that night and it was impossible for me to swim underwater the entire way and keep my sense of direction. The water was so cold. I was only wearing shorts and a black t-shirt.

I surfaced and saw the island directly in front of me, approximately one mile away.

I swam underwater roughly twenty-five yards and resurfaced. I repeated this exercise until I reached the beach. I crawled onto the black sand and pulled off my diving equipment, hiding it behind some rocks. I had carried a dive bag that kept my boots, socks, knife, handgun and three clips of ammunition somewhat dry. I had no choice but to put on my semi-wet boots. I then crawled up a series of jagged rocks at the base of a cliff. As I climbed up the rock face, I could hear gunfire and mortars going off nearby. Flares that were being fired by the Marines helped to illuminate my path. My climb up to the expected location of the Japanese General was unabated. Reaching the top of the cliff face, I hid behind some large rocks.

I listened intently for the Japanese; I did not have to wait long. I heard a few Japanese soldiers off to my immediate right. I silently worked my way around to them. Two Japs lay on the ground with obvious wounds to their upper bodies and heads. I carefully came up from behind them and killed the first Jap by slitting his throat from ear to ear.

As that Jap bled out, I put my arm around the other Jap's head and neck and pressed my bloody knife up to his left eye. He was in no shape to fight so I knew I had the advantage. I immediately whispered to him in his native tongue, "Where is the General?"

He did not answer. I asked a second time and still he refused to answer. I then added more pressure with my knife and muffled his scream with my hand. He then gave me the information I needed; informing me the general was in a cave roughly fifty yards behind me. I asked him how many soldiers were with the General and he said only two. I felt confident that I now had accurate information, so I slit his throat and left him to die.

I hiked further up the sloping backside of the island, looking for the cave that contained the Japanese General. As I maneuvered, I surveyed the backside of the island, which fit the description of a living hell. The island was on fire, the thick smoke and sulfur from the island, made it challenging to breathe. The palm trees all had their tops blown off, most likely from concussion blasts, and there was no sign of life anywhere. Massive craters dotted the ground, thanks to the hundreds of bombs dropped, compliments of my brothers-in-arms. Dead Japs were all around me and the smell of rotting flesh was overwhelming.

I soon found the cave the Jap had given up just before he died. My instincts told me something strange was going on. How could a Japanese General be in that cave without anyone guarding it? I slowly and carefully approached the cave. I did not hear any voices. What I did hear surprised me. Coming from deep in the cave was the sound of a radio playing, clearly a Japanese song of some kind. It sounded liked Japanese children, and they were singing about their brave Japanese fathers fighting on Iwo Jima. As I worked my way into the cave, I grabbed a Japanese rifle propped up against the cave wall. It was loaded and ready to fire. Counting on three Japs to be in the cave, I figured a rifle might be my best option against three.

The music got louder as I neared the rear of the cave. I saw a flickering light, so I knew I was getting close. I overheard three men speaking in Japanese about committing hari-kari, a Japanese ritual for suicide. I had learned that the Japanese refused to surrender, feeling it was a disgrace to do so. I remained out of sight and in less than a minute, I heard the first Jap ram a sword into his abdomen, shouting, "Long Live the Emperor!" in Japanese.

I then heard another Jap do the same. Who was left alive? I hoped that the Japanese General was still alive. I was not going to let him take his life as I was going to do that for him. I immediately rushed around the corner, with the rifle pressed against my right shoulder. I spotted my target, the Japanese General, sitting on his knees with his sword in his hands. He was startled to see an American in shorts, with a Japanese rifle pointed squarely at him. I immediately fired, hitting him right between the eyes. The backside of his head blew out and sprayed against the wall of the cave, as he collapsed to the dirt floor. The music, coming from the radio nearby, was still playing. I fired another shot into the radio and silenced it.

I had been instructed to kill the Japanese General and remove his body from the island. It was believed that it would convince the remaining Japanese troops on the island that he had deserted them. I laid the rifle down and proceeded to drag the dead General out of the damp cave. Upon exiting the cave, I picked up the General and put him over my shoulders. I carried him down to the rocky edge of the cliff face I had recently climbed. I unceremoniously dumped him over the side and onto the beach below. I climbed down the rocks and located my diving equipment. I removed my now somewhat dry boots and replaced them with diving flippers. I left the remaining diving equipment. I then filled the dead General's uniform with hand-size rocks, rocks that would force him to sink in the cold, dark ocean.

With all my strength, I pulled the Jap General's body out into the water with me. Once we cleared the beach, it became a little easier, but immediately his body wanted to sink. I was able to generate enough force to swim out and still hold his body up. Blood still oozed from his head, or what was left of it, as I continued to drag him further out into the depths. In the back of my mind, I hoped there were no sharks nearby.

I pulled his body about two hundred yards offshore and let it sink. Emotionless, I watched as his body sank, disappearing into the blackness beneath me. I immediately looked for that familiar red light blinking from the sub's conning tower. I scanned the darkness and soon spotted it approximately half a mile away. I swam on the surface most of that distance. Upon reaching the USS Redfin, I simply tapped on the outer hull three times, my signal that I was back. The sub completely surfaced this time and I climbed up a side metal ladder. The conning tower hatch opened, and a young Navy sailor greeted me.

As I removed my diving equipment and handed it to him, he asked me simply, "Did you have a good swim, Sir?"

I replied, "As a matter of fact I did sailor. Mission accomplished."

With that, the USS Redfin sank back beneath the waves. I provided the details of my mission to the sub's Captain, who transmitted the information via cryptic code to my OSS superiors in Hawaii. Word reached the USS Redfin on March 26th that the Japs on Iwo Jima had surrendered and that the island was secure. The B-29 bombers now had an island they could land on in the event they encountered damage or mechanical problems on their flights to and from Japan.

The USS Redfin was ordered to head to the waters off Japan and survey two particular cities called Nagasaki and Hiroshima. The war against the Japanese had turned in our favor and the number of missions that were required of the OSS was slowing down.

My new instructions were soon transmitted to me from Hawaii. I was simply to remain on the USS Redfin, awaiting further orders. Those orders would not come for several months. I spent the next five months with the USS Redfin and its crew. The UDT divers were still on board, as well. I never left the sub during those five months. The only relief I got was when the sub surfaced each night to take on fresh air. I took advantage of that surfacing and walked the deck of the sub a few times. The cool air was such a relief from the humidity and smell of the inside of sub.

During my lengthy time on the sub, I befriended the sub's navigator, a young sailor from Ringgold, Pennsylvania, named Ted Breisch. He took the time to explain to me how he navigated the sub through the water and all the various obstacles it presented. He also showed me the new radar system recently installed. I was fascinated by how it all worked.

We found out in May 1945 that the Germans had surrendered in Europe. After all this time, Hitler and the Nazi Party had finally been defeated. All that was left was the Japanese and we were intent on making that surrender happen soon. We were all eager to get home.

By late August 1945, the USS Redfin had successfully navigated into the bay near Hiroshima and the entire southern tip and western shores of the island near Nagasaki. The sub had avoided the mines that the Japs had laid in the waters near both cities, thanks to Ted.

On the evening of Sunday, August 5th, the USS Redfin got within five hundred yards of the port of Nagasaki. The sub then surfaced to periscope depth and we all took turns looking at the lights of the city. Most of us wondered why we were there. Then word came down that the Navy wanted the UDT frogmen to plant explosives on as many of the Japanese Navy destroyers anchored in the bay as they could. I asked if I could join them. It did not take much to convince them as word had spread about the details of my Iwo Jima excursion.

The same exercise that deployed me from the sub at Iwo Jima was repeated for the UDT frogmen and me. Nine of us exited the sub that night. We each carried magnetic explosives that could be attached to the outer hull of a ship and set with a timer.

The UDT frogmen were much quicker in the water and had swum about one hundred yards ahead of me. Not long after we exited the sub, out of nowhere, a Japanese PT boat cut the water between the frogmen and me. The PT boat opened fire from its deck machine guns and sprayed the water where I had last seen the frogmen. The firing continued for over a minute. I assumed the worst. I looked back and the USS Redfin was gone, escaping beneath the waves, looking to avoid any depth charges from the Japanese PT boat. The information the USS Redfin had secured over the last five months, could not be compromised. I was on my own, floating in the port of Nagasaki. I swam over to a nearby anchored Jap destroyer and floated near its side. I bobbed up and down, cold from the water and coolness of the night.

The Japanese PT boat left the area a short time later. As it pulled away, I saw my dead American brothers floating in the water, some face down and others face up. All were dead; there was no sign of life.

For the first time in my military career, I had limited options. I had to get out of the water, but once I stepped foot on Japanese soil, I was a dead man. There was nowhere to hide. After bobbing in the water for over two hours, I was prepared to take my chances on land. Suddenly, I saw the conning tower of a sub surface out in the middle of the bay. The USS Redfin was back, or at least that is what I thought. I immediately swam out to the sub but as it began to surface, I saw that it was not the USS Redfin but a Japanese sub with the identification of I-401! My heart sank and I immediately turned, trying to swim in the opposite direction.

I had not gotten far away when I heard the crack of gunfire and bullets hit the water all around me. I stopped swimming. I heard a voice shout in Japanese behind me, "Halt! Swim toward me now." I turned and saw a Japanese sailor looking down at me with a machine gun pointed directly at me. I thought about sinking beneath the waves, figuring with my diving equipment, I could swim a mile underwater and escape. I placed my mask on my face and immediately the Jap sailor fired off another volley of bullets around me. If I wanted any chance of surviving, I had to follow his instructions.

I swam to the Japanese sub. I removed my diving equipment and let it drift away. I then climbed up a metal rung ladder, with the thoughts in my mind growing heavier with each grasp of the rung. I reached the deck of the sub and the Jap sailor motioned me to enter the sub through an open hatch. As I placed my legs into the hatch first, my upper body was still exposed. A Jap sailor took the butt of his rifle and cracked it over my head. I blacked out and my body fell down into the sub.

I woke up hours later chained to a torpedo rack in the rear of the Jap sub. The compartment was damp with puddles of salt water everywhere. A small red light about ten yards in front of me illuminated a small door. I saw no one and received no food or water for two days. On what I figured to be the third day of my capture, I was jolted awake by a kick in the head, only to see a Jap sailor with a cup of water in one hand and a small ball of rice in the other. He threw the ball of rice on the floor of the sub and threw the cup of water in my face. The sailor left the torpedo room and slammed the door behind him. Regardless, even though handcuffed to the torpedo rack, I was able to maneuver my body enough to enable me to lick up a few grains of rice and drops of water off the floor of the sub. The water tasted metallic and salty, making me even thirstier.

Over the next few days, my awareness of days and nights was completely lost. My arms would constantly fall asleep, forcing me to reposition my body as much as I could to allow blood to reenter my arms. I was alone, cold and hungry but I endured by thinking of Alice and her own fight with the Japanese. Somehow, I had to find a way to fight through this. Every inch of my body wanted to kill every Jap on the submarine. My endurance training, all those years prior, was now paying off. I had not received any psychological training in the Army but I somehow found a way to endure the pain and isolation.

I slept a few hours each day and tried to keep my mind sharp, by speaking to myself in German and Japanese, reciting as many memories as I could. It was hard to determine how many days I had been handcuffed to the torpedo rack. My mind continued to wander, thinking of Alice, what I could do to escape, revisiting boot camp all over again hour by hour and finally what I would do if I managed to get topside. Days turned into weeks.

The door to the torpedo room opened suddenly with a resounding clang. A brilliant shaft of light blinded me and I blinked rapidly, desperately willing for my eyes to adjust from the darkness that had surrounded me for so long. I recognized the outline of a Japanese Lieutenant, walking hurriedly through the door towards me. His uniform was crisp, clean and easily recognizable. He stopped directly in front of me, knelt down, and silently began to unlock my handcuffs. After the cuffs fell away, he turned his attention to the locks and chains on my ankles. For a month, those cold steel bonds had held me prisoner in this rear compartment of a Japanese submarine. I heaved a shaky sigh of relief now that the bonds were off. The stern face of the Lieutenant told me he was especially upset as he impatiently motioned for me to stand. Having lain in such an awkward position for so long, it was very difficult for me to even move, let alone stand. Nevertheless, I gathered my legs beneath me and prepared to defend myself from an expected execution. When

I rose, the Lieutenant placed his hand on his pistol, but he did not remove it from its leather holster. Instead, he gave me a belligerent shove toward the door, where another Japanese sailor awaited us. I stepped through the narrow hatch with an initial feeling of relief, but I remained on my guard as we proceeded down the small corridor.

I was astonished when I saw ten or more Japanese sailors lined up at attention on the left side of the narrow passageway. All of the enemy sailors were looking at me. I could see their hate for me in their eyes and in their body stance. As I walked forward, with the Lieutenant directly behind me, several of the sailors cursed at me in Japanese and spat on me.

We paused near the sub's conning tower for a short moment as the Lieutenant and the Captain conferred in a seemingly calm but debating tone. The Japanese crew was not aware of my training in Japanese linguistics and that I understood their conversations throughout my entire internment. As a result, I was able to read the sub's depth gauges and clearly understand the discussion between the Lieutenant and the Captain. The two Jap officers had now concluded their brief conversation, bowed to each other with neither man looking in my direction. The Captain made it clear he wanted me released but the Lieutenant was clearly against it. My fate was in debate, I did not know what my outcome would be. I could sense the sub rising rapidly. We would soon be breaking the surface of the water and exiting the sub. My mind raced, my heart began to beat even faster.

After a few minutes passed, a Japanese sailor then proceeded up the conning tower ladder to open the outer hatch. I watched him intently as he turned the dial and slowly opened it. A sudden rush of cool air met my face, a stark contrast to the humidity I had endured during my time in the sub. Saltwater dripped in, splashing all over me. Bright rays of sunshine lit up the interior of the sub, and I squinted, looking up at a brilliant blue sky. The Captain pushed me from behind and briskly motioned for me to proceed up the ladder. Even though the Captain had ordered me released, I remained on guard to defend myself, in the event they had any last minute ideas of shooting me and throwing me overboard.

During the last few weeks, as a prisoner of the Japanese, I heard various conversations that revealed to me that the United States had unleashed two atomic weapons over the Japanese cities of Hiroshima and Nagasaki during early August. From the limited conversations I could pick up, both bombs had caused a brilliant flash of light over each city. Both cities had been destroyed and thousands of Japanese had burned alive or where completely vaporized. I thought to myself, "What American weapon could unleash that kind of power?" My capture by the Japanese near Nagasaki linked me to those events.

I exited the sub and took a deep breath of fresh air. My eyes continued to adjust, temporarily blinded by the sunlight. The Captain exited behind me and motioned me to the rear of the sub. I started toward the rear, still expecting the worst to happen. Even in my debilitated state, I knew I could take out both Jap officers if it came to that. This red-blooded American was not going to die without taking them with me.

My eyes finally adjusted to the sunlight and my vision cleared. I looked around and was astounded by what I saw. The Japanese sub had surfaced behind a mighty flotilla of American Naval vessels. I saw battleships, destroyers, and cruisers. There were frigates and even submarines scattered in between the larger ships. On each vessel flew the red, white and blue American flag, snapping proudly in the wind. It was at that point I knew my life was spared.

The Japanese submarine Captain turned to me and, speaking in clear English, said, "You are free to go."

To his surprise, I replied in Japanese. "*Domo*", which meant "thank you". The Captain then directed my attention to a small raft that was tied to the side of the submarine. I carefully worked my way down the slippery rungs of the small ladder on the side of the submarine and eased into the raft. The same Lieutenant that had just moments earlier released me from the cold handcuffs and chains, let loose of the rope holding the raft to the sub. I hastily picked up the two oars in the raft and began to row backwards toward the nearest American Navy ship. I estimated the closest one was approximately four hundred yards away.

My progress was painstakingly slow. During the last week of my capture, my consistent meals of small balls of rice and cups of water were improved with the addition of a slice of bread and extra cups of water. The limited sustenance overall had left me weak and tired. I estimated I had lost close to thirty pounds.

With sheer adrenaline and excitement, I somehow managed to row farther away from the Japanese sub and as I did, I looked up and noticed a single white flag secured to the top of the Jap conning tower. I tried to increase my pace but my legs and arms protested with every single dip of my paddles in the water. The wind was against me, and the waves were choppy, but the sky was mostly clear. I constantly turned my head around to check my progress. I tried very hard to keep my course steady as I fought my way through the water. After an agonizing forty-five minutes, I finally reached the starboard side of an anchored destroyer, the USS Nicholas DE-449.

As my raft lapped up against the sides of the destroyer, an American Navy sailor peered over the railing and called down, "You look like an American, but what are you doing in that raft?"

Before I could answer, he continued, "Are you a pilot? If you were shot down, you must have been adrift in the ocean for a long time!"

I answered with my dry throat and parched lips as loud as I could, "I am Captain Allen Voigt. I'm a member of the Office of Strategic Services and I've just been released from the Japanese submarine I-401."

The astonished American directed me to a set of collapsible stairs that had been lowered for me by some other sailors observing our conversation. I gingerly got up from the raft and started slowly up the stairs, letting the Japanese raft drift away. A crowd of sailors gathered to watch my ascent. When I wearily stepped aboard the deck of the USS Nicholas, the sailors did not say a word as they observed my tattered t-shirt and shorts, bare feet and matted beard.

I looked around and finally asked the group, "What's going on here? Where are we? What is the date?"

From the back of the crowd, a loud voice shouted, "We're in Tokyo Bay! The Japs have surrendered!"

Then from another direction, someone bellowed, "It is Sunday, September 2nd!" I had been a prisoner of the Japanese for twenty-eight days.

I looked at the faces around me in astonishment. I did not believe what I was hearing! Then another announcement came over the loudspeakers on the ship, this one perhaps the most surreal of all. "The Japs are surrendering to General MacArthur! And you're about to witness it!"

I was given fresh cloths, some water, something to eat and for the next five hours, I joined the other sailors of the USS Nicholas, peering over the deck of the ship. We had a front row seat to the surrender of the Japanese. The ceremony took place on the deck of the USS Missouri. General MacArthur was there, along with most of the United States senior military leadership. I even spotted General Wainwright standing with them. I asked some of the men around me about General Wainwright. They informed me that he had been a prisoner of war the last four years, and had just been released by the liberating Russian Army. He had lost a lot of weight but was standing proud. The Japanese dignitaries were dressed in top hats and coat tails, a strange sight, for sure. American and Japanese officials signed the surrender papers.

Naval gunfire erupted all over Tokyo Bay from the surrounding Navy ships. The sailors of the USS Nicholas and I congratulated each other and gave each other high fives and hugs.

The war was finally over.

EPILOGUE

"America was not built on fear. America was built on courage, on
imagination and an unbeatable determination
to do the job at hand."
Harry S. Truman

After the Japanese surrender ceremonies ended on the deck of the
USS Missouri during September 2, 1945, I stayed aboard the USS
Nicholas for two weeks as it ran clean-up maneuvers around the
islands of Japan, looking for any remaining hostile Japanese activity. I
was informed we were also sitting ducks, acting as bait for belligerent
Japanese submarine commanders who refused to surrender.

By late September, I was back in Hawaii, a place I had come to
claim as my home away from home. The first thing I did was try
to find out the status of Alice and her fellow nurses who, as far as
I knew, were still prisoners of the Japanese in Manila. I tried hard
to get the OSS to allow me to conduct a solo rescue mission, but
they would not hear of it. The war was over on both sides of the
globe, and as far as they were concerned, they were not risking any
more American lives. The nurses were going to be released through
diplomatic channels.

I was frustrated that I had to wait, not knowing when I would see
Alice. We had not spoken or seen each other in so long. Would she
still be interested in me? Maybe she had fallen for an Army, Navy or
Marine officer whom she had cared for. Finally, in mid-November

1945, word came to me that a ship with several American nurses from the Philippines was due to arrive in Honolulu in less than five days.

The day the ship came in; I waited at the dock, hoping to catch a glimpse of Alice on the deck or gangway when she walked off the ship. After three hours of waiting, there was no sign of Alice. I even asked a few nurses who had just gotten off the ship if they knew Alice or her whereabouts. No one did.

February 1946 came and I received orders to report to Fort Meade. I did not want to leave Hawaii without knowing that Alice was safe, but orders were orders. Maybe my connections at Fort Meade and the White House could help me find out more.

By March, I was back at Fort Meade and was beside myself. No one could tell me anything about Alice. On April 2nd, word finally arrived, and it was information that I did not expect. I was told by senior OSS officials that the nurses in Manila had been rescued a year earlier, in February 1945, by the Army. Alice had suffered a head injury during an American bombing run over the city of Manila in December 1944. A section of the hospital roof had collapsed and killed several patients and nurses. Alice survived but had been in a coma for over three months while the swelling in her brain subsided. She came out of her coma sometime in March 1945, just before she and her fellow nurses were transported back to the United States. The other nurses cared for Alice during their trip back to San Diego, California.

To make matters much worse, Alice was suffering from amnesia and did not even know her name, let alone remember me. She was transported home to Jacksonville, Florida, to live with her parents with the hope she would eventually regain her memory. By this point, she had been at home with her parents for over a year.

With uncertainty, apprehension and excitement all mixed up in my mind, I secured a month leave from the Army and traveled by train to Jacksonville in early April 1946. I did not know what to expect when I walked up the front step. I was wearing my Army uniform, hoping that would help bring some memories back to Alice.

By this point, I had not seen Alice for four years. Would she know me? Would she still care for me?

The door opened and an older man, presumably Alice's Dad, greeted me. "May I help you, son?"

"Yes, Sir, my name in Allen Voigt and I am a friend of Alice's. Is she home?"

"Are you making this up, son?" he replied.

I paused for a moment before answering, thinking to myself, why would he think that? "Yes, I am Allen, the only Allen Voigt I know, Sir."

The man motioned me in and asked me to take a seat on a couch in the living room. The house was so quiet; I heard a grandfather clock ticking in the corner. Before too long, I heard motion coming from the hallway in my direction. I rose to my feet and saw Alice for the first time in a long while. She had no bandages on her head and showed no signs of head trauma.

My eyes filled with tears as I walked up to her. She looked at me and said, "Allen is that really you?"

"Yes, it's really me and I'm really here right now." I replied as I pulled her into my arms. "I was afraid I'd lost you forever, Alice."

She laid her head on my shoulder and said, "No, I'm right here."

"I'm never losing you again, Alice," I whispered in her ear.

I spent the entire day with Alice and her parents. While Alice and I sat on her parent's couch, her parents told me that Alice had moved back home almost a year earlier and did not even know them. Three months prior to my arrival, Alice's memory had come back to the point that she remembered she had been a nurse, knew she had been overseas and now recognized her parents. She had mentioned to her parents that during the war she had met a man named Allen but could not recollect his last name. She also told her parents that she remembered falling in love with him, but could not remember much more than that. This explained why, when her father greeted me at the door, he thought I was making things up.

I found a nearby hotel and spent the next few weeks going back and forth to see Alice. Slowly her memory returned, and we recalled our limited time together over the last thirteen years. She also regained her ability to walk on her own, which allowed us to go out on the town a few times, catching movies and dinners. I was able to secure an Army post in Jacksonville and we spent as much time together as we could. We walked on the beaches of Jacksonville, Florida and watched the sun set many a night. We had been apart for so long but were now making up for it.

In November 1946, I asked Alice to marry me, something I regretted not doing during the time we spent together in Hawaii during the War. Looking back on it, I should and could have asked her, but it never felt right due to the dangerous nature of my assignments. We were married on Saturday, December 14, 1946 in Jacksonville, in the Riverside Presbyterian Church. My parents were able to attend the wedding and my father was the best man. Our honeymoon was spent in Naples, Florida on the Gulf Coast.

Alice and I built a home near the beach, in-between Jacksonville and St. Augustine, Florida. The sands of time rolled on and we raised a son and a daughter. We had both of our parents pass away in the mid sixties but not before, they all saw our children born and grow into teenagers.

I retired from the Army in August 1947, having served faithfully for over twenty years. I never fully parted ways with the Army, as I spent another thirty years as a contract employee. I initially helped train young Army recruits that were heading to the Korean War with counterintelligence and weapons training. By the fifties, the Cold War had escalated with the Soviet Union and I was asked to train, what were now CIA (Central Intelligence Agency) personnel, how to blend into the society of a foreign country, and maintain a false identity.

I made good money as an Army contract employee, working all the way up until 1978. Jimmy Carter was in the White House and I had seen enough. For fifty years, I dedicated my life to the Army and the United States' safety. It was time for me to concentrate on nothing but my wife, grown children, and, by that time, my grandchildren.

The relationships I had forged with Tom Beckett, Joe Yates and others were special to me, but they had all passed away by that time. Tom ended up going to Korea as a counterintelligence officer. Sadly, he was tragically killed in a firefight during July 1953. Joe died of old age in the fall of 1962. Up to that point, we had managed to correspond via letters over the years.

I am now an old man. I have lived an exciting life and traveled the world in defense of my country. I have no regrets and thank God for His providential hand of protection over me all these years. I saw my two children and five grandchildren grow up in a free country. Their freedom was inherited from all those who have fought and died on their behalf. I am just glad to have played a small part. The Army made me into the man I have become. I have no regrets.

ACKNOWLEDGEMENTS

My interest in World War II started at a very young age. I have my two Grandfathers' to thank for their military service during the war. Archie Houston served in the Army, as a member of the 558th AAA AW BN, Tech Sergeant. Maurice Drake served in the Navy, as a member of the USS Culebra Island, ARG7, Electrician's Mate. They both inspired me to learn more about the war, who fought in it and what the war meant to America's freedom.

My Father, James Drake served in the United States Air Force from 1959-1963. He served his country stateside with pride, learning skills that allowed him to work for IBM close to thirty years.

My Uncle, Wayne Drake, served in Vietnam from 1970-1972. He earned a bronze star, as an M-60 door gunner on a Huey helicopter, a member of the Army's First Calvary Division.

My Father-in-Law, Ed Clements, Jr., served in the Army Reserves for close to seven years during the late sixties, learning traits that have given him a successful business career.

All of these men have inspired me in different ways. That collective inspiration drove me to write Solitary Vigilance.

AUTHOR

To contact Tim and learn more about his books, visit **inheritedfreedom.com**. He can also be reached via email at **inheritedfreedom@comcast.net.** He lives in Cumming, GA, a suburb of Atlanta.